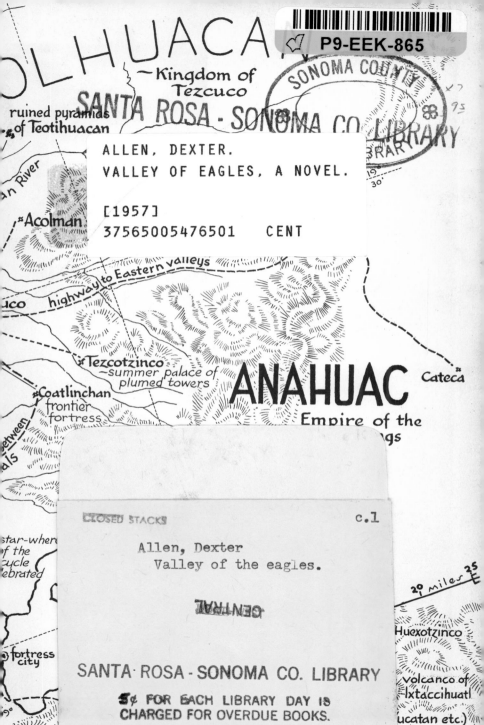

OLHUACAN
~Kingdom of
Tezcuco

ruined pyramids
of Teotihuacan

an River

*Acolman

19
30'

highway to Eastern valleys

uco

*Tezcotzinco
~summer palace of
plumed towers

ANAHUAC

Cateca

*Coatlinchan
frontier
fortress

Empire of the
...gs

star-where
of the
cycle
ebrated

20 miles 25

Huexotzinco

fortress
city

volcano of
Ixtaccihuatl
ucatan etc.)

Valley of Eagles recounts the third and concluding phase of the great Nezahual's reign, subject of *Jaguar and the Golden Stag* and *Coil of the Serpent*. These are the final years of Anahuac, just before Nezahual's arrogant successor played host to the Conquistadores.

The Valley of Mexico lay quietly under the rule of Nezahual, the last of the great Tezcucan emperors. The eventuality of his abdication never occurred to his ministers. There were vague premonitions of disaster, but nothing the high priests could be sure of. The affairs of state progressed normally enough. There was no dearth of slaves to attend the palaces, or to be sacrificed atop the pyramids to assuage the gods.

Then in the third month of the year 1510 Nezahual was presented with two sons, each of a different mother. One was the only child of the dying empress; the other, merely the youngest son of a royal concubine. Their births were separated by several days. Because of the differences in rank, their destinies should have been as unrelated as if they were born in totally different cities. By an odd coincidence, however — a coincidence that could only entail tragedy — the emperor had been reborn in his last sons together.

The two princes were exactly alike in feature, except that the heir apparent was fair and his half-brother as dark as black obsidian. As the one inherited, along with his rights of succession, the gentleness and sensitivity of his father, the other prince revealed, even in his infancy, a terrifying viciousness. These were the conflicting elements of Nezahual's nature. Unreconciled, the two temperaments could destroy the kingdom, united, they might have saved Anahuac *les* from the ravages of war. The conquest was inevitable; but a strong leader among the Aztec armies would have prevented the massacre.

Valley of Eagles is a novel of two youths unknowingly and disastrously at odds, of the beautiful Princess Nicte— whose loveliness frightened the nobles that desired her, and whose strange intimacy with the heir apparent sealed the fate of the three cities.

Through the cities of the lake, bent on irrational vengeance, deadly in spite of his youth, stalks the black prince—personifying the brutality Nezahual had long sought to control in himself: the black prince, known in history as the destroyer of his people, the one Indian chieftain who contributed most to the downfall of Anahuac.

Valley of Eagles

a novel by
DEXTER ALLEN

*The darkness of death is brilliant
light for the stars*

Coward-McCann, Inc.
New York

TO CECIL GOLDBECK

*—not only for his insight
but for his even greater patience*

Valley of Eagles

1

IN THE year 1510 the Valley of Mexico (particularly the lake region) provided an amazingly beautiful site for the cities that ruled a subcontinent. There was a remoteness—a calm, impersonal loveliness of water, earth, and rock —that caused even the princes to rise at daybreak in profound albeit anxious reverence.

Perhaps the very beauty of the valley, which overawed the alienated whoever came, provoked the inhabitants to strive fiercely against rejection—to open their arteries in unending sacrifice; for cults of the most exacting brutality held sway over the lake cities, as though with all the fruitfulness there was a need of anguish and the bitter taste.

The land was then a sanctum of forests and birds, not the wasteland of parched gullies. Mountains many thousands of feet high girt the inner region of the Three Lords. The earth was rich and dark with the loam of spring torrents. In seasons of harvest the wind wore the sheen of russet-gold chaff. Beyond the fruit and cypress groves lay acres of white, bursting cotton. Reedy swamps, held in the shallows of the plain or extending the irregular shores of the five lakes, were rife with quail and deer—the haunt of strange, implacable little cats and of hares wild and furtive by turns.

Forested ridges descended into the valley; and throughout the meadows rose abrupt islands of volcanic stone, the naked quarries a porous earth-red. Fastened to the crags were pulpy, dark-green nopals where the cochineal alighted. From its attenuated body came the scarlet of the nobles' robes, the deeper blood-hue of the priests'. The merest flutter of a trogon's wing glanced sudden incandescence in some distant field, such was the deceptive clarity of

9

the atmosphere; for even the valleys of the Mexican plateau lie at high altitudes.

Fifty miles of luxuriance, of overripeness, stretched between the adobe ruins of Cuicuilco (once a city against the southwest mountains, long covered with lava before the first of the present tribes) and the gigantic, desolate pyramids to the northeast. Despite the ceaseless activity of the rulers, however, the building of roads and aqueducts, the assertions of pyramid and fortress along the slopes, a disconnection yet remained.

For ten thousand years the Valley of Mexico had sheltered wanderers, had offered up the yield of its dark fields. The bereft had come, to be nurtured on maize and the knowledge of past ages. The destitute remained to found empires. So it was. No one had hitherto come in strength. Whatever the seekers brought with them, chastened by misfortune until only what could not be done without remained, was grafted on the sturdy and primitive stock of another time.

There was a profound underconsciousness, the spirit of all those sundry peoples who had come and slowly lost the memory of their source, a vaster recollection of a myriad fountainheads and all the happenings in ten thousand years, that dwelt in the valley. And in the thoughts of this spirit (as in the fantasies which so convince a madman that he deems them real) were creatures oddly composed of jaguars, serpents, and birds—in short, the gods.

Being quite discarnate, without immediate sense of touch, or sight, or other faculty to curtail a whim, this spirit of the valley could imagine what it chose. The priests, if ardent enough in their penances, were often allowed to enter deep trances and behold the divine ones. Through the hours of darkness, when no one except the desperate ventured out, the Lord of the Night Winds rushed angrily along the highways in search of a victim. Because they knew he was lurking in the shadows, and their inner minds held the link to his reality, there were many merchants who had glimpsed the sinister, pale umber of his body in the foliage beyond them.

Throughout the valley of the lakes were many cities that paid homage to the gods and to the capitals of the war lords: often unique in language, yet akin in sustenance. The dark fields, the memory of ten thousand years' loneliness amid such impartial beauty, held them in communion.

In the year 1510, however, a moment occurred—the sudden, terrifying insight into ruin. Not that there hadn't been other signs. This was the awareness, at once incontrovertible and not clearly to be understood, that disaster already existed. It waited in the near future for reality. Kites not yet in flight were glimpsed on the carrion of warriors that on this morning were mere youths in the houses of instruction.

An ominous hush fell over the cities. Not a wind swept into the valley. Even the scattered, forlorn cries of marsh birds were quieted. The people stared up at their temples atop the great pyramids; and the priests, equally nonplused, stared back. It was the first hour, that of the white hummingbird. The season: the beginning of the rains, which was in the fifth month and named *Toxcatl*.

Eastward, the Sun God hesitated on a ridge of the sierras, brightness fused into ice. A last, strident echo of conch horns was lost in the terraced groves of cedar and sycamore. It seemed that the spirit of the region (an energy common to men and herons alike) had drawn a deep, restricted breath—in a moment of intense self-perception had started in dismay.

It was the critical point of day. Throughout the three lake capitals the glass blades of priests had struck into a thousand breasts. Now they stood, high priests in vermilion robes and plumed miters, offering the still-pulsive hearts to the Sun, the blood of flowers to sustain the vigor of the Fire God. But Tonatiuh himself faltered, high on the rim of the valley.

Holding the torn hearts aloft, the priests looked down in consternation at the cities below. The fire had entered—but wavered, a pale incandescence. The wind as suddenly lost its life movement. The earth sighed, as though the spring had gone from its furrows. The elements were unaccountably checked; the plainsong of day would not begin.

The princes and their followers waited. Montezuma II, Lord of Anahuac, hid his face as the chiefs about him moaned. It was a terrible quietness. The insensible slaves, whose very urge to procreate had been destroyed, felt the silence that originated in their bellies.

And then, without so much as a tremor of earth or wind, Lake Tezcuco (the central lake, and the largest) was seized by a violent agitation. The Goddess of Waters began to thrash in mounting paroxysms of rage, or of fright, deep in her abiding place under the cities. Fearsome waves swept across the surface, lashing in preternatural fury against the shores. By midday the surrounding hamlets were engulfed. Salt torrents flashed through the canals, and poured into the avenues of the chief capital. Several great palaces on the island of the Mexican ruler were washed from their pilings.

All the while the populaces scurried about in silence—so overwhelmed with the initial threat that their attempts to stem the flood were completely disorganized. The nobles had fled to the higher terraces (which was certainly inauspicious) and stared in dismayed anger at each other over the sudd-clogged, widening currents that ripped the street gardens. The priests remained on their pyramids.

Except for the lake turbulence, the occasional grind of falling walls, no other sounds accompanied the upheaval but the hysterical barks of stag and fallow deer, or the howls of foxes and wolves; the outer islands, which the Mexican lord kept stocked with game, were all but submerged by the second hour of afternoon.

Then, as unaccountably, the waters subsided. The sun throbbed with restored vigor, became steady, and firmly carried the day into evening. The wind rose, whisking over the fields of green corn. At nightfall a slight rain hurried through the valley, leaving streaks of silver to shine in the furrows. The weather-burnished stucco on palaces and temples glistened in the light of an early moon. Lesser buildings and the shattered causeways gleamed dull, violet brown under the foliage and above the dark, now quiet, lake. The night was aromatic with herbs and nocturnal flowers.

The moment of insight, the anticipation of a profounder violence (internal, and yet to be thoroughly manifest) was forgotten. Several barges set out over the lagoons, as though the chagrined nobles preferred to ignore the day's happenings. On the next morning, reconstruction was begun on the dikes.

But this wasn't the end of it. In the following year another symptom of cosmic disorder appeared to the princes. A tower on the chief Aztec pyramid was suddenly wreathed in flame, and quite without apparent cause. The porphyry itself burned—as though the masonry were of the soft, black stone from the eastern provinces. All attempts to quench the fire were to no avail; and again the people felt the dread that welled inside them, as from a secret nexus holding every spirit to a common source.

Again the nobles were temporarily deprived of authority, and could do nothing but watch from their terraces (though the priests were aggressive enough).

At last this too abated, in obedience to the hand of someone not yet satisfied with his warning. An unconscious, fretting tension began to divide the tribes. The priests understood. These were portents they had awaited since the rise of their cities. They remembered the lost god, He-of-the-Wind, whose ruined temple lay among the desolate pyramids to the northeast. Long ago, when the first wanderers from the north, the People of the Broad Shoulders, entered the valley, he had been persecuted and driven away.

Hummingbird Wizard and Smoking Mirror, the gods of the newcomer, had taken the exiled deity's titles to themselves. He-of-the-Wind (or Feathered Serpent, as he was also called) relinquished his Crowns of the East and of the Morning Star; but as he went, humbled in his once great dignity—fleeing down the mountains to the sea, his fair attendants stricken one by one with thirst and cold—Feathered Serpent left the promise to his enemies that he would come again. All should then be wasted by fire.

This the priests remembered . . . and knew the signs of the dread Wind God. The time of his return was near at hand. Not tomorrow, but one of the days thereafter, Feathered Serpent would come.

And in the third year after the lake cataclysm, the first of three eerie comets fell through the sky at midday. Still the prows of war canoes and pleasure barks glanced idly through the swells, casually averting flower-laden rafts. Caravans brought tribute of chocolate and gold, and bevies of slaves to attend the lords—or perhaps to be immolated by priests.

13

The empire seemed to progress normally enough. Cities were conquered or reconquered at the whim of the princes or perfidy of the vanquished. (It must be admitted, however, that the Three Lords often declared war, and raised the dreaded *quaxolotl,* the death's-head standard, for the mere purpose of extorting additional slaves from their vassals.)

There were rumors that great sea birds with billowing wings had been sighted from the island of Cozumel in the eastern sea. The savage Caribs, who descended unexpectedly on the coast cities, had mysteriously ceased their ravagings. But all in all, nothing happened that could definitely be ascribed to Feathered Serpent.

It was in this year of the first comet that one of the most disastrous moments in the civil history of Anahuac occurred.

The unnatural catastrophies, the sudden turmoil of the lake, the burning tower, the appearance of a comet, were beyond the scope of the citizens' existence. These were seemingly unrelated incidents, staggered through the calendar of seasons and festivals that set the rhythm and the continuity of years. Life itself, the successions of kings, the birth and rivalry of princes, followed a separate pattern of crisis. But on that most detached of levels, the private level where the individual follows the curve of his willfulness into death, there appeared to be at least an accidental synchronization of social and cosmic event.

Through the long, summer afternoons, the rival princes wandered in their gardens or strayed out along the causeways, their awakenings to manhood watched by jeweled courtesans. And in the year of the first comet, a pathetically unnecessary tragedy occurred: a tragedy ironic and individual, when a civilization was preparing itself for destruction. An innocent prince did stray out along the causeways of his city; an unknowing courtesan inadvertently caught his eye.

The Lady Nicte, daughter of a Mayan prince and an Aztec slave from the city of Tulán, was so very beautiful in her youth that no one dared touch her. There was a rather cynical high priest who played an interesting if obscure role in the over-all tragedy, privately observing that the courtesan was as remarkably stupid; and later, several judges of the Supreme Council were discreetly of that opinion. Nevertheless, Nicte provoked the same uneasy reverence as the other phenomena of the valley. If stupidity, or sheer remoteness, was part of her loveliness, it was this more than her wantonness that exacted self-destruction.

As we view the last emperors of Anahuac, from a vantage now of over four hundred years, and attempt to penetrate the intimate motives of their lives—apart from their civic function as anonymous spokesmen—perhaps their personal failures will seem to coincide with the collapse of an empire . . . events part and parcel of a common disaster, preordained by an outraged god.

Apparent throughout these last years was the hand of a malignant genius. The dark Prince Ixtlil was the constant, a youth that in his very beginning was possessed by the baleful forces at work in the valley. Unlike the serene, disinterested Nicte, Ixtlil was the alien, the rejected suitor who fell under the influence and became an expression of the wanderer's sickness.

Over the cities, like cypress in pleasure gardens, rose the temples of the gods; no longer thoroughly reassuring to the Emperor Montezuma, whose elder cousin had before him erected the foremost pyramid in the lake region. Another, more distant cousin had given him the realm, installing the young Aztec not only as prince of the southern islands but as chief of the three confederate states. Lord Nezahual had taken the diadem of Anahuac (the *copilli* of three crowns, designating the supreme war lord) from his own brow, and set it on the Mexican ruler's—though Montezuma had barely attained the age of reason, and had certainly not equaled the early exploits of the former emperor.

But Nezahual's unexpected abdication was only eleven years before the first comet. Not yet enough time had passed for the three courts to appreciate the irony of his words as he relinquished the copilli.

"And surely, *more* than a brother in tenderness . . . in sympathy," Nezahual had said, as though he completely forgot how insidiously Montezuma encouraged rebellion against him. Wishing the Mexican many long and glorious years, and "yet more abundant blessings," the Lord of Tezcuco retired to his rural gardens on the outskirts of the lake. Nearby, on the northeastern shore, lay the city of Tezcuco, capital of the kingdom of Acolhuacan.

15

From the great palace in his capital Nezahual once had ruled the continent. Even self-deprived of supreme authority, he gave his name to the final era of his father's empire. Through the eleven years that stretched between his retirement and the apparance of the first comet, he had isolated himself on his hill of the Plumed Towers. He returned to the scene of his boyhood, to become again but an emperor of terraces. To his sons, he was nothing more intimate than an aging patriarch whom one of them should succeed. On his rare appearances in Tezcuco, Nezahual the Lord was attended by ten thousand warriors: an eclipsed god, though one still remembered rumors of his grandeur, of the strange friendship that had brought about his ultimate disgrace.

Secluded or no, abstaining from judgment, refusing to participate in the affairs of his kingdom, Nezahual could not escape the historic, impersonal role that his birth and unwitting genius had conferred on him. The intimate, final tragedy of his life was more a state disaster than the mere cause of one man's despair. Even his grief mocked him.

During his last three years, each marked by the appearance of a comet, Nezahual gazed down on the lake region from his hill. Before he left his capital he had ordered a throne cut in a cliff near the summit. And now he waited, staring north at his city, or south at the islands of the Mexican lord. Perhaps his eyes might wander westward toward the third capital, which ruled the petty kingdom of Acatlapan. These last princes were of little consequence in the balance of power.

Immediately below Nezahual's throne was an oval basin hewn in an enormous block of porphyry. The proportion followed the Rule of Three, with a length of twelve feet by a width of eight. The curved rock jutted out into space like a bee-martin's nest; and from the throne a stairway descended into the well, which was over five feet deep in the center. Lodged in the tracery beneath the water was a medal engraved with the sign of fire. The dark stone, polished to a mirror fineness, caught only the pale ochre of Nezahual's thin body, the green of his royal vestments, the glint of gold. An occasional leaf would strike the pool, for only a moment disturbing the quiet tension of the surface.

16

And now, these centuries later, when the pyramids are all leveled, the palaces destroyed and no vestige left of other thrones, this one persists.

Here he sat, through the summer afternoons when a son was forfeiting life, in contemplation of the realm he had even relinquished for his future generations. Lord Nezahual was the last of the great princes to rule over the valley. Let the Mexicans, who had tormented him long enough, wear the copilli. One by one he watched his barons leave, to pledge their loyalty at another's throne. Of the eight original nobles who were his chief support, but half remained at the time of the comet. A few cities yet guarded the approaches to his capital; and the lake on the west, the swamps northward, were protection enough.

Not only was everything lost to Nezahual that he himself had gained, but most of his inheritance. There were eight groves and gardens about Tezcuco, each under the care of slaves who were sent as tribute from one of the provinces. Half of these had become a mockery, parks of defection. The waters that eight great fountains spewed forth came to nurture the earth with Nezahual's bitterness, as his tears had once nurtured all those he had loved.

One could not be certain why the Lord of Tezcuco sat in such strange contentment on his hill; for here Nezahual waited, through the eleven years of an era his abdication had begun— remote, nonparticipant, and yet responsible.

Had he grown merely weary of the endless challenges? Perhaps he did foresee the calamity that waited in the near future. He could not have been defeated by the rival princes, whatever coalition they managed against him. The only one who might have undone him on the battlefield was Montezuma's elder cousin; and this wily chieftain contented himself with his conquests in the south. Ahuitzotl had been accidentally killed as he was superintending work on the great dike, on the eve of Nezahual's abdication.

Nezahual was in his fiftieth year when his own laws last called him to account. He still had his vigor; his military genius was well established. His ministers were convinced that out of sheer perversity the lord allowed his provinces to be wrenched away. Even at this time, after the long era of his inactivity, had he taken to the field the empire would have shaken. There was no estimating him.

It was rumored that Nezahual often spent days without food or drink. Though he ordered that no attendant approach him during these periods, there were those who, guided by anxiety, violated his injunction. They would find the ruler by his pool, his breathing to all appearances stopped. And putting their ears to his chest, they could barely hear the heartbeats that punctuated long intervals of silence. It seemed that shallow breaths accompanied the intermittent pulse.

But this was court talk. It was a commonplace that Nezahual the Lord often spent entire nights watching the heavens from a tower on the crest of his hill. He was not a high priest; and yet he was given to rising at midnight to observe the North Star and its wheel (the constellations that revolve about the pole). When the seasons allowed, he carefully watched the Pleiades and the other celestial groups. Though he refused to participate in the solemn festivals of his people, it was said he paid his own homage at the rise of Venus. There were further rumors that at the morning appearance of the Dog Star in the tenth month, Nezahual gathered his favorites about him for celebration.

What he was celebrating is quite unknown. Though he had withdrawn from his people, and refused the purposes his high position allotted him, the Lord of Tezcuco apparently enjoyed an eventful, self-significant life in these latter years.

He left three young princes behind him in his capital, their instruction confided to his ministers. The heir apparent, Lord Temozin, had reached his sixteenth year when the first comet appeared. His mother, the unfortunate Lady Tecui, had died at his birth; and though Nezahual had taken an Aztec princess for his next consort (such was his power at the time, that he could break with tradition and bring yet another wife to his throne), Temozin's priority was not openly disputed.

His half-brother Cacama, second in the line of succession, was in his twentieth year; and the youngest son of the Aztec princess, the dark-featured Ixtlil, was Temozin's age. These were the immediate heirs in the eleventh summer of Nezahual's seclusion.

18

Through Temozin and Ixtlil in particular, the exiled ruler unwittingly continued to manifest himself in the capital.

The differences between the two boy princes were the more startling as one compared their likenesses. Their features were identical: the thinly arched eyebrows, the narrow nose, the strong yet sensitive chin with its slight cleft. In profile and at dusk they were very much the same. That is to say, under certain circumstances one might for the briefest moment mistake one for the other.

The first difference was an obvious one. Whereas Temozin had a pale, gold cast to his skin, Ixtlil bore the darkness of black obsidian. Both inherited the deep-set eyes of their father; but as the heir apparent's were a light, hazel-green, Ixtlil's seemed all pupil—and even in his early childhood expressed such a ferocity that other children were afraid of him. "Vicious . . . yes, *vicious!*" one of the chief high priests in Tezcuco had declared to an underling, when Ixtlil was only three years old.

Temozin's full, boy's lips were gently curved, melancholic; his brother's, arrogant and vindictive. Both were of the same stature, the usual height for youths in their sixteenth year. Their bodies were lithely muscular, from the exercises and competitive games (especially *tlachtli,* played with a hard rubber ball) of the nobles; but there was an underlying asceticism in Temozin, a suggestion that his muscles would never harden to the strength required on the battlefield.

To those who remembered the Lord Nezahual's own youth, such as Tizoc the High Priest, it seemed as though the middle-aged cacique had been reborn in his two youngest princes: as though the dual nature that had characterized him were now separated into two parts. The conflict of energies that brought about Nezahual's downfall was given, by some peculiarity of inheritance, an even more disastrous expression in the city.

In the very beginning Tizoc suspected this—and after his first attempts to rid Tezcuco of the threat, sat back in the security of his temple to wait. He unwisely countered Ixtlil in the prince's twelfth year (the year of the lake upheaval), however; and in spite of his several thousand warrior attendants, did not survive the breach gracefully.

Tizoc had anticipated this fatal division of Nezahual in his

19

princes many years before the year of the comet. The Lord of Tezcuco was then a young man at the height of his prowess—still Emperor, the formidable commander of armies.

A messenger brought Tizoc seemingly trivial news from the palace. One of the many princesses at court had borne the Supreme Lord another son . . . as though such an occasion should have any more than routine significance! The Empress herself had given birth to the heir apparent nine days past; and the nobles were still in celebration. Temozin had been given the name of a king. The chief physician, aware of the Lady Tecui's failing strength, had succeeded in forcing her labor.

But Tizoc not only heeded the second birth; he took exception to it. He consulted the zodiac again, reconsidered the sinister aspects he had observed in the heavens at midnight—and quickly summoned his attendants.

In the third hour of morning, the hour of the Falcon, the High Priest of Hummingbird Wizard hurried through the gates of the Imperial Palace.

It was unusual for even a high priest to come before Nezahual unbidden. The guard, surprised by Tizoc's feverishness (and by his very presence, as the pontiff of the War God was held in particular awe), sent an attendant to announce him to the Emperor.

At the moment of the high priest's entrance into the throne room, as if heralding his approach, a death knell echoed through the city. Lady Tecui, Nezahual's empress for so short a time, had departed from the valley.

2

Tizoc faltered at the low, reverberant clangor. He continued a few steps into the dark hall, then abruptly stopped. An uneasy thought occurred to him; and he felt the measured, slow impacts of a mallet on tempered stone in the pit of his stomach.

With an unconscious gesture, Tizoc crossed his arms and pressed his long fingers into his shoulder blades. It seemed to him that the veiled concussions were the pulsings of an enormous, invisible heart. He glanced for a brief moment at the priests about him, then at the throne a hall-length away. In the faint light there was only the indistinct glimmer of gold and orange. The bare, dark-red floor stretched a vast distance to the dais and reflected with a waxy luster the tapestries of plumage and metallic thread.

A door was opened somewhere in the throne room; and in the draft the fantastic designs that covered the low walls became a movement of long-crested birds devouring jeweled insects, of flowers shedding amethyst calyxes. Startled, the high priest quickly reached out his hands to touch his subordinates, who reacted to his gesture with surprise and concern.

A figure in the robes of a noble approached the group of priests and knelt before Tizoc. "Your Eminence . . ."

Tizoc regained his composure, and gestured for the Cacique of the Palace Guard to rise.

"Your Eminence, this is an unfortunate time. The Serene Lord Nezahual is not here to receive you." The warrior spoke with a bland determination, fully aware that the Emperor's presence in the palace was known, and finished his words in a slight bow. After he had risen, Tizoc skeptically returned his gaze.

The high priest considered the situation briefly, decided it might be unwise to insist on his announcement to Nezahual, and closed his heavy-lidded eyes: "The Lady Tecui . . . the knells are for her death."

"Her Serene Excellency is gone from us."

Tizoc studied the man before him, slightly opening his lids. He rubbed his hands together, feeling the heavy metal of his rings chafe. "There was a priest with the Lady Tecui during her last hour . . . ?" His remark wavered between attentive respect and more purposeful questioning.

"The Empress died alone."

"Then a priest has surely been summoned." Tizoc opened his eyes wider.

"Yes, Your Eminence," was the level reply. "The High Priest of Tloque."

Tizoc compressed his thin lips, and the nervous movement of his hands stopped. He was plainly annoyed. Nezahual was forever holding this inconsequential God of the Unknown above the two great divinities (who were at least equal rivals). Even the naming of the heir apparent five days past had been given to this minor prelate. Tizoc's high voice was calmly defensive: "Last night, at the hour of the Earth Mother, a son was born to Nezahual."

The cacique was puzzled by the high priest's attitude. Certainly, another son had been born. "At the seventh hour—" he said aloud in agreement.

"The child of an Aztec princess," Tizoc insisted trenchantly. The other noble was more disconcerted. Surely the chief priest of the War God hadn't come out of concern for a mere concubine's child. Tizoc, pained that another should be called when circumstance had already brought him to the palace, vindicated himself: "I have come on a more important errand than the saying of prayers over Tecui . . . over a dead empress."

He noticed the shocked expression on the cacique's face, and casually fingered the jade gorget that hung over his shallow chest. Tizoc turned to his priests: "I have not come on the call of death, but *with* its call—" The slight tilt of the jeweled crescent betrayed his overly prominent sternum. Unlike his followers, who were unkemptly robed in black, their hair matted and their ears shredded from self-inflicted penance, the high priest was fastidiously clad in scarlet, his drawn face unmutilated and oddly youthful in repose.

22

He followed some vagary of thought for a moment, then spoke again to the custodian of the palace: "When you decide the time is opportune, tell your master . . ." Tizoc paused, and the sarcasm had left his voice when he spoke again. "Tell your master that a viper has been hatched from the hummingbird's egg. In its jaws is a poison—a poison virulent enough to destroy eagles." He raised his hand to dismiss the warrior: "Tell Nezahual I have come—"

"*With* the call of death, Lord Tizoc?" a low, clear voice answered him from a distance.

Barely discernible in the darkness, a lone figure robed in white stood beside the dais. The high priest and the Emperor briefly confronted each other, separated by the length of the great hall. Tizoc, taller than his companions, his height accentuated by the tall plumes of his headdress; Nezahual, of average stature, appearing slighter below the massive throne with its high baldaquin. Of the two, it was the ruler that seemed alien in the Chamber of the Kings. With his jeweled miter, his mantle of cardinal plumage, Tizoc was akin to the long-crested birds that fluttered down the walls.

In the half-light, against the glimmer of gold and orange, Nezahual the Lord was alone in his bereft majesty. Except for the thin diadem about his head, he was without adornment or indication of rank. It was his voice, low and clear with the detachment of one in supreme command, that gave his presence an immediacy. There was a sad mockery in his attitude—an overtone of restrained excitement.

Tizoc recovered from his surprise almost immediately; and gathering his plumed mantle about him with a sweep of his long arms, fell to his knees. As the priests touched the pavement with their foreheads, the Cacique of the Palace Guard quickly strode to the center of the hall and genuflected.

After a slight pause Nezahual spoke again. "This is not the opportune time, Lord Tizoc." He took a few steps up the dais, then deliberated aloud—turning back into the room: "My second empress has also betrayed me . . . but innocently, innocently, and to death alone. Rise and come to me, Tizoc." His last words seemed almost gentle, as though he were calling to an intimate.

The high priest rose unsteadily, hesitated, and approached the dais. He knelt again, his half-closed eyes fastened on Nezahual. Tizoc was exhausted from his night's vigil on the pyramid; but he was one of those men who find in exhaustion a ready stimulant. A deeper faculty than mere cleverness was given to him. He was aware that the Emperor was in a state of shock, that the sudden familiarity Nezahual affected could be dangerous. But Tizoc, momentarily free of his self-conscious dignity, was prepared to meet the supreme war lord on equal terms. He felt secure in his mission.

There was a long interval of silence—which did not, however, cow the kneeling priest. It added greater purpose to his trial encounter with Nezahual, with this forlorn young man who held in himself the central pivot of an empire. A thousand cities balanced their might in him. The consideration of Nezahual as another human being, in travail and need, was foreign to the scarlet-clad prelate; instead, Tizoc saw before him a potent lord, the axis on which revolved the power of three kingdoms.

Nezahual was the focal point, besides, of a vast physical energy. The gestating wealth and military resource of Tezcuco converged and took direction in him. Only he could co-ordinate the countless warehouses of his merchants and the warrior hordes of his barons: the coffers of cocoa and jewels were transmuted by his will into armies, and converted back again—with a gain of captives to quench the avid thirst of the gods in exchange.

The young Emperor, as he attempted to humble Tizoc by forcing this prolonged obeisance to the throne, was well aware that no one felt a genuine concern for his happiness, much more for his grief. Tizoc, or whatever dignitary, was interested in Nezahual's thoughts and emotions for the advantage that might accrue. A gesture from the throne—and after all, one might become possessed of a city, or of a thousand slaves to dispatch at will.

So the two men confronted each other for several moments— not as mere personalities, but as instruments somewhat tempered with human idiosyncrasy. At last, as though he had decided how to ward the high priest off, Nezahual spoke: "Have you seen the threat of violence and death in the heavens, Your Eminence?"

Tizoc opened his eyes and unabashedly stared at the ruler. It had been his private foreknowledge of calamity that gave him courage enough to approach Nezahual. He was startled to find that the Emperor already knew of the revelation which had brought him pell-mell from his temple.

But surprised or not, Tizoc was not to be disconcerted so easily. He rose unbidden to his feet, discreetly aware that Nezahual's position on the dais more than compensated for their differences of height. There was an obvious correspondence, an equality of purpose that the high priest had considered while he had been obliged to kneel. Surely both must be aware of it. Together they forged the link of the War God to actual desolation, the nexus to destruction and the bloody shield. Tizoc represented the principle of conflict; Nezahual, the means and the purpose. Where they touched each other, the idea fused with the occasion into active hostility.

The high priest trembled with determination as he waited for Nezahual to continue.

"Have you seen an evil aspect in the stars?" the Emperor asked again.

Tizoc nodded vigorously.

"A prince is born—"

Tizoc raised his eyebrows and shrugged.

"Perhaps you have too hastily associated *prospects* of misfortune with an unrelated birth, Your Eminence." There was a quality of detached amusement in the ruler's voice. Tizoc sensed the taunt and raised his hand in protest; but Nezahual interrupted him. "Do you think too much of death and war?" he chided with an attitude of slight indulgence, gesturing to the Commander of the Palace Guard.

Tizoc imagined that he was about to be dismissed. "But the seventh hour, Serene—"

"Merely an unfortunate circumstance, Lord Tizoc. The seventh hour of night bodes an evil outcome . . . ? Very well, so let us say my latest son was born in the ninth. A common enough deception, Lord Tizoc."

"But the general aspect of the planets, Excellency," the high priest insisted, knowing very well that the ruler had also cast the horoscope of the newborn child. How else could Nezahual have anticipated his mission? Both had seen the threat of total disorder and ruin that accompanied the birth. This infant, who was at the moment no more than a mere concubine's son, was destined to great and evil influence. Tizoc hesitated, controlling his eagerness to insist further on the child's death. Nezahual had his heir now, a prince to delight any royal sire—and twenty other sons besides. And should Temozin die, there were five legitimate uncles and their offspring. The electors of the Supreme Council had many princes to choose from.

But the prelate lost his opportunity to demand the unnamed child's death. Nezahual refused to correlate the hour of birth and the frightening position of the stars. Instead, he remarked again on Tizoc's abiding interest. "You worship such a god of violence and warmongering, Lord Tizoc. Indeed, you are his chief minister in my city." There was the implication in his voice that really nothing more could be expected of the high priest.

Nezahual watched his cacique kneel, and nodded to himself. Without glancing at Tizoc, he tentatively concluded the audience. "You have come, my Lord Tizoc, an anxious minister of death. The gods, who we agree invest the stars with their intentions, have anticipated you. Death is here. Death, Tizoc—" he stared direct into the other's face—"*death* is here, and its knell proclaimed your entrance."

Tizoc felt a strength, not anger, in the Emperor's associating him insistently with death. He was vexed, however, by Nezahual's purpose. Tizoc, high priest and instrument of a god, whose scarlet robes announced the bearer of the sacrificial knife, could nevertheless not openly dispute the Lord of Acolhuacan. Nezahual now said the sign of calamity had forewarned the cities of his Empress's death. Both he and Tizoc understood the actual meaning. The infant son that had been born in the seventh hour should be sacrificed. Otherwise the ruin of the cities was assured.

But why should the Emperor, who had already sacrificed himself to the state, remain so obstinate?

Nezahual, aware that the priest would not dare contradict him, waited on the steps of his dais. Tizoc continued to return his stare, agitated yet observant. The ruler would be thirty-five within a month—though he seemed no older than the youth Nezahual, on the eve of his first major victory thirteen years before. There was the same disturbing energy in him now, constrained by the sheerest will. For a moment Tizoc understood the nausea, the sigh too deep for tears inside this prince of the Acolhua. He was humbled by the other's loss, and heard the endless corridors within himself awake to a common despair. The high priest intuitively grasped the more immediate significance of the Emperor's attitude, however. He noticed the sudden, repressed smile on Nezahual's lips.

Confronted with disaster, one might either falter in dismay or rise defiantly. But disaster on disaster, at last ridiculous to some, provokes the outraged laugh. Nezahual had begun to realize the strange excitement in despair, to find in loss a secret means of gaining his release. Both were elements of that faint smile: a yielding to the ludicrous, a tragic exultation in the ultimate, longed-for escape—as though the pain of love were more oppressive, less, far less endurable than the final hurt that seizes in a fit.

Nezahual, lord yet man . . . yes, he could rejoice in his beloved's death.

And Tizoc, with his intense perception, for a moment felt close to weeping himself. He didn't share the depth of Nezahual's emotion, nor the capacity to love so deeply and to lose so much; but in another age, another city, Tizoc should have been a great tragedian. He had the actor's genius of suggestibility; the aptitude for ferreting out by some obscure process the emotions and unconscious thoughts of others. In almost a trance, the high priest gained an alarming intimacy with those about him—became one with them, as though a part of his consciousness deep in the abysm of selfhood were disengagable and could interlock with the secret parts of others.

Fortunately, there was a gap between this untoward perception and his intellect. From temporary anguish, his mind turned and fastened for an instant on a similar occasion many years ago. He remembered the tall, wistful boy he had brought before Nezahual to be blessed and sent off to the pyramid. The Emperor had refused the boy's sacrifice, as he was refusing now the death of an inconsequential son. Nezahual would have spared himself considerable grief had he given Tizoc his way then. The awareness, not of being slighted but of being checked in his ministry, brought Tizoc in focus again. And that smile—perhaps it implied that the

Emperor's stand was not conclusive. The high priest wondered how he might manage a counter humor that should find the ruler sympathetic.

He must help Nezahual to see, or at least to accept, the only course open. The unnamed child really must die. Tizoc had to maneuver cautiously, however: in no way could he show insolence to the throne. Perhaps five minutes passed before he was prepared to speak. And all the while, the death knell echoed in the corridors outside. Both, spent by the night's ordeal, had lost a sense of time. Nezahual gazed at the warrior kneeling below him, as though he were lost in the contemplation of his temporal might. The high priest formed his comment, the oblique suggestion, and then—

"Yes, Tizoc, the knell is for *Tecui.* . . ." Nezahual again forestalled him. "Tecui, who always thought of herself as a captive spirit, the black pheasant of the southern coast: the delicate bird with the golden eyelids, *with its crown of curly feathers.*" He spoke his final words in the language of the Maya.

The ruler, as though telepathic himself, knew what had occurred to Tizoc in the sound of the knell.

"Death is here," Nezahual had said a few minutes past. But one only struck the knell for a specific person, for someone by name— for an old warrior who, to assure himself of paradise, had bared his chest to the priest's knife. But this infant born in the seventh hour was yet without a name. If its life were detached from it before the fourth day, not even an entry could be made of its momentary existence. No lament would sound through the city. It could be drowned, and the immature spirit assured of a place in the Water God's heaven. Tlaloc loved children, encouraged their sacrifice; and this was the month of his worship. Indeed, such a death was most fitting.

Immediately on Nezahual's associating the knell with the death of Tecui, no-longer-adequate phrases ran through Tizoc's mind. "Your Serene Excellency is wise," he might have said. ". . . Irresponsible evil, a mere tool of the malevolent . . . difficult, even when an entire people were at stake . . ." So his unvoiced thoughts went. "Essentially innocent, the child—but once historical, fitted with a name, the expedient will only then seem the more murderous."

28

Caught in Nezahual's turn of the erratic conversation, however, Tizoc's attention was drawn to the Emperor's last words about the black pheasant. Though he had known the dead Empress only slightly, the high priest was familiar with Tecui's whimsical manner if not with the Maya tongue. He had frequently sought audiences with her; and on several occasions, when Nezahual was not in the valley, she had received him in the gardens of the Plumed Towers. Tecui had been such a frail, lovely woman. The chief of the War God's cult remembered her mouth, the full lips that tapered to the slightest breadth at the corners.

Again Tizoc had faltered, and Nezahual called out *"Quantzin . . ."* The high priest, unaware that there had been others listening nearby, suddenly noticed the two men in the doorway of the anteroom behind the throne.

The chief physician left his companion, whom Tizoc recognized as the Lord Marshal, and approached the dais. Nezahual had continued up the steps, and stood watching from his throne. He had withdrawn. The High Priest of Hummingbird Wizard wished that he had been dismissed, or had possessed the foresight to take his own leave. His self-conscious dignity returned; and with an air of defensive superiority, he watched the physician cross to the steps. Tizoc was below no one in the empire but Nezahual himself—yet *he* must kneel in homage to the throne.

Quantzin stopped before the dais, nodded his head to the Emperor, and offhandedly contemplated the high priest. Tizoc, abruptly aware of his own kidneys and liver, fought against his sense of nakedness. *Wretched, prying man,* he accused with his stare, and closed his eyes disdainfully.

"Would you say, Quantzin," Nezahual asked with a trace of sad capriciousness, "that our Lady Tecui died in childbirth . . . that her travail has lasted these nine days?" He spoke to his confidant in an easy, conversational voice, as though Quantzin had been standing beside him for some time.

"The Night Wind put his mouth to hers. Excellency, nine days past, to draw her breath into him," the squat, preoccupied physician answered, without taking his gaze from Tizoc. A slight perspiration stood out on his forehead. He spoke almost curtly in spasmodic phrases, his irritability ill disguised. There was one virtue, one state of mind, that dominated Quantzin's every action: disinterested, all-inclusive compassion. And as this yearning to succor a child, faun, or young plant (anything, in fact, that held the fluid of life, the potential of growth) consumed him, so his political sense was the more irresponsible. He had watched over both Tecui and her undreamt-of husband in their early youth . . . yet his position at court was not to be envied.

Nezahual, in a happier day, had watched the two men below him in passing arguments. At that time, however, Tizoc had been second to the great Lord Cacama: the most irascible, wily, impossible old man imaginable. The young ruler had likened the present high priest and Quantzin to gardeners. Left to his own devices, one would utterly destroy the trees and flowers in his care by unmitigated selection—the other, by allowing such luxuriance that the foliage should eventually stifle itself.

They were not equals, however. Without Nezahual's protection, the physician would have been struck down before this on a gesture of Tizoc's hand. As Quantzin passed judgment on the Empress's death, he stared with an unfocused contempt at the priest. There was a moment of silence; and he repeated *"Nine . . . days . . . past,"* slowly.

"Tizoc," Nezahual called out in his low, clear voice. The prelate, who had seemed to be studying a plume of his great headdress that arched down several feet to the right, gathered his mantle with a wide sweep of his arms. He was on the point of falling to his knees —then hesitated, clenched his frail jaw in this humiliation before Quantzin, and began to sink down. The Emperor, however, immediately inquired: "Do you accept my physician's opinion?" A curious eagerness had entered his voice.

Tizoc crossed his arms, and bowed in assent as he pressed his fingers into his shoulder blades. What he was agreeing to, unfortunately, had slipped his mind.

"Very well, then." Nezahual beckoned to the Cacique of the Palace Guard. "Let it be announced to my people that Lady Tecui, dying in childbirth, has gone to the Paradise in the West." It was important that one of the chief prelates concur.

Tizoc, not disdaining to look at the little physician, compressed his already thin lips, which in turn exaggerated his long, overly spare nose. Quantzin continued to stare with petulant curiosity at the high priest, his short fingers intertwined on his paunch. Both listened attentively to the Emperor's words. His exhaustion and pent-up grief suddenly swept out in a strange, disordered lyricism.

"Say that Tecui will dwell forever in the western Mansions of the Sun, and forever bathe the fiery Tonatiuh in the waters of Night. She is become another's handmaiden. She is become the gold-lidded pheasant, my lord Tizoc . . . and nourishes her beauty on seeds of a fruitgrove never to be sown. On fermented honey, little Tecui, and on delicate rinds of bitter, bitter melon—

"And at eventide, *tell my people, Lord Tizoc* . . . at eventide, the Sun God, plunging into the lake of his worshipers' dreams, quenches his measuring fire in our timelessness: strikes fire in a pool of long bitter leaves, leaves and nectar that past seasons yielded past memory. My love drinks her fill of forgetfulness. . . ."
A repressed laughter lay behind his sudden flow of sentiment.

"Go now, Tizoc. And Paltzin—" Nezahual turned to the warrior-noble who knelt beside him on the upper tier—"order the chief steward to prepare our Lady's pyre in the court below my throne room. Lay her on cedar and rosewood, and strew copal on the flames. This afternoon will I have her ashes. Go at this moment, Lord Paltzin."

As the commander left on his errand, Tizoc stared dumbfounded at the ruler seven steep tiers above him—then turned apprehensively to the physician. Quantzin dejectedly contemplated the pavement. His lips trembled, and he slowly shook his head as though refusing the profound accusation within him. For Quantzin, who had listened through the previous conversation from a distance, this last tangent of Nezahual's was too much. Through almost twenty minutes, which seemed as many hours—so far-reaching were the implications, so nervous and inconsistent the moods—he had listened to the tragic farce played out at the foot of the throne.

Nezahual, his heart numb, committed himself to this false, effetely clever identity. Paralyzed with despair (Quantzin had seen the moment of affliction: the blood drain from his face, the flicker of coldness in his eyes), he yet persisted in the most inconceivably banal subterfuge. The physician could not even faintly understand Nezahual's need of abandoning himself to the ludicrous. Why should the Emperor play this nonsensical game of evasion?

At least Tizoc had come in the forthrightness of his mission. Nezahual, adroit in his mockery (for a reason no one but the high priest himself could imagine), had ridiculed not only Tecui's death. By confusing it purposefully with the terrifying aspects at midnight, he had passed verdict on his own utter desolation. His despair should have been left in the remoteness of himself—at least, so far as Quantzin could understand.

This last, wild lyricism of bitter leaves, bitter melon and impossible fruit groves derided the people's faith in paradise, the incarnations of the nobly dead as exquisite birds to attend the gods with song. Yet Quantzin could recognize the yearning against hope that such a visionary realm existed, the bitter excitement of disenchantment that ironically protests a lost dream. It was this summit of pretense that completely destroyed Quantzin's restraint.

"*Tizoc* . . ." he demanded harshly, "go *back* to your temple!"

The high priest took a quick step backward. He flung his long arms straight behind him, his body bent slightly forward and his head turned to the side. He stared at the outrageous physician, his eyes dilated with fury.

Quantzin stepped toward him, raising his plump hand palm upward in the priest's face. He shook the hand in angry determination: "Go back to your temple, Tizoc. We have no use of you here." Quantzin vindicated Nezahual's high dignity. "The Emperor knows as well as his priestlings the significance of the stars. In his own time Nezahual the Lord will decide whether the newborn child shall die. That is his prerogative."

"Then you do know," Tizoc answered, his voice shrill. "You know that the child of the seventh hour must die. The aspects were *not* for the Empress's death—"

"We know very well." Quantzin's attitude was suddenly quieter, more contemptuous. "Leave the palace, Tizoc."

The high priest raised his head, a smirk on his lips. He partly closed his eyes as his long arms folded the scarlet mantle about him. "Has a dog from the western mountains, straying too long in a palace, imagined itself the master? Do you mimic your lord's

32

ways? There will not always be those to protect you, Quantzin." He seemed to forget that open quarreling in Nezahual's presence showed a dangerous contempt. His threat, however bona-fide, was the height of indiscretion.

And Quantzin took his advantage. "No, not always, your Eminence," the physician answered, forcing his thick fingers together again on his belly. "But my protector sought *me* out. . . . No," he reassured himself, pursing his thin though protuberant lips, "nor do I lean on him." He stared direct at Tizoc, absolute conviction in his voice and ostensibly without malice: "I am true to my nature; death threatens no defeat." He was beholden to no one—though granted, there had been extremities.

The high priest nodded in approval, deigning a slight smile. The physician had apparently decided not to challenge him further.

Quantzin, however, was not finished. He paused before the great prelate, robed in his short silver-gray tunic. The ends of a worn mantle were tied about his neck, and its rumpled folds of pale-blue and orange plumage overlapped about him to the floor. "But you, Lord Tizoc . . . you were prepared for your exalted station. A master of your priesthood taught you your purpose. You listened, and took the meaning another offered you as your own. Has this a particular significance, Lord Tizoc?"

The priest coughed. His energy had spent itself, and he wanted to be gone. "Significance? Yes . . . yes, Chief Physician. At fourteen I was chosen by Lord Cacama to be his successor—destined in the first spring of my youth to the highest throne of my priesthood."

"You were entrusted with your priesthood, in your own eyes, in early youth?"

"Yes," Tizoc answered, weary yet vaguely amused, "in my own and others' eyes, entrusted."

"You were intended for authority, obliged by the strictest vows to protect the dignity of Cacama's throne . . . ?"

"Obliged, and robed in the scarlet vestments to nourish our lord Hummingbird Wizard on the blood of flowers—to counsel the temporal princes of our empire, Quantzin, not to feed them herbs." His voice was almost gentle, quietly chastening. He started to raise his hand and summon his immediate subordinate

33

from the hall behind him. They could pay final obeisance together.

"Obliged, Tizoc . . ." Quantzin repeated, "meant to be something you have not become." There was a slight pause. The physician pursued his denouncement in a low, intimately contemptuous voice: "Lord Cacama, were he to observe you now, might be galled by your ineffectuality. You have come in his scarlet robes, his heavy jewels, to ask a necessary death . . . necessary, at least, in the eyes of your priesthood. You have not even found an opportunity to put your question. You appear so elegant, *so* formidable!" Quantzin raised his hand, indicting the high priest. "Here you stand, before the Supreme Lord of Anahuac—a scavenger in wind-serpent's plumage—and behave as a common death-merchant. Are you bartering for the life of a child? High priests are above fearing offense taken to them. Cacama demanded.

"I am as nothing in this land of yours: yet you disgrace yourself, your priesthood, and your Emperor, by threatening me in his presence. Out of respect to Nezahual, Lord Tizoc, I must ask you again to quit the palace. This is a time of sorrow. One does not come to take away, but to comfort. Stray dogs are nevertheless capable of sorrow; and here, in the halls of sovereignty, after *me* the scavenger."

Tizoc, subjected first to Nezahual's evasions, was altogether unprepared for the physician's final attack. He had been led into exposing himself, then summarily slapped. Overwhelmed with his humiliation, which he had not only permitted but unwittingly aided in, the high priest stared up at the throne through bleared eyes. For a moment he was unconscious of his sudden tears. His lips twitched nervously with soundless, half-formed words. Surely the Emperor would not allow this sacrilege.

Above him, he could only see an indistinct shimmering of orange, gold, and white. *Wind-serpent's plumage . . . scavenger!*

Still uncollected, Tizoc raised his hand to summon the prefect of his temple. Quantzin had touched on a fatal weakness: the prelate's desperate need to identify himself with his office. Had Lord Cacama been confronted in such a manner, the old noble would have been highly amused. He had imperiously flaunted his personal weaknesses. Tizoc, though he had reached forty-three, was still

34

firmly confident that high priests were high priests, and princes princes for all their human frailties. In fact, in great offices a man had no choice but to lose his mere humanity. His self-image had become that of his robes. It was sacrilege to question a man's fitness after he became so exalted. (The irony was that one could only lose "humanity" by such outrageous humor as old Cacama's.)

Nezahual summoned others to his throne, but Tizoc didn't listen. The high priest watched his prefect kneel, and gestured for him to rise—then quickly reversed his order, shaking his head in confusion and anger. The obeisance was to the Emperor. Nezahual, ignoring the under-priest, left him on his knees.

". . . and those are my wishes, Baron Tupil," the ruler was saying. He had seated himself on the throne at last. The Lord Marshal of Tezcuco bowed, and stepped aside. Another state dignitary, the Cacique of the Private Guard, also stood on the platform; and halfway down the dais waited the infamous Lord Tlamec.

"Baron Itzco . . ."

"Yes, Serene Excellency?" the Cacique of the Private Guard asked, tilting his small head intently.

Nezahual leaned forward. "Lord Tizoc . . . is it your pleasure to wait in the palace until the pyre for Lady Tecui is prepared?"

"Serene Excellency," the high priest answered faintly, "I am very tired. With your permission—" He knelt beside his prefect.

"Very well, my lord. I will send a messenger for you later. Lord Itzco, accompany your exalted uncle to the gateway. And Tizoc . . . on the fourth day my new son will be acknowledged before the people. Look through my family records and bring me his name."

The priests waited for Itzco to descend the seven tiers, and all together they crossed the hall. The Lord Executioner continued up the steps to where Nezahual and his marshal waited. Quantzin, the chief physician, walked slowly toward the anteroom behind the throne. Perhaps he was thinking of his two sons, who had accompanied him in exile to this savage land of abundance. Tizoc might very well take vengeance.

"There is too much blood in that priest's brain," he might have observed with sympathy—and no little satisfaction. But why . . . why had little Tecui survived the night, to die in the third hour of daylight?

35

3

"Ixtlil . . . it's the name for a prince, my lord Tizoc," the young cacique answered, incredulous and amused.

"So—"

"But this is a mere concubine's child!"

Tizoc glanced at his nephew, then walked casually toward the doorway onto the court. His outstretched fingers were pressed firmly together. After a moment he asked: "How is it, Itzco, that you are the commander of our Emperor's private guard, and yet know so little of palace rumor?"

There was no reply.

Tizoc nodded to an attendant, and the heavy drapery was pulled aside. A slight but continuous rain had been falling since the early hours of morning. The mosaics outside glowed a deeper, liquid hue in the sunlight—the dusty, worn colors now brilliant blue-vitriol and yellow chalcedony. Even the dull, intricately carved jasper façades of the buildings reflected scarlet on the wet pavement.

In the center of the wide enclosure, rising tier on tier of white, polished stucco, stood the War God's pyramid, casting light into verandas that were usually hidden by its shadow at this hour.

It was a common enough phenomenon, the rain and the sunlight together. That the pyramid should reflect such brightness from the eastern sky, however, was an optical freak. The light seemed to flutter through the confine, illusive yet distinctly illuminating, while the turrets on the side were painfully afire and blurred in the direct rays of the western sun. Tizoc, almost morbidly sensitive to the visual, forgot the significance of his question.

He stared into the court for a time, watching the fragments of a myriad rainbows glance on the stone—and then said at last, in a low voice: "Yes, we shall call the new prince *Ixtlilxochitl. A little black-flower prince,* my dear Commander." The high priest was himself obviously amused by the name he had chosen for Nezahual's latest son. So an insignificant rival had named the heir apparent nine days before—and then been asked to sanctify the Empress's death: to a lesser man, Tizoc assured himself, this would be taken as an affront. (But for one so in need of recognition, it was no more than a shift in emphasis, and ridicule became acceptance.)

Tizoc stepped backward and half-turned into the room: "Though our Emperor seems not aware, he has done *me* the greater honor. And, Itzco . . . the rain has come." He waved his left hand gleefully toward the open doorway. "It is but the second week into the third month. Drought was expected this year. But see, my nephew, rain—rain for the young corn." Without question, this was also a personal achievement. Tizoc was not only chief of the War God's cult; the High Priest of the Rain God was his companion and lieutenant. The child sacrifices to Tlaloc had brought the water.

"But, my lord uncle . . ." Itzco tilted his ferret head, clasping his arms together behind him and bending forward . . . "how do you know the infant is black?" He wondered at the coincidence; for no one had been allowed to see the child but the Emperor's immediate staff. Not even the Lord Chancellor—

"Surely, Itzco, *not* because you told me. You are the chief knight in my order of Eagle Warriors, yet you seem to have more loyalty to Nezahual's guard." The prelate abruptly faced the room, but avoided his nephew's gaze.

"Only through omission, Lord Tizoc," the cacique answered coldly.

"Whatever you intend by that!" the high priest exclaimed petulantly. He decided not to press the matter, however. Itzco was a cautious, extremely adroit leader of men (although perhaps inclined to be a little too eager for blood), and a decided asset to Tizoc's knighthood. The cacique was quite small and slender, and his head was habitually thrust forward to one side. He bore a family resemblance to Tizoc, his features sensitive and boyish. Standing alone in his warrior's gear in the center of the apartment, he seemed a child armed for practice combat—except that the hatchet that hung at his side could be put to immediate and lethal

37

use. Itzco's nose was unnecessarily aquiline, though this one feature the high priest thought was quite attractive. The young cacique was also raptly curious about everything.

His uncle noticed that Itzco had paled, and that his small, rounded ears were unusually pink. Tizoc quickly added: "But black the infant is, though his concubine mother is fair and Nezahual as bright as the sun. Tell me, my nephew, who will be present at the ceremonies this afternoon?" He appeared undecided on his next position in the apartment, then stared sideways again into the court outside.

Itzco cleared his throat and sniffed thoughtfully. He sauntered past his uncle and, pausing in the doorway, stretched out his hand to catch the rain. "Tlamec the Executioner . . . and Tupil the Marshal . . . and old Prince Quaupo the Chancellor . . ." His attention was caught by movement high on the pyramid.

"And who else?" Tizoc asked impatiently, withdrawing farther from the willful young warrior.

"The Lord Mictla, High Priest of Smoking Mirror," the cacique answered, turning to see Tizoc's expression. It was this prelate that was his uncle's great rival in Tezcuco, the other great ecclesiastical prince. Smoking Mirror was the patron god of Nezahual's kingdom, and Mictla was in theory the supreme pontiff. Only because the previous emperor had chosen to ignore both gods, and took the God of the Unknown as his protector, were Tizoc and Mictla competitors at all.

"Mictla the fantastic," Tizoc remarked with casual disdain. "And who else, Lord Itzco?"

"Quantzin the divine healer—"

"Is our Emperor inviting his slaves also?"

"Not that I know of," Itzco replied with a thin smile, turning back into the court. "But Acatli, princess of Tulán, will be there, and Lord Ahuitzotl, the ruler of Mexico."

"Oh?" Tizoc rubbed his hands together, not sure whether he was pleased or distressed. "When did he return to the valley? Are Nezahual and he still on intimate terms? *Ahuitzotl* . . . well, this promised to be a strange afternoon." He had decided to confront Nezahual with further proof of his son's malignancy. But the Lord of Mexico, Nezahual's brother king: one really didn't know what course Ahuitzotl might pursue if there was further argument. And besides, the Mexican High Priest of Hummingbird Wizard and Tizoc were not particularly congenial. "Is the Lord—?"

"No," the cacique answered, anticipating his uncle. "Ahuitzotl is bringing none of his prelates or ministers with him. Several household nobles—and the young Montezuma, his priest cousin."

"Montezuma must be at least twenty-three now," Tizoc commented, wondering how he should manage the afternoon.

"He is twenty-three," Itzco stated offhandedly. "Have you heard what happened last week?"

"No," the high priest said, and walked toward his throne.

"As you know, the present high priest in Mexico is very old. Almost seventy, isn't he?" Tizoc murmured something, and Itzco continued: "Last week he offered his miter and robes to Montezuma, with a plea that the prince in turn should offer up the old man's heart to the War God. Montezuma was sweeping out the temple when he was told—and burst out in tears, humbly begging the messengers to find a worthier successor. Another should wear the vermilion robes."

"A modest youth. But tell me, Itzco: are there others the Emperor has summoned?"

"Lord Catzin, chief of the merchant guild, and . . . oh yes, what is his name? The four-year-old Cacama and his mother."

"By the Feathered Serpent, who are *they*?" The high priest turned on the dais and sat down. He shook his head in exasperated humor. "Tell me, my dear nephew, who . . . who is Cacama?"

"Your predecessor's namesake, I suppose. His mother was your great Cacama's niece. Nezahual himself named the boy."

"So . . ." Tizoc waved his hand impatiently. "Who is Cacama the child? Why did the Emperor bother to give him the name of a high priest?"

"Well, the child's mother is a princess in her own right, and at the time was Nezahual's favorite concubine . . . and because, my lord Tizoc, our Emperor *is* the boy's father."

Tizoc leapt to his feet, struck by the sudden revelation. In a low,

39

strained voice he asked: "Itzco, do you understand at all what you tell me?" He rubbed his throat with his long fingers and sat down again.

The commander walked quickly to the dais and stared up at his uncle questioningly. Itzco actually knew very little of palace rumor. Cacama and his mother were asked to the naming ceremonies because the infant involved was his brother and the concubine's son. It was merely a thoughtful gesture.

So it was not an unfounded rumor, Tizoc thought to himself— or an imperial whim. "Nezahual does intend taking her for his next empress," and probably with dispatch.

"What, Eminence?" Itzco put his foot on the first step of the dais.

"What is the concubine called?" the high priest asked in a tired voice.

"I don't recall," the cacique answered. "She is an Aztec princess, the cousin or niece—"

"You will know her name soon enough. This very afternoon she might be recognized as the new Empress of Anahuac. Child Cacama is about to be a prince—second in line to the throne of Tezcuco. Listen to my words, Itzco."

"But Lady Tecui is so soon dead!" The warrior was bewildered, and walked away from the dais. "Nezahual has his heir . . ." He stopped in the doorway, facing his uncle as though to ask confirmation: "It is prohibited. Nezahual must not take another wife." The Sovereign Lord of Anahuac could at least wait a year or so, if he chose to defy the council of electors.

"Prohibited or no, that is apparently his will. I suspect the Lord Ahuitzotl will support him. After all . . . if Nezahual was contemptuous enough of his nobles' approval to set a boy consort over them, he surely won't be deterred from placing another empress on the throne."

"Will you challenge the Emperor's right?"

There was a long pause. Tizoc clapped his hands and several attendants crossed the room to kneel before him. "Has the High Priest of Tlaloc come?"

"Yes, Your Eminence," they answered in unison.

"The prefect of my temple?"

"Yes, Your Eminence."

"The Chief Vicar of my pyramids throughout Acolhuacan?"

"Yes, Your Eminence."

"Then bring them before me immediately."

As he waited, Tizoc composed himself on his graceful wicker throne. He felt his heavy ceremonial rings chafing together. From the doorway onto the court a low voice called: "Uncle, will you challenge Nezahual's right to bring yet another empress to his throne?"

The high priest, without glancing toward his chief knight, answered: "No . . . no, Itzco. I dare not." It was even more imperative that the infant born four days ago in the seventh hour of darkness should be slain. Perhaps—perhaps this *was* Nezahual's perverse humor. He would first give the child the means to destroy Acolhuacan, then order his sacrifice.

"Once before Nezahual tormented me this way . . ." Tizoc commented aloud.

"What did you say, Uncle?"

The high priest waved his hand, as though to say *never mind,* and followed his thoughts privately.

By middle afternoon the rain had ceased falling. Tizoc, on entering the palace grounds, found an expectant group of nobles in the court that separated the two chief buildings. To the left was the Tribunal of the Gods, where the lords of the city were crowned. It was here that the decisions affecting the commonweal were given to the people. In the Tribunal of the Kings across the way was the throne room of Tezcuco. Here the sovereigns carried out their reigns.

There was a particular significance in Nezahual's choosing the former building for his present ceremony. Immediately on the high priest's arrival, Lord Itzco perfunctorily touched the pavement at his uncle's feet, raised the hand to his lips, and disappeared into the Tribunal of the Kings. Tizoc exchanged slight bows with the High Priest of Tlaloc at his right, then with the Lord Chancellor, who stood a little apart from the others. The fourteen great barons of Acolhuacan waited about him. Alone among the nobles, the old prince was jeweled and robed according to his dignity. His expres-

41

sion of awe comforted Tizoc, who was quite perceptive of the subtlest reaction to himself.

Through half-lidded eyes the prelate caught the glint of sunlight on metal. Tupil, the Lord Marshal, pointedly ignored the entrance of the four dignitaries of the temple and continued speaking with his companions—the executioner and his aide, and a deposed Prince of the Maya. Everyone seemed completely unaware that only princes, religious or secular, were allowed to robe themselves otherwise than in the coarse mantles of the lowest *macehual*.

In the center of the nobles stood the aging but still lovely Acatli, princess and courtesan. Near her were the insolent physician Quantzin and the Chief of the Merchants, who in another day had been so powerful. Tizoc respected, almost admired, the paternal merchant-baron, however. Lord Catzin, whose father had been the greatest of Nezahual's chancellors, had protected him on several critical occasions in the high priest's youth.

On the steps of the Tribunal, with an expression of surprising disdain for one reputedly so humble, waited the priest-prince Montezuma. Tizoc wondered why he wasn't with his cousin and Nezahual, wherever these lords were.

Suddenly Tizoc felt a peculiar shock run through him. It was as though he had unexpectedly discovered a red-and-gold snake coiling a short distance away. Repulsion, *yes!* —but he quickly discarded his fear, and turned to speak with his prefect about some dubious ritual that had taken place in the temple. ". . . and must be stopped, really," Tizoc mildly insisted, staring at his chief vicar for support.

Mictla, High Priest of Smoking Mirror, watched the rival prelates with fierce contempt for a moment longer, then crossed from the gateway to the gardens and mounted the stairs of the sacred Tribunal. He paused a few steps from Montezuma, but did not trouble himself to recognize the prince. Mictla faced the gathering (who had carefully watched his entrance), his narrow shoulders curved in and his chin high. His elbows bent, he raised his hands palm outward in sickly blessing, the fingers limp; but the high priest's eyes were intense and darkly smoldering. Montezuma left the platform and merged into the crowd.

"I . . . have just . . . returned from the *moun*tains," Mictla announced in a harsh voice that was placed high and back in the palate. "The god . . . of the mountains, lord of *beasts,* Jaguar God . . . sends you warning and blessing." The high priest spoke in a halting monotone, oddly accentuating his words. He was no older than Tizoc—in fact, Tizoc had undergone the tribulations of rule somewhat longer; and yet Mictla seemed worn and distraught with years. They were both tall, gaunt. But Tizoc was proportionately emaciated; the other's belly protruded morbidly, as though he harbored death in his entrails. His self-hatred, the disgust of life, had found a visceral lodging.

As Tizoc was intensely preoccupied with policy, so Mictla was rabidly engrossed in the spiritual life. Agonizingly enough for the priests of Hummingbird Wizard, it was Mictla that achieved greater and greater temporal power.

Tizoc continued talking to his subordinates, ignoring his rival and unconsciously raising his voice. Murmurs of awe, however, soon distracted his attention.

Mictla had waved to his guard, who stood closely pressed near the Tribunal of the Kings; and as the warriors parted, a remarkably well-favored youth stepped forward. His nakedness was barely covered with wreaths of flowers interwoven with gold and tufts of feathers. There was a proud melancholy in his bearing; and as he passed to the stairway below Mictla, the nobles fell to their knees and touched their foreheads on the pavement. The youth cast petals from his garment about him. In his wake the rising dignitaries caught the leaves and pressed them to their lips. Even the Lord Montezuma paid homage to the passing god of Tezcuco.

Tizoc trembled in annoyance. His cult offered no such spectacle. More than to any other god were the blood offerings made Huitzilopochtli, the Hummingbird Wizard—but not with such absurd selectivity. The prelate muttered to his companions: "Why don't they rip out his heart, and be done with it!" Every year it was the same thing. A captive warrior, chosen for his physical perfection, was taught by the opposing cult to impersonate the god Smoking Mirror. Throughout the duration of eighteen months he wandered the streets of the city, robed in jewels and flowers, attended by warri-

43

ors of the Ocelot Order. As he passed, playing on gold instruments or singing sad little liturgies, the people worshiped him as Smoking Mirror, the Perpetual Youth, descended to earth.

At night, garbed as the dreaded Night Wind and armed with darts, he rushed possessed along the dark highways. He lurked in the shadows of the roadside, blowing weird night sounds through his whistle. Sharp, chirping bells were tied to his wrists and ankles, and the cult warriors followed after him. (Often, however, the sinister god was glimpsed in separate parts of the city at the same hour. Only one could be the incarnation.) And a brief month before his dramatic and pathetic end, four lovely princesses, becoming goddesses, attended the last needs of the consecrated youth.

"Six weeks, *Tezcatlipoca*," Tizoc called out in a hoarse whisper as the youth passed. "The fifth month nears—"

The captive god glanced sadly at the high priest who mocked him, and smiled as he lifted his flute. The guilelessness of the boy's manner caused Tizoc to feel ashamed; and he bowed, not to the manifestation of another god, but to the young warrior himself. Not over eighteen years, and as lithe, as pure and virile as . . . "An antelope, Cihua," the high priest said aloud in quiet appreciation to his nearest companion.

The prefect kneeling beside him stared up in surprise. Since Tizoc had become a prelate he rarely spoke in such an intimate voice to his childhood friend. Tizoc turned to the other high priest, who was rising. "Soon enough he'll visit the little pyramid across the lake." His voice was both sarcastic and tender. This was the way of life. Indeed, one's career often began in glittering brilliance, attended by great honors and feasting—so soon to be brought to its end, an end darkened by bitterness and fear of the terrible pain.

The thin, sweet wail of a reed flute fluttered on the damp wind. The faint coughs and rustling of robes, the involuntary murmurs and striking noises that arose from the crowd for a moment simulated the restlessness of the woodland.

Tizoc was on the verge of compassion when a conch trumpet blasted several notes nearby. Again the assemblage fell to the pavement, this time, together with Tizoc and Mictla. Only the foredoomed youth stood, one foot casually raised on the stairs as he continued to play his gilt pipe.

44

The strident, impersonal voice of the steward called out: "Neza-hual the Lord," and after a pause, "Ahuitzotl, Prince of Mexico." The two rulers quickly strode across the court. With them was the white-robed Coatl, High Priest of the Unknown God to whom but flowers and incense could be sacrificed. Coatl's name was called out also, but only two or three of the nobles heeded him. The merchant-baron and Tupil made the cross of the four winds on their chests as he passed.

As though appearing from nowhere, Itzco's elite guard lined either side of the stairway to the Tribunal of the Gods. The palace warriors knelt at every entrance that let into the wide court, their naked, glass lance blades pressed lightly against the paving stone. The commandant of the palace, the bland cacique that had so care-lessly received Tizoc on the morning of Lady Tecui's death, genu-flected a moment afterward in the doorway to the Tribunal of the Kings. Beside him on the low platform a young woman fell grace-fully to her knees. She wore a flowing mantle of shining green, the imperial *tilmatli* of quetzal plumage.

Standing between the two was the four-year-old Cacama, his little hands tightly clutching his mother's robe. The cacique's arm encircled the small prince to support and reassure him. In the new Empress's arms, a mere bundle of hummingbird down (though strangely animate for a child only several days old), waited the ill-starred Ixtlil.

As Nezahual crossed the court, it seemed to Tizoc that fast per-cussions accompanied the Emperor's steps. The high priest again felt the impacts in the pit of his stomach. He did not look up, but Tizoc was aware that the Empress had appeared. He knew that the infant, his and the empire's nemesis, was waiting to be recog-nized. And with his odd sentience, he was sharply conscious of the animosity between his own warriors and Mictla's. Tizoc earnestly prayed that the spirit of his dead predecessors might come and advise him. Then, suddenly, the poundings inside him stopped.

Nezahual paused before the consecrated youth at the foot of the stairs across the court from his empress. He bent his head slightly, attentive to the melody the other persisted in playing. As the sov-ereign listened, seemingly unconcerned that he had brought an abrupt halt to the ceremony, he toyed absently with the gold medal

45

that hung over his chest. A slight smile hovered on his lips. Ahuitzotl, a man who had been infamous even in youth for his bloodmongering, reached down and touched his young cousin's arm. Montezuma hesitantly rose, his expression one of absolute humility, and bowed his head to the Lord of Mexico. The young priest's hatred of Nezahual was well known throughout the three cities; but in the Emperor's presence, it was at least adequately disguised.

At last the spurious god ceased playing, and withdrew the flute a few inches from his mouth. The Lord of Tezcuco, clothed in a white robe embroidered with leaves of pale-green plumage (and seeming a little like a martyr prince himself, awaiting his assassin), nodded his head as though in agreement to something. Nezahual put his hands together and bowed his head, then stretched out his arms in exaggerated obeisance, lowering his head still farther. The Emperor called out his own name: "Nezahual*pilli*," which was also one of the god's titles in his guise of Death Dealer.

The youth replied: "Hungry Chief," repeating the name, and bowed in the same manner. The two paid their private though sympathetic mockery to each other. Like this mild boy, Nezahual periodically became possessed himself by the Death Dealer. But seven years before, he had accompanied the lord waiting beside him on the bloodiest expedition in the entire history of his people —and had himself aided in the sacrifice of twenty thousand victims, the climax of the sacrificial cults that dominated his lake cities.

Nezahual straightened up, his mood abruptly changing, and quickly climbed the stairway. The two Mexican lords followed him halfway, and paused on the middle steps. The High Priest Coatl, with an expression at once stern and gentle, blessed the boy with open palms—then followed the Emperor to the platform before the Tribunal of the Gods. Mictla, kneeling nearby, was outraged by the other high priest's behavior. Nezahual sensed his anger and glanced sharply at him, as though to say: *This afternoon I will* not *be amused by your outbursts;* and Mictla, still glaring furiously, held his tongue, sacrilege or no.

Tizoc, on whom this brief scene had certainly not been wasted, raised his head and smiled delightedly at Mictla, who appeared even uglier in his hatred. The heavy wrinkles in the fanatic high priest's forehead became welts, and the scars of recent mutilations were fiery. Tizoc stared curiously at the flower-bedecked youth, who stood in a strange confusion near the foot of the stairway. The flute stem rested idle on the captive's chin as he gazed up at Coatl in resigned yearning. Not even Nezahual could save him. The Emperor gestured toward the opposite building.

Tizoc turned to watch the Empress descend into the court, followed by the commander and her son. As she passed, the high priest stared at the bundle in her arms—and drew back dismayed. Two very black, and decidedly evil, eyes returned his gaze in a focus that was quite unnatural; and when he thought about the incident afterwards, it seemed to Tizoc that the infant Ixtlil *had* grinned malevolently.

At this moment, Tizoc felt accused, as though the child were very much aware that the grotesquely elegant priest hankered after his death. Tizoc's gaze fell on the small Prince Cacama; and he wondered for a moment what had happened to the heir apparent. He glanced quickly about the court, but there was no sign of the fair Temozin. As though Nezahual's mind were also on the absent heir, and the common thought momentarily associated them, Tizoc suddenly felt a profound melancholy.

The Empress had shyly mounted the low stairway, and knelt before her lord. Nezahual took her gently by the elbows and raised her up. With his arms still about his new consort, he presented the Empress to his nobles: "My lords, prelates and ministers of my city and the empire . . ." He paused, and pressing his lower lip between his teeth, contemplated the young woman beside him. He had lain with her dutifully, as he had with his other concubines; and yet at this moment he judged her, took account of her features and manner, as though like his nobles he were viewing the Lady Ilan for the first time. It was too late to love her.

Nezahual stared down at the congregation, his expression becoming almost supercilious. He withdrew his arms and stepped back, his left hand catching up the hems of his imperial mantle. His right fingers covered the gold medallion that lay on his chest.

47

"Warriors and priests of Anahuac," he began again, "behold and pay homage to the consort of Nezahual*pilli*. Gaze carefully upon her, the Lady Ilan, for she is become your Empress."

Montezuma and his ruling cousin fell to their knees on the steps below. A murmur of surprise ran through the crowd, who had not expected such an immediate and secret coronation but at most an announcement of Nezahual's intention. No one, however, raised his voice in denouncement. "Gaze upon her carefully, my lords," Nezahual repeated. "When she is borne through the streets, press your foreheads to the earth." Nezahual hesitated again, and stretched his hand behind him. The white-robed Coatl took the Emperor's arm and stepped forward. Lady Ilan moved aside and allowed the high priest to take her place.

Nezahual raised his head and with closed eyes announced: "The infant son Lady Ilan holds now at her breast is the *last* prince Nezahual the Lord shall give to his people." He opened his eyes and stared out over the court: "Out of my early searching has come a strong city, an empire that continues a few years longer the golden age of my father."

He looked down again at his kneeling courtiers: "Out of my longing for women, the mothers of men, has come an heir to the throne of my ancestors. I give you yet another prince, and another, for the security of our city. And now . . ." Nezahual motioned for Ahuitzotl to rise and come to him, "my brother in sovereignty, nobles of my city and the land of Acolhuacan, I shall retire to the realm of my own thoughts." It was a moral if not an actual abdication. To the electors of Tezcuco, his words were an indirect command that his successor should be chosen from among his immediate sons.

He turned to the Lord of Mexico standing beside him: "Do you dispute the wisdom of my actions, now or in the past, Ahuitzotl?" The Aztec shook his head and said something no one but Coatl could overhear. "My lords Mictla and Tizoc," Nezahual called, gazing intently down into the court and ignoring the prelate behind him, "accompany me into the Tribunal of the Gods." As the High Priest of Hummingbird Wizard reached the platform, the Emperor asked in a low voice: "And what, Lord Tizoc, shall be the name of my last prince?"

"Ixtlil, Serene Excellency. His name shall be Ixtlil*xochitl,* youngest and final son of the great Lord Nezahual." Serious words, but the comic sense had somehow entered. Tizoc, by the slightest inflection, had thrown a mock-heroic cast on the whole proceedings. Little Black Flower—!

Nezahual glanced at him in mild surprise, and nodding his head, returned Tizoc's thin smile. The high priest appeared in unusually good spirits—in fact, actually jubilant with a wicked insight. The humor was infectious. The young Emperor opened his mouth, exhaling a short laugh. He turned to Coatl, who himself seemed amused, and then stared down at the dour Mictla. The situation was suddenly ridiculous . . . as though Tizoc's incorrigible predecessor had wandered spirit-wise into the group.

A sudden idea struck Nezahual and the sovereign took a few steps into the court. *"Telpochtli,"* he called out. "Warrior Youth, come to us." He stretched out his hand and waved the young captive up the stairs. Then the supreme war lord of Anahuac took the infant swaddled in hummingbird down from its mother and held the prince out. Nezahual spoke reassuringly to the quasi-god, who then reluctantly took the child in his own arms. Those most intimately concerned with the ceremony about to begin completely misinterpreted the gesture. The Empress seemed frightened. Mictla was appeased; Tizoc, further elated.

Nezahual indicated that he was ready to proceed. The gateway of the Tribunal was thrown open, and the Emperor passed into the great apartment with the sacrificial youth at his side. Immediately behind them came the lords of Mexico, then the Empress, little Cacama, and the four high priests. The nobles in the court rose quietly, and followed the fourteen chief barons into the sacred building after the minor dignitaries of the various temples had entered.

Itzco, Tupil, and Paltzin exchanged a few words on the platform after the last courtier had passed into the hall. Then the commanders returned to their stations.

The hall was brilliantly illumined with torches. Near the center, before the pedestal on which lay the skull of an earlier king, a large fire had been kindled—set aflame by the embers that priests had

49

ignited at the moment of the infant's birth, to nourish its frail life. No one but Tizoc seemed to notice that the pile of javelin staves and shields with which the barons pledged their loyalty had provided the fuel.

On the shining skull lay an immense emerald of the most sacred hue; and on this, the miter-crown of the three cities—its long, jeweled plumes rising and curving down like fronds of some fantastic fern.

At the farther end of the hall was a throne of gold inlaid with turquoise and jade. A tapering baldaquin stretched overhead, surmounted by a jewel that glistened alone in the darkness above the torches. Its color was such an intense red that the seemingly detached orb appeared likely enough to be a crystallization of sacrificial blood and fire. The jewel was a miniature sun, the changing glints on the dark, burnished ceiling its firmament; and Tizoc was not at all sure but that the solar god did inhabit (at least with a fragment of his spirit) the slowly turning, pulsing fire above Nezahual's throne.

The high priest stood a little to one side of the dais, watching the nobles begin their feast of celebration. Across from him was the impromptu throne on which Ahuitzotl had been seated. The Mexican lord talked quietly to his cousin, who half-reclined on a pillow near his feet. Despite the gloomy grandeur of the place, Tizoc was still in his strange humor. He should really be seated himself. His own throne was behind him, next to Mictla's; and a moment ago the Emperor had glanced at him questioningly, in wonderment why the High Priest of Hummingbird Wizard was not content to remain with his fellow prelates.

But Tizoc, unaware as it were of his own erratic behavior, had returned Nezahual's stare with all aplomb. Nezahual glanced away, an expression of amusement again on his lips, and continued his conversation with the Lord Marshal and Quantzin. Waiting also before the dais, a few paces from Tizoc, stood the flower-robed youth. It seemed as if the captive imagined himself completely alone. He stared in awe and sad curiosity at the infant in his arms, gently rocking the evil child.

Little sounds of pleasure arose from the bundle of hummingbird plumage—but Tizoc was not to be discomfited. He ignored them both. The high priest watched the slaves enter with salvers of quail and citron, of jellied duck and avocado. Pitchers of pulque and mescal were brought, in seemingly endless relays, for the libations to come. Urns of chocolate and coffers of copal gum were placed beside the pedestal of the skull.

Suddenly a hush fell over the nobles. Nezahual had risen. He took the goblet of chocolate and mescal an attendant offered him, and descended to the floor. Tizoc genuflected as the Emperor passed, then rose to follow behind him—his sense of the burlesque gone.

4

NEZAHUAL faced his high priest over the sacrificial fire: "My lord Tizoc—"

"What do you ask, Nezahual the Lord?"

"Was it on the fourth day past that our son was born?"

"On the fourth day past, Nezahual*pilli*."

"The judgment of the gods is determined . . ."

"Yes, determined," Tizoc replied in an expressionless voice, the questions and answers mere rote. He paused now, as though to say more. Nezahual stared at him intently, expecting the refusal and denouncement; but Tizoc cleared his throat, suddenly convinced this was not the moment to confront the Lord of the Three Cities. (Besides, there was still the suggestion that Nezahual was indulging his perverse humor. Perhaps he intended to give the child a momentary position in the empire.)

"The *tonalamatl* has revealed the course of the infant's life, Serene Excellency," Tizoc answered after his hesitance. He had deliberately committed himself. Had the high priest, in the brief silence that again ensued, demanded the rites of death, Nezahual might very well have conceded and turned the festivities into a sacrifice to the Rain God.

The Emperor pursed his lips, then asked in form: "What shall be the name of my son, Lord Tizoc?"

Again the high priest answered: "Ixtlil—" There was no touch of levity now, no misunderstanding. If the day and hour of a child's birth had evil significance in the Book of Fate, custom permitted the naming ceremonies to be set for a later time. By this religious fiction Tizoc might have contrived an excuse for himself . . . but he had accepted the actual hour of the prince's birth, formally acknowledged the full import revealed in the almanac. And now, he had pronounced the name.

At the sound of *Ixtlil,* Nezahual emptied his goblet of chocolate and mescal into the fire. A sharp, momentary hissing, a burst of steam—and the child's compact with life was made. An attendant approached Tizoc and knelt. The high priest solemnly gathered a handful of copal nodules, and staring intently at Nezahual, cast the incense into the coals. It was done. Tizoc had only delayed his defiance of the Emperor's will.

Ironically enough, Tizoc's misunderstanding of Nezahual's intention had now assured Ixtlil his life. The ruler actually expected the high priest to renege his previous stand and sanction another day for the ceremony. As the incense billowed up, Nezahual glanced toward the throne, gesturing for the flower-robed youth to approach; but the captive had no understanding of the rituals. The exchange between the lord and the priest, the brief crisis, were without meaning.

Nezahual beckoned again, and the youth hesitantly stepped forward—then paused in confusion. No one near him would take the liberty to direct the personification of a god. The infant in his arms suddenly began to struggle violently, as though it wanted to leap away. The folds of hummingbird down were thrown aside, and a black little head and shoulders thrust into view. The startled captive firmly seized the child about the waist and, holding Ixtlil out in front of him, he strode hurriedly toward Nezahual.

If it were possible, Tizoc would have been even more alarmed than the rest of the gathering. Directly beside him, held out at arm's length over the fire, was a possible heir to Anahuac. It was proper for the infant to be purified in the flames—but hardly in this manner. Perhaps, for the briefest moment, Tizoc had the impulse to put his foot in the captive's path and give him a slight shove. His obvious reaction, however, was more considerate. He raised a restraining hand to the youth's shoulder, and calmly (not to say graciously) stepped back . . . as though he were enacting some ritual of reclamation. The captive followed him, bending his elbows in a little but still keeping the child at a distance.

The high priest stared down at the now-quiet prince in what he imagined was well-disguised abhorrence. Tizoc wetted his fingers in the bowl of water offered to him, and touched Ixtlil's lips and forehead as he pronounced the name—this time invoking the Goddess of Childbirth, ". . . that the sin, which was given us before the world began, might not visit this child; but that, cleansed by these waters, it might live and be born anew."

Nezahual, having taken the weapons from his attendant, stepped forward and pressed a toy bow and several arrows into his son's outstretched hands. Ixtlil gave a low, feral sound of satisfaction; and the youth holding him, reassured by the Emperor's nearness, drew the prince closer to his chest. Nezahual patiently guided the child's hands in the motions of the bow's use; then took it and the arrows away, and offered a miniature javelin to him. With an odd eagerness, Ixtlil tried to wrench the straight, thin weapon from his father's grasp. Nezahual, amused and surprised, removed his hand. Untaught, the infant pulled back the javelin as though he were about to cast it.

Nezahual glanced at Tizoc, who stood at his left, with a slight smile. The high priest was not impressed—at least, visibly. The Emperor reached out to take the weapon, and completing this part of the ceremony, placed a ribbon of woven gold about his son's head. Lady Ilan, who had waited beyond the pedestal of the skull, now approached her husband. Without a word, Nezahual indicated with a disinterested gesture that the child should be given to her. Until his weaning in the third year, Ixtlil would remain in his mother's trust.

The Empress and her two sons withdrew to a low dais set back between the chief throne and the chairs of the high priests. Nezahual, taking the captive youth with undue familiarity by the arm, followed behind her. Tizoc waited by the sacrificial fire and watched the other high priests pour out their libations to the Old God. When this had ended, the feast began, the nobles of the empire periodically rising from their mats to cast pulque and spiced partridge into the embers. The soft, grating percussions of notched deer bone set the complicated, pleasantly confused rhythms. The accents were strengthened by the resonant thumps of a water drum, an inverted gourd floating in a large tub—the favorite instrument of the god Tlaloc.

A dancer, an extraordinarily beautiful girl in her sixteenth year, was performing below the throne, the meaning of her movements described by a singer in a wailing chant. The emphasis of her gestures was caught by the sharp tinkles of copper bells tied about her slender wrists and ankles.

Tizoc had retired to his throne, and casually watched her, preoccupied with his own thoughts. He had suddenly felt exhausted and feverish. Not quite an hour had passed since Nezahual's libation to the Fire God, yet the utter tedium of the continuing ceremony weighted the high priest's spirits. It seemed that he could hardly even catch his breath, and he began to breathe with a conscious effort.

In an attempt to rouse himself, Tizoc watched the dancer with greater interest. "Yes," he nodded to himself, "her waist *is* amazingly small . . . hips full, heavy and round . . ." His associations caused a mild excitement, a focus of intellect, and he glanced across the hall. Sitting on their low, wicker chairs were the four chief dignitaries of Nezahual's kingdom. The old Prince Quauhpo, Lord Chancellor (or Snake Woman, as he was officially called), was nodding senilely at the others' words—as though he had the vaguest idea what they spoke about! Beside him was Baron Tupil, chief of the armies, who with the chancellor constituted the highest judicial authority. This last noble had grown extremely sullen and peevish of late, Tizoc observed to himself. Tupil was but a year or so older than the Emperor . . . "thirty-six or seven, yet absolutely consumed by black bile." He had been such an aggressive, talkative youth.

A little behind Tupil, and turned to face the room, was Tlamec, the Lord Executioner. Tizoc had a mixed reaction of pity, awe, and what he imagined was contempt, for him. Tlamec was evidently holding a monologue with the fourth minister, the liaison chief in civil and military affairs, and the exiled Mayan prince who sat with them. Beyond their specialized functions in the Supreme Council, each of the four ministers was the military head of one of the quarters into which Tezcuco was divided (and into which the twenty clans were evenly distributed).

As he talked, the executioner stared out into the apartment, apparently unconcerned with his listeners. It was difficult to imagine that Tlamec was among the most brilliant and efficient of the Emperor's commanders. He was short, light-boned, and heavy-set;

55

his voice was high and quarrelsome, his gestures effeminate. Once, it was said, he had had great difficulty in exercising direct authority over his warriors. Only after his caciques realized that by obeying him they had the better chance of winning honors in the field, much more of surviving, did they wholeheartedly support his actions.

Tizoc had often spoken out in defense of the Lord Tlamec, particularly because his rival Mictla openly tried to have the commander stripped of tribal honors and sacrificed. Tizoc glanced to the right, momentarily catching sight of the evil-breathed prelate of Smoking Mirror, and then turned to the High Priest of the Rain God: "Who is that child dancing?"

"The Princess Nicte," the man answered without hesitation, obviously fascinated by her himself. "Nicte of Tulán . . . or rather, Your Eminence, a princess of Chichén-Itzá."

"Of Chichén-Itzá!" Tizoc exclaimed in amused disbelief. "Why, she is so obviously a slave. You were more correct in imagining her of Tulán."

The other, not wishing to contradict his superior, bowed his head. Tizoc persisted, however: "There is only one high noble of the Maya in Tezcuco. There . . . over there," he indicated, waving his hand towards the prince sitting at Tlamec's feet.

"Nicte is his daughter," the High Priest of Tlaloc replied self-effacingly. "Her mother was the personal slave of the Lady Acatli, Princess of Tulán and Baroness of Coatepec . . ." As he spoke, both prelates carefully watched the dancing girl. Her full though delicate breasts were sharply conical under a blouse of fine cotton interwoven with gold and with violet plumage. It occurred to Tizoc, while he listened to how the Maya prince discovered her mother, that Nicte was voluptuously enjoying the movement of her body . . . as though the slight friction of the fabric over her breasts aroused her.

The high priest became conscious of the copal fragrance, the scent of lilies on the stagnant air, and the faint reek of burning flesh that was offered on the fire. ". . . But though the prince desired Acatli's slave," the other prelate was recounting, "he was thoroughly ruined. His city had deposed him, and he was quite without funds to purchase her." Tizoc felt the raspings of the

56

notched bone as though he held the scraper in his own fingers. Nicte moved so naturally, and yet with the greatest practice.

". . . And at last, Acatli made him a bargain; for she had already allowed him to lie with the slave, and the girl was with child." Tizoc was a little surprised that his companion had so completely informed himself of Nicte's origin. The children of slaves were not born into servitude, yet Acatli (who had tragically lost her own daughter) now wanted her slave's. So the princess agreed to give the lovesick Mayan her attendant, and a villa in the capital with the income to support it, in exchange for the yet unborn child . . . "whether it be a boy or a girl."

"So Nicte became Acatli's slave," Tizoc commented.

"She is also a princess, by right of her father," the other added.

"And undoubtedly shall be a courtesan—"

"In the manner of the gracious Acatli herself, a courtesan," the High Priest of the Rain God stated respectfully.

Tizoc stared out into the hall, and quickly found where the Princess Acatli was watching the ceremony. Beside her sat the merchant-baron Catzin, who had been her constant companion for the last ten years. There was little sign of it from this distance, but Acatli must surely have been in her early fifties, and Catzin was sixty-five at least. Oddly enough, the high priest decided, they were still carrying on the most romantic relationship in the capital of Nezahual the Lord.

About the couple were the "speakers," the representatives of the clans, who composed the Supreme Council. Their class had become almost permanent before the end of the last reign, the hereditary body politic. They still represented the clans, however, not themselves. The weapons they had offered Nezahual in fealty were among the token shields and javelins of the fourteen great barons —who were the suspensive factor in the government that embodied the chieftainships of the Tezcucan provinces. Eight of the barons who sat near Acatli ruled in Acolhuacan proper, the remaining six in the valleys adjacent. Together, they were the unofficial electors, subtly influencing the four ministers of the Supreme Council though subservient to the collective speakers.

Tizoc raised his head and looked directly across the hall at the Lord Ahuitzotl, Prince of Mexico. He himself had been an admirer of the great courtesan's, and had given her the estate of Mexical-tzinco on the rich peninsula just south of his own private holdings. In fact, Tizoc's predecessor had given Acatli one of her chief titles; and Nezahual had taken her daughter for his first love. There were those at court (among the fourteen chief nobles, who detested the merchant class) that had sought to punish Catzin for his insolence in taking the beloved of princes as his mistress; but this was not adultery. Acatli was unmarried, and no law breached. They could only stone Catzin to death in effigy. The merchant was still in Nezahual's favor and, as Chief of the Merchant Guild, a man to be reckoned with.

"She is, I believe, Your Eminence, the most beautiful child I have ever seen in the valley . . . and but sixteen, the age of ripeness," the High Priest of Tlaloc concluded, his judicious tone ill disguising cupidity.

Tizoc, whose mind had already wandered from Nicte to the courtesan Acatli, and then to Catzin, turned abruptly to his subordinate. He pursed his thin, lower lip and raised an eyebrow: "I'll purchase the *Princess* Nicte tomorrow, and send her off to your Temple of the Frog. She may attend the divine tadpoles in the sacred pool." The other winced, regained his composure with an arch expression, and answered in an innocent, truly reverent tone: "My lord Tlaloc, God of Rain and Nurturer of our Mother the Earth, would be pleased with your thoughtfulness." He raised his hand to his chest and bowed. Tizoc, not amused by hypocrisy, turned away. He noticed the flower-robed youth cross the lower hall on his way out. The captive god was closely followed by Mictla's warriors.

As he passed, the nobles again touched their foreheads to the pavement. And after he had gone, the low swell and fall of voices again filled the hall. The musicians resumed their playing; and other dancers knelt before the Emperor's throne. A dwarf attempted to bedevil the Lord Executioner. Acatli sent her attendant off, probably to ask something of Nicte; and the physician Quantzin, who had slipped out of the hall, reappeared on the dais beside Nezahual. In his arms was the Prince Temozin, heir apparent to Anahuac.

Tizoc heard the shrill, distant sigh of a whistle, and wondered if it were from inside the Tribunal or had been wafted in from the streets.

From the dais set back and to the left of the main throne, the four-year-old Cacama stared shyly at his other new brother. There was no sound from Ixtlil himself, who had nursed quietly at his mother's breast and had seemingly gone to sleep.

Five days after the ceremony of name-giving, Tizoc stood in the doorway of his apartment and stared into the court before the pyramid. Everything had decidedly gone awry. The rains had refused to stop, though he had sent an urgent request to the High Priest of Tlaloc to cease further sacrifices. The drainage in the compound was insufficient for such a downpour, and the water had risen to within an inch or so of Tizoc's sill. For two mornings now, at the first dawn, the high priest had been forced to mount the pyramid in the chill rain and officiate at the rituals that commenced the day.

This morning a catastrophe had happened. One of the priests that were to bear him to the altar on the summit slipped as they were crossing the courtyard. Tizoc found himself suddenly waist-deep in the stagnant, cold flood. The Sun was near his appearance; and there was absolutely nothing else for the pontiff to do but continue up the pyramid, drenched and shivering. His hand shook so much when he took the sacrificial knife that Tizoc was ashamed of the clumsy incision he made in the victim's belly.

He lifted the heart up, afraid that the Sun should be angry, and hurried down to his apartment. Then he went about his next chore, the divination by means of wild beasts' entrails. It was at best a bothersome task. Tizoc had an extremely acute sense of smell; and the odor of fowl entrails especially nauseated him. In the beginning of his reign, he had forbidden quail or duck gizzards to be cooked anywhere in the temple enclosure. The stench of human hearts from the tower was quite enough for the copal incense to disguise, and there was an uncontrollable association.

But on this morning his divinations proved more than bothersome. Despite the rain, he was all for hurrying to Nezahual with his new proofs; but the Emperor had left the capital for his estate some thirteen miles to the southeast. Tizoc ached in every nerve

59

and muscle of his body, and his head was feverish. The temple physician was brewing him something now; so the high priest decided to wait for a more favorable day and stood brooding over his latest illumination. Cihua, the temple prefect, had already removed the wretched beast; but Tizoc still shuddered from what he had seen.

A young prongbuck had been brought to him from the mountains north of the valley. It was unusual for the strange, antelopelike creature to be found in this forested region, and Tizoc had been extremely interested in the results of his probing. The circumstances promised something of importance. When the animal was brought in, it appeared to be a splendid specimen of its kind. It struggled frantically to free itself from the priests, not weakened in the least by captivity or the rough hands of its captors. The wide eyes were glazed in the stupor of fright, and the savage creature had actually attempted to impale its tormentors before an attendant regained his hold on the long neck. The sturdy, sharp horns were equipped with short snags in front, and especially wicked.

Tizoc quickly ordered the animal to be stretched across the onyx table, eager to examine its viscera. Cihua offered him the thin obsidian blade, and the high priest ripped open the belly with his usual deftness. The creature didn't even cry out, but stared at Tizoc with an expression of equally rapt curiosity! The intestines were lifted out and thrown on the floor. Tizoc and Cihua bent down on their knees to inspect the patterns nervously formed. This was ghastly enough. Neither had ever seen such dire expressions of warning, not even in the handbooks.

They glanced at each other without a word, and the high priest rose. Tizoc returned to the table and inserted his hand again in the wound. He studied the liver for a moment, then the spleen. Suddenly, without removing his hand from the cavity, he stared at Cihua in utter amazement, his jaw lax. He probed again, then stared intently into the animal's eyes. It was dead now . . . it should have never been alive! Tizoc frantically probed again; then removed his hand with a jerk, and strode angrily across the apartment.

It was quite obvious to his fellow priests what he had discov-

60

ered: Tizoc had been unable to find the animal's heart. Apparently, it hadn't any. For several minutes there was a stunned silence in the apartment. Finally Tizoc turned from the doorway and abruptly commanded—*"Take it out!"*

And once in the corridor, the priests immediately carried the animal into Cihua's quarters. Their attempts were equally futile. Within half an hour the entire temple had heard of the incident. In the lecture halls the novices left their studies, and the older priests brought out the codices of divination. The priests who had attended Tizoc were asked to draw the configurations of the entrails. Cihua was forced to threaten punishment in order to restore discipline, or he might have been held responsible to the two assistants of the chief vicar of Tizoc's pyramids (who looked after the novices).

In the midst of the temporary confusion, the prefect was summoned to the high priest's quarters. "Take out this trash," Tizoc commanded, as though he blamed Cihua for bringing the monstrous prongbuck to him in the first place; and the under-priest, afraid of the prelate's ill-temper, stooped down and swept the quivering entrails onto the skirts of his robe.

Tizoc had been on the point of calling back the apprehensive Cihua and asking that his litter bearers be alerted. But no . . . his plunge into the icy water earlier in the morning was already having an effect. After all, he was in his early forties, and his constitution had never been particularly strong. "Sheer will," he thought, shaking his head. "Only my extraordinary will has kept me alive." He felt his forehead. Tizoc became aware that his legs were unsteady, and wondered sadly why the physician hadn't come with his herb tea. Really, he must lie down.

Tizoc slowly crossed the audience room and paused for a moment at the entrance of his sleeping chamber. He felt a profound sentimentality for the place where he laid himself down to rest . . . perhaps to die. Why, why must he be tormented by the threat to Anahuac? It was Nezahual's empire, and Tizoc controlled but a handful, a scattered handful, of pyramids. And he shouldn't have been harsh to Cihua. He must send for the prefect later. Perhaps if he listened to poetry, it would quiet him, prepare him for the unknown.

61

Nezahual the Lord, when he was informed of the incident of the prongbuck, had no reply. Several other evil portents were related to him (for Tizoc had journeyed to the rural palace in company with three other high priests and their astrologers); but still the Emperor was not particularly concerned.

In exasperation, Tizoc exclaimed: "But Your Serene Excellency, if the child Ixtlil lives, disaster . . . absolute, unavoidable, disastrous disaster . . . will ensue. The very elements assure us—"

Nezahual nodded pensively, his mind apparently on something else.

The high priest insisted: "Ixtlil is destined to overthrow your city, to destroy your people and your gods."

"Yes . . . yes," an old astrologer agreed in a faltering voice. "The eastern heavens, Excellency—they're not at all proper." The others murmured.

The Emperor stood, surveyed them for a moment, and began to walk away. He stopped a few yards distant, however, and faced the dignitaries. Nezahual had noticed the foreboding aspects of the stars several weeks before anyone else had accounted them. He had had a tower built in this very palace, high on one of the outlying crags, in order to observe the warning he long knew would come. In a quiet, deliberate voice, turning away as though to address the commander Tupil standing nearby, he said: "If death is to come with evening, why fret the afternoon away? My father left me an empire, my lord Tizoc . . . an empire of a thousand tribes, and the warning of my ruin." He paused. "Do you remember, my lords, how our city was first built? Do you remember the god who was driven from the valley, so that we might prosper? In the very beginning our day of atonement was set. Not tomorrow, Tizoc—but one of the days thereafter, the weight of eternal balance will carry us down."

He strode back to the kneeling priests: "The approaching years are described in our most ancient writings. The signs and portents are already recorded. There is no need to make further entry of what has now begun. The future has existed long ago; we have only to wait and perceive it. The last years are upon us."

"But my lord," answered one of the prelates, "would you have one of your sons be the traitor? These are but warnings of destruction. With foresight that is given us, we might avert the ruin of our cities."

"Have you yourselves not taken vengeance by warning victims who could not escape of your approach?"

The high priests exchanged glances. "The very gods that once deposed the Feathered Serpent are our gods still," another replied. "We nourish them on the blood of flowers, Serene Excellency," Tizoc added, intent on his purpose, "and they are terrible in anger. Give us the blood of the child Ixtlil to offer the Sun. There will be no further prodigies to frighten us. The children of your children, and the children after them, shall inherit your palaces and gardens."

"You are difficult to convince, Lord Tizoc. Why did my father write a lament for my losses as he gave me his scepter? I was but in my seventh year, and Tezcuco at the zenith. Have you listened to his verses, Tizoc? He promised that the realm should soon be wrenched away, *our moon diminished rise* . . . And these words, Tizoc, were spoken even before my birth. The children of my children, and the children after them, shall inherit ruin. Their rank shall be forgotten; and in their exile, only the memory of lost cities for a little while persist."

Nezahual hesitated again, then spoke with absolute finality: "If my youngest prince is to aid a vengeful god in destroying our land —if this is so, then I will not dispute the Feathered Serpent's claim. Ixtlil is to live. This is my decision. If you would protect your temples from his wrath, my lords—well, then, pray to your gods to deliver you. Ask your Hummingbird Wizard and your Smoking Mirror to turn aside the threats of the bright god they plundered."

And with these words, Nezahual dismissed the high priests. If the Lord of the Three Cities had been undecided in his first encounter with Tizoc, unsettled and in such momentary anguish that he had sought evasion in self-ridicule, he now had reached a firm conviction of his obligations to his last prince. The laughter of his hurt had spent itself. Tizoc's effort to deter him, particularly the high priest's refusal to set another day for Ixtlil's birth, further convinced the Emperor of the role his son must play.

". . . The weight of the eternal balance will carry us down," he had told the priests; but how could they understand? Let them think the god would come with their destruction, conceive the death of the cities in a primordial image. The essential truth was there: the return to the opposite. The zenith had been reached. Collapse was inevitable, the running contrariwise.

Ixtlil had become, at the moment of his naming, an expression to Nezahual of a secret part of his nature he had long restrained . . . an expression of energy that the last Tezcucan ruler of Anahuac would force into the future. As Nezahual watched the band of prelates leave the lower terraces, however, he thought of his heir apparent. Temozin would be a gentle lord, woefully unsuited to the bitter years to come. And that other verse of his father's:

> *The darkness of death*
> *is brilliant*
> *light for the stars . . .*

5

THREE years passed without particular incident. In a land far to the northeast of Anahuac (an unimaginable distance over great wastes of water where forgotten sea gods quarreled and fretted), the turn of a century was celebrated in the court of an aging queen. Isabel the Catholic, Queen of Castile and Leon, had already seen a mighty empire fall to her warrior's swords. A Genoese navigator had founded an outpost in the islands of the Carib chiefs, to the south of the Maya cities; but the sea beyond Yucatan was swept by treacherous winds. Even the most venturesome of Nezahual's merchants rarely penetrated the low, wild forests to the southern shore.

And in the first year of the new century, the child Don Carlos was born of a mad princess—heir to the thrones of Isabel and her husband. But this was an event in another world and in another time; Nezahual and his princes lived in the past of mankind, their cities belonged to the days of Nineveh and Tyre. As they wandered through their palaces and gardens, the rulers of Anahuac were akin to the ancient priest-kings of Erech. Only by the most flagrant confusion of era could one imagine the two cultures confronting each other. Surely whatever the eventual disaster to befall Nezahual's line, it must arise out of a people's weakness, out of their inability to govern themselves or to repel the invaders of their own time.

In Anahuac there was no halt in the sequence of festivals. Every fifty-two years there occurred a terrible moment when the rhythm of the universe was broken—then life began anew, another count was begun. This was yet seven years away when the new century was welcomed in Isabel's land. It seemed to the inhabitants of the lake cities that the valley had at last become theirs. Summers were long; and the warm, dark earth was watered by frequent, light rains. The fields were white and gold with produce. The fragrance of fruit groves filled the valley.

Over the highways from the south came the caravans laden with chocolate and *xtabantún,* the slightly narcotic liqueur made by the Mayas of fermented honey. The slave market of Azcapotzalco, on the westernmost shore of the lake just north of the great Tlacopan causeway, was teeming with strong youths and beautiful maidens taken as tribute from conquered tribes. It had been in this city that Nezahual's father had defeated a tyrant's warriors and had then proceeded to put the wretch to death in the palace baths.

In the great market of Tlaltelolco, the companion island of Mexico, the people of the lake region could purchase rare perfumes and dyes from the southern jungles or the delicate whitefish from Lake Pátzcuero in the rival empire of Michoacan. It had been at the hands of a Tarascan prince that the Aztecs had suffered their only important defeat. With lands that stretched from Lake Chapala in the northwest to practically the Tropic of Cancer on the northern shore of the Carib Sea, that reached south into what is now Salvador, up the western coast to Acapulco, then inland to the great plateau—with these thousands of square miles under their domination, and ten major races paying them homage, Nezahual and his fellow monarchs had little need of the barren ranges fronting the western ocean.

And actually, had either Nezahual or Ahuitzotl desired it enough, they could have defeated the Tarascans. All the nobles in the three cities had agreed that this was so. One of the Mexican commanders was harrying the tribes of Nicaragua (continuing the exploits begun by Ahuitzotl); and the merchants of Tezcuco and Tenochtitlan were planning the caravans they would send into the conquered territories. It was rumored that cities as wealthy as those of the Maya in Yucatan had been discovered.

It was obvious that the erratic Nezahual's nature had deepened and quieted. During the three years since Lady Tecui's death, his capital of Tezcuco took on more the appearance of an enormous warehouse than that of the nervously garrisoned stronghold of a war lord. Perhaps the priests chafed a little under the young Emperor's rule—for Nezahual had returned to his earlier attitude and restricted the sacrifice of slaves; but this was in keeping with the golden age. The reign of Nezahual's father seemed to be revived. To some of the Emperor's ministers, it appeared that their sovereign granted amnesty to the Mexican lords too easily when undercover actions against Tezcuco came to light. These incidents were not infrequent; but as Nezahual explained to his merchants, the loss of a city here and there was of no practical importance.

The chief power of Tezcuco lay in its being the fulcrum of the empire, the pivot on which the other cities balanced one against the other, weight against counterweight. The authority of the imperial city was unassailable, even though its princes were to throw in the copilli of Anahuac. "The value of a cask of chocolate, a bale of hummingbird feathers, a skein of cotton—the very act of bartering is controlled by us; for we hold the scale on which all loss and gain is measured. The market of Tlaltelolco, though policed by Aztec officials, is the actual seat of our power." This Nezahual assured his merchants, and quieted the restlessness of his nobles by the other observation.

The city-states of Anahuac balanced their might on the steadfastness of Tezcuco, exchanging conquered towns and levying warriors with the surety of purpose. Were Tezcuco deprived of authority, even the vast armies of Ahuitzotl would be unable to hold the plateau itself in subjugation. When the Aztec commanders ventured out to quell one rebellion, twenty others would flare up. Conquest was a state of mind agreed on by the victor and the vanquished. A city could accept slavery, if by so doing its own vassals were held by a common understanding in fealty. This common understanding was focused in Nezahual's capital. Tezcuco was the gauge.

Even the most ambitious Aztec would be afraid to touch one hamlet of Acolhuacan proper. "Let them take some wretched mountain village here, a sterile valley there"; whatever the Mexican overlord might wrench from the inhabitants would be exchanged to Tezcuco's profit in the market place.

The barons listened, skeptical but not too openly complaining. After all, their chief wealth did exist in valley holdings, and Nezahual promised them protection of these. Nezahual held court in his capital with greater infrequency; and his Supreme Council was extremely flattered by the authorities he delegated to them. Indeed, it did seem there had been a return to more democratic days, when the clans ruled and the "chief of men" was only their spokesman. The citizens of Tezcuco heard that their Emperor had ordered a throne cut in a cliff near his rural palace, and wondered at his caprice. It was undoubtedly a gesture of complete self-assurance. They took heart at his actions, at his apparent decision to withdraw actively from the mere business of governing. If they had need of him, Nezahual would come.

The capital seemed to have forgotten the existence of the Prince Ixtlil. Prince Cacama reached his seventh year, and his formal instruction in the warrior craft had already begun. The four electors gave him a small residence near the Imperial Palace, outfitted his household with slaves and warriors, and appointed a high noble to oversee his education. The heir apparent himself had been taken to Nezahual's estate of the Plumed Towers after his weaning; and the Emperor decided to keep the boy until his sixth year.

Ixtlil remained in the Imperial Palace with his mother. During his third year, however, the unfortunate Empress began to wonder if she were capable of handling him. It was perhaps in the ninth month, the Birth of Flowers, the third month into summer, that Nezahual heard again of his controversial infant.

The afternoon was waning. The air was filled with the low, steady drone of yellow bees. An occasional dragonfly skimmed along the stone water trough that led from the well into a grove of fruit trees. A low wall overgrown with honeysuckle skirted the path leading to one of the palace buildings above; and a slave girl had paused for a moment in her descent to catch the salt taste of the lake wind. She balanced the empty wicker pail on her hip, her eyes closed, and felt the summer weight of the sun on her lids. The flattened arch of her naked, sturdy foot was pressed over the worn edge of the step; and as she hesitated in her thoughts, the girl slowly worried it against the stone.

Then she smiled to herself with some simple pleasure and threw back her head. Raising the pail, she glanced out over the canal beyond the wall—then setting it firmly on her head continued down the path. The stone was shaded here by cypress branches. She enjoyed the damp, rough coolness of peat moss between her toes. The leafmold confused the flower fragrances and the salt wind into an earthy, dry sweetness.

The girl stopped before the well; and putting the tightly woven jar on the narrow ledge, she sat down beside it. She rubbed her full, dark arm, then languorously reached up to take the cord that dangled from a long pole attached to the post behind her. The girl carelessly fastened the pail, and without moving her body stretched out her arm to tilt the pole down. She leaned over to watch the slow descent, absorbed in her musing. The pail, carried by the downward movement of the lever, alighted on the surface ten feet below without turning on its side and began to float at the end of the lax cord.

The slave girl reached down into the well and seized the rope, intending to jerk it and upset the pail—when she suddenly felt a slight shove. Startled, she turned awkwardly to catch her balance, but the girl had leaned out too far. Her fingernails scratched over the stone, and with a wrench she plunged down into the water. Her frightened screams echoed up hollowly from the cistern.

The girl rose quickly to the surface and grasped the thin rope. Ixtlil quietly watched her pull herself up until her hands reached the end of the pole. She stared up at him in terror, but did not call out again. Her hands were not strong enough to hold her heavy body, and she slipped back into the water. She struggled again to rise, but it was futile. The frightened girl began to thrash about, trying to force her fingers into the crevices of the stone. If she had kept more presence of mind, she might have steadied herself with the rope and found the shallow footholds sufficient to carry her up. In her terror she quickly spent her energy, however.

As Ixtlil watched, a cold, satisfied grin on his little lips, the slave's efforts to save herself became weaker. She went down into the water . . . returned to the surface and feebly attempted to seize the now-submerged pail . . . sank again. Within but a few minutes she succumbed; and the three-year-old child, who had climbed to the top of the wall, peered into the quiet darkness beneath. Then he swung himself back on the post, jumped to the earth; and with that utterly detached attitude of a young child, walked to the stairway leading to the palace.

He really was an extremely attractive youngster in his change of mood. He was slender, and his little shoulders unusually broad for a child that had just begun eating venison and berries and unleavened corn meal. A thin gold diadem encircled his head; a small carnelian amulet with crystal pendants hung on his bare chest; and a loincloth with gold fringes fell from his waist. His feet were sandaled in soft leather, the thongs carefully crossed up his calves. It was perfectly obvious that Ixtlil was a prince; and when he was with the other children at court, even the older boys gave him his will. He had decisive little ways of avenging himself. At this moment, however, the alarming fierceness that often lighted the prince's eyes was absent. His full, already firm lips turned upward at the corners. He seemed not in the least vicious as he mounted the stairway, playing a little jumping game. His cheeks were fuller, his short nose less formed. The slight cleft in his round chin gave him an appearance of childhood innocence.

He paused midway on the stairs, about where the slave girl had stopped to enjoy the lake breeze, and tried to lift himself up. He wanted to look over the wall onto the canal. It was too difficult, and Ixtlil continued on. Sometimes he would stay alone in the gardens until it became very dark. Then the prince would wander stealthily about the grounds, trying to catch some warrior supposedly on guard asleep. When he did discover such a miscreant, Ixtlil would devise an immediate punishment, and thereupon carry it out.

The slave's disappearance was almost immediately noticed, and attendants were sent to find her. It wasn't until the following morning, however, that her body was discovered. Another slave had been sent to fetch water, and returned to the palace in great agitation. The Empress was quite upset, as the dead girl had been one of her personal attendants. Ixtlil did not find it necessary to commit himself. He had passed judgment on the errant girl, carried out his sentence, and the matter was closed. It wasn't deception that caused the child to hold his tongue: he merely would not disdain to vindicate himself.

As circumstance would have it, however, several other children had followed the prince to the well; for though they were afraid of him, or because of their fear, they found Ixtlil completely fascinating. The children had watched from the bank above the stairway as Ixtlil silently approached his mother's attendant, who sat so unawares at the well. They had wondered, when the prince stopped a few yards away from the girl, what he intended. The rigid, expressionless set of his face was a familiar warning.

Ixtlil had waited until the precise moment (as though he had prearranged the entire incident), then quickly walked to the low guard wall. He struck the leaning girl on the hips just below her waist with the entire weight of his little body, and immediately stepped back. As the girl fell, the watching children froze in a moment of terror, then turned and fled up the slope to the palace. They were too frightened that night to tell their parents; and it seemed to one particular five-year-old boy that when he encountered Ixtlil in a patio the following day, the prince had stared at him in warning. His fear of Ixtlil had caused the child to seek out his father, the chief of the frontier town Aticpac, in the main palace, and confide the story of Ixtlil's crime.

At first the chief was angry with his son, imagining it to be no more than an idle tale; but when he realized that the boy was almost hysterical with fright, he decided to look into the matter himself. Before calling in higher authority, even a baron of his standing had to be certain. He questioned his son about the other witnesses, and by late morning had gathered the fathers of the children together. Though it seemed ridiculous that a three-year-old could manage the murder of a strong, young woman, even if he chose, this was exactly what Ixtlil had done. What the prince's motive had been was impossible to judge, but the circumstances were clear.

The Baron of Aticpac, reassured by the anger of his friends, went directly to the old Prince Quauhpo, Lord Chancellor of Tezcuco. Quauhpo stared at him in momentary disbelief, then smiled blandly. Surely the baron was mistaken. There was prejudice against the young prince because of his birth. The other children had heard their elders talking. Surely . . . But the baron insisted that the Emperor be informed. This step could not be taken, the chancellor assured him, until the three other electors had discussed the matter fully.

"And what is to happen to my son in the meantime?" the chief demanded, convinced that Ixtlil knew of his child's actions.

71

The minister raised his hands in an unconcerned hopelessness. There was absolutely nothing Quauhpo could do. Another chief, one of the clan judges below the rank of speaker in the Supreme Council, stepped forward and bowed perfunctorily: "If Prince Ixtlil *did* drown the unfortunate girl, it was most likely with good reason—"

"Who are you?" the cacique asked angrily, aware of his actual if not official superiority.

"He is the Lord Zalmec, a judge in the precinct of Hummingbird Snake," the chancellor said, rising from his wicker throne. The old man was obviously upset by the situation, and he lowered his palsied head to dismiss the baron.

"You should at least have Ixtlil confined to his nursery!" Aticpac insisted. "Last week he cut off another boy's finger because the child was caught cheating at patolli . . . the prince wasn't even concerned in the game. He takes it upon himself to punish his own mother, the Empress herself, when she displeases him. He is possessed by the evil spirit of vengeance—"

"I can do nothing," the chancellor repeated in a monotone. The baron stared at him for a moment longer, completely outraged and alarmed. Then he turned and left the audience chamber, convinced that something monstrous would happen to his son if the boy was not immediately sent away. As he returned to his chambers he worried the question; for it was by law that the eldest sons of Nezahual's barons be kept until their sixteenth year in the palace confines. There was nothing to do, he at last decided, but to go to the Empress himself.

While the Baron of Aticpac was seeking out the chancellor, however, two of the children who had witnessed Ixtlil's escapade were searching for the child prince. One of them especially was intent on finding him: the eight-year-old Lord Nopal, whose father was baron of the great fortress city of Chiconautla at the edge of the northern swamps. Nopal had been as frightened as the others the night before; but when his father summoned him, and he was confronted with the testimony of the other children, Nopal experienced an odd surge of loyalty to Ixtlil. He determined to warn the prince that his crime was found out.

It was a little difficult to escape the group of fathers, as it was decided to keep the children under surveillance until Aticpac's return. The latter baron's fear for his son had been communicated to the others. Nopal had waited his time; and under the pretext of going to his mother (who was a confidante of the Empress's), he was at last able to leave the main palace. One of the other boys, however, had asked to accompany him to the women's quarters. Nopal waited until they had passed onto one of the intervening terraces before he confronted his playmate.

"I'm going to find Prince Ixtlil," he stated firmly. The other boy, who was a year younger and the grandson of the king of Tlacopan, turned pale. He stammered something, and turned as though to retreat to his father. Nopal seized him fiercely by the wrist: "You are a coward!"

"I am *not* . . ."

"You betrayed the prince."

"I did not. It was Mayo," the young lord answered, standing his ground.

"You told our fathers that what Mayo said was true." Nopal released the other, and stared at him in contempt.

"So did you," Tochtli said defiantly, glaring back.

Nopal, without admitting that this was also true, remarked offhandedly: "You'll never be a great warrior. Ixtlil will be a great leader of men . . . maybe even Chief of Men. Go back to your father; I'll find him on my own."

Tochtli hesitated a moment; then smiling ruefully, asked: "Where will we find him?"

"In one of the courts outside his mother's apartment . . . or down on the lower terraces."

"We'd better hurry," the younger lord said expectantly; and together they started off in search of Ixtlil. They found him playing by himself near a wide, shallow fountain. The two boys entered shyly, and genuflected to the three-year-old prince—who stared at them with wild curiosity. "Excellency . . ." Nopal began, then paused in embarrassment. Perhaps the knowledge that he had been found out would antagonize Ixtlil.

Ixtlil stood up and walked over to the newcomers. He smiled at them disarmingly and touched Nopal's ear. The long silver pendant swung back and forth; and the infant prince gave a little laugh.

73

"Excellency," Nopal began again, "our fathers know what happened to your mother's slave." Ixtlil stopped playing with the ornament, but the smile remained on his lips. "Mayo told his father, and everyone knows . . . and Mayo's father has gone to the chancellor. Everyone wants to punish you, and you'd better run away."

Ixtlil studied them, and without a word nodded his tousled head. He had scraped his knee on the pool wall; and as he thought about what the other boys had said, he licked his fingers and stooped to rub the scratch. "Go away," he said at last, and turned back into the court. Nopal and Tochtli stood up uncertainly and waited for him to say something else. Ixtlil, however, climbed into the giant pepper tree over the pond and ignored them.

As the boys left the court, the prince called: "Nopal . . ."

"Yes, Excellency?" the child answered, kneeling again with his companion.

"Nopal . . . Nopal and Tochtli." The prince repeated their names to himself and nodded, obviously delighted by their loyalty to him. The boys waited a moment; and as one child understands the intentions of another, both Nopal and Tochtli knew that Prince Ixtlil was now their friend. Had their fathers known the royal infant's sense of protectiveness was as prodigiously developed as the vengeful side of his nature, they would have immediately forgotten the episode of the slave's death and returned to the problems of government.

As it was, Aticpac shortly visited the apartments of the Empress. He tersely informed her of her youngest son's perversity, and added that his presence in the palace was a threat to the other children. The baron earnestly besought her to advise Nezahual of the situation. The high priests had warned at his very birth that Ixtlil could bring only misfortune to those around him. It would be an act of mercy to the warped child if he was quietly put away. The punishment of his unwarranted act was set by law.

Lady Ilan did not question the young man's sincerity. She began to weep; and the noble, touched by her wretchedness, attempted to comfort her. The Empress then begged him to leave her, promising to send a courier to Nezahual immediately. After Aticpac left, Lady Ilan summoned her attendants and told them the cause of

74

her slave's death. She asked Nopal's mother to dispatch the courier to her husband, and herself went in search of her son.

She found Ixtlil quietly sitting in the fork of the pepper tree. She gazed up at him sadly, and unable to think of anything she could say, sat on the bench below. She was an attractive woman in her middle twenties—not beautiful, but delicately formed and gracefully feminine. How could she reproach him, this evil son of hers? She put her hands together in her lap and rested her head against the tree. With a sudden pang of remorse, the Empress turned her head and scratched her cheek on the coarse bark as though chastising herself. Back and forth she scraped her face, unaware that blood had risen to the sensitive skin.

At last she stood up. "Ixtlil . . ." she called.

There was no answer, and Lady Ilan looked up at her son. "Ixtlil, I have told your father what you did yesterday." Still there was no answer. "He will send for you, and you must go away." Then she turned and silently left the court.

Nezahual gave no immediate response when he heard of his son's brutality. He was standing in a pavilion that lay at the bottom of a ravine several miles west of his summer palace. The stone was discolored with age, and bits of the broken tracery were held from falling by the thick tendrils of vine. There was nothing in the low, wide room but a couch, several pillows, and a thin rush mat that stretched to the edge of a pool. At the far side of the shallow basin, growing so close to the water that their branches swept down and trailed on the surface, was a brake of fern trees. Small, plump-bodied *axolotls,* the salamanders called "servants of water," wandered in erratic lethargy along the brim.

The slopes about the ravine were irregular with deceptive cliffs overgrown with low, thorny foliage. Midway on one of the rises there was a naked outcrop of porphyry; and below the narrow ledge, a sheer fall into the gorge. To the west beyond the pavilion, a conduit from the higher gardens emptied out; and the cascade churned and foamed down a stretch of sharp rocks to the floor. It was in a wild, secluded section of his estate that Nezahual often chose to spend his afternoons.

Even as he turned from the courier and strode to the edge of his pool, a covey of quail rose suddenly in flight a short distance away. In his early youth Nezahual had once commanded his companions to wage a mock though arduous battle along these ridges, so that he might choose his lieutenants. Those that had won in the contest, and survived the battles of the intervening years, now held the highest military posts in Tezcuco. Tupil was Lord Marshal, Itzco the commander of the elite guard. It was strange, however, that a man not yet in his full prime should return to the scene of his boyhood exploits. But here Nezahual came frequently; and here the courtiers found him on the day after his youngest prince's violation of the palace.

"My son Ixtlil deliberately pushed the girl into a well . . ." the Emperor said at last, raising his voice slightly and turning again to the messenger.

"The Empress is convinced that he did, Serene Excellency," the young man answered, averting his head in embarrassment. "Lady Ilan is prepared for whatever sentence you decide. She fears for the other children.

"What has Ixtlil said to defend himself?

"The Empress was going to find him when I left the Imperial Palace, Serene Excellency."

Nezahual gazed out across the ravine, his attention suddenly caught by a movement on the slope where the quail had been flushed. As he watched, a large golden-brown cat marked with black rosettes stalked into view. He watched the animal's approach as he considered his son's fate. It was in the fifth hour of afternoon, and the surrounding slopes quavered in the heat. A slow vapor rose from the pool, undisturbed by any breeze. The dusty odor of sage brush filled the room; and from the near distance there came a faint, dry rattle of some casually annoyed snake. A brightly colored wasp settled for a moment on the pool, then whisked to the side and away.

As Nezahual considered the problem, the slave squatted on his heels in the apartment behind, absently tracing a figure in the gritty silt past winters had washed in. A low cry of alarm suddenly rose from the youth; and the Emperor, aware of what had frightened him, turned from the pool with a slight smile. The courier, still on his knees, supported himself on an arm he had flung to the side and cowered away from the door.

Pausing on the sill, in a momentary attitude of fierce ruthlessness, was the aged and feeble jaguar that had been Nezahual's war companion for over ten years. The beast had fought at the Emperor's side in the great Oaxaca raid that had culminated the sacrificial cult of the three cities. It had strode arrogantly through the avenues of Tezcuco in the midst of victorious warriors, and had sprawled with feline disdain on the dais in the Imperial Palace as the barons feasted below. But now, wearied and almost blind, the royal jaguar was finishing out its already overlong life in the secluded gardens of Tezcotzinco.

It still had its moments, however. Even a very old jaguar could rip out a man's entrails in an instant of antagonism; and though Nezahual's pet was above this temperamental weakness, it enjoyed the respectful awe accorded a jaguar. It paused now in the doorway, switching its long tail and baring its yellowed, broken fangs. Nezahual called out its name, and the cat answered with a guttural moan of greeting. The jaguar crossed the room to his side, rubbed its ears against the Emperor's hip, then stretched out beside the pool, half turning as though to warn the slave of its potential.

Nezahual had reached a temporary decision. "Return to the Imperial Palace. Before the hour of Centeotl bring my son Ixtlil to me. I will decide on his punishment then."

The messenger touched his forehead to the pavement and rose quickly to depart. "Bring Baron Aticpac with you," the Emperor added; then once more alone, sat down on the low couch. Within the hour his litter bearers came, and he was borne to his summer palace on the hill of Tezcotzinco. The evening passed in a simple meal of maize cakes, a pepper stuffed with venison, two avocados filled with a sharp, delicate fish sauce, and a goblet of guava juice and mescal. Only a handful of his favorite chiefs attended him, among whom were Tupil, Itzco, and the merchant-baron Catzin.

During the performance of dancers afterwards, Tupil inquired his master's opinion on a decision of the Supreme Council. It concerned a recent rebellion in a city north of the valley. The council had decided to appoint a Tezcucan judge as temporary military governor, a man who was severe yet without brutality; but the judge favored by Itzco and Quauhpo was the Lord Zalmec, of the precinct Hummingbird Snake.

"I know nothing of the man," Nezahual commented, watching one of the dwarfs mimic the affectations of a dancer.

"He is straightforward of manner," Tupil stated without particular concern.

"I have known of him," Catzin remarked. "Scrupulously honest, but unsympathetic and hard. He would as soon take off a man's hand for some trifling thievery as give him a good beating and let him go."

Itzco leaned forward: "But this is the second time in the last five years that this village has defected. We must send a harsh governor who knows and strictly abides by the laws of Tezcuco."

"But we have agreed that the man we choose must not be brutal," Catzin insisted.

"Brutality is but strictness unwarranted," Itzco countered—then paused, delighted with his own phrase. "The very quality that gives Zalmec the appearance of harshness in our capital will bring him honors in the mountains. The northern plateau is continually on the verge of rebellion . . . and the Mazahua, they are a fierce, cruel, degenerate people."

"Only because there is little water for their cornfields; and in these long summers, the game flees the parched mountains for our valleys," the Emperor said. "It is easy for a tribe to remain loyal when the harvest is plentiful, and there are grains of gold and sleek otter pelts to trade in our cities."

Neither Itzco nor Catzin had anything further to say, but Tupil observed after a moment: "It is true, Excellency, that the northern tribes only respect the heavy hand. Remember your own vengeance on the Huaxteco in the mountains north of the Otomi. You gutted twenty villages, and threw their walls into the ravines below. For seven years their chiefs have remained peaceful, and the merchants report the tribesmen speak of you as a great, benevolent ruler of men."

"Do you want Zalmec to carry the *quaxolotl* to the Mazahua, Tupil?" Nezahual asked, rising from his throne.

The marshal nodded his head thoughtfully.

"Very well, give him the appointment. Let him carry the standard of retribution into the northern mountains. Is it nearing the hour of the Corn God, Comtzin?"

The twenty-three-year-old attendant, son of the Emperor's long-dead boyhood companion, stared across the hall at a thick beeswax candle. "Yes, Excellency, the fourth hour is near at hand." He had been long accustomed to giving Nezahual the time; for the ruler had an odd aversion to sundials, candles—anything, in fact, that interrupted the steady movement of sequence on sequence.

Nezahual stood for a moment gazing down on his nobles. He did not appear tense, but his companions understood his dread of the coming encounter with Ixtlil. Then without further comment, the Lord of Anahuac crossed the hall and entered the corridor. The slave Comtzin followed behind him.

6

THE attendants stepped aside, and after a moment the infant prince wandered into the richly furnished apartment. Nezahual sat on a chair above a dais of several steps. He watched his son approach without speaking, carefully examining the boy's manner. Ixtlil appeared to be an average, not particularly precocious child, the only singular characteristic about him the early refinement of his features. He had been dressed in a white tunic, which accentuated the darkness of his skin.

As Ixtlil approached his father, his little sandals made slight scuffing sounds on the coarse matting. He stopped before the throne and gazed with open curiosity at Nezahual; and as his father did not address him, turned his attention after a moment to the jaguar that lay on a thick rug nearby. The jaguar lifted its head from the powerful old paws and returned the prince's stare without blinking. Ixtlil, without a backward glance at the quiet ruler, walked over to the animal and pulled at its ear.

The jaguar purred deep in its throat, and stretched its neck. Ixtlil thereupon sat down between its paws and rubbed his head against its shoulder. In its satisfaction, the jaguar's long claws slowly curved out of their soft paddings and caught at the boy's garment when he tried to move. Instead of being frightened, Ixtlil carefully tore the sheer cotton away—and then began judging the sharpness of the nails with the end of his forefinger. Without knowing, the prince had given his father an important insight into his nature. For reasons of his own, Nezahual decided on the honesty of the child; he would believe whatever Ixtlil was to tell him. The prince had inherited the dark nature of the jaguar that had for so many years driven Nezahual to acts of destruction. It was a cruel, scrupulous temper.

"Why did you drown her, Ixtlil?" the Emperor asked at last, his voice calm, his manner quietly curious.

The child rose gravely to his feet, stared intently at his father for a moment, then turned his head away: "She made herself dirty." His tone was peevish, and he glanced toward the door in impatience.

Nezahual considered the answer. "Did you push her into the well to wash her, Ixtlil?"

"No," was the immediate reply. The prince turned back to his father, and Nezahual noticed the fierce brightness that suddenly came into his eyes.

"Why, then?"

"To punish her." The words came out in a low surge of anger. The child averted his head slightly and closed his eyes, his little jaw clenched. He apparently had nothing more to say on the matter. Nezahual rose and approached his son. He raised Ixtlil's head with his forefinger: "The girl must have been very bad . . ." Ixtlil closed his eyes tighter. "She must have been very dirty indeed. But a little water, and some soap, and a scouring with henequen—"

"She was dirty inside."

The Emperor was surprised by this, and let his hand fall. What could a three-year-old know about someone's being dirty inside?

"I saw her . . . down in the rushes. No one goes there . . . but *I* go. She had a man with her. They took all their clothes off. And the man had ugly hair—" Ixtlil interrupted himself. His little mouth sneered in revulsion. The idea of having hair anywhere except on one's head was apparently outrageous to him.

"But she took care of you . . ." Nezahual said in an attempt to end the description.

"She kissed *him* on the mouth," the prince insisted. "Then they acted as though they were fighting . . . and I called out, because he was hurting her, but they didn't hear me. Suddenly they stopped, and she didn't try to hurt him with her legs any more. She liked fighting with him . . . but they weren't fighting at all!"

Nezahual, abashed by the circumstances, continued to stare at his son. The child had paled with anger, and clenched his fists as he concluded: "I have seen my mother's dogs in the courtyard."

The Emperor turned and walked to the edge of the court

beyond his apartment. It was amazing that his small son had even guessed what was happening. Nezahual wasn't absolutely sure that the prince's ire had been merely aroused by the girl's impropriety. Nevertheless, though the girl had been unmarried, and her offense not punishable with such severity, Ixtlil's actions must be condoned. Nezahual gazed back into the apartment thoughtfully, wondering how he might quell his son's premature passion for justice. Surely so young a child could have no idea of death. Ixtlil could certainly not have intended taking the girl's life.

Ixtlil had returned to the jaguar and was stroking the cat's head as though he had completely forgotten his moment of anger. Nezahual called out: "Comtzin . . ."

The youth appeared immediately and knelt at the Emperor's feet.

"Comtzin, take Prince Ixtlil to his mother's attendants. Tell the courier that the prince is to remain with Lady Ilan, and that he must be kept under closer supervision. I have decided not to see Baron Aticpac, who has nothing to fear for his son . . . though I think the child should return to his parents' city. Aticpac may send his wife with him."

After this incident, Nezahual the Lord kept himself better informed of the happenings within his Imperial Palace. In the spring of the following year a crisis of more general import took his attention. At first the rains promised a bountiful harvest. Tizoc was immensely pleased; and the High Priest of Tlaloc suggested a pilgrimage to the Temple of the Frog—built in the centuries before the present empire, when the great Mitl ruled over the all-but-forgotten Toltecs in the valley of Teotihuacan.

When the rains persisted in falling, however, and the sluggish Acolman river, which drained the valley of the ruined pyramids, became a torrent rushing into the lake above Tezcuco, the high priests decided to let well enough alone. Of all the gods, Tlaloc seemed the most difficult to control. The more to honor him, his idol was placed atop the highest mountain near Tezcuco; and over the surrounding slopes artificial ponds were consecrated to his worship. Beside each of the five pools a child was annually sacrificed. During the festival just past, that of the sixth month, the priests plunged into Lake Tezcuco and imitated the sounds and movements of frogs to appease Tlaloc and his wife, the Goddess of Waters.

Every eight years, when the nameless, dateless day was introduced to right the calendar, a special festival was held. Throughout the fast the inhabitants of the lake cities ate nothing but maize porridge and water, and returned to their ways of life in savage times. They appareled themselves as birds and animals, and performed long dances mimicking the creatures of the forests and deserts. The lake before Tlaloc's chief temple was filled with frogs and water snakes; and into this the priests and nobles leapt, catching the reptiles in their mouths and devouring them. Whatever anyone could possibly imagine to please the Rain God was done, so that his wife should bear the *tlalocs,* the cloud children. Occasionally through the years the god would be usurious, and demand an exorbitant amount of blood before he allowed the use of his rain. Sometimes he might be overstimulated by the fertility rite (which consisted in drowning a boy and girl together in a canoe filled with hearts), and would deluge the valley.

This was what had apparently happened. Tlaloc was overwrought. The rains would not continue for long. They should take away the vase (which contained a kernel of every known grain) from his altar; remove the gold serpent, which signified the lightning, from his jewel-green idol. Tlaloc would then be angered— and to spite them, would hold back the rain. So Tizoc suggested; the High Priest of Tlaloc obeyed. Unfortunately, there was no cessation. The rain continued to fall: not heavily, but hour by hour, one week into the next. A tributary of the Acolman River became so flooded that its course was diverted into a side ravine; and the little city of Tepechpan, which had given Nezahual his greatest commander, was practically destroyed.

Through the month the sun continued to shine warmly despite the mistlike rain; and the valley shimmered in the humidity and a thousand arcing rainbows. The high, burnished tower of the War God's temple was absolutely opalescent against the gray-blue sky. The terraced gardens glistened a deeper, waxen green; and the rich fields were a darker, richer umber. The far-stretching swampland that connected the northern edge of Lake Tezcuco to the two higher lakes, however, had become ominously flooded. The cause-

83

ways that held the island capital of the Aztecs in communication with the mainland were but several feet free of the rising water. The low cornfields about Aticpac were flooded; and the shallow river that entered the lake at that point threatened to submerge the city. The baron, on leave from Nezahual, hastened to join his wife and son.

At Coatlinchan, the chief frontier fortress on the southern verge of Nezahual's kingdom, the dam crossing the river was washed out; and the main highway between the capitals was all but closed. By the second week of the seventh month, the little Feast of Princes, it became obvious to the Aztec engineers that their great dike—which stretched ten miles across the narrow inlet of the southern lakes and the marshes to Iztapalapan—could no longer hold back the mounting pressure; and Ahuitzotl sent to the Emperor for aid in fending off the threatened disaster.

Before Nezahual had dispatched the several thousands of men he intended to send, news arrived in the imperial capital that the Lord of the Mexicans was dead. The dike had been breached; and Ahuitzotl, without waiting for his cousin's reinforcements, had himself gone to supervise the frantic efforts to stem the downpouring waters that surged into the lower basin. A block of stone, weakened in its embrasure, was thrown down by the force of the escaping torrent. Ahuitzotl, who had been standing near the safety opening, was struck a glancing blow as it fell. At first he had seemed not badly injured; had risen by himself and continued directing his men.

A quarter-hour later, however, he collapsed. Though unconscious, the lord began to thrash about the platform, calling out eerie, animal noises of anguish and mortal hurt. His caciques restrained him and bore Ahuitzotl back to his island palace. A physician administered a quieting narcotic. Before the following day Ahuitzotl, the strong and vicious conqueror, the vindictive and relentless foe, was dead.

The Mexicans were left without a ruler. Coincidentally, the rains stopped falling. The islets about the Aztec capital were temporarily flooded, a few retaining walls collapsed, perhaps a thousand slaves were drowned; but surprisingly little of consequence resulted from the flood. Nezahual sent Tupil to Tenochtitlan; and under the

84

supervision of the Tezcucan marshal and a brother of the dead Ahuitzotl, the dike was quickly restored. Several days after the disaster a deputation of nobles presented themselves at the gate of the War God's temple in Tenochtitlan. They demanded to see the priest Montezuma, the twenty-seven-year-old cousin of the late king—and found the youth sweeping down the stairs of the pyramid. Encountering him on one of the wide tiers, the nobles knelt and pressed their foreheads to the pavement; and Montezuma, feigning complete surprise, begged them to rise. He shyly asked them why they had interrupted his duties to the god.

"To offer you the crown of your forefathers," they answered.

Montezuma again burst into tears, as he had when the dignity of high priest had been offered him; and earnestly beseeched the four electors to choose another prince. There was the lord Cuitlahuac his brother, who was known for fairness and generous nature . . . and there was young Prince Cuauhtemoc, who had inherited the dead lord's estates of Iztapalapa and had already given proof of military genius. Why should the electors insist on elevating a humble priest? There had never been a ruler of the Mexicans who had not first proven himself on the field of battle.

But the more Montezuma protested, the more the nobles insisted. His very humility impressed them . . . and perhaps they were further assured by his passive nature that the control of government should rest the more firmly in their hands. At last Montezuma pleaded with them to return to the palace. The priest promised to spend the night in prayer before the idol of Huitzilopochtli.

In the following morning, when the leaders of the Supreme Council again presented themselves, Montezuma received them in a quiet court under the pyramid. He had thrown off his black robes and was now appareled in a plain white tunic. With heavy sadness in his voice, he accepted their offer of the throne and allowed them to place the band of jewels about his head. Then he rose; and taking leave of his brother priests, Montezuma entered the royal litter and suffered himself to be borne to the palace.

A day in the tenth month (the Fall of Fruits) was set for his crowning; and his foremost caciques were sent into the rebel province of Oaxaca to take captives again for sacrifice. His relative, Nezahual, was asked, as was the custom, to give the coronation address and set the diadem of Mexico on Montezuma's brow. Nezahual, as formally as he was petitioned, granted the request. The months passed; the harvest was gathered in, and the famine—such as one which had occurred some fifty years before, after a severe storm had inundated the valley—was averted. At last Nezahual, Lord of the Feathered Scepter, journeyed the twenty-five miles over the lake to the Aztec capital.

Before the assembled nobles of the empire, he spoke of Montezuma's humility. He praised the line of Aztec princes in the most extraordinary terms. After a long oration (his exaggerations only appreciated by those of his caciques who knew Nezahual's ironic eloquence), the Lord of Anahuac concluded with a question: "Who can doubt whether the Aztec Kingdom has reached the zenith of its greatness, since the Supreme God has placed over it one whose very presence fills every beholder with reverence?" Nezahual paused, and caught Tupil's eye.

"Who, indeed," the marshal thought to himself. Mexico had reached its height only at the expense of Tezcuco.

"Rejoice, oh happiest of people!" Nezahual exclaimed, raising his hand palm upward. "You have now a sovereign who will be to you a steady column of support; a father in distress . . . and surely *more* than a brother in tenderness, in sympathy; one whose aspiring soul will disdain all profligate pleasures of the senses and the wasting indulgence of sloth.

"And thou, illustrious youth . . ." with this, the Lord of Tezcuco turned to the waiting Montezuma, "doubt not that the Creator, who has laid on thee so weighty a charge, will also give strength to sustain it. He who has been so liberal in times past will shower yet more abundant blessings on thy head, and keep thee firm in thy royal seat through many long and glorious years."

Nezahual, to the surprise of the gathering, knelt at the young man's feet; and Montezuma, momentarily overcome by his cousin's graciousness, wept as he lifted Nezahual up. The Aztec prince himself then knelt below the Supreme Lord; and Nezahual gestured for his attendants to approach. Then, to the complete amazement of the watching lords (his own barons utterly appalled by his gesture), Nezahual presented the copilli, the tiara of absolute sovereignty over the lake cities, to the people. As their murmurs of awed delight and moans of despair rose in the hall, the Lord of Tezcuco pressed the supreme diadem onto Montezuma's head. Never again would the miter-crown rest on the skull of Nezahual's forefather in the Tribunal of the Gods. The sacred emerald would bear only the modest diadem of Tezcuco.

Nezahual—now in his fortieth year—left the island of Tenochtitlan before the feasting was over. On the following day the first of twelve thousand victims were offered to the War God; and the Lord of Tezcuco had at last retired to the seclusion of his rural palace in the gardens of Tezcotzinco. The end of the Tezcucan emperors had been accomplished.

The five years that brought to a close the fifty-two-year cycle were attended by further weird prognostics. Nothing outward seemed to change in the structure of Anahuac. Montezuma evinced a greater aptitude for war than his ministers had expected, and frequently led the armies himself. During the festivities after his coronation, a group of Tlascalan nobles—who were hereditary enemies of Mexico—disguised themselves and entered Tenochtitlan in order to watch the entertainments. They were straightforward found out, despite the precautions, and their presence reported to the new emperor. Montezuma, magnanimously disposed, took it upon himself to see that his courageous visitors be provided with special receptions and given the best places for witnessing the games. Then they were given jewels and cocoa, and allowed to depart intact.

A year or so afterwards, he declared war on the mountain republic and drove the tribesmen from their valleys. In the fastnesses of the eastern mountains, however, they were unassailable. One of the Mexican allies, the Huexotzincans, had entered into one of their endless wars with the Tlascalans; and Montezuma seized the opportunity of finally avenging himself on Nezahual for the death of his half-sister. The intemperate Princess Chaciuh had been Nezahual's first empress. At first their marriage had strengthened the relations between Tezcuco and Tenochtitlan; but when the beautiful but vicious Chaciuh was discovered to have passed her days in sexual excesses of the most antisocial nature, the Lord of Tezcuco took advantage of his rights and commanded her execution. It was warranted, but the child Montezuma had sworn to avenge her public dishonor. And copilli or not—Nezahual paid a further price. Montezuma had encouraged his brothers to despoil Tezcucan provinces whenever opportunity afforded; and when he himself gained the throne, immediately set about breaking Nezahual's military strength.

On this occasion he innocently requested several companies of Tezcucan warriors to accompany him on his raid into Tlascala. Nezahual's electors agreed; and both Lord Tupil and Lord Tlamec were given command of the troops. Sending the Tezcucans into a valley to the side of his main approach, Montezuma quickly fell back and left his victims exposed. The Tlascalans quickly took advantage of what they supposed was a mistake—for Montezuma could not possibly benefit by his maneuver—and ambushed the unsuspecting warriors. The companies were wiped out; and Nezahual learned soon afterwards that his two councilors were dead. As ministers, Tupil and Tlamec could be replaced; as commanders, they were an irremediable loss.

When he heard of the disaster, Nezahual seemed but little affected. Itzco was immediately chosen in Tupil's stead, and left under protest for the capital. He was never to have an intimate contact with the ex-Emperor again. Though the ruler was a solitary man who never avertly gave himself in friendship, his caciques found themselves devoted to him in a measure beyond that normally given the most generous princes. Here was something both tragically ineffectual and awesomely competent—a contradiction of nature that aroused sympathy and demanded loyalty. The Lord of Chiconauhtla, whose son had secretly become an accomplice of the Prince Ixtlil's, was appointed cacique of the elite guard on Itzco's graduation to a higher rank. The fifty-year-old baron had been childless until the end of his thirties, when his wife had unexpectedly after twenty years borne him his heir, Nopal. His brother was once the Lord Marshal of Tezcuco; and though old Teuhtli had been disgraced, he was restored shortly before his death, and his son was now commandant of Nezahual's chief palace.

Because of this connection, the lord of the warden city on the

northern swamps had a decided though unknowing claim to
Nezahual's favor. Teuhtli had given his daughter to the great
Tepechpan, the sovereign's esteemed commander who had been
killed at the height of his career. The girl had borne the warrior
twin sons; and when her father also died, the Baron of Chiconauhtla had taken the boys of his niece into his household. He had
cared for them as his sons. For this, Nezahual was prepared to
honor him by the highest posts—even though the lord was among
the fourteen hereditary nobles whom the ruler continually checked
in their pretensions. Even after his own son finally arrived, the
baron continued to give a father's affection to the children of the
unfortunate Tepechpan, who left his sons a rank also among the
fourteen. The marshal had in his youth been reduced to the merchant class and was therefore held in particular estimation by the
common citizens. Not a city-noble by birth, Tepechpan's rise had
not been resented by the people, despite the Emperor's elevating
him without the council's consent in a time of emergency.

The twins, Tepech and Macuil, were sixteen now. Nezahual had
watched their approach to manhood from a distance, his personal
interest in their welfare expressed in the most oblique manner—as
though he chose to protect the boys from the effects, both subjec-
tive and social, of his immediate patronage. He had begun to fear
for those that he bore affection. When the twins had reached their
sixth year, the ruler took advantage of their foster-father's reluctance to bring them from his home to the capital. Court ruling
was waived; and Nezahual—under the pretext of merely honoring
an old man with semi-retirement in comfortable surroundings—
sent an exceptionally learned and able teacher from the palace. The
boys were destined, not only by their precedents, to be the coun-
sellors of kings.

And now, when they must continue on to the *telpuchcalli,* the
house of youth, for special training before their formal induction
into the tribe, the ruler arranged that Tepech and Macuil be sent
to the palace of Prince Cacama, where the private schooling of the
Lady Ilan's eldest son was pursued. Cacama was in his tenth year,
a year important in the lives of all children; for at ten the full rig-
ors of the law were exercised against a public offender. The state
was substituted for the father. For a prince who was potentially a

ruler, and who at least would take an active part in government, it was a major turning point in his development.

In addition to his slaves and attendant warriors, Cacama was given the companionship of a select group of nobles' sons who should eventually assume positions under him in the state. Usually the boys chosen to accompany a prince were older, and just beginning their war studies. In this way Cacama's attention would be unconsciously focused on the competition of arms. Nezahual himself, his precocity in war tactics legendary, had actively entered the mock battles when he was nine years old; and had exhibited such a peculiar, though perverse, aptitude that the regent had interrupted his pursuits in the capital to spend an afternoon watching the boy-king's maneuvers.

Cacama did not seem more than normally inclined in this direction; and his bent seemed more toward the role of a wise prince who might depend on his war chiefs to carry out his claims. Though Nezahual could not have contrived a close friendship between Cacama and the twins, he was extremely pleased that the prince had taken Tepech and Macuil as his intimates. Because of the brilliant instruction of their tutor, and their inherited vigor from the dead Tepechpan, the two barons would prove an asset to any court.

Had Nezahual felt any particular concern for his heirs, it would have been for Prince Temozin—who had now attained the age when he would be separated from his father, and also be given a palace. Though he was only six, the child had already amassed a formidable collection of codices. The ruler would often find his chief heir involved in conversations with court poets—who spoke to the boy as though he were their complete equal. By an odd coincidence (for Nezahual had not consciously arranged it), Temozin had been given the apartments of a long-dead poet-prince of the Aztecs, the young Emperor's companion through his tortuous rise to power. Someone had once observed that Axaya, the Aztec prince, was similar to a beautiful but hybrid flower: singular and alone. "He will last for a brief time, to depart without casting or receiving seed." Acatli the courtesan had commented that Axaya suffered from a strange malady no one could discern—that as soon as a maiden sought to hold him in her embrace, the life that gave meaning to his beauty would go out into the wind.

And so it had been. In Axaya's twentieth year, the year of his betrothal to a girl of his father's court, the prince had been laid on a funeral pyre in the island capital. Nezahual had grieved bitterly for a time; but those were the years of Mecatl, Mecatl the daughter of Acatli—the most enchanting, and tragically possessed, of Nezahual's loves. Now Temozin had spent his early childhood in the dead prince's apartments. The ruler recognized the similarities of nature, and wondered sadly what would become of his heir apparent. Perhaps he also recognized how Axaya had paralleled a side of his own nature.

Ixtlil himself seemed to behave properly enough. There were unfortunate incidents, to be sure; but nothing dire occurred. What attention Nezahual gave to Anahuac was focused on the new Emperor. His own kingdom was in competent hands. Itzco quite adequately managed the reduced armies (which was his forte anyway); and the Lord Zalmec, who had been sent against the northern rebels, was an efficient Lord Executioner. He had by-stepped the ranks of clan leader and speaker in his rise over the Supreme Council. It was strange that the nobles submitted to his almost inhuman, depersonalized brutality; but Zalmec never acted against an offender without due consideration of law. He was like a superior, undeniably exact conscience—never at fault in the aptness of his vengeance on ill-doers, never to be questioned. Those about him often felt accused of their secret shortcomings; and had he confronted them, would have accepted their punishment without murmur.

It was obvious to Nezahual that his new executioner had usurped the authority of the two rightful judges among the chief electors. Zalmec intimidated the court, unquestionably; but for reasons of his own, the Lord of Tezcuco did not interfere . . . not even when he heard that Ixtlil, who had at last been given a palace of his own, had Zalmec as his mentor. Both Nopal and Tochtli, who had witnessed the slave girl's assassination, accompanied Ixtlil into his new way of life (at the prince's particular request).

The change in Montezuma's condition was more interesting to

watch. After his betrayal of Nezahual's army in the second year of his reign, the Emperor's nature radically altered. The Aztec ministers were not only surprised by his activity on the battlefield; Montezuma developed an inordinate passion for the chase. He reclaimed the many slightly submerged islets about his capital with retaining walls and silt held firm by shredded husks and the roots of transplanted trees. It had been by creating such *chinampas,* the so-called "floating gardens," that the Tenochas had first made their end of the lake at all habitable. The ruler then commanded that his barons bring him animals of all descriptions, and enlarged the royal zoo to unexampled proportions.

He stocked the surrounding islands with stag and fallow deer, with foxes and wolves and ocelots—everything, in fact, that he could hunt. Not content with his own pleasances, he often invited himself to his cousin's estate at the farther end of the great causeway; and the annoyed Prince of Iztapalapan watched his prize deer and sounders of peccary slaughtered in an afternoon or so. This is not to say, however, that Montezuma forgot his priestly duties. Never had there been a monarch whose reign was attended by such festivals and rites. Oracles were consulted on the most trivial pretexts; and absolute torrents of blood cascaded down the stairways of the island pyramids.

Montezuma elevated the High Priest of the War God over the other prelates, and placed him at the head of the Supreme Council itself. He was given the title Mexican Lord of Divine Matters, and not only continued in his function as supreme pontiff, but took over the authorities of Chancellor. Thus given control over the internal affairs of all the priesthoods, and second only to the Emperor in civic rank, Tizoc's Aztec counterpart thereupon summoned the Tezcucan high priests to pay him homage. Tizoc, begging the protection of Nezahual, refused to go. He shut himself up in his temple compound, and stayed there in almost entire seclusion.

Then Montezuma took to patrolling the streets of his city in disguise; and attempted on occasion to bribe his judges, to test their integrity. Those that were swerved from their duties by such bribes were immediately tried—and strangled. The humility he had displayed as a priest disappeared by no slow degrees. After his destruction of the Tezcucan companies, the Emperor gave way to intolerable arrogance. He refused to take his evening meals with his barons, and forced them to eat in an adjoining room. Out of complete disdain for his courtiers he secluded himself from all but his closest ministers; and when he chose to leave his palace, he exacted the most slavish obeisance.

Only those of the highest rank were allowed to perform even menial tasks for him; and he discharged council officials of common blood but important service because he decided their attendance dishonored him. The Supreme Council of clan speakers was in effect dissolved, for barons alone could hold the rank of minister. In Tezcuco, only the immediate city nobles (who also had clan affiliations) could aspire to these posts, in their capacities of mere tribal elders. What had been the exceptional rise of a landed chieftain now became the order of the day. His councilors advised him against these actions. Such impolitic conduct could bring unfortunate consequences . . . the citizens would not abide chieftains of other cities on their council. But Montezuma, unaware that his haughtiness disgusted his subjects, further infuriated them by raising both taxes and tributes. Even the distant provinces felt the effects of his lavishness at court; and though this oppression led to frequent revolts, it only gave the Emperor an excuse for falling on the defected cities and making off with additional captives to sacrifice on his altars. The merchants of his city were deprived of the little class imminence they had achieved.

Soon after the Tezcucan loss in the valleys of Tlascala, Montezuma even presumed to summon Nezahual to his court. Disinclined to leave the serenity of his woodlands, Nezahual sent the youth Comtzin with a curt reply. "I am not well. When my health improves, you may visit me in Tezcotzinco." Though reportedly enraged, Montezuma was politic enough on this occasion to leave the Tezcucan lord his dignity. Apparently unaware of the fretting tensions that had begun to divide his own clans and dependent tribes, the Mexican at least was circumspect enough not to stir up his brother kings to rebellion. It was wisdom to abide even the independence of the Tlacopanecs, out of respect to Nezahual's alliances. The latter city-state, however, was completely under Aztec domination.

93

And perhaps the Emperor suspected that Nezahual the warrior had no equal now in the valley. The fourteen great nobles of Tezcuco were still loyal to him—the "claws of his battle mace," Montezuma called them—and it was best to leave Nezahual in his strange contentment on the hill of the Plumed Towers. The Lord of Tezcuco was forty-one when Montezuma had attempted to humble him; and he was at last alone. Temozin was given his little palace across the park from Ixtlil's, a short distance off the main plaza. Cacama had been four years installed on the western outskirts of the capital.

Situated throughout Tezcuco were the eight groves and gardens that continued to represent the potency of Nezahual's will. About his chief palace wandered the city barons, who often shared in the Supreme Council and would follow their lord in whatever extremity. And Tezcuco still remained the fulcrum of the empire. Montezuma's increasing power must gauge itself, weight against counterweight, by Nezahual's standard. Unwittingly, the new Emperor had taken an important step forward by inviting non-city nobles into his own council. Had he been given time the resentments would have subsided; and with Nezahual's concepts of economy, Anahuac might have remained intact despite outside defeats.

7

So THE intervening years be-
tween the abdication and the end of the ninth cycle were spanned.
Suddenly the quiet was broken by a general alarm. For weeks preceding the last fire ceremonies, unwholesome apparitions crowded
each other, to the further agitation of the inhabitants. Reports were
brought from the southern chieftains that sea monsters with billowing wings were sighted; and the descriptions of men pale as
dry sand, with black beards that hid their faces, were brought to
Nezahual and Montezuma. The Emperor watched the gloomy aspects of entrails and stars; and the citizens approached the last
five indescribably unlucky days of the cycle in even greater despair
than usual.

It was written in the sacred almanac, in a time beyond memory,
that the world's destruction would occur in these drear days of a
"year's binding." The sun was no more than a sickly, warmthless
flame in this season, guttering its substance away—a pale seepage
from the southern sky. Heavy, murky clouds would overcast the
valley, and chill winds sweep down from icy ridges, striking sudden affliction in the bellies of the poor. Commanders returned
from the southern cities; but neither merchant nor warrior would
venture from the plateau into the hot jungles of the lowland, for
such a change could cause the throat to thicken and a man to die
of strangulation. It seemed as though the gods wanted none to
leave the valley.

It had been threatened that a time should come when the sun
could no longer nourish his children; when the source of fire, at
last depleted, might no longer burst anew with the blood of flowers. How oppressive it was, to inherit a valley of such fruitfulness!
One knew the gods themselves were forever on the verge of exhaustion in the unending round of seasons. Montezuma felt the

weariness, the bitter taste. Perhaps he was tempted to gaze northward at the hill of the Plumed Towers, and envy the peacefulness of his cousin's life. Nezahual was not a priest—yet he lived in a monastery of his own making.

The Emperor knew the eventual end of Anahuac was assured—only the moment was uncertain. The season of the faltering sun was forever the crucial time, whether cycle-end or no. With the final days of an era upon them, his subjects destroyed their furniture and cooking utensils (as though they never again expected to nourish themselves). The little images of their household gods were broken, for minor divinities were of comfort in daily distress, no succor in a holocaust. Throughout Anahuac, even in the cities of the Maya, hearth fires were put out. In the temples atop the great pyramids the fires that consumed offerings to the gods were extinguished. The people rent their garments. Pregnant women were locked in granaries to gain protection of the corn goddess and her ever-dying, ever-resurrected son. They might otherwise be changed into wild animals, and bear monstrosities that should haunt the desolate woodlands.

Profoundly troubled, the wicked frantically searched out the priests in order to offer confessions, and their hearts for sacrifice. When Montezuma was borne through his city, moans of lamentation followed his progress. It was during these last days that the young emperor, out of his own anguish and despair, came to an understanding of Nezahual's withdrawal. When he learned that the Tezcucan lord would not attend him in the sacred toasting of the corn supply at the first of the month, he earnestly requested his kinsman to accompany him in the succeeding ceremonial hunt. Nezahual replied that as he no longer indulged in the tiresome excitement of slaying wild animals, he no longer felt it necessary to placate Mixcoatl, the Cloud Serpent.

Montezuma, not immediately grasping the other's mockery of his over-indulgence in the chase, reminded his royal cousin that the welfare of the hunters was at stake. After Nezahual refused to participate in the bird killing and the arrow sacrifice at his city of Cuauhtitlan on the western shore of Lake Xaltocan, the Emperor was stricken by a sense of his own complete aloneness. These were cities of the marsh. Generations of Aztecs and Tezcucans had sustained themselves on the birds snared in reedy swamplands, on the fish netted in the lakes. It was Opochtli, the left-handed, that was god of fishermen and bird catchers—that gave the trident, the fishing rod, and the bird net, to the people. The ceremonial slaying of birds was Opochtli's due, though the lake dwellers were no longer dependent on his bounty.

Nezahual seemed to have accepted the turning away of the gods; even his obligation to attend the important arrow sacrifice to the Rain God was ignored. Montezuma, cut off now by a great gulf from his own nobles, must face the gods and offer homage for his realm alone. For all his arrogance and vindictiveness, he admitted a profound need of Nezahual's confidence. And the Lord of Tezcuco, though he ridiculed the superstitions of his priests—and had only sporadically taken part in the rituals to comfort and reassure his tribesmen—felt a corresponding need on the final day of Montezuma.

In the evening of the fateful night, Nezahual gathered his nobles and his boy princes about him and set off over the lake. In the cities about him the small children had begun their ordeal. Throughout the night they would be kept moving, in fear that sleep should result in their being turned into rats. Nezahual might have scoffed at this; he was not too sure but that at the moment of the Pleiades' zenith the rhythm of the universe might break, however, and the cities suddenly become funeral pyres on which an entire civilization should be burned. The fourth age was to be ended in a general conflagration, the last of the elements to be accounted for.

The first era had been destroyed by floods; the second, by earthquakes. The third had been brought to a close by furious winds that devastated the land. Then began the fourth age, the Sun of Fire, when the vengeful White God of the East was to reappear in the valley. If mankind survived, his condition would be wretched beyond imagining. The greatest lords would grovel in the ashes of their cities.

The royal barges slowly navigated the canals that led into the lake. Rising about them were the terraced villas of barons and powerful merchant-lords, sustained above the shallow marshes by massive

97

stone pilings. The rich silt had been dredged for the passage of boats, and deposited basket by basket through the years of Tezcuco on the masonry above. The sere branches of fruit trees stretched over the waterways.

In the faint moonlight the tiered gardens gleamed with the dull waxen reflections of cypress leaves. The glazed plaster of the palaces shone a pale, reddish umber behind the foliage. The night was bitterly cold, the fitful wind acrid with salt. A quiet brooded over the lake, broken only by the occasional cry of a frightened night bird. There was no light to mark the cities, just the indistinct whiteness of the Mexican pyramid rising over the dark water in the distance to guide the steersmen.

Nezahual sat on a low wicker throne in the center of his barge. Over his head stretched a frail canopy of plumage and woven gold, which rustled sharply in the brief gusts. The ruler drew his heavy mantle close about him, with clasped arms, and thoughtfully watched his breath turn to vapor. It was like the sigh of speech in the priests' writing. Though he was chilled, despite his feather mantle and heavy cotton robe, an irritant, nervous sweat covered his body. His mind was feverish and confused, his thoughts changing as fitfully as the wind. Outwardly, he was serene and unconcerned. His hair was drawn tightly to the back of his head; and about his forehead extended a simple aureole of brocaded gold fastened with quetzal plumes.

Sitting at his right, carefully watching the screen of canoes filled with warriors, was the Baron of Chiconauhtla. The prows of the swifter craft threw up silver spray as they crisscrossed in the path of the royal barge. The chancellor, Itzco, and another minister, were grouped at the stern beside the steersman; and at the ruler's feet sat the six city nobles of Tezcuco.

Immediately following in the procession came the barge of the heir apparent. The nine-year-old prince was accompanied by his teacher, and his half-brother, Cacama. The barons Tepech and Macuil, within a year now of their betrothals, waited quietly on the low dais below him. The six remaining provincial nobles had taken their places about the walled platform. Temozin was flushed with restrained excitement, and worried his pearl-brocaded cuffs with his slender fingers. He wore a long, white tunic interwoven with rosettes of gold thread and plumage; and a full mantle of quetzal plumage shrouded him. From his shoulders hung the jade gorget that designated his first place in the line of successors. He sat with knees drawn up, agitatedly speaking with his brother. ". . . But I don't want to watch. What if no fire comes when they try to kindle it in his belly? Wouldn't all that blood put the flame out?" The prince shuddered at the thought of the night's sacrifice. "Father doesn't believe in inflicting death—except accidentally, on the battlefield. Why must we go, Cacama?"

His brother put his arm about Temozin's shoulder, and gave a low, quiet laugh of reassurance: "It is politic for us to go . . . and particularly for you, Temozin. You shall one day be the Lord of Tezcuco . . ."

"But I don't care to be!" the heir apparent insisted, raising his voice against the wind. "Give me our father's palace of the Plumed Towers—and you may rule in the capital."

"Ssh . . ." Cacama admonished him, shaking him with his arm and glancing to see if the barons beyond Tepech and Macuil had overheard. An abrupt lull had fallen. Then the older brother, with an insight unusual in a thirteen-year-old boy, asked in a sad voice: "You have no thought of me, have you, Temozin?" He withdrew his arm and caught his mantle closer. A sudden gust threw cold spray over the barge.

"Why?" Temozin asked, letting go his knees and sitting up straight. His wet tilmatli glistened in the darkness, and the odor of damp plumage further discomfited him. He looked at Cacama, ashamed of his retiring nature yet earnestly wishing he were back in his own villa.

"Because you know how I wait for the day when we are men— when you are the lord of our father's realm, and I am your most trusted minister." The heir apparent lowered his head in accept- ance, and listened to the other's words: "Tepech and Macuil will command your armies, and bring you vast tributes to share with the people." Cacama was sincere; in his mind his brother was *the anointed*. Had he instead been selected, the older prince would have accepted the throne without reluctance, determined to fulfill that obligation.

Temozin glanced out over the water toward the shore. The

99

barges had swerved farther into the lake to round a sharp peninsula; and nine miles away lay the palace of Lord Cuauhtemoc, at
the end of the great dike, where Nezahual would disembark. From
there he would continue some four miles along the causeway on
the dike itself, to the junction where the Emperor Montezuma and
his court were to pass in procession. The Hill of the Star was but
a short distance farther south. Through the hours of waiting,
every eye would be fastened on the temple that crowned its summit. Tribesmen had left their secluded mountain villages at sunset
and watched now from the ridges enclosing the valley for the first
sign of fire. The night was clear; and the moon, nearing its short
span, would leave the skies to the sharp radiances of the stars.

As Temozin considered his older brother's words, his dread of
the coming sacrifice momentarily forgotten, a conversation of a
less gentle nature was in progress on the barge behind. "Why do
they offer *one* slave to keep the sun well?" Ixtlil demanded in a
low voice. He sat with his mantle apart, in utter disregard of the
chilling wind. His robes were drenched; and as though he seemed
unaware of his bedraggled state, he raised his head in satisfied
defiance to the gusts of water.

"This is the ritual," his mentor the Lord Executioner answered.
The prince's gaze fell on Nopal, hesitated, then shifted to Tochtli. It was a matter of the simplest deduction. Gods were fed on
blood. This was a season of the sun's weakness. Ixtlil rose without
explanation and crossed to the guardrail. He leaned out and stared
up toward the eastern sky, narrowly estimating the progress of a
small, bright group of stars. Immediately behind the star cluster
(a band of four hundred youths once hurled by a furious giant
into the skies) came the Follower, a red flicker moving high over
the ridges. Ixtlil could discern seven of the youths, though only
six were visible to the average eye.

Why did they drench the temples with gore during other festivals and at times of minor calamity, when now—the most critical
moment—but a single captive was brought forward? Ixtlil exhaled
sharply in disgust and returned to his throne. He was robed like
his brothers in an embroidered white tunic and a mantle of quetzal feathers. The soaked material clung to his small, lithe body. In
the darkness his face shone with a hard luster—as though he were

of carved stone. He sat down on the jeweled wicker stool, and let his hands fall to the platform. The striking of his rings against the wood startled his companions, and the fourteen-year-old Nopal quickly asked: "Will we join the Emperor's procession in time, Excellency?"

Ixtlil stared at him without answering, a slight expression of hostility entering his eyes. He soundlessly pronounced the name *Montezuma* with his lips. Temozin, though he seemed already to have the intellect of a man, still retained the mannerisms of a child. Ixtlil, obviously not gifted in the usual sense, already tasted the bitterness of a revengeful nature. The two boy princes were of the same height. Both were slender and well formed, their features almost identical. The careless defiance of Ixtlil's attitude, however, implied the approach of early adolescence—which his physical immaturity belied. His odd habit of ignoring his companions, of often repeating words silently to himself, and suddenly commenting disjointedly on something else, would have given an unknowing observer the impression that the boy was retarded.

Ixtlil would ask abrupt questions, weigh the answers, and turn to other matters. His refusal to explain either his actions or his purposes was deceptive. He seemed to brood when others were around him. The prince had taken easily to the war games; but he displayed such an unexpected ferocity in the mock battles that even the older boys were frightened by him. Once, when his group was losing ground, Ixtlil had produced several arrows barbed with glass—and would have felled his afternoon's opponents had not one of the instructors immediately interrupted the game.

No one could imagine what possessed him. He had lost many times without showing anger . . . and the afternoon just before the first of the unlucky days (after he had become victor of the field), the prince tried to break another boy's arm with his blunt battle mace. On both occasions Ixtlil's anger had been aroused by one of the other boys disobeying the rules. And no one understood. Not even Nopal had his confidence. As the barges slowly veered in toward the shore, the outer canoes passing but a few yards from a low island, Ixtlil rose again and sullenly walked to the guardrail. He stared out into the blackness, listening to the warning calls exchanged by the steersmen. In the near-darkness he seemed but an average boy: slightly built, and as vulnerable as children were supposed to be. No one, however, gave a thought to his being drenched and in the cold wind.

The warriors and the two other boys behind him shifted restlessly on their benches. The movement of the stars was hidden from them by the canopy; and one of the nobles, having leaned out to glimpse the heavens, turned back with a terse comment. They looked out over the water toward the causeway, in an attempt to discern the procession of priests; there were occasional glitters on the stretch between the midway fortress and the mainland. If there was no interruption, the two bodies of nobles would join together at the appointed time. The youths that glimmered faintly in the sky would not reach their zenith for another three hours.

Ixtlil, anxious to reach the Hill of the Star, leapt ashore while the barge was being drawn in. Without waiting, he walked quickly up the wide stairway to the first platform—and found himself before the Lord Cuaúhtemoc. The young cacique, who was only in his twenty-fifth year, stared at the disheveled prince in mild surprise; the first noble to present himself should have been Nezahual himself. Identified as he was by his robes, and by his aggressive attitude, Ixtlil was immediately recognized. Cuauhtemoc bowed his head out of respect to Nezahual, and welcomed the boy: "We are as slaves at your bidding, Lord Ixtlil . . ." He had been waiting apart from his attendants, at the head of the desolate, branch-strewn stairway. As he spoke, the great noble stepped back from the edge, holding his cape in from the wind.

Ixtlil gave no reply; and the Mexican prince raised his head and glanced at him in further surprise. Nezahual's son returned the commander's stare for a moment with an expression of impatience and amusement on his lips, then turned to search for his father in the darkness below. Nezahual waited for his nobles to line the stairway before he left the barge. Accompanied by his chief ministers and the cacique of his guard, he strode to the landing where his cousin was awaiting him. His manner was intent, but not hurried. The narrow steps were dangerous without torchlight, over-strewn as they were with fallen branches and pine needles.

At his approach, Cuauhtemoc knelt and touched his forehead to the pavement. Nezahual stooped, and with both hands raised him up. The youthful prince was moved by the ex-Emperor's humility, and for a moment forgot his greeting. "We are as slaves, Nezahual*pilli*."

"We are as brothers," Nezahual formally corrected him, catching sight of Ixtlil in the twilight nearby. He turned back to Cuauhtemoc: "So my youngest son has hastened to present himself."

The Lord of Tztapalapan nodded his head, a rueful smile on his lips.

Nezahual turned to the stairway: "Come, Temozin and Cacama. Present yourselves to your cousin who rules these gardens."

Temozin advanced to his father's side and shyly bowed his head: "The hands of the gods lift you into high places, Cousin and Lord."

The cacique leaned forward to catch the prince's words, then glanced at Nezahual in delighted amazement. The boy had used an ancient form of address. "My greeting to you, Lord and Cousin . . ." It was bleak, uncongenial weather for such formalities. Perhaps, on this ominous night when sudden ruin might descend, when the wind was bitter and the nobles shivered under their elegant robes, wincing at the touch of their jewels—perhaps etiquette *was* in keeping.

Cacama stepped forward and self-consciously bowed: "My greeting to you, Lord and Cousin."

Cuauhtemoc returned his salutation; and Nezahual raised his arms about his princes' shoulders. The lord stared curiously at Ixtlil, who had made no attempt to join his father, then spoke to his cousin: "Montezuma's procession is nearing Mexicaltzinco. We must hasten to meet him."

"The litters are waiting, Your Excellency . . ."

As the two men and their attendants moved up the second stairway, Temozin and Cacama briefly confronted their brother. There was a moment of silence; then Ixtlil turned to the attendants behind him impatiently. Temozin, glancing at Macuil—who was angered by Ixtlil's insolence—remarked gently: "The litters are waiting." He started up the steep stairway. Cacama, humiliated by Ixtlil's disrespect to their half-brother, paused a moment and then followed the heir apparent with his attendants. Ixtlil ascended behind them with Nopal and Tochtli. The nobles and high priests had watched the incident quietly. They exchanged thoughtful glances and followed the royal princes to the upper terrace.

The litters were quickly assigned according to precedence; and within a quarter-hour Nezahual had set out to meet the Aztec procession. The rain that swept over the valley earlier in the evening had left the causeway slippery. The bearers slipped frequently, and the heavy litters had to be caught by attendant nobles that walked beside. At either edge of the dike stretched the winter-barren swampland, a lonely, threatening waste in starlight. Sudden black shadows would flit skyward—the movement followed by thin, desperate shrieks.

In the spring these low fields would be gardens of flowers and fruit trees. Weary nobles, escaping to their coolness, would stroll along the endless stairways and paths. Young courtesans would rest in secluded pavilions. Fishermen would cast transparent nets into the shallows under the cypress that leaned from the banks. But all was desolation now, deserted and treacherous. Only malignant spirits haunted the waste, the dreaded *ciuapipiltin*—the spirits of betrayed women who had died in childbirth. Their eyebrows were golden; and their faces, arms, and hands were the dead white of *tisatl* powder.

The baleful creatures frequented crossroads, and pleasure gardens in forsaken seasons: eager to infect mortals with dire maladies, to possess the bodies of susceptible people and work their evil wills. They were down there now, below the causeway, wandering in the darkness and robed as princesses. A foul odor of decay blew up from the swamplands; and as he watched from his litter, high on the porters' shoulders, Temozin saw a spectral light suddenly quiver a moment beyond the causeway. He winced at the tiny shrieks—as though an owl's claws were ripping at his own entrails.

The prince shuddered and sat back in the litter. He drew the heavy mantle about him, his thoughts turning again to the sacrifice on the Hill of the Star. His mind was feverish with terror and expectation. One of his bearers slipped on the glazed pavement, and Temozin frantically clutched the strong poles that held him.

He tried to imagine what the captive would be thinking now; and pretended for a moment that he was confined in a wicker cage, and his robes were those of the Sun God's. He felt the chafing murderousness in the warriors beside him. Their glass-barbed javelins glistened faintly in the starlight.

Several priests quickly strode past, each masked and plumed in the guise of a different god. There was a wrench in the boy's stomach, then a cold breeze seemed to sweep up through his body toward his head. They were nearing the city of Mexicaltzinco, and the buildings were frighteningly familiar. Vague, terrible, half-remembered incidents occurred to him, though Temozin had never been to the south of the lake before. The child was on the verge of weeping when there was a momentary halt. Attendants sped past him toward the rear of the company.

Then the bearers were moving again. The Tezcucans had joined Montezuma's procession. The priests of the three cities now led the way, glittering with jewels and feathers, a grotesque, fearsome array of the valley's gods. Tlaloc was there, with his tusks and the hideous volute issuing from his mouth over the lower lip . . . and Hummingbird Wizard, his left leg covered with feathers and live gilt snakes wriggling sluggishly about his waist. Smoking Mirror, robed as a young prince, hurried in front of the other gods—his obsidian shield glancing in the half-light. In their midst, borne forward in a cage held on gold shafts, was the solitary victim. Several paces behind the priests came the nobles of Anahuac, led by Montezuma in his blue-and-white tilmatli, the sweeping plumes of the triple crown falling about him. Eight nobles bore his throne along the roadway to Culhuacan, whose chief once ruled the southern valley and held the Mexicans in bondage . . . and now felt the weight of the Emperor's litter against his shoulder.

Behind Montezuma, several yards to his right, followed Nezahual and his princes.

The procession passed through the city, and took an ancient path that led up the slopes of the hill. The pace was quickened now, the confused chanting of the priest-gods more intense. At last the summit of the hill was reached; and the procession quickly circled the base of the low pyramid, collecting itself about the ancient, tiered walls. Then the high priests curved in toward the almost perpendicular stairway and slowly mounted to the platform. Before them, in the center, stood the altar of the Sun God carved with the tables of his progress through the seasons.

The voices became more insistent, rising in controlled hysteria as the entire roster of gods pleaded with Tonatiuh. Metztli, god and goddess by turns, the consort of the Sun, raised his elbows in anguish and swept in weaving circles about the altar—reminding his lord how he had sacrificed the first mortal to hasten the dawn. And after Nanahuatl the leper had been cast into the flames, as the starry night was consumed by the Sun, so the Moon himself leapt into the pyre.

Remember . . . remember, the gods wailed. They too had sacrificed themselves to sustain the newly created Sun. And as the Pleiades reached their apex high over the valley, the gods became more frenzied in their fear of the Sun's death. Their spirits seized entire the bodies of the priests—convinced in their despair that these likenesses were themselves. Eerie lights flickered from their wide eyes; as from the vast, dark reservoir of memory, of racial fear amid ten thousand years' loneliness, surged the fiercely yearning realities of the gods.

The victim, robed in scarlet striped with white, was thrust from his cage and borne to the altar. From the back of his head rose the white plumes sacred to the Sun God. His staff was tipped with feathers; and his shield was marked with tufts of cotton. A bundle of eagle plumage and paint was tied on his shoulders: the captive was prepared for his long journey. He was the lone mortal on the platform. The gods surveyed him for a moment, their voices quiet. Then Smoking Mirror, who was god of the sacrificial knife, approached him. "Lord," he called out, and paused. Then his words rushed out, strident as if a wind blew through his throat: "Go to our brother the Sun, and offer him the blood of flowers—that he may drink his life from your cupped hands . . ."

Again the fast, wildly intricate rhythms began on the taut serpent skin. The gods moved about the altar in the death dance. Several of their number grasped the terrified, unprotesting captive and tore off his robes. With an easy co-ordination of movement, they seized his ankles and wrists, and bent him backwards over the

106

convex stone. Smoking Mirror stood aside from the dancing priests, his gaze fixed anxiously on the Pleiades.

The victim uttered a low, continuous moan—his body limp as though the life had already been torn out of it. There was an abrupt silence, and he tightened in a convulsion of fear. He opened his eyes, no longer glazed but intense and desperately searching. A scream caught in his throat as the heavy razor edge cut into his belly and rapidly arced to his pelvis. A cold, inhuman hand reached into the cavity of his chest, and quickly wrenched out the throbbing of pain. The attendant gods relinquished their grips as the pulsing heart was lifted up to the sky. The victim, already dead, rose up as though in worship of his own blood—then slowly fell back on the stone, his white plumes touching the pavement below.

The heart was immediately taken into the small temple nearby and placed on the solar altar of sacrifice. The *quauhxicalli* was engraved with the sun disk, the center hollowed into a cup to receive the offering. Smoking Mirror waited for a moment in quiet adoration, then turned from the Cup of Eagles and hurried out onto the open platform. The quiet gods were narrowly observing the Follower. As the body gently shook in diminishing tremors, one of the deities stuffed his gaping chest with wood shavings and cotton lint.

There was a short, anxious wait. Then the attending god fastened a fire stick in the wound and began to twirl it. A moment passed. The Follower seemed to pause threateningly at his meridian. There was no breath drawn throughout the valley. The gods and the inhabitants together were caught in the spasm of bitter yearning as the stick whirled in its socket of softer wood.

Suddenly there was a wisp of smoke, a faint glow at the point of the fire drill, then a small flame that quickly spread to the tender. The crisis was past. As the victim's belly filled with a sputtering, leaping fire, a murmur rose from the foot of the pyramid. Its volume swelled into a loud ovation to the absent sun. Overcome by a happiness that was almost unendurable, the nobles began to laugh and call out to each other incoherently. Nezahual, however, withdrew to the edge of the hill. He quietly gazed out onto the dark valley that would soon be filled with a thousand lights.

Smoking Mirror descended the pyramid with a flaming torch, and the waiting couriers quickly caught the fire on their own. Eager with the promise of continued life, the runners sped throughout the valley to rekindle the altars in the great temples. The citizens waited expectantly below the pyramids for the brands to light their hearths. Tribesmen intercepted the messengers that left the valley of the lakes for every city in Anahuac; and the fire bearers, without faltering, passed the sacred gift of Tonatiuh to them.

8

WITH the dawn, thick clouds of incense rose from the pyramids—caught the wind currents, and drifted out over the valley. The altars brimmed with the blood of a thousand offerings. For thirteen days the lake region would be re-dedicated by rejoicing. The priests set about restoring their temples; and the citizens, eager to end the long fast with nourishing food, began shaping new utensils for their households. Shuttles deftly skimmed over stretched looms; wicker was pressed into hot water, then quickly woven into furniture. Clan leaders distributed the freshly roasted corn; urns of pulque, octli, and mescal, were brought from the public warehouses.

No one thought of the winter bleakness. And the auguries of disaster? Tizoc himself was too exhausted by the ordeal to thrill much at the fortunate outcome, or even to grimace inwardly at his thoughts of the future. He really didn't care much in the next few days that there was to be a future. It had been by sheer will that he had managed the ascent of his own pyramid on the first dawn, and performed the necessary ritual. Then his priests had carried him down again; and Tizoc had collapsed into unconsciousness. A violent nausea churned inside him, rising to his throat when the attendants brought him nourishment. If he tried to rise, a severe throbbing struck him at the base of his skull; and a searing light would blaze in his eyes.

The high priest had betaken himself to the Hill of the Star in the guise of *Mexitli,* Hare of the Aloes (one of Hummingbird Wizard's manifestations); and had returned to Tezcuco much the worse for it. He remembered the miserable journey across the lake clearly enough, and the tediously agitated march along the dike. The High Priest of Tlaloc accompanied him; and as the chief altar of the Rain God lay on a Tezcucan mountain, this particular Tezcucan prelate was allowed to deck himself out with tusks and a multicolored robe representing the four points of the compass. His costume was further ornamented with streaks of silver, for the mountain torrents.

He had really appeared quite awesome, Tizoc admitted—annoyed that his own trappings were less spectacular. It amused him that the Aztec High Priest of Tlaloc had been forced to come as the god's wife, Our Lady of the Emerald Robe, carrying a jeweled frog for scepter. The chief priest in Tlacopan (a vulgar, fat little man) had appeared as Four Times Lord, who was merely one of the minor rain gods. At least in the representation of the Lord of the Rains a Tezcucan was predominant; and here in Nezahual's capital that Tezcucan was subservient to Tizoc.

As he lay through the first days of the festival, too nauseated to writhe much, Tizoc forgot his cramps—and reduction at the hands of the Aztec Lord of Divine Matters—in an attempt to analyze what had happened to him. He had obviously been possessed during the ascent of the hill . . . but it hadn't begun there. He could remember the journey in detail as far as the junction of the dike. It was when he beheld his rival, resplendent in gilt serpents, with a fistful of gold arrows tipped with plumes and a headdress that outdid the Emperor's for sheer grandeur, that Tizoc felt the first giddiness.

And the wretched Mictla was there too, in the guise of Smoking Mirror—his ugliness hidden by an exquisitely wrought mask. At that moment Tizoc was put down, relegated as it were to insignificance. Tlaloc arrogantly stepped forward and took his place among the great gods; and Mexitli . . . well, the minor gods, and the deities merely personifying a phase of the chief lords, were reduced to bringing up the rear. Tizoc's vanity could not endure the humiliation. After all, a god was a god; and Mexitli, though he shouldered the litter bearing the Sun's victim, had his own, undoubted grandeur. The distressed priest concentrated on the Hare of the Aloes' attributes so intently that by the time the procession reached Culhuacan he actually felt the god's presence hovering near him. And halfway up the hill he noticed the vague outlines of a figure walking beside him in step.

In a state of submission and awe, Tizoc had accepted the god's reality. But think as he would, the point of actual connection escaped him. He somehow confused the god with himself, as though he had passed into a dream and watched himself from a vast distance without being anywhere. Then the vision of Mexitli and himself were one, and farther and farther away from the observer until the link was broken, and Tizoc lost from himself.

When the high priest recovered his senses he was lying on the summit of the pyramid. Several yards away, the charred body of the victim had broken from its midsection and lay on the pavement. The sacred fire had become a pyre; and the attendant priests would shortly cast the remaining sections of the offering into the flames. Cihua, the temple prefect, was bending over his master in an attempt to revive him. An unbearable aching throbbed through his body. His entrails twisted and jerked. There was the taste of burning, retching gall in his throat and on his lips.

He had begged Cihua to go away and leave him; but the other priest insisted on holding him up. A quantity of bitter powder was forced between his lips. After a time the prelate, his pain pushed away from him (though still pulsating nearby), managed to stand. A peculiar, half-conscious sense of well-being swept through him; and on the arms of his priests, Tizoc was able to descend the pyramid to his waiting litter. The succeeding hours until dawn passed in a vague, timeless rapidity. He could not recall the end of the homeward journey, nor the moment he was finally laid on his own couch. Obeying Cihua's gently urgent ministrations, Tizoc had stood and allowed himself to be robed in his usual vestments. He was borne across the compound and up the steep pyramid. Cihua guided him to the altar, where the victim had been prepared; and with the prefects practically steadying his hand, the High Priest of Hummingbird Wizard in Tezcuco commenced the first day of the new cycle.

The day Two Reed thus painfully begun, Tizoc again collapsed in the arms of his attendants. In the following days it gave him no little satisfaction to learn that most of the prelates that had participated in the fire ritual had fared in very much the same way. By the fifth day Tizoc was able to leave his bed (he had given the chief vicar his duties of sacrificer, for someone had perforce to offer the Sun blood) and join in the festivities. He had a sense of grim satisfaction to learn that the old High Priest of Humming-bird Wizard in Tenochtitlan had had a hemorrhage of some sort, and after a brief resurgence, died. Whomever Montezuma should now elect to succeed as Lord of Divine Matters would be accept-able to Tizoc.

Mictla, however, had recovered almost immediately—accustomed as he was to seizures. He had gone about his business with the manner of one almost completely contented in life: *his* hand had offered the Sun the gods' sacrifice. Cihua thought it circumspect to keep this information from Tizoc until the latter had recovered. The month was a fairly quiet one for the priests of Humming-bird Wizard; but the High Priest of Tlaloc, who was perhaps a little sicker than Tizoc, was forced by the calendar to leave his se-clusion and direct—at least nominally—the sacrifices to the lake goddess and her children. Her chief priest in Tezcuco was under the jurisdiction of Tlaloc's temple, though her cult was of the ut-most importance and quite the equal of her husband's. In the first month fell the ceremonies for rain, the child sacrifice; and the prel-ate paid for his moment of arrogance by days of demanding ritu-als . . . without a vigorous spirit to buoy him up.

As a gesture, Tizoc went on an excursion to Coatlinchan, the powerful frontier fortress some ten miles southeast of the capital. On hearing of his rival's death, the recuperating high priest de-cided to leave his self-imposed seclusion and enjoy the bleak coun-tryside. Coatlinchan was a pleasant city in any season, with its sloping terraces above the river perennially green. The baron was a close relative of his; and Tizoc had frequently wandered about the dense groves of cypress and fir trees in his youth. In a ravine a half-hour's walk from the city lay a massive, unfinished statue of the Water Goddess, the greatest, however unsuccessful, attempt at sculpture in the valley. Forever to be bound to its matrix of living rock, as though the stone itself had once tried to take her form, the goddess seemed to strive through the centuries to emerge.

Tizoc, his life completely ordered as it was by refined and exact-ing rituals before exquisite idols so stylized as to be mere abstrac-tions, found in this weather-darkened figure lying unworshiped on a hillside a profound expression of the forces that ruled over the valley. For all the triviality of his nature, his self-defeating search after power, the high priest earnestly worshiped the fierce creatures his people had formed and given substance to in their age-old communion. He was not brutal, only obedient. And the afternoon he set out for the frontier city was on the eve of his forty-sixth birthday. The old baron, who still considered his august nephew as a child, had demanded that Tizoc come. Itzco, who by an involvement of marriages was both a city noble and one of the old man's immediate heirs, was not invited—Lord Marshal or no.

On the afternoon Tizoc went to visit his maternal uncle, which was the seventh day of the new cycle, a strongly contended ball game was begun in the royal palace of Tezcuco. Most of the nobles that had come to settle disputes of one sort or another quickly forgot their appointments and hastened to the court. Apparently all business had been set aside in the excitement; and one litigant would find himself with the other, leaning over the wall and exchanging words in utmost camaraderie—while the judge of their case glared antagonistically from across the long, narrow enclosure. From either end of the court below them, a stone hoop stood out vertically more than a man's height above the pavement.

Tlachtli was a passion among the merchants and nobles of Anahuac; and especially the inter-city matches were irresistible. Any game, however, presented an excuse to ignore one's commitments and join in the rivalry. Barons wagered estates against warehouses that their teams would win; in obstinate exasperation, a partisan of the losing players might stake a villa against a slave girl on a goal. In fact, just such an agreement was being concluded when Lord Itzco took his place above the court. The marshal glanced at his friend in astonishment, then gave his attention to the game. All eight of the youths below were his commanders' sons.

Neither side had made a goal so far that afternoon; and the winners were ahead by several points in the second set, having just won the first by a decided margin. They were in the second of the usual three games, each of which was brought to an end by one team's gaining five points. The outcome of the afternoon should be decided in the next several minutes, as this game could give the leaders two out of the total three. If the other team was unable to manage at least a tie, it would be unnecessary to play out the final set . . . unless the losers would try for what practically required the intervention of the god Flower Prince.

Itzco, his mind half on a message he had received from the governor of an outlying province, mildly interested himself in the players below. The game, the set, and the afternoon's encounter, would be over before he could judge the merits of the two teams. "Ha . . . !" the noble beside him called out. The hard rubber ball had deflected from an end wall and bounced, an inch off the hole, against the hoop. The losers had gained a point, and one of their team quickly struck the ball again with his elbow—sending it in a straight line toward the opposite end. "Two points . . . two points more," the man exclaimed, further delighted. If the ball could be immediately retrieved by a man of the same team that had scored on a hoop, and sent the length of the long court, an extra point was granted.

"They're only a point ahead," the noble confided to Itzco.

"You wagered your villa on a goal, not on a game," the marshal answered; but the other had turned again to the players and seemed not to hear him. The ball could only be struck with elbows, hips, or legs; and it was an extraordinary feat to send it through the center of a hoop . . . so extraordinary that in the event of a goal, the players and backers of the scoring team had the right to snatch whatever jewels and clothing their adversaries were wearing. The set, even if two games were lost, would be accorded them.

Under these conditions, it was difficult for Itzco to remain in his place without becoming concerned. Had he not been thinking of military affairs, he would have first sent an attendant to discover the score. He couldn't leave now without offending his companions—so he covertly handed his attendant a jeweled ring he favored and sent the man after a decanter of chocolate, with instructions not to return until he had deposited the ring in a safe place.

The winning team suddenly feinted, gained position; and one of its members caught the ball deftly on his knee. It glanced up; and as the ball fell, a sharp elbow sent it straight as a stone from a sling at the opposite wall. By a fraction of miscalculation, the ball flew back into the court without touching the hoop. There was a moment of confusion among the players. The two judges left their position near the hoops and bent over one of the losing team's men, who half-stood with his hands pressed against his stomach. It was no more than a slight, even if painful, injury. The judges hesitated; and the court was instantly filled with loud disputes.

The nobles, who had risen in excitement with the last play, remained on their feet and hurled thinly veiled curses at each other. One of the judges, without gaining the agreement of the other, waved his hands sideways, palm out. The injured youth must leave the court. There was a lull as the backers waited to see who should replace him—then a surprised murmur. Ixtlil's presence had gone unnoticed until he strode defiantly out onto the court. The boy threw his mantle to his attendants, and roughly intercepted the wounded player. He demanded the wide orange-and-silver brocaded belt and fastened it about his own waist.

He stood barefoot, clad in a short tunic and fringed loincloth, near the center of the court. After a brief hesitation, the three players of the losing team grouped about him. The nobles above the enclosure were incensed. What right had a boy within several months of even being ten to interrupt the match? Villas and slaves, coffers of cocoa and of gold sand, bundles of costly feathers and spindles of fine cotton dyed with cochineal—a great deal of wealth was involved in the afternoon's diversion. What right indeed . . . ! There was no hope at all for the losers now. Those that supported the winning side, reconsidering Ixtlil's appearance, settled back on their benches and waited for the game to begin anew.

The losers accepted the prince, reluctantly perhaps; and the judges indicated that the ball should be thrown into the air. High into the air it sped, then down almost direct from where it had risen. Ixtlil, whose head reached his companions' shoulders, stepped a little to the side and struck the ball with his elbow. Off it flew towards his opponents' goal. One of the other team intercepted it with his arm; and as the ball rose from the pavement, struck it lightly with his knee. Another on his side caught it with a quick, turning movement of his body, sending the hard, resilient sphere to the court away from the players. He quickly drew back his arm, when a small shoulder struck him in the chest.

The ball skipped off. Another of the winners swept down with a sharp turning of his thighs and dealt a well-aimed blow with his hip; but the same little figure bent forward and caught the ball in the sensitive curve between the shoulder and the neck. The ball fell aside; and before the surprised player who had cast it recovered, Ixtlil paused—fastened his eyes on the precise block of stone to one side of the hoop before him, and flung out his elbow.

The ball sailed in an outward curve toward the wall, flicked the stone, and rebounded into the hoop. It seemed for an instant to hesitate on the thick lip; then sprang through the opening, slightly deflected back toward the wall. Before the ball hit the pavement the watching nobles had risen without a sound to their feet. The unexpected victors were glancing at each other in such amazement that no one thought of despoiling his opponents.

Ixtlil stood by himself near the hoop. After a moment he called out something to the judge several yards away and turned to leave the court. They watched him go, his own players and the general onlookers, without ovation. A decided, oppressive sense of the unnatural communicated itself through the nobles. The youth who had been injured earlier in the preceding game advanced from the stairway leading into the court, and stood undecided near his fellows.

One of the judges called out: "One to one." A low confusion of voices rose from the stands as new wagers were made on particular plays, but the excitement was subdued. Several of the younger nobles of the goaling team half-heartedly demanded a jewel or a pair of sandals from the losers, both to revive the spirit of the match and to satisfy Xochipilli, the Flower Prince, who was god of gaming; and were answered by good-natured howls of protest.

The marshal's nearby companion accepted the reassurance that the slave girl was his, in an attitude of forced delight. And as Itzco rose to leave, the returning player tied his belt again about his waist. The ball sped high into the air. Itzco paused a moment in the middle of the stairway leading to a higher level. He half-turned into the court, his small head to one side. The nobles had resented Ixtlil's interference . . . but no, their behavior could not be construed as insulting to Nezahual. The murmurs against the prince had been momentary; Itzco had had no opportunity to admonish them.

The War Minister quickly reached the square open platform

above, then turned aside and walked along the edge toward the palace proper. The terminus was cut by a wall of carefully glazed stucco that extended over half its length beyond the platform, the lower face bounding one end of the narrow I-shaped court. At the bottom of the earthen rampart the ball game was still in progress; and on the tier immediately below Itzco were the gamblers, crying out in suppressed anger at their opponents. Behind the outer line of spectators stretched the terraces of the royal estate. The gray-blue of Lake Tezcuco shone in the near distance. Though the sky was overcast, the air was clear; and one could easily discern the Aztec pyramid looming over the islands at the south.

The marshal nodded curtly to the warriors who guarded an entrance through the wall, and passed into a small patio. He paused by the empty pool, decided on his answer to the provincial governor, stared a moment longer at the knotty vines that covered the enclosing walls, and skirted the pepper tree. As he entered his own apartments, which were directly across the patio from the absent Nezahual's, Itzco made up his mind to call a session of the Supreme Council.

A wide, square court—similar to the platform behind the royal apartments—lay in the center of the palace. The area was walled on two sides; and a broad stairway flanked by serpent balustrades descended from the ruler's private chambers. It was here that Nezahual had often reviewed his caciques and vassal chieftains on the eves of his early battles. Set back beyond the right wall were the low storehouses filled with the tribute of his conquered cities. On the left of the plaza was the celebrated hall of science and music; and behind the building stretched the patios where the learned of Tezcuco wandered their lives away in a seclusion of fountains and colonnaded paths.

Facing the ruler's apartments over the courtyard, set high on platforms and connected with the central area by flights of stairs, were the rooms of the War Council and of the visiting ambassadors respectively. A narrow passageway separated them, the chief entrance into the inner palace. Outside, the Tribunals of the Gods and of the Kings flanked either side of the great market place— where every twenty days Nezahual allowed his merchants to gather and hold a fair. A high mound, faced on both sides with intricately carved stone, walled the enclosure; and along its summit patrolled a perpetual guard. Still another plaza lay before the palace, the central junction of the highways and canals that led from the city into the countryside and gave access to the lake.

It was against this massive embankment which divided the court of the Tribunals and the main plaza that the citizens once flung themselves in despair. An invader, coarse with the primitive brutality of the northern mountains, had besieged the eastern walls of the capital and threatened to enter Tezcuco momentarily. Like agitated, crazed insects without directive, the people attempted to force their way into the palace in search of the missing Nezahual; and the late-arriving nobles, hastening to the center of Anahuac where authority began, had no alternative but to command their warriors to cut a passage through sinew and bone.

But this had happened over twenty years before—when Nezahual was young in his rule, and all Anahuac acknowledged his supremacy. The blood that covered the pavement had long been worn away, scoured by caravans without number, the rains of many winters. The summer sun had bleached the half-acre of concrete of all marks of violence. Nezahual had come in that last hour to defend his city; and the threat that the canals were arteries that should carry Tezcucan blood into the lake came to nought.

A wide thoroughfare led away from the palace into the city, turning in a gradual sweep to the northeast. The way was lined with the villas of powerful merchants and city nobles. Cool parks lay under the shadow of cypresses and plane trees. And in the distance, its sanctuary a forty-foot tower crowned with plumes, rose Tizoc's terraced pyramid. How many times the young Nezahual had set out along this avenue, guarded by ten thousand warriors. Across that little park, a quarter-league this side of the War God's pyramid, lay Lord Catzin's villa, in the merchants' section that fronted the Square of the Lions.

Northwest of Nezahual's stronghold, rising out of the swampland over the water, were the terraces of Acatli's villa. The boy ruler had once fled his palace (when fortune had seemed against him, and his regent to have usurped the throne) to demand Princess Acatli's protection. From her villa on the outskirts of the city he had heard the hollow, wooden ring of the *teponaztli*—and knew his ambitious uncle was dead. From a low island neighboring Acatli's villa rose the pyramid to the Rain God; the princess had often watched the high priest officiating at the morning sacrifices. The death offerings had always distressed her, yet she often watched—compelled by the exquisitely panoplied ritual of viciousness.

On this seventh afternoon of the new year, the serenely gracious courtesan of the golden age sat in a patio with a group of admirers, still a focus in the capital. Near her, resting on a wide wicker chair, was Catzin himself—chief of the merchants and advisor to the Supreme Council. He was a robust man, projecting an aura of endurance and strength despite his seventy years. He was quite bald now. A scant ring of white, close-cropped hair passed around his head from ear to ear. His shoulders and neck were powerfully built, though ostensibly the noble had never done manual labor; he had been far too busy throughout his life managing the affairs of the merchant guild.

He listened attentively to one of the other visitors, then leaned forward. Catzin rubbed his short, stocky forearm as he turned it thoughtfully in the grasp of his other hand: "No . . . no, Cihua. That is not a good exchange."

The prefect of Tizoc's temple, a man in his fifties now himself, shook his head. "I know. It isn't a good exchange at all. The holy Tizoc will be annoyed." He was an extremely handsome, efficient priest, totally without initiative and therefore absolutely trustworthy. Both Tizoc and his predecessor had employed Cihua on the most delicate missions; for he carried out their instructions, and when an unexpected question arose did not take it upon himself to supply solutions. His deportment had a quiet grandeur. When Tizoc found it necessary to demand greater tribute from the cities under his jurisdiction, Cihua was the very man to send with the edict.

At the moment the prefect seemed mildly upset. Tizoc had demanded that all the temple vestments be burned, and his priests be outfitted with new ceremonial robes for the beginning cycle. Unfortunately, there was a temporary shortage of certain plumages; and the funds the high priest had allotted his prefect were apparently insufficient. Tizoc, however (following in the footsteps of the perverse old Cacama), refused to trouble himself with the discrepancy. That further monies should not be assigned from the temple treasury was clearly understood.

Cihua sat on the wall about the fountain, his hands stretched out at either side of him on the masonry. He leaned forward, bowing his head in dejection. "I know," he repeated. "But I have spoken to the merchants, and within slight variance they are in accord."

"What have you already managed to purchase?" Catzin asked without glancing up.

"Twenty bales of hummingbird down, as many of eagle plumes. This morning I agreed to take two bales of trogon feathers . . ."

"How much?"

"Five coffers of ground cocoa and a piece of tin," the prefect answered, raising his head.

"Ridiculous!" Catzin stood, moving with a suppleness unusual for a man of his age. "What are you particularly short of, outside of the quetzal plumes?"

"We have enough *green* hummingbird down . . ."

"You need a little more white? Two bales?"

"Yes, that would be sufficient. And at least four bundles of the blue cotinga."

"How much are they asking for cotinga plumage?" Catzin raised his eyes and acknowledged the young woman that stood at the doorway.

"Three pouches of cochineal; and with a pouch of gold dust, five cotinga and two bales of the rose-colored spoonbill." Cihua glanced up and nodded his head. Princess Nicte hesitated, as though she were afraid of interrupting the men.

The older princess waved to her. "Come, my child . . . sit with me." Acatli moved to one side of the bench. Nicte smiled in acceptance (that strange expression of inner amusement hovering at the ends of her mouth), and crossed the end of the court.

Catzin watched the twenty-four-year-old girl take her place beside his beloved, then turned to Cihua: "Very well. Quetzal plumes, white hummingbird down, cotinga, and roseate spoonbill." He paused for a moment, glancing again at Acatli as though addressing her. "Five pouches of gold dust, and five orange bowls from

120

Cholula . . ." The old courtesan nodded her head, and Catzin turned to the prefect with the offer.

Cihua thought a moment, hiding his satisfaction, and asked: ". . . Five plumbate bowls from Maya Kiche?"

The merchant was delighted by Cihua's tact. The bowls from Guatemala were a decided rarity in the valley. Pretending to protest Catzin's demand, he had offered something of far greater value.

"Done!" Catzin exclaimed, smoothing the scant hair at his temples. "You shall have your feathers before the end of the week."

"You have no need of cardinal plumage?" a young noble who had been sitting quietly behind the fountain asked sarcastically. He stared at Nicte and nonchalantly twirled a broken stem of the rose tree between his fingers. His meaning was perfectly obvious to every one; and Cihua did not deign an answer. That Tizoc should assure himself an ample supply of feathers for his own mantles was only proper.

"*Tepoh . . .*" Acatli chided. "Should you be disrespectful?" She spoke to the young grandee as though he were a small boy; yet there was a gentleness, a subtle admiration in her voice that could have offended no man. She rose with a slow, graceful movement, and stood for a moment gazing toward the fountain. A finely webbed veil fell from her coronet, erasing the few lines in her face. The lids of her large eyes were shadowed with kohl; and in the even, diffused light of the court, the most celebrated of courtesans seemed perhaps a year beyond forty . . . certainly no more.

Acatli's features were still defined: the narrow-ridged nose, the clearly molded cheekbones and chin. Her mouth was similar to Nicte's: full yet perfectly chiseled, a slight ridge that followed the curve of the lips. Her smile was calm, detached, approving. With her maturity, however, there had come a subtle, almost melancholy warmth that she had never possesed in her youth. She had had a life of power, of great wealth. Emperors and princes had sought to amuse her; but until the last years, Acatli had been alone. Now she paused beside the low bench, one jeweled hand raised to her shawl, and seemed to gaze into the fountain.

Catzin waited nearby, admiring her beauty as though he had seen her for the first time. Then the merchant lord said, his voice formal: "My Lady Acatli . . ." She turned to him, tilting her head quizzically. "Are you weary of us?" Acatli opened her lips, feigning amazement that he should imagine such a thing. "Nevertheless, I fear that we have tired you," he concluded in a decisive tone. "It is time for your afternoon rest."

The princess was amused by his allusion to a private understanding of their youth.

"Let me accompany you. My lords," Catzin said, turning to the others, "excuse us. Lady Acatli would retire."

"I must also leave," Cihua stated, rising to his feet.

"Oh, no," Acatli protested quietly. "I will send an attendant with chocolate and maize cakes, and your favorite honey of the xtabantún flower . . ."

"But I must—"

"No, no," the great courtesan exclaimed with a laugh. "I'll send the girl." As she kissed Nicte on the forehead, the young noble crossed the court and bowed. Acatli touched his cheek gently with her fingers and, leaning on Catzin's arm, left the patio.

"Before three days have past, you will have your plumage," the merchant called back from the corridor.

Cihua turned to the fountain and sat down again. Nicte and her gallant were together on the bench, staring into each other's eyes without a word. The young princess's face had no expression; and the priest wondered if she were bored by the youth's infatuation. At last Cihua called out in a gentle but firm voice: "You two should go down on the lower terraces and be alone. It won't offend me . . . go along," he added with a slight laugh of understanding.

The noble glanced at him, an expression of momentary resentment in his narrowing eyes. The youth was quite aware of his own position among the fourteen barons. He stared at Cihua as though to say *I am the Lord of Tenayuca.* The prefect was not cowed, however—whether the noble came from the same lineage as Nezahual or no. It was quite a long time ago that the chief Tlotzin had quarreled with his brother in Tenayuca, and removed to Tezcuco—thereupon founding his own line of princes.

The two men stared darkly at each other for a moment, and Nicte rose. *"Notlazomahuizteopixcatatzin,"* she addressed the prefect, using the proper title for priests. Her tone was one of disinterested respect. "Venerable minister—if you *will* excuse us . . ." The noble reluctantly stood beside her, and they bowed their heads together. Cihua was left to his chocolate and his thoughts of the temple. Though Nicte had been dedicated to Tlazol, the Earth Mother who in one of her guises protected courtesans, it was rumored that no man had yet known the princess intimately. Aggressive or not, the proud young baron would find little satisfaction for himself in Nicte's company.

And down on the lower terraces a little later, Lord Tepoh was in the process of discovering this. They had withdrawn to a small pavilion overlooking the lake. Below them was a quay; and Nicte, sitting at the edge of the open building, watched an official canoe being docked. A courier with Nezahual's insignia on his helmet stepped to the landing; and after a moment's delay, began ascending the stairway to the villa.

". . . but I have a remarkable little palace at the mouth of the river," the baron was repeating. "Quite remarkable—the king of Acatlapan himself envies me. Directly east lies the great causeway leading into the Mexican capital. Across the inlet is the city of Tlacopan . . . and the slave market just above it. I would purchase you twenty attendants of your own—lovely, graceful girls who should add to your beauty."

"How?" the princess asked simply, turning from the canal.

"An extraordinarily beautiful rose in a garden of merely lovely flowers is the more beautiful," he answered easily, drawing closer to her. "The delicate petals are more jewel-like as the garden echoes their color." Under his flamboyance, however, there was an unmistakable susceptibility.

Nicte, who had begun to shrink away from him, relaxed and nodded her head in acceptance of his words. "You are of the same blood as Nezahual," she commented, half questioningly. The young cacique, accustomed to reminding others of this himself, was surprised.

"Yes," he answered suspiciously. "We have the same ancestors. Why do you ask, Lady Nicte?"

"You don't look much alike." She raised her thin eyebrows in a higher curve. Her loveliness was an odd mixture of elements: the austere, clear-cut features of the Toltec softened and rounded by the Mayan blood of her father. Under the fullness of her cheeks was the cold, symmetrical perfection that characterized Acatli's beauty. Nicte's jaw was a little more rounded, a little more set back, which gave her mouth a slightly pursed appearance. Her dark eyes were slanted at the corners, and her lids had heavy lashes. Pendants of jade incised with the precious blue turquoise hung from her small ears, the color accentuating the dark, warm ochre of her skin. As the courtesan commented on Tepoh's dissimilarity to the ruler of Acolhuacan, she drew back again and coldly appraised the baron.

The youth was momentarily nonplused. There was a strong, self-conscious virility in his manner; and his features were well formed, if commonplace, for one of the forever-intermarrying aristocracy. He had the slender, almost gaunt, facial structure of his race, and the hard compactness of a warrior's body. His cheekbones were too broad, though; and his lips hadn't the sensitivity of Nezahual's. Nicte thought about the ruler for a moment and threw back her head—as though she were completely unaware that Tepoh's hand rested against her breast.

And the noble, guessing her thoughts, said at last in a disdainful voice: "The Lord Nezahual is an old man."

"Only forty-four," she answered without expression. "His lips are so strange . . ."

Tepoh murmured something, and roughly drew her closer to him. Nicte allowed him to take her hand without objection, then wondered at his extreme forwardness. He pushed her hand down against himself and held it there demandingly. The more intimate contact with his body was less immediate than the simple grasp had been. His approach didn't seem at all obscene, or ludicrous. It was a young man's inexperience that led him to believe all women could be aroused by the mere tactile assurance of male need.

Nicte, gazing down at her jeweled fingers, in her own innocence did not correlate the exact physical nature of his excitement with herself. The obvious mechanical correspondence escaped her . . . or, if she understood, only occasioned mild surprise and even vaguer curiosity. Her mind gave much more significance to his excitement than the pulse she felt constricted in her hand. Her own heart felt no urgency whatsoever.

"He is a great lord," she insisted, referring again to Nezahual; and the courtesan thought to herself that at least the king's ardor was not a plaything—not to be taken lightly. Then she wondered where she had overheard these words. Nicte seemed to recall them from her early childhood. *In his being are countless rulers, past and unborn.* Where could she have heard this? Nezahual was already twenty when she herself was born; yet Nicte was certain these words were spoken of an even younger Nezahual.

Her reminiscences were cut short by Tepoh's angry voice: "I am a prince also, as much . . . as much as any Tezcucan lord. Once *my* line of chieftains ruled in the valley."

"Why, then you are of noble birth also. . . . I am a princess of the Maya. My forebears were the great Tutul Xius, the priest-kings of Uxmal and Chichén-Itzá . . . a warrior race." Her voice was far-away; and an odd, soft glaze covered her dark eyes.

Tepoh stared at her in surprise, his ardor subsiding briefly. Then he understood that she wasn't ridiculing him. She was more than a slave, than even a courtesan. Her father was a deposed prince, deprived as he by untoward circumstance of an empire. In fact, Nicte's father had actually experienced dominion. The youth's desire rose again. "Yes," he answered in a quietly persistent tone, discarding his conceit in the need he had created in himself for her; and with a sudden intuition, added: "Yes, Nicte, and we hold a dynasty in ourselves." He had shared the secret of his striving, the mythic eroticism that man gave to his journey through life—to make the utterly monotonous endurable. Tepoh weakened himself to her; and the absent chafing of her hand caused a sharp, irritant throbbing in his throat. His grasp tightened to hold her fingers still.

Nicte's longing was not to bring forth rulers, but to find a meaning for herself in the past. Misunderstanding the intent of his words, the courtesan stared at him in awakened curiosity. Yes, they were prince and princess—he of Nezahual's blood, she of the great Tutul Xius. In the darkness of themselves they held a link to the past. With an awe that was unfamiliar to her, Nicte examined her suitor; felt the restrained eagerness in his longing, the girth of his secretness that seemed to swell with her own yearning for the hidden generations long, long past—yet on the verge now. Nicte was aware inside herself of the flooding, painfully checked memories of empire, the ecstatic purposefulness of other ages. She suddenly, almost spitefully, resisted the tightness of his grasp, and stretched out her slender fingers under his. It seemed that something in her earliest childhood—beyond childhood itself, but in a vast, universal darkness that was warm and heavily, dampeningly fluid—glided over the barely perceptible ridges, over links of gradually quickening purpose.

Suddenly her hand was wrenched away, the strange, emerging glide broken. For an instant she felt a great undercurving crest of the elusive, gelatin warmth of earliest beginning—then emptiness and anger. Tepoh seized her in his arms and drew her back on the couch. He laughed at her struggles, assured at last of his conquest, and deftly unfastened the courtesan's blouse. As he folded the loose garment from her breasts, Nicte ceased moving and stared up at him through half-lidded eyes. She watched him coveting her, the momentary anger quieted. This was familiar to the courtesan now: the mere physical desire of a man for a woman's body. She allowed him to undo her jewel-brocaded skirt. Reassured by her attitude, Tepoh allowed her to rise. As Nicte disrobed, the young baron lay back against the pillows and further untied his loincloth. He threw the long, fringed scarf away from him, then leaned forward a little, pulling off his tunic. Tepoh rested again on the pillows, enjoying the prolongation of his need now that his eventual pleasure in her was certain. The princess's unexpected curiosity had almost undone him. He could well believe she had never been with a man before.

Nicte had momentarily associated Tepoh with her fulfilment— not as a woman, but as one deprived. She had been awakened by the vigor of the past in him; and in a way known only to women governed primarily by primitive instinct, the courtesan had participated in his very maleness with him. But the link she had imagined was broken. His yearning, his body, were outside the field of her consciousness . . . no longer hers to search with; and as Tepoh watched the late afternoon sunlight glance on her dark ochre skin, molding the distended fullness of her breasts, the soft litheness of her waist with its shadowed moon-navel, Nicte herself stared at him in the most disinterested curiosity. He was only a young man who admired her. That he was also unclothed did not occur to her; the courtesan was only conscious of her own nakedness, and of the excited admiration her beauty aroused.

She began to dance about the small pavilion. Nicte moved with a peculiar naturalness that was at once stylized, practiced, and decidedly feral. The fleeting movements of wild creatures could be discerned under the cadenced gestures. Had the watching noble been less naïve he would have taken warning in the easiness of her expression. Nicte danced in too great a completeness of herself, seeking and discovering within the compass of her own body the tensions and releases that nerves and muscles require.

He had unwittingly aroused in her a need of him, and as carelessly destroyed it. And as Nicte danced, her gestures and momentarily arrested stances less impromptu, more patterned, it seemed to Tepoh that he almost heard the sharp tinkle of bells in accompaniment. The rhythm of her heels on the pavement, the angular, catching pauses of her hips and arms, began to build in mounting, flowing cadences; and through her movement, the courtesan projected the low, vibrant percussions of a water drum. Her outstretched, fluttering fingers echoed the wailing melody of a single string, the shrill, plaintive hesitance of a reed flute. Nicte incited the under memory of the body, which recalled and gave meaning only to tactile impressions.

As he watched, the baron felt the raspings of notched deer bone at his own fingertips. If he had destroyed the illusion that might have given Nicte to him, the princess now evoked an impassable aura about herself that rose from the dark consciousnesses of both. Fearful insinuations flitted through her, a terrible mime confused of serpents and jaguars, the rending beaks of eagles and spiders with hummingbird wings.

Tepoh's nerves sustained his excitement. The aching of a need too long held back tightened inside him; but he watched now in another anxiety. An uneasy, strange feverishness swept through a thousand nerves, as though the excitement were a venom released through a secret duct. The pulse gathered momentum in his blood, building against itself. Nicte, knowing only her own urgency, had involved the youth in a deeper search than the pursuit of his particular maleness. He was the one deprived now; and the yearning of the ever-rejected flooded against his temples, burned with the quiet fire of the annelid over his belly. He longed for his meaning in her—yet accepted the desperate impossibility of gaining the princess. She somehow ridiculed the purpose he had given himself —his secret goal of dynasties that gave his maleness a far, golden mystery. This was no self-provoked self-mysticism of sexual identity.

Confronted by the greater mystery, no longer unique but only an expression of his kind, Tepoh submitted to the courtesan and passively allowed her the pulse of his own loins. His blood ebbed and flooded to her movement, rising almost to the verge of itself, then falling away. Nicte's beauty encompassed the women men had searched for through ten thousand years of loneliness. In the remoteness of herself, the courtesan princess focused the impersonal loveliness of the valley that seemed forever alien, forever requiring fierce abnegation.

The youth's desire and fear of her was too great; had Nicte come to him now, Tepoh would have feared to touch the dancer who could so easily evoke the frightened reverence that belonged only to the gods. Her strange genius alienated him, even as it altered yet sustained an intense distress.

Nicte swept in increasingly rapid gyrations about the pavilion, her fingers outstretched and seeming to flick over smooth, invisible ridges. Higher and more quickly her hands rose; and Tepoh, his body no longer responding outwardly, felt the surge of his blood rise beyond the aching, quiet fire of endurance. His breath caught in his tightened throat, and the pulse struck—impersonal, insistent —against his forehead.

Suddenly Nicte leapt into the air, her hands sliding up and out —as though pressing the thick crest of a giant arum beyond its slenderer spike. Then she fell in a slow, turning collapse to the floor, tearing down with her the loose spathe of an invisible flower. A scalding, full release swept out of the barely conscious youth, a slow flooding of exhaustion that carried away the ache.

When Tepoh at last opened his eyes, the princess was clothed again. She was raising the shawl of plumage and woven gold over her shoulders. She glanced at the baron, a slight, noncommittal

128

smile on her lips, then turned away. Tepoh stared for a moment at the vacant doorway, and closed his eyes again. No customary sadness called out to him from his hidden self—no sigh of pathos. His body had expressed itself in elemental terms, its uniqueness not involved.

Nicte was completely unaware of her victory over him: she wasn't concerned. She had danced in the great courts of the empire . . . and when she felt the subtle rhythms finding cadence in her movement, the thin melodies fluttering at her fingertips, Nicte was no longer the child of a slave mother. She was no longer a mere courtesan in the cult of the goddess Tlazol, but the daughter of a Maya prince. The legend she portrayed, the ancient rites that only princesses of the Tutul Xius performed—these were her witness.

9

Nicte hesitated on the path above the pavilion, suddenly aware of her own exhaustion. It was a warm, easy tiredness: a thoughtlessness that hovered between sleep and sad, not-quite-remembered memories. Her body was numb, yet vaguely aware of itself, of the marvelously satisfying ache that trembled over the nerves.

She stood for a moment by a bench, her hand lightly rubbing against the spiny trunk of a honey locust. She remembered the fragrant white flowers, and almost imagined the elusive odor that was now only an inert factor in the motionless sap. A faint orange haze outlined the western mountains; and the canals below the revetments of the lowest terrace were already dark. A chill was in the lake breeze. The courtesan decided that the afternoon really had been unusually mild for the season. She drew away from the bench; but her shawl caught on the sharp roughness of the tree, and Nicte turned back to release herself. She noticed that Tepoh had walked out on the little platform beside the pavilion, and she waved to him as she continued up the stairway. The young noble waved back, but did not attempt to join her. He was apprehensive even of himself now: he would admire the courtesan from a distance.

After a short walk, Nicte passed into a court in which the Fountain of the Turtle stood. She paused again, leaning over to examine the dried bulbs of water lilies in a nearby box. The princess, idly wondering at the gardener's carelessness, replaced the cover and rose. As she raised her eyes, she caught the gaze of Princess Acatli—who stood watching her with an expression of remote gentleness from the doorway of the apartment where the aging courtesan received callers.

"Nicte . . ." Acatli's voice expressed her affection and approval.

The younger woman crossed the court and bowed her head to kiss Acatli's hand.

"Nicte, the Lord Nezahual has sent for you." Acatli brushed the girl's hair with her palm. "Yes," she continued, as Nicte raised her eyes in surprise, "His Serene Excellency has accepted an invitation to attend the court of Lord Montezuma. His steward has asked if you will accompany Nezahual*pilli* and the barons to the island of Mexico."

Nicte pressed her lips tightly together; and Acatli, knowing her rare expression of amazement, added: "It won't be for another two weeks, the celebration of seed time. And your mother is to visit us tomorrow . . ."

The women entered the apartment; and Nicte sat quietly beside her mistress. Acatli rearranged a bouquet of winter roses. "Has the young Lord of Tenayuca gone? He *is* a vigorous youth, isn't he?" The great courtesan, seeming to study the rose she had taken in her hand, glanced at Nicte. "Not quite twenty-five, and has already distinguished himself in battle. Did he mention his palace? It's built at the very mouth of a river . . . in the rainy season, one might really find it difficult to escape." She laughed, and threw back her head. "I once visited Tenayuca. Tepoh's father was a delightful man—a little vain, perhaps, but generous and well-meaning. He was clever when we were alone. In company he always talked too loud, and repeated himself so much. . . . Once Ahuitzotl—or was it that impetuous Axayacatl?—well, *one* of the Mexican princes once became so annoyed that he whispered quite audibly (while Tepoh's father was speaking) that if a man repeats a stupid phrase enough, even the gracious among his listeners will exhaust the possible implications they loan him."

She withdrew the rose. "Tepoh is not offended . . . ?" Her voice was mildly curious.

"I danced for him," Nicte answered, stretching out her arms as she turned on the divan. She rested her chin against the high bolsters and stared into the court beyond. Acatli recognized the movement and smiled to herself. Really, Nicte was quite like her in many ways. The young courtesan wasn't actually dull-witted: she had a very practical mind. Nicte would listen to the most complicated conversation, and unexpectedly offer a comment that summed up the whole affair. Acatli, who had herself once been a dancer, understood the girl's seeming stupidity. When dancers think too much, they lose that peculiar tie between movement and the under-awareness of beauty. Acatli had wondered before if rhythm hadn't a visceral inspiration the mind could easily inter with.

Often during these long winter evenings when Catzin was away in the capital, Acatli would have Nicte dance for her. Sometimes the older princess would devise poems, have one of the slaves follow the meter on wood blocks, and ask Nicte to interpret the words. There was a decided esthetic excitement in the way the dancer somehow grasped the subtle meanings and projected them into movement. She envisioned legends so completely that her body was merely a part of the whole dream—not even a vehicle. It was similar to the visionary playmates of childhood.

Acatli watched Nicte, and wondered whether the young woman she had taken as a daughter actually returned her love. Acatli herself had been the finest flowering of courtesanry in the golden age. Her poetry had been acclaimed as well as her severe beauty, which she had often tried to subdue. Conquerors had sought her; early in her maturity she became an image of sensual devotion that often alarmed the younger nobles.

Acatli had not been succeeded. Nicte was something else: not a culmination of the line of courtesans that had wandered in whimsical, childlike boredom through the halls of sovereignty. Nor was she a little wicked, as princesses and courtesans were, because she had also been taught to wait while others bartered a destiny for her. Nicte was a cumulation, a reversion to the basic woman that had attended, if not thoroughly comforted, the men of the valley through the rise and ebbing of dynasties. In Acatli, men had arrived at the perfect companion. Contradictorily enough, Nicte had no personal need of their intimacy: the male excitement found no correspondence in her. The pulse in their bodies was alien.

Acatli promised her protégé villas, and had already assigned her the tributes of several estates. There was no necessity for Nicte to offer herself to a protector. The young courtesan's need of reassurance was answered by the excitement she could arouse through her dancing. Nicte, even because she could participate in Tepoh's maleness—not as a woman, but with a sympathetic proclivity—was the natural female aware of the essential difference, the sexual disparity. Her profound envy of Tepoh was an impassable gulf, even as it had led her into momentary rapport.

It was Acatli that was less the woman. With all her elegance and femininity, her formidable accomplishments, the courtesan of the golden age had no little of the male in herself. How else could she have been the perfect companion to the rulers of Anahuac? She did not envy the male possessions. Her own psyche held the pattern of both sexes. She had been able to join herself to men easily, as to an intimate, familiar part of her own nature.

Had she found herself alone in the little pavilion with the youth Tepoh (and he had drawn her hand close to him), Acatli would have merely been amused; without the need of projecting herself into his vigor, she would have brought him into her own warmth, as though returning something lost to its proper lodging. As she gazed at the beautiful girl beside her, Acatli derived the same abstract pleasure that she would have felt had Tepoh himself been lounging against the pillows. The minor difference was the lack of mechanical correspondence.

Acatli fell silent after Nicte had answered that she had only danced for the young lord. Her mind turned from the girl to Catzin; and she wondered if the merchant would be able to finish his business in the capital and return for a late supper. Catzin answered almost exactly that part of the great courtesan's temperament which was efficient and invariably assertive (elements that Acatli had learned to keep adroitly hidden in herself), and she undisguisedly loved him.

Without turning from her pillows, Nicte asked: "Is my father coming tomorrow also?"

"No . . . no, I believe not."

"Where is he, Princess Acatli?" Nicte slipped down from the bolsters and leaned away.

"Most likely in Tlaltelolco. He mentioned last week that he wanted to buy some ashlar—jasper or onyx." Acatli stood up as she reached out her hand to take a small, long-handled bell.

"Will he accompany our Lord Nezahual to Montezuma's court?"

"I don't imagine so. Only the high nobles are to go," the other answered, her thoughts now on summoning the attendant.

Nicte was annoyed, and said peevishly: "I don't want to see my mother tomorrow. These dreary days oppress me, Princess Acatli . . ."

The older courtesan glanced down at her in gentle concern, shaking the bell as she asked: "What do you want, Nicte? Your mother will be upset if you don't visit with her." She walked to the divan and affectionately brushed Nicte's cheek. "What do you want?"

"I . . . let me go to your palace in Mexicaltzinco."

"When? Tomorrow?"

"Tomorrow morning. Perhaps I could stay there until I go to the island and dance for the Lord Nezahual."

"But everything is in disrepair, Nicte . . . oh, 'Chitl. Yes, my child, come in." Acatli paused, thinking both of what she wanted to say to her attendant and of Nicte's request to leave Tezcuco. "Nicte, do you want to have your supper now, or wait a little? Perhaps Lord Catzin will be here shortly, and I should really wait."

"I'll eat now, if you stay with me awhile," Nicte answered, her voice shyly demanding.

"Very well, though I really should . . ." Acatli turned to her favorite attendant: " 'Chitl my dear, bring the Princess Nicte her supper here. I'll wait until the fourth hour after sunset. Perhaps Lord Catzin will be back from the city by then." After the girl departed, she answered Nicte's request: "Certainly you may go to Mexicaltzinco; but I fear it will be drearier in the south of the lake now. Why don't you visit Lord Cuauhtemoc? It's much livelier in his palace . . . and he should be back with his army by now."

There was no immediate reply; and Acatli understood the young woman's disappointment. She had wanted Nicte to become at least a friend of Montezuma's cousin that ruled over the province of Iztapalapan, the peninsula separating the southern lakes from Lake Tezcuco. Acatli had actually expected Cuauhtemoc to be chosen Lord of Mexico instead of Montezuma. It was odd that the grimly charming Ahuitzotl had himself preferred the priest's succeeding him, and not his own son. The nobles of Mexico would have elevated the present emperor's brother, who was known for his extreme generousness in granting revenues. Montezuma was increasingly parsimonious, despite his personal extravagance. He only spent great sums when it was for his own amusement.

Though she stared at Nicte, Acatli's mind followed a far-removed train of thought. She had suddenly become very sad. Nicte, as though she had forgotten what she was asking of her mistress, said in a gentle voice: "You are thinking of your dead brother, Princess Acatli . . ."

Acatli appeared a little startled, and turned her head in momentary embarrassment to hide her sudden tears. "Yes . . . yes, Nicte. He has been gone now over twenty-six years—though sometimes I remember our last conversations so clearly that it seems only a day has passed since we spoke together." She turned to Nicte, the faintest suggestion of despair on her lips: "It was shortly after his death that you were born . . . a month or so." Acatli rubbed her hands together as she spoke.

"Your brother lived in Mexicaltzinco, didn't he?"

"Yes, his last years were spent in fair luxury, though I could never retrieve even a fragment of our forefathers' empire for him. Had he lived, I might have given him the governorship of Cholula . . ." Her voice had become distant. "He would have had a throne again."

It had been for her brother that she had first left Tulán and journeyed to Tezcuco, the capital of her people's conquerors. Throughout her youth she had satisfied the needs of powerful men, had reassured them when their gains seemed empty. She had strengthened them in endeavors when the vigor of their own youth failed and when mature insight into acquisition either foreboded defeat or caused ennui.

When at last the confidence of Nezahual himself was gained, her brother was already dead. Acatli had come near to ruin and exile in her alliances; her eventual triumph accomplished nothing. Then her daughter had died, afflicted with a tragic malady of the spirit. Only for a moment the signs of her profound, recurrent distress appeared on the princess's face. Then she was again impassively beautiful, her gestures again calculated and refined. The slight trembling in her voice passed. "You may go to Mexicaltzinco whenever you choose," Acatli said, as though the references to her brother, the mere thought of him, had never occurred.

"Tomorrow, in the morning?" Nicte was almost joyous.

Acatli paused, wondering why the girl yearned for the solitude of the now-desolate swampland. "Yes, tomorrow." She decided to send a messenger to Culhuacan, whose lord had once fallen heir to the southern cities of the Toltec empire before the Aztecs had in turn wrenched the ancient palaces away. The Baron of Culhuacan pretended Toltec blood in his own veins, imagining himself a cousin of Acatli's; and the princess, prompted by polity, accepted his friendship. She would ask him to send his youngest son to visit Nicte. The two cities were barely three miles apart; and perhaps he might carry the young courtesan off to his father's capital. Two weeks was a long time for Nicte to be alone—though Acatli had been given to secluding herself for months in some mountain citadel.

The attendant entered the apartment with Nicte's supper. Several slaves accompanied her; and as the young courtesan began to eat, they sat at the entrance, adjusting their instruments. Acatli crossed the room and stared from the narrow casements onto the quay below. She could see the torches of her guard, but no sign of Catzin's return.

And shortly after daybreak on the following morning, Nicte and her own slaves set out for the southern shore of Lake Tezcuco. The Lord Nezahual had not yet arisen, as he had taken to living mostly at night; and the Emperor Montezuma had just left the chief pyramid, where he had attended the first sacrifice to the sun. Before the courtesans barge should round the sharp peninsula that jutted out halfway down the lake, a funeral procession would have already left Tlaltelolco and crossed the short span of causeway between the Mexican islands. The governor of the great market city had died during the third hour before sunrise; and as he had been one of the Emperor's most illustrious servants, Montezuma decided to inter the body beneath his own palace.

On receiving the triple crown, Montezuma had married his eldest sister, the Princess Papan, to the governor; and he heard of the cacique's death with keen regret. Papan*tzin,* who had looked upon her marriage to anyone with an attitude of complete distaste, unexpectedly found her husband more than satisfactory. Virginal until her fortieth year, and quite past the time of convenient child-bearing, Princess Papan took less than a month to discover the childlikeness in her consort (to the amazement of the courtiers, who were in dread of him), and thereupon gave the lord her complete devotion. Montezuma, perhaps unduly fond of his sister, was delighted, then annoyed by the change in Papan's affections; and under the guise of considerations, added titles, and further obligations, to his brother-in-law.

The increased duties had taken six years to break the middle-aged cacique's health. The governor's death, however, now depressed Montezuma. To assuage his sense of guilt, and to honor Papan, he immediately commanded that her husband be placed in a subterranean vault in the foundations of his chief residence. The princess, unaware of her brother's perfidy, was grateful to him for his generosity. She requested that Nezahual be asked to Tenochtitlan immediately; and Montezuma, though he resented her love for their cousin, agreed to send a courier to the palace of the Plumed Towers.

Papan, as though she had forgotten the unfortunate consequence of Nezahual's earlier marriage to her half-sister, insisted on addressing the Tezcucan lord as "Brother." During the years of her stay in Tlaltelolco, she had only left her husband to visit the royal cousin who ruled over the Acolhuans; for alone among her relatives, Nezahual was the congenial spirit to whom she could confide her most intimate thoughts.

So, as Nicte's barge approached the peninsula marking the middle point of her voyage, an official canoe that bore the imperial standard swiftly sped past. Before his accustomed hour to arise, Nezahual was awakened by Comtzin and Tlatoa, his personal attendants. Unlike Montezuma, the Tezcucan ruler preferred his slaves to his nobles; and as he grew older, no one was allowed to approach him except through their agency. With his peculiar humor, Nezahual had conferred on both youths fantastic titles of his own invention when he heard of the Emperor's refusing the attendance of anyone but the highest nobility.

And as he was awakened by Comtzin, he sat up on his couch

and demanded quietly: "What, Lord of the Three Reservoirs and Keeper of the Hummingbirds, is the reason for this interruption?"

"A messenger from Montezuma has just arrived, Excellency," Comtzin answered.

"And his purpose? Lord of the Gold Caymans, fetch me some chocolate." As Tlatoa exited, Nezahual sat up and rubbed his arms. He yawned, and then glanced at Comtzin expectantly: "Is Montezuma displeased by something? Every day seems to bring some new threat that alarms him."

"Excellency, the Princess Papan's husband died last night. She wants you to come immediately to Tenochtitlan."

"Oh . . ." Nezahual became serious, and thoughtfully swung his legs over the edge of the couch. "That is unfortunate. Certainly I'll go to her. Draw my bath, Comtzin."

"It is already drawn, Excellency."

The ruler stood and began to cross the room. The appearance of the steward, however, arrested him. "What do you want?"

The noble knelt and touched his forehead to the pavement. Then he looked up: "Do you want your barge made ready, Excellency?"

"No. It would take too long to descend the river. Send a messenger to Tezcuco immediately, and have a barge wait for me at the end of the marshes. I'll travel more quickly if I take runners to the lake. Have my litter made ready. Go on . . ."

"Yes, Excellency. But . . . but you really should eat before—"

"Send the messenger to my capital. I'll take something to eat." Nezahual quickly passed into the anteroom, where the sunken pool had already been filled with warm water. Comtzin helped him to bathe; and within a quarter-hour the Lord of Tezcuco was on his way to join in the interment of Papan*tzin's* husband. The Barons of Chiconauhtla and Aticpac would be awaiting him at the lake. Nezahual had commented to his steward before leaving Tezcotzinco that this trip to the Mexican capital would cancel his attendance two weeks later. A messenger was sent to Coatlinchan with instructions for Tizoc's uncle to join his master at Montezuma's court. Tizoc would have to spend his birthday alone.

Further instructions were sent to Itzco and Prince Quauhpo. These ministers were to be in Tenochtitlan by evening also. The steward took it upon himself to send after Nicte, unaware that she had that morning set out for the opposite end of the lake. It wasn't until the early evening that the courtesan, who had only been several hours in the palace of Mexicaltzinco, was informed that she was to attend the lords Nezahual and Montezuma immediately. The funeral and lamentation were over and a feast was in progress.

Princess Papan alone seemed to be dispirited. She sat solemnly between Nezahual and her brother Cuitlahuac, who was about Nezahual's age: taller than either his cousin or the Emperor, burly and given to a peculiar, aggressive silence. On the other side of Montezuma sat Cuauhtemoc; and beyond him, the Baron of Chiconauhtla. The table of the high lords overlooked an empty hall (in accord with Montezuma's dislike of the minor nobility); and the other lords that accompanied Nezahual were feasting in the adjoining hall with the Emperor's courtiers.

Several of Montezuma's children sat at the left end of the U-shaped table, across from the lords of Tlacopan and of Culhuacan (who was Acatli's supposed kinsman). One of the sons, though his mother was a concubine and he was therefore without title, was conspicuous among the children by his height and the refinement of his manners. Beside him sat the lovely little Princess Tecui, whom Montezuma (after he had allowed the Tezcucan forces to be ambushed in the valleys of Tlascala) had penitently named after Nezahual's second empress. There was a strange bearing in these two that distinguished them from Tecui's royal brother and the daughters of Princess Acatlan, the ruler's second wife.

Nezahual, as he listened to Papan, watched Princess Tecui with a careful intensity, as though he sensed something of her future. She seemed very much aware of herself for a four-year-old child.

". . . and really, Brother," Princess Papan was repeating to her cousin, "do you think I should . . . take on the responsibility of governing myself? Montezuma wants me to, but I'm forty-six. I must admit it, *forty-six*. It's all I can do to manage the household affairs of my own palace. Imagine having to govern one of the largest cities of the empire . . . having to know exactly where to levy warriors in case of an emergency, and decide cases when my judges are confused. Really, Brother dear . . . would *you* do it, if you were a—well . . . actually a middle-aged woman? And dear Chimac . . . oh, Nezahual—what shall I do without him? He was so pressed these last years, I hardly knew him anyway. But do you know, Brother, I'm absolutely sure he will come back from the dead and spend evenings with me."

Nezahual, who hadn't been listening closely, caught the meaning of her last words and stared into her eyes. "What are you saying, Papan?" he asked rather sternly.

"That Chimac will come back to me. In fact, I think in the early morning he might first come . . . down by the baths, early some morning when no one is about." She seemed suddenly annoyed at herself, as though she had broken a promise, and looked away. Her eye fell on the illegitimate prince who watched her from the foot of the table. "Come, Cahua . . . come to your aunt," she called out distinctly, waving her hand. Montezuma glanced at her in disapproval, and Princess Papan arched her delicate eyebrows in unconcern. Nezahual smiled to himself, and watched the seven-year-old boy approach.

As Cahua paused beside her, Papan put her arm about his waist and drew him closer, kissing him on the cheek. She moved aside, as though she had forgotten her added bulk, and indicated for the child to sit between Nezahual and herself. Cahua, in awe of the Tezcucan king, was embarrassed—then delighted, when Nezahual made a little more room himself and took the boy by the arm to help him.

Montezuma, staring peevishly at his sister, remarked: "The dancer Nicte is about to perform for us. We should give her our attention, Papan. She is quite accomplished."

"Oh?" the old princess questioned. "And what, Serene Excellency, will she interpret for us?"

"A poem on how Smoking Mirror turned himself into a spider, and descending out of the sky on the sleeping Feathered Serpent, bit him so that the god, intoxicated by the poison, might tell where he had hidden his gold and jewels." Montezuma spoke in a priestly monotone, his voice rising slightly at the ends of his phrases as though he were chanting.

"Oh," Papan answered again, rather impressed by the serious-ness of the dance. The musicians were adjusting their instruments, and sporadic, discordant runs and trills echoed faintly through the hall. She turned, goblet in hand, to a passing slave. "You know, Nezahual, I really *have* heard of her before. Nicte . . ."

"I have brought her to attend the Emperor," Nezahual prompted the talkative, independent lady. "She was trained by Princess Acatli." He had always enjoyed Papan's company, and was pleased she had come to the feast.

"Princess Acatli? Why, how is she? It's been so long since I've seen her, Brother. Do you think she'd come and visit me in Tlaltelolco?"

Nezahual nodded his head in assurance.

Papan leaned in front of the child between them and asked Nezahual in a whisper: "Why did Montezuma choose to watch so macabre a dance? Spiders! Really, he's been absolutely morbid this last year. He never sleeps, and wanders about his palace all night. He certainly had a fright several mornings ago . . . in the early hours, just before daybreak—" She interrupted herself to stare into the hall. The musicians had finished tempering their assortment of drums and pipes. Papan cleared her throat and spoke rapidly: "He was down near one of the canals, gazing over the wall into the water. Suddenly he heard a woman's voice calling out to him. *My child, my child, we are lost! We are lost.* . . . Imagine, Nezahual. And do you know who Montezuma thinks it was?"

Nezahual looked at her. He paused, then stated: "It was Chalchivitlycue, the Goddess of Waters."

Papan seemed rather taken aback, as she knew the Tezcucan ruler did not believe in the Aztec gods . . . or, at least, considered them no more than vicious spirits without cosmic significance. Before Nezahual had the opportunity to explain how Montezuma dispatched a messenger to him on that very morning and earnestly beseeched him to come, the deep, splattering concussions of the water drums sounded through the hall. And a moment later, the scraping glide of notched bone added a gently rough texture—carrying over on the offbeat. Cymbals scoured dissonances in brief crescendos, ending in sharp crashes that glanced between the ceiling and pavement.

As Nicte appeared, a speaker rose near the musicians: "The forest was dark on the road to Cochtan, and the weary god . . ." As the narrator began his tale in a high, wailing chant, a single-stringed instrument entered with a shrill, plaintively discordant melody, followed by a confusion of flute voices. Papan stared at her cousin for a moment longer, then gave her attention to the dancer.

". . . and as Feathered Serpent slept, another god watched him from the branches of the tree above." Nicte stalked toward the center of the hall, her movements tentative—her arms held out before her, with elbows high and bent. She approached with a sidling movement that was the more terrifying as it seemed jerky, hesitantly co-ordinated. Montezuma leaned forward on his throne, his narrow face impassive and taut. Nezahual had a slight expression of abhorrence on his lips. He glanced down at the boy beside him and reassuringly put his arm about Cahua's shoulders. The child started at his touch, then drew closer to the ruler without taking his eyes from Nicte.

The accompaniment became tenuous as the giant spider descended gradually on its thread. Nicte's accomplishment was such that one actually felt that she hung suspended from the branch where a few moments before she had anxiously paused. At last she reached her destination, the imagined breast of the sleeping Quetzalcoatl. As the spider struck with its poison, Princess Papan convulsively drew her hand to her bosom and shuddered. She turned to Nezahual, who was quietly smiling at her, and closed her eyes. Then Princess Papan slowly stretched out her hand to the goblet, brought it to her pale lips, and took a deep swallow.

The dance ended after another several minutes; and the spider, unable to coax his secret from the delirious god (though Quetzalcoatl, in a lust created by the poison, had corrupted a maiden and shamed himself before his followers), retreated from the hall. The fountain of *Cozcaapa,* Water of Precious Stones, would never be found until the exiled god himself returned. The musicians were quiet now, and the nobles sat staring into the vacant room.

Princess Papan rose deliberately, glanced at Montezuma, then spoke to Nezahual: "This has been an unpleasant day, and I really must be alone now. Brother Nezahual, do come and spend tomorrow morning with me."

"I will, Papan."

The princess took the child's hand. "Come with me, little Cahua

. . . the men will want to talk. I'll tell you a story, and you can sleep with me tonight. Farewell, Nezahual*pilli,* great and honored lord, prince among princes." She paid casual deference to the Emperor and the other nobles, and hurriedly left the hall.

Montezuma, without preamble, turned to his cousin: "I told you of the woman wailing at me from the water. This morning a fowler from the mountains brought before me a weird bird he had caught in his net. It had only one eye . . . one eye, Nezahual, and the lid was closed. But when I looked at it, the lid flew open. There was no eye underneath. When I stared into the cavity, I saw a curved mirror, and all the heavens were reflected in it."

Montezuma winced, and pursed his thin lips for a moment. He was a small, delicate man in his thirty-third year now. His features were fine, and his color as light as Nezahual's. A thin beard covered his jaw, which for reasons of his own he allowed to remain. He hesitated a moment, then stared intently at the Lord of Tezcuco. His voice had a determined edge, as though he were not sure Nezahual would believe him. ". . . All the heavens were reflected—I recognized the constellations. I was startled, and looked away. Then I peered again into the bird's eye—and I saw a great army of warriors. My astrologers were immediately sent for; but before they could come and witness this new threat, the bird suddenly stretched its wings. The fowler was frightened by its strength and allowed it to fly away."

There was an unusual feverishness in the Emperor's manner. "Nezahual," he demanded, "what is the meaning of the warriors? Why do my people bring monsters to me . . . sinister, cruel-looking creatures, that as soon as I see them disappear? What shall I do to appease my gods?"

Nezahual quietly returned the Emperor's stare. "There is nothing that you can do, Montezuma."

Montezuma suddenly grimaced in anger: "Nothing, Nezahual*pilli?* These are warnings; and we must discover the intent. Something has been left undone . . ."

"Nothing has been left undone," Nezahual calmly insisted, gesturing for an attendant to bring him tobacco.

"Then what is the purpose of warnings?" the Emperor asked with a slight sneer.

Nezahual, not inclined to speak further on the subject, turned to take the tube of tobacco. "The army you saw were strangers to our land. They will come to conquer us, to lay waste our provinces. Our valley will become a desert; and where the lake swells wash now against our palaces, there will only be salt plains."

"Absurd . . . *absurd,* Nezahual." Montezuma stood up, a mocking laugh in his voice. "My soothsayers know the meaning of the warriors in the bird's eye, and in the warnings called to me from the water. We are lost only if we are unable to satisfy the gods' thirst. A blight will fall on the land—not because unknown conquerors will come, but because our gods intend to punish us. You are neither priest nor astrologer, Nezahual." The Emperor walked away from the table.

Nezahual called after him, his voice low and deliberate: "Montezuma, have you three turkey cocks?"

The Aztec ruler turned in surprise, then his expression changed to one of outrage. Did Nezahual dare to ridicule him? "Three turkey cocks, my cousin . . . ?"

"Let us play a game of tlachtli, Montezuma. If I win, you forfeit your cocks to me. Should I lose, you may have my kingdom. You already possess my empire. Acolhuacan, Montezuma, against three turkey cocks: my interpretation of strangers against your fear of the gods' displeasure."

Montezuma stared at him in disbelief. He hesitated, glancing at the nobles that had heard Nezahual's challenge. "Very well, my cousin: three cocks against your kingdom. A wager. When shall we play?"

"Tomorrow afternoon . . ."

"As you will." Montezuma stood for a moment beyond the table. He decided not to leave, and returned to the gathering. He indicated for the musicians to play again.

"You have only seen Nicte in a grotesque expression of her art," Nezahual commented. "Shall we have her dance again for us? Something graceful . . . whimsical?"

"As you will," Montezuma answered again, without interest.

Nezahual turned to a waiting attendant: "Ask the Princess Nicte to dance the story of the prince and princess who went to found a city." He stared thoughtfully into the hall, adding as though in explanation to Montezuma: "It is an ancient legend of the Maya . . ."

The ball court in which the Emperor himself often played was smaller than that in the Tezcucan palace. The game was to begin at the third hour of afternoon, but the audience had gathered well before the time. Nezahual and Montezuma at last entered together. Cuauhtemoc and the Baron of Chiconauhtla were appointed goal watchers; and without further ado, the ball was thrown high into the air. The observers watched silently; there were only the voices of the judges calling out points, the sharp impact of the rubber ball against the walls.

Both lords were barefoot, and clothed only in the long-sashed loincloth fringed with gold. Montezuma, who was more practiced than his older cousin, quickly won the first set. Without pausing, the rivals began the second; and the Aztec took the necessary five points that credited the game to him. Nezahual played with an easy carelessness, undisturbed by the other's apparent mastery. In the second game of the set the long-disused techniques of handling the ball recurred to the Tezcucan prince. His movement became more assured, though his attitude of carelessness remained.

Montezuma's slender body glistened with his exertion as he leapt and turned, frantically striving for the points that came less easily. Nezahual, as though unconcerned with the count, concentrated more on the Emperor's movement about the court than on the ball's. It seemed that his points were made accidentally. Both had gained four points when Nezahual set the ball up for his opponent and stepped aside. Montezuma, unaware that Nezahual quickly sped past him, sent the ball glancing against the stone hoop. Before it rebounded to the pavement, and the play was broken, the Tezcucan intercepted the ball with a powerful thrust of his elbow.

The ball shot in a straight line the length of the court and struck the wall. The game was tied, the ball retrieved; and the last game of the second set was begun. Again Nezahual concentrated on sending the ball, not toward his particular goal, but into awkward angles of the court. Montezuma expertly recovered it each time for his score; at unexpected moments, Nezahual would turn a passing play to his own point. The Aztec no longer found an opportunity to catch the ball as it ricocheted after touching his goal, which had added to his score throughout the first set. At last Nezahual won the third of the three games with a miraculous play that sent the ball in a seemingly futile curve toward the goal. Midway in its flight the arc straightened, the twirl of the small, hard sphere somehow deflecting its course. The ball passed without a tremble through the stone opening. The lords were equal.

Montezuma's co-ordination was beginning to fail. He realized too late the Tezcucan's plan to exhaust him. Of the two players, the Emperor's form was the more finished. In comparison Nezahual seemed inept; but as Montezuma's timing failed, his cousin's gradually improved. Nezahual took the first game, seemed to lose ground in the second, then (in a quick succession of points) won again.

There was a hesitation in the court. Montezuma refused to play out the last set. Nezahual had won the three turkey cocks. The contest had taken barely an hour; yet it was an incident that would be remembered long after Nezahual's greater triumphs were forgotten. Later that night the Emperor's scribes were accounting the game in their codices. Montezuma left his island before evening for his summer palace of Chapultepec on a hill overlooking the lake. Not only his fear of the future oppressed him. Nezahual had held the Aztec diviners in such contempt.

10

Nezahual escorted Princess Papan to her palace in Tlaltelolco. He spent several days with her; and together they watched Nicte perform the graceful ceremonial dances of her father's people. Papan seemed unable to have enough of her. Nezahual was on the point of presenting the young courtesan to the vicereine when his disinterested admiration changed to a more personal approval. Nezahual returned to his hill of the Plumed Towers with Nicte. Within the month it was rumored in Tezcuco that Acatli's slave was manumitted by decree of the Supreme Council, and absolved by royal injunction from her vows to the goddess Tlazol. Nicte had become a concubine in the household of Nezahual the Lord.

It was not until the year of the lake cataclysm that Nezahual journeyed again to the island capital of the Emperor Montezuma. Soon after his return to Tezcotzinco he appeared to have tired of the rural gardens. Once again he took up residence in the royal palace—more to satisfy Nicte's curiosity than for the mere pomp he had long discarded. Perhaps the young concubine, gazing over the two leagues that separated the retreat from the royal capital, coveted the luxuriance hidden in the great pile of buildings which formed Nezahual's chief palace.

Nicte had doubtless heard of the long arcades of marble and porphry shafts, the dark, warm paths through terraces that were overgrown with ancient cedar. Nezahual, aware of her longing, not for idle display but for the lost grandeur of her father's race, might have purposefully taken the princess into his vast palace in order that Nicte should find a momentary proof of herself. Even the great Tutul Xius, the priest-warriors that had once vanquished the southern jungles, would have found the late Imperial Palace of Tezcuco splendid enough for their feasts.

The palace proper extended twelve hundred and thirty-four yards from east to west. It was nine hundred and seventy-eight yards deep. A wall six feet thick and nine feet high protected the lower terraces that overlooked the swampland. The terraces toward the city were fifteen feet in height. About the two central courts rose terraced buildings that contained three hundred apartments, those intended for the chief barons not less than fifty yards square. At least two hundred nobles were in constant attendance, each in turn accompanied by twenty warriors and an odd number of slaves. Including the palace guard, the elite guard, Nezahual's personal slaves, the Princess Ilan and the royal concubines (together with their attendants), the establishment often amounted to well over six thousand persons.

The palace was not mere stone mortared on stone, a line of warehouses confronting a court across from the hall of science and music. It was the concentration of a people's yearning through uncountable centuries. *Nahua,* People of the Rule—so the tribes that had built the three cities called themselves. Many thousands of lives, with all their tortuous complications of ambition, momentous or petty gains and tragic outcomes of vindictiveness, lent an immediate dimension to the gigantic pile of earthen work and stone. The warehouses held cocoa and emeralds: one perishable, the other a constant treasure; yet both constituted an exact, necessary part of Nezahual's wealth.

There was a desperate urgency, not of the past finding expression in the present hour—but of merchants and judges, avarice and verdicts. The threat of an executioner hung over the great outer court, the reminder of the disciplines that had carried savage war chiefs to jeweled thrones. But Nicte, as she paused outside Nezahual's apartments and gazed down the stairway flanked by serpents, saw nothing of the practical functioning that gave reality to Nezahual's rule. The four hundred lordly villas that stretched out beyond the massive embankment were peopled with her imaginings. That they might be converted into fortresses never occurred to the princess—nor that the graceful drawbridges that spanned the canals could be lifted the moment an alarm was given from the palace.

When she turned, disturbed by the endless activity, to enter the royal apartments, the ruler would take his concubine by the hand and lead her through rooms faced with soft pumice stucco rubbed with gold. Jewel and feather tapestries rustled in the slight drafts; and Nicte could see her reflection in glazed obsidian. The ruler would not have told her that these apartments had once been decorated for Acatli's daughter, the unfortunate Mecatl . . . nor that the Empress Tecui had also strolled in the evenings with him through the arcades of alabaster. There had been others who had waited for him beside onyx fountains, sheltered from the wind by the cedar branches.

But it was not important for Nicte to understand these things. And at last, when Nezahual had tired in turn of the dream and the confusion, he left the young concubine in his capital and fled again to the seclusion in Tezcotzinco. He built a villa for Nicte in the lee of the palace walls, where she could sustain her dreams of the Tutul Xius without banal interruption. But even as the construction of unburnt bricks and cement began, the facings of jasper and translucent chalcedony were cut and polished, the conduits brought from the reservoirs for her fountains, Nezahual knew that his stronghold would not long protect even the functioning reality of his people's myth.

Through the first months of the year preceding the lake upheaval, while five hundred workmen fastened stone to stone, raised earthen platforms for the terraced buildings of Nicte's villa, a column of fire appeared over the eastern mountains at midnight. At first the phenomenon excited open alarm in the citizens; but Tizoc and his fellows devised some explanation which seemingly convinced their followers that the priests understood the nature of this new threat.

The people were quieted—for whatever disaster it was that impended, the foreknowledge somehow mitigated their anguish. Only the paralyzing fright of the unknown could disorder the cities—and this was Montezuma's secret burden. Beneath the apparent calm, however, the clans began to fret, to vacillate under the exacting rule of the Supreme Council—as though deep in their consciousnesses men knew the fatal indecision of their leaders. A subdued shudder of fear had accompanied the pillar of fire that wavered over the mountains beyond the valley. A quiet, desperate hysteria almost imperceptibly rose throughout the cities.

For centuries the people had unquestioningly accepted the rule of their chieftains, had allowed the unseen, unknowable factors that were the state to control their very pulse. Gradually the clans had begun to tighten inwardly, to draw away from the central authority of the tribe and the community of each other. Within the clans, small groups of men unconciously strengthened their bonds —as though they feared the laws sustaining and guiding them might be removed. The courts were unable to cope with the increase of public offenses; and Prince Quauhpo and Lord Itzco were forced to appoint more and more judges. Without purposefully ordaining it, the marshal placed Nezahual's capital indirectly under martial law. Warriors were seen as frequently as police officials patrolling the avenues and squares.

It was a futile action, however. Tribal authority was based on the spiritual concentration of the clans toward a center: the center was nothing in itself but a political tension, a field of power magnetism that only seemed to have a permanent outer limit. A new force had entered now, a slowly accelerating movement that carried the clans apart. But (as is so often the case) the central moments of power, the princes themselves, seemed completely unaffected by the change beyond them.

The princes Temozin and Ixtlil celebrated the completion of their eleventh year under the watchful eyes of their mentors; and Cacama began the final stage of his instruction before he assumed the full rights of manhood. He would not be allowed to marry; but concubines would be his, and the permission of the Supreme Council to join in war expeditions. Lord Cuauhtemoc, who had first met the sons of the Tezcucan king on the desolate terraces of Iztapalapan during the night of the cycle end, had invited Cacama to join him in a raid on an obstinate city of Maya Kiche the following year. There were rumors that the young commander had fallen into Montezuma's disfavor, and would probably quit the valley for some time.

The year 1510 commenced properly enough with the sacrifices to the Goddess of Waters. In the second month the fields were duly planted, and the god Xipe honored by his priests wearing the skins of captives. In the third month of the third cycle-year, what seemed at first to be merely a family tragedy occurred. The Princess Papan died. Nezahual gathered his nobles about him and journeyed for the final time to the Aztec islands. Cacama attended his father. Nezahual had decided to present the sixteen-year-old son at the imperial court. Cuauhtemoc would be there, and Cacama was to be placed in his keeping.

Only one unfortunate incident first marred the funeral. After the pomp and the customary sacrifices, Papan*tzin* was interred in the vault beside her husband under the Imperial Palace. The entrance was secured by a stone slab; and as the final ceremonies prescribed for the burial ended, Montezuma was on the point of retiring. He stood for a moment, quietly contemplating the stairway to the royal baths—which lay in a secluded part of the gardens, just outside the palace. His court knelt quietly near him, waiting for the sovereign to dismiss them.

"Cuauhtemoc . . ." the emperor called out suddenly.

The prince rose and knelt beside his cousin, wondering what it was that Montezuma could want. Without a word, Montezuma reached out his hand and grasped the jade gorget that hung from Cuauhtemoc's shoulders. He hesitated for a moment, though not in indecision, then deliberately wrenched it away. The breaking of the cord startled the courtiers, who murmured in amazement.

The Emperor turned quickly toward them, his face dark with anger as though he imagined their whispers to be against him. "Cuitlahuac, come here."

The prince, who had been kneeling beside Nezahual and Cacama (who alone stood before Montezuma), rose and walked solemnly toward his brother. He fell heavily to his knees and touched the earth with his right hand. Montezuma waited until he had raised it to his forehead in submission, then almost roughly placed the broken gorget about his shoulders: "I give you custody of Iztapalapan, and appoint you my heir to the scepter of Anahuac."

The Emperor thereupon gathered his robes about him and walked toward the palace gate. Cuitlahuac, who had caught the medallion before it slipped to the ground, watched his brother leave with an expression that was at once surly and appreciative. Suddenly the clear, low voice of Nezahual broke the awed silence: "Cuauhtemoc . . . come to me." The Emperor paused, and turned to face the gathering. Cuauhtemoc rose from where he had been left kneeling beside his successor, and approached the Tezcucan monarch. Nezahual took his hand before the humiliated prince could genuflect, and gestured for the youth Cacama to draw closer. Then he pressed his son's hand into Cuauhtemoc's: "I leave my eldest son in your custody. A palace is nothing to you, Cuauhtemoc. There will come a time, and *you* shall briefly taste the bitterness—the full bitterness, Cuauhtemoc—of supreme rule."

"What do you intend, Nezahual?" Montezuma demanded, stepping toward him threateningly.

"Why do you humble your princes, my cousin?" Nezahual asked with a sad smile. "Let them rejoice in their spring. The day nears when only the gall of distress shall quench their thirst."

The Emperor blanched in rage. With a guttural exclamation, he turned and strode into his palace. The nobles recovered, and silently followed after him. Nezahual and Cuauhtemoc spoke for a while above the baths; then, together with Cacama, walked out onto the terraces. In the near distance they could see the lights on the opposite shore. Chapultepec was directly across from them; and farther away, the capital of Tlacopan glittered over the marshes.

At daylight next morning the little Princess Tecui escaped her governess and wandered by herself along the terraces near the baths. She had been told that Princess Papan, who was the favorite aunt of the royal children, had gone away on a long trip and would never come back. Tecui had wept herself to sleep the previous night; and even this morning the six-year-old child felt the grief of losing someone she had loved. There was a solemn, tomblike quality about the baths when no one was there: the quiet, confused murmuring of water pouring down the open channels. The slightest sound echoed desolately between the high walls. Children know the meaning of death, they only have no fear of it.

Tecui slowly descended the long stairway. Suddenly the little girl called out in a shrill voice of amazed delight. *"Papan . . . Papan,* you haven't gone!" She leapt down the remaining steps and ran to the end of the pool. Princess Papan was standing in the shadow of the wall. As the child embraced her, the old princess took Tecui tenderly in her arms, admonishing her to be quiet. "But where have you been? Tell me, Papan. Your robes . . . your jewels are *cold*."

"Never mind, little Tecui," Papan answered gently. She firmly took the girl by her shoulders and held her at arm's length. "I want you to take a message for me . . ."

"Must I go, Papan?"

"Yes . . . for now. Ask your governess to come to me here. Tell her I am waiting . . . be absolutely sure, now: tell no one else you've found me here. No one, Tecui—"

"Yes, Princess Papan." The child walked away, then turned several steps above: "May I come back?"

"Later, Tecui . . . hurry now, and do as I told you."

Tecui reached the terrace above the baths, and paused to wave at her aunt. Then she crossed to the wall, entered the gate, and went direct to her own apartment. The governess, who had been searching the women's quarters for her, asked in exasperation: "Tecui, where have you spent the morning? Princess Teçalco has been completely upset."

"Mother isn't even awake yet. And besides, I've been talking to Princess Papan—"

"I hope she was as instructive as your teachers, Princess Tecui. Now come along." The woman walked toward a door leading into an adjoining room. "Have you finished your needlework? After all, a six-year—"

Tecui hadn't moved. The governess, suddenly aware that the princess was waiting behind her, stopped and turned into the room. "Tecui . . ." she commanded in an annoyed, long-suffering voice.

"I have been with the Princess Papan and she said for you to come to her."

"Where is she?"

"Down by the baths," Tecui answered, raising her chin.

"So that's where you've been. Oh . . . how you plague me, a wretched slave!—and you, a great princess, daughter of Monte-

153

zuma the lord. The wind blows cold over the terraces. The baths are damp and unhealthy this season. Why, why, Princess Tecui, must you torment me?"

"Papan*tzin* is waiting for you," the child said, unmoved.

"Are you so lonely for her, Princess Tecui?" The governess's manner changed, and her voice was gentle with pity. She walked to the little girl and caressed her. "There are real playmates for you, right here in the palace: children who can laugh, and tell you how pretty you are, Princess Tecui. Now, come with me—"

"Princess Papan will punish you, Xihui. She is very cold down there. Her jewels were like ice, and burned my cheek. Her robes are wet. She must have walked all night through the gardens. And she didn't go away. They didn't put her in that cave under the palace. Princess Papan wants you to come . . . and no one else must know she's waiting."

The governess, both incredulous and curious, stared intently at Tecui. She really couldn't believe the old princess was waiting by the baths; but her feminine penchant for the supernatural came to the fore. "Where, by the baths, Princess Tecui?" she asked skeptically.

"At the right, near the wall. She was beside the pool when I was there. You'd better hurry, Xihui."

"I must have my shawl." The governess started toward the outer door. "Are you coming with me?"

"No, I'll wait here. Princess Papan said she would see me later. Don't tell anyone . . ."

"Are you sending me down to the baths this hour of the morning for nothing, Princess Tecui? If you are, your mother will be told of this." After a backward glance, Xihui entered the court and quickly walked to the gateway. Once on the outside terrace, however, her steps faltered. She cautiously approached the stairway leading to the baths and stared down into the shadows. Unable to see anything near the pool, and more to give truth to what she intended saying later, the governess descended into the hollow beneath the gardens.

She walked uncertainly along the edge of the pool, absorbed in her mounting anger at Tecui's having made a fool of her, when a voice called out: "Xihui . . . over here." The governess was stricken. A little beyond her she saw what appeared to be a familiar figure sitting on the steps. Without a sound, Xihui pressed her hand to her throat and collapsed.

Tecui, who had disobeyed her aunt, was watching from the terrace above—not out of disrespect, but to assure herself that Xihui actually intended to enter the dark baths. On seeing the governess faint, the little princess hurried back again into the palace. Within several minutes she had managed to awaken her mother and explain what had happened. Princess Teçalco, encouraged by two of her attendants, hastened out of the royal apartments.

Papan was waiting for her; and after she had reassured the frightened princess, asked to be allowed to accompany Teçalco to the apartments of the royal consort. Papan insisted that the whole affair should be kept secret until she could send for her chief steward. Almost immediately on gaining the privacy of the royal chambers, the supposedly dead princess asked that Teçotzi be found and summoned on no matter what pretext to the women's quarter.

When he at last appeared, however, the chief steward of Papan's household was even more terrified than Tecui's mother had been. The old princess asked him to tell the Emperor that she had returned. "Ask my brother to come here immediately, Teçotzi. Tell him that what I must say to him is of the utmost importance."

The steward declined to carry her message to the Emperor himself, not at all convinced that Papan was who the princess said she was.

"Then go to the Lord Nezahual. Is he still in the palace?"

"Yes, Your Highness," the steward answered, averting his head but examining her with a sidelong stare.

"Then at least ask Nezahual to come," Papan insisted. The Princess Teçalco intervened: "We are patient, Teçotzi. Your cowardliness is understandable. If you refuse this wish of the Princess Papan, however, I will have you lashed and deprived of your offices. Now leave . . ."

Nezahual, on hearing of the vicereine's return, did not question the circumstances. Without robing himself properly, he hastened from his apartments.

When Nezahual was brought before the Princess Papan, she was beside herself with the urgency of her message. "Do you believe that I *am* who I am?" she asked tersely, if a little illogically.

"I know my love for you, Papan. I feel it now," the lord answered as simply. "What would you have me do?"

"Go to my brother Montezuma immediately . . . without loss of time, Nezahual*pilli*."

"But you still have your death shrouds on, Papan," Nezahual observed.

"Oh—I do, I do!" The princess wrung her hands. "I really *shall* change this moment. Go now, Brother, and fetch Montezuma to me. You have no idea how urgent this all is. You know I'm no longer dead, don't you? Do I seem pallid? But go . . . go." The distraught princess watched Nezahual pass through the door, then immediately asked for a mirror. Princess Teçalco sent her attendants for fresh robes.

Montezuma stared at his cousin in disbelief. ". . . how do you know, Lord Nezahual? Are you sure it isn't one of the haunters? Are her eyebrows golden?"

"Yes, they are—partly; and the white powder is streaked on her face. Papan apparently tried to wash herself in the bath. After all, she was prepared by your attendants for the interment. There is nothing unnatural in this."

"No one returns from Mictlan. My sister is dead. It is an apparition. How do you know otherwise?" The Emperor sat stiffly on his couch, nervously toying with the fringe on his pillow.

"Have you seen apparitions, Montezuma?"

"Of course not, but my seers have."

"If you reach out to touch a spirit, Montezuma, your hand encounters nothing. If you watch it pass in front of a table, you can see the pitcher and the cups behind. Spirits are transparent and insubstantial. Papan's hand trembles, but the touch is actual. When she stands between your gaze and Teçalco's attendants, she hides the women behind her."

"What proofs are these, Nezahual?"

"Come to your consort's chambers and discover your own." Nezahual turned abruptly away.

"Wait," the Emperor called to him. "Where are you going?"

"To see Papan again. I was fond of your sister in her last existence; I am nonetheless fond of her now."

"You are convinced it is she?" Montezuma stood, and commanded the noble beyond him: "Tell my ministers to attend me immediately." He addressed Nezahual again: "Pray, Cousin . . . wait for me to accompany you."

"Why must you have your entire suite, Montezuma? You are both a priest and an astrologer. Your senses are not only regally acute, your standards are approved."

"Will you wait?"

"You are the Supreme Lord, Montezuma. If that is your request, I must certainly obey."

"We must hurry," the Emperor remarked in a low, self-conscious voice. Nezahual's mockery unnerved him. "Why don't my ministers come?" As he spoke, there was the sound of rapid footsteps in the corridor. Montezuma and Nezahual strode to the door to meet the approaching nobles; and without further words, the group crossed the patio beyond and hurried to the seraglio.

The ministers about the royal cousins knelt as Papan entered the room. She went toward her brother as though to embrace him; but Montezuma flinched. "Is it you, my sister?" His voice was hard and unsympathetic . . . he might as well have admonished her for not remaining among the dead. Papan, obviously pained by his coldness, turned to Nezahual—her eyes filling with tears. "Or are you some evil demon who has taken the likeness of the departed princess?" The Lord of the Aztecs bent his head forward to inspect her.

"It is I, Serene Excellency . . . indeed, it is your sister."

Montezuma appeared to be satisfied, and seated himself on a nearby chair. He stared at Papan speculatively, noticing for himself that it was quite impossible to see through her. Her perfume had a pleasant fragrance not at all sepulchral; and he could see that Nezahual's hand encountered firm flesh. His attitude seemed to demand: *Very well, Papan . . . just why have you troubled us by coming back?*

Papan, hurt and angered by his demeanor, said after a long pause: "Listen, Montezuma. I have seen signs of your destruction . . . and not your destruction alone, my arrogant brother. Allow me, dear Nezahual . . ." She pulled her hand away, and crossed the room to take the chair facing Montezuma's. Nezahual followed her and sat on a couch several paces away. The ministers sat on pillows about them.

"You have seen me dead . . . very dead, Montezuma. The sight had gone from my eyes, and my ears were closed. Remember? They found me on my side in the morning; and my left side was violet, as though bruised. Dead, my brother . . . and you have seen me buried. Now behold me alive again."

Montezuma nodded his head, his attitude still one of disapproval. Papan had always insisted on doing what others considered unseemly, and refused the proper occupations of women in turn.

The princess glanced at him severely: "By the authority of our ancestors, my brother, I am returned from the abode of the dead to prophesy certain things to you . . . things of prime importance."

The Emperor glanced uneasily about him, avoiding Nezahual's gaze. He cleared his throat—then stared at his sister, impatient for her to begin.

Papan gazed down at her hands, thoughtfully rubbing the little age stains. She adjusted her rings, and lifted her head for a moment. Her eyes were closed as she began: "I found myself in a spacious valley . . . not really too wide, but spacious, and seemingly without beginning or end. Steep ridges rose on either side; and at the foot of the eastern cliffs flowed a river . . . a great, rushing flood of water that crested high over its banks and swept violently past cataracts. The whole valley echoed with the uproar. A frightening torrent . . .

"I didn't know that my death had come; and on perceiving myself on the desolate plain, I was really quite bewildered. The brightness hurt my eyes. Then I was annoyed, and began to walk quickly in a chance direction. The earth was rich and dark, yet nothing grew. At last I neared the middle of the valley and came upon a road with a confusion of branching paths. The river wasn't too far away, now. Without particular surprise, I noticed that a young man in a long robe was waiting for me on the bank. His mantle was fastened with a jewel that glistened as brightly as the sun. An aura of pale iridescent light emanated from him; and as I drew closer, I recognized the sign of the four winds on his forehead.

"He had wings, which didn't strike me in the least as unusual . . . full, sweeping wings; and the plumage shone with the most resplendent colors. He moved slightly with mild impatience, and the light glanced from the feathers as though through a prism. His eyes were green, like translucent jade. His glance was shy. Really, he was fair as alabaster: not white and deathlike, but the color of pale ochre gilt with rose. His aspect was beautiful, and his bearing—that of the greatest lord's. He was surrounded by an unimaginably sweet fragrance, like that of night flowers and of copal.

."He took me by the hand and said: 'Come, Papan*tzin*. It is not yet time for you to cross the river.' Then the youth led me through the valley, along the roadway I had previously come upon. The earth about me was strewn with the heads and bones of countless dead men. I watched a number of black people, who were horned and had deer hooves for feet, busily at work on a house—a nearly completed house—and I wondered what fearful creatures would inhabit it. The workmen were engulfed in a depressing, dark mist of muddy color; and their stench was wretched . . . utterly cadaverous.

The river beyond us had become broad and smooth; and I suddenly beheld a vast number of boats on the water. They had great timbers held upright on their decks, and crossbeams. Billowing shrouds of white material were stretched between the beams to catch the wind. The people that manned these strange barges had clear, gray eyes . . . yes, and ruddy complexions, and peculiar clothing of striped cloth, and folded tissue about their necks and wrists. They carried banners and ensigns, and wore helmets without plumes. They smelled like mice.

Papan paused, then stared deliberately into the faces of her listeners: "They called themselves Followers of the Son, and exuded avariciousness. The youth who conducted me through the valley allowed me to see all these things. 'It is not the will of the Supreme Lord that you should cross the river,' he repeated to me. 'You have been given sight of the future preparing itself.' I could not understand him, Montezuma . . . but I asked: 'What is that house that was building? Who will inhabit it?'

"The youth answered: 'It is for those of your people that will fall in battle with the seafarers.' Then he convinced me that I was actually dead, despite my illusion of having a body and all my perceptions. 'You merely remember your senses,' he said. 'But what meaning have these visions to me?' I questioned further. 'Go to your brother and tell him. Without your knowing it, Papan*tzin,* you have lived by the law of the One God—the Unknown God of your people. You shall not be lost.' "

The princess had finished her story. Montezuma gestured for her to continue: "But what *is* the purpose of this warning? What, Papan?"

"I understand nothing of it, Brother . . . nothing, nothing. Before he brought me again to the place where I first beheld the valley, the celestial youth said that my message to you was urgent . . . that I should have you brought to me immediately, though no one outside the princes of Anahuac and their ministers were to know of what I had seen." Papan turned from Montezuma, and instinctively raised her hand to Nezahual as though to ask him the meaning of her travail.

Nezahual nodded his head thoughtfully and appeared disinclined to speak. "Why, Nezahual!" she exclaimed in a startled voice, "You had the fragrance of pine rosin and berries for a moment. Tell me, who was the youth that led me through the valley? Oh . . . he was the angel of the Close Vicinity!" Papan was amazed at her own words, and repeated the youth's title several times to herself in an attempt to divine meaning in the sound. "It was strange. When the angel spoke to me, a thousand associations rang from his words . . . a multitude of meanings, from a simple phrase, the slightest inflection." She lowered her eyes. "I really can't remember now—only the bare words themselves."

Nezahual rose and stood hesitantly by the couch: "He was an angel of Tloque, the god of my fathers."

Papan answered with a tone of conviction: "The unknown god, the cause of causes, He of the Close Vicinity—it was his angel, Nezahual, his manifestation in our valley that we worship with flowers and incense. The celestial youth is our god of fragrance, the deputy of the Supreme Lord."

"And who are these seafarers?" Montezuma demanded, standing also. "Are they messengers of the Supreme Lord? Avengers of the exiled God of the Wind? Are they supernatural beings, Papan?"

"This I cannot remember, Montezuma. But the seafarers, though they worship the One God as we do, and the One God alone, had the odor of mice. Perhaps they are avengers . . . but not the messengers. Some of their leaders were revengeful and cruel, and smelled of death. Their chief had the odor of burnt maize, of self-admiration." The princess stared at her brother in distaste: "You have the odor of burnt bread also, Montezuma. And the ministers at your feet . . . they have the stench of vomit, of hypocrites."

The Emperor could endure her revelations no longer. He left his sister's presence without another word, and went direct to his private apartments. Nezahual, aware that little more could be gained from Papan, left the capital of the Aztec princes the following day. The Lord of Tenochtitlan had not yet left his seclusion, nor had he partaken of any nourishment. The ministers, appalled by Papan's unnatural perceptions, kept the interview to themselves.

11

___

IT WAS RUMORED that Papan had told her brother the gods were monstrous figments of imagination —horrible expressions conceived in ignorance and fear of mankind's bestiality.

"Figments!" Montezuma supposedly exclaimed. "When we offer blood to the idols, why do they cry out in pain and relief? I have heard their shrieks in the temple . . ."

And Papan answered that the dead as well as the living were given to hallucinations. In the world of death, however, there was no immediate material proof to deny the false; and the imagination, unrestricted by and cut off from the senses, could create the reality of what it had ignorantly contrived in a previous existence. Jaguars, serpents, birds, and spiders—all the creatures that symbolized viciousness and deadliness could be confused with those that reflected the quiet virtues into composite deities. The living, who held continual though unknowing intercourse with the spirits of their ancestors, shared in this fearful reality of the gods; and when they themselves left the physical world, did indeed pass into the regions of the various heavens that existed intact in the communal consciousness of a myriad dead. During the sacrifices one was held by a common intent to the spirits, and heard the groans of relief with their ears . . . as though the idol itself called out.

What Montezuma's reply to this had been was not included in the rumor. Shortly after Papan's return to the living, however, her brother ordered that she be shut away from the people. Nezahual himself was refused audience with the princess, and retaliated by declaring he would no longer visit the Aztec cities. This was no loss to the Emperor, who found his cousin's insistence on ruin intolerable.

The fourth month commenced with the celebration of the "long fast," which was in worship of new corn. Throughout the lake cities the dwellings of lord and subject alike were strewn with bulrushes on which blood drawn from the extremities of the inmates was sprinkled. Even the numerous statues of the little *tepitoton* were robed in bright paper garments. Then the worshippers, leaving their household gods, proceeded to the fields. Tender stalks of the growing maize were pulled from the earth and, interwoven with the stems of flowers, were taken to the clan houses in the cities. A mock combat was fought before the altar of Seven Snake, an ancient corn goddess that had ruled in the valley before the Nahua had even ventured onto the plateau from the northern mountains.

During this time the youth Centeotl, the male maize spirit, was also worshiped (though his mother, the Nahua corn goddess and earth mother, was ignored). Young girls presented Seven Snake, whose name alluded to the fertilizing power of water, their bundles of maize of the last season's harvesting. The seed corn blessed, it was returned to the granaries for the coming year. Before the goddess's household image a basket of provisions was placed, surmounted by a cooked frog that bore on its back a piece of cornstalk filled with maize flour and vegetables. This frog represented the goddess of waters, who assisted in providing the harvest.

In order that the earth might be further benefited, a frog was sacrificed; and with this the rites of the fourth month concluded. Those of the fifth month began. This was a particularly important moment in the priests' calendar: the moment of truth. The youth who had for a year impersonated the god Smoking Mirror approached his final day. Throughout the eighteen months he had wandered the streets of the three cities robed in jewels and flowers, attended by warriors and eight guardian priests. In the next to final month four beautiful maidens of noble birth were brought to him. They were given the names of the principal goddesses, and shared the last secrets of his youth.

At the final day the earthly representative of Tezcatlipoca took farewell of his companions, who would now bear in themselves the expression of his yearning—for anguish would lend potency to ardor, and the women were often with child. As he was carried along the avenues for the last time, the citizens paid homage and mourned his approaching death: the bitterness and fear that should end a term of great honors and feasting, a career begun in glittering brilliance.

A barge carried the youth and his retinue across the lake to the western shore, where the chief pyramid of Tezcatlipoca lifted the god's tower high over the valley. As he ascended the steep stairway, the weeping impersonator broke the instruments he had played on, tore the garlands from his body and cast them away. Mictla, the brooding High Priest of Smoking Mirror, waited on the summit with the sacrificial knife.

This particular year, Tizoc had selected a captive from his own reserve of victims; and having anointed him, presented the young man to his people as the god Hummingbird Wizard. He paraded the warrior god about Tezcuco in great pomp. When the day arrived for Smoking Mirror to be sacrificed to himself, Tizoc distracted the attention of the populace with his own spectacle. There was precedent, to be sure. The old Lord Cacama had occasionally ordained gods and presented them to the awestricken citizens. Tizoc's gesture, however, seemed a little too impromptu. Mictla was outraged, and demanded that the war god's festival be canceled. The sacrificial victim had not been chosen until a month before the day of the Toxcatl; and it was quite apparent that cult rivalry was more involved than ill-timed piety.

The Supreme Council supported Tizoc's claim, despite the powerful Mictla's contention. Tezcuco was given a reinforced example of life's tragedy. It was several mornings after the particularly dramatic death offerings that the lake disturbance began. Tizoc was on the summit of his pyramid, at the crisis of the morning sacrifice. He had only a moment before deftly ripped out the heart; and as he lifted it skyward in dedication to the sun, the high priest instantly became aware that something had gone awry.

He stared up at Tonatiuh, and his brows drew together in consternation: the sun faltered on the rim of the valley, had not moved that customary fraction since the moment of first appearance and the elevation. Tizoc had never before been conscious of that slight progression; he wasn't actually aware of the solar lag now. It was an animal susceptibility in his marrow that sensed the instant of cosmic disorder, a reflex in some hidden nerve near his heart. The breath caught in his chest, as though something had struck him sharply on the throat and arrested his pulse.

At that instant, the still-fluttering heart in his hand was also affected; the wild convulsions immediately ceased. The high priest, his hands continuing to offer the blood of flowers to the sun, glanced over the valley in frightened dismay—his eyes seeking out the other prelates atop their pyramids. Together, they stared down on the cities and fields. Uncontrolled, a deep sigh escaped Tizoc's throat; and the abruptly stilled wind, which a moment before had threshed the folds of his vermilion robe, faintly moaned into quiet —as though the primitive, strong vigor of the spring itself, the life in the maize shoots, suspired.

An uncanny trembling began on the surface of the lake. Then the sun took his course again, a pale, sickly incandescence that coagulated the eastern clouds. Tizoc, suddenly aware of the faintly pulsive heart he had held overlong above his head, quickly strode across the summit and cast the offering into the cup of eagles below the War God's idol. The hoarse, pained whisper that vibrated in the stone went unnoticed. The quietness was suddenly broken; and the high priest, annoyed and relieved, turned to rebuke the excited murmurs of his attendants. Far below them the lake had wrenched through the inert tensions of its surface, and began to surge violently against the shores.

Tizoc gruffly ordered that the now-useless corpse be cast down the steps of the pyramid. Only Cihua heeded his command, and demandingly seized the arms of several nearby priests. As the body was borne to the edge, the high priest agitatedly waved his gory hands; and the chief vicar, after a moment of confusion, stepped toward him with a bowl and pitcher. Tizoc quickly cleansed himself, took the drying cloth, and then walked anxiously to the end of the square platform. His deep-set eyes were wide in amazement, and his long, lax jaw twitched in nervous excitement.

Cihua approached his master for instructions; but Tizoc, glancing at him as though without recognition, turned back to the spectacle—his arms crossed and his fingers pressed into his shoulder blades. He was completely fascinated. For several hours he stood watching from his pyramid, his priests kneeling about him. Behind him rose the high tower of his god's temple, the giant panache

165

drooping in the still air. The dull, filmy clouds were ash-gray. The lake below gathered in a momentum of convulsions. Thick, mounting waves, curdled with orange silt, swept over the shores—tearing out fruit groves and hurling down the buttressed terraces. An eerie, sucking noise followed the upheaval as the water drew back into deep troughs.

Swift, sudden torrents swept through the canals into Tezcuco, leaving in their shorter and shorter wakes the debris of villas. From his vantage, Tizoc watched the destruction of Chimalhucan, a city eight miles south on the lake. Only its single pyramid could be seen above the thrashing waves of mud. The outlying palaces of Aticpac were being submerged; and the highways leading into the fields were congested with motley survivors. Petty nobles, unable to command their clansmen, fled on foot. Along the shore, crews of abandoned slaves strove in mechanical, disordered feverishness to stem the rising flood. Those nobles whose escape had been cut off formed little clusters on the higher terraces, watching the haphazard, futile efforts of their attendants.

Even more frightening than the unexpected upheaval was a spiritual paralysis of the leaders. Montezuma watched in angered despair from his palace, temporarily unable to command his caciques, accepting the impotence of human will in the face of the incoherent, unbalanced energies now turned against him. He accepted the cataclysm, the scattering of his power. And Tizoc, viewing the whole catastrophe, the quiet, strangling death below him, the mockery and cowardice, derived a peculiar, profound satisfaction. "There is no cause . . ." he had murmured hoarsely to his priests, his attitude triumphant. No tempest had swept down from the outer plateau, no earthquake ground in the recesses under the valley. This was a direct expression of the gods. That it was a warning, an act of anguish, was something else again.

The high priest watched in an ecstasy of worship. Once he gripped Cihua's shoulder as a torrent surged along the canal a short distance away. The wall of thick water rose high above the banks, breaking against the buildings in advance of the main body. Along the narrow avenues that flanked the canal fled crowds of citizens—desperately, silently attempting to escape. Again and again a man or a woman was seized in the foaming torrents and

166

swept down into the channel. The air trembled with the low roar of rushing water, the abrupt, grating slides of broken masonry. There seemed to be no human sounds, just the frantic cries of drowning animals.

As the cataclysm reached its climax, Tizoc could no longer contain himself. Without speaking to his attendants, he hurriedly strode to the stairway and began the descent. Cihua turned to follow him, hesitated at the edge, and watched the pontiff cross the second tier. In his eagerness, the high priest almost lost his balance several yards above the compound, then fortunately caught himself on the balustrade. A sudden sweat drenched him, and he continued to the temple court with greater care.

Tizoc walked quickly to the chief gates and passed out into the stricken city, compelled by his nature to join in the violence of the gods' rage. Later in the evening he was found by a patrol of Itzco's warriors and returned to his apprehensive priests. During the second hour of afternoon the waters had quieted as inexplicably as they had risen. Order was restored among the cities of the Nahua, the rule of the princes re-established. The wind arose from the northeast, setting the fields of new corn in careless motion.

After he had regained consciousness, and his physician had poulticed the deep cut above his left eye with coral dust mixed in crerus juice, Tizoc stoically allowed himself to be bathed. He had apparently lain exposed to the onset of the rain that was falling, for his robes and feathers were completely drenched when the warriors brought him home. The slaves and common tribesmen who had seen the great prelate sprawled unconscious near a canal had doubtless been afraid to touch him.

"I could have died, unattended," Tizoc murmured as a priest robed him. "A macehual, the *low*est laborer, would have been cared for the moment he had fallen."

"Yes, Eminence," the attendant answered him solemnly.

"Ah . . . how wretched I am in my greatness, when my very dignity causes the people to desert me, to abandon their father who has striven to guide them." Tizoc raised his hand to the bandage and winced. With exaggerated feebleness, he took the cord from the priest's hand. Carefully drawing it about his thin waist, he stared out across the apartment, a wistful earnestness in his eyes:

167

"But I have survived. It is my will to serve that strengthens me to live."

Tizoc turned and wearily made his way to the dais. "Where is my prefect . . . where is the gentle Cihua?"

"I am here, Eminence," a voice called from the doorway.

The high priest followed Cihua's approach through half-lidded eyes. "Ah, Cihua . . . have you watched over me?"

"Yes, Eminence."

"Was I bleeding badly when the warriors brought me in? Where are my robes?"

"They have been taken away, Eminence. Why are you not on your couch? The physician said—"

Tizoc waved his hand to silence the prefect. "In a little while, Cihua, a little while. Was there much damage done the temple?"

"None, Eminence."

"Is there any report on the losses of our property?"

"Not a thorough report. The lowlands south of Tezcuco were flooded. The grain is ruined on our estates that front the lake. How far the water reached into the fields is not yet known. At least one of our villages in the marsh north of the capital is destroyed."

"Grievous, grievous!" The high priest rose and started down the five steps. He stopped suddenly, however, and pressed his fingers against the pain above his right ear. He paused uncertainly, then returned to his throne. "There was a great general loss, wasn't there? Has the Lord Nezahual proclaimed anything to the people? Where is my nephew Lord Itzco? I should really lie down."

"Yes, Eminence, you really ought to rest. Here, let me help you." The high priest rose as Cihua mounted the dais; and together the two men reached the floor. As they walked slowly toward Tizoc's sleeping chamber, the prefect answered his questions. Nezahual had dispatched no courier to his capital. Tezcuco had not suffered the losses of the other cities; but due to the confusion, the Lord Marshal had been asked to place all of Acolhuacan under martial law.

"The Supreme Council is in session, then?" the prelate asked as he sat on the edge of his couch.

168

Cihua arranged the pillows behind him. "Yes, Eminence. Do you want some broth, and a little partridge? A breast?"

Tizoc thought for a moment, then reluctantly answered: "Yes . . . just a little, and a goblet of chocolate thinned with mescal. Come right back, Cihua."

"Yes, Eminence."

As he lay waiting for the prefect to return, Tizoc reconsidered his experience in the city during the cataclysm. He attempted to recall his excitement; but the high priest was emotionally spent. His thoughts were too confused to focus on anything distinctly. There were fleeting impressions of collapsing walls, of hurtling waves crested with reddish foam, of broken trees lying quietly in a backwater. He had joined a crowd of sullenly hysterical citizens rushing pell-mell along one of the channelways—and then found himself alone, not having had the slightest idea what they were drawn to. He had recognized someone floating with the current below him, had watched a feather-mantle ripple in the dark water, the jewels glistening through silt. He tried to recall the familiar crest; but a thousand insignias fluttered in the disordered reflections of his mind.

Under the exhaustion, the slow throbbing in his forehead, Tizoc was aware of a quieting satisfaction. He murmured something, as though comforting himself, and closed his eyes.

The nobles had begun the reconstruction of their villas immediately, anxious to obliterate the signs of their misfortune. At the moment the water had begun to quiet, a shock of willfulness jolted through the caciques. Without immediately conferring among themselves, the barons and their overseers took the measure of their diminishing losses: noted the precarious tilt of walls, the earthen works about to be disastrously undermined.

With the ease of controlled urgency, the clan chiefs, who had a moment before been lost in the frightened confusion of escaping crowds, suddenly became aware of their authorities. Throughout the cities the hand of order was raised, and recognized. The fear was gone. Warehouses that fronted the overflowing canals were quickly screened with mounds of rubble. The out-branching canals were locked from the larger channels, the hitherto untouched gates forced close and reinforced with tree trunks. Each leader concentrated on the situation at hand, setting up a discipline to allay further loss. Bodies were retrieved; and the identified nobles put on litters to be borne to their respective villas.

The barons of outlying villages, who had found themselves isolated on their higher terraces, rejoined their attendants to supervise the buttressing of the outer palisades that still remained. Walls were raised along the terraces too far weakened to be saved, and the remained earth further undermined methodically. The petty nobles that had managed their escape from the shore suddenly realized their lack of dignity. Litters were commandeered and bearers seized. The fleeing clansmen were checked; and the movement on the highways turned back toward the inundated shore. Ravines were closed. At natural weaknesses along the lake embankments were thrown up.

Later in the afternoon couriers from the Supreme Councils sped through the valley in order to ascertain the exact degree of misfortune. The lake had receded from the ruins of Chimalhuacan. All but the pyramid was beyond repair; everyone except the cacique, his family, and the priests, had been drowned. The surrounding fields were banked with coarse silt—but there would be no need to open the granaries in Tezcuco to avoid starvation here. Atipac presented a graver problem: the people remained, deprived.

And Montezuma foresaw an even greater tax on his surplus grain. He had no alternative but to be magnanimous. Angered by the defect he had been forced to acknowledge in his own will, he energetically accounted for himself by summoning councilors and barons and demanding thorough reports on the disaster. His brother was appointed responsible for an immediate reconstruction, at a pace that should take the toll of many thousands of slaves. Despite his overbearing harshness, the Emperor did not question the previous ineffectuality of his nobles.

The Lord Nezahual seemed not to have even concerned himself with the catastrophe. He had watched from the summit of his hill, dispassionate and hardly curious. And in the evening, after the commotion had died down, he had gone for a walk along his terraces—apparently much more interested in what nocturnal flower might be budding than the travail of his people. Tizoc was awakened from his feverish sleep by his prefect; and after taking a little nourishment, dictated a few dispatches. Several barges had set out over the now tranquil lake; and the strains of music, the relieved outbreaks of laughter, echoed in the lagoons outside Tezcuco.

Above the wreckage of her terraces, the Princess Acatli—serene and undisturbed—entertained several guests from Tezcuco. The lake immediately to the south had not been disquieted; and her villa at the juncture of the great dike had not suffered in the least. At Tenayuca the baron's palace had been washed from its pilings. The little pavilion where Nicte had danced for young Tepoh had fallen into the water also; and Baron Catzin offered to help in the expense of building new revetments. Acatli was delighted by the merchant's projected designs for her future gardens. There would be paths and stairways without memories attached. Later in the evening the courtesan agreed to remove herself to Mexicaltzinco until the constructions were finished. Nicte, who was loath to leave her villa in Tezcuco for longer than a few hours, demurred—then accepted Acatli's invitation.

In another section of Nezahual's capital, his two eleven-year-old princes viewed the day's happenings with disparate reactions. Temozin, in an anguish of sorrow, wept for the people's misfortune. He sent a message to the electors, begging them to be moved more by compassion than by mere exigency in dealing with the citizens' need. He wrote several long verses on the dead and the despair of those left in the ruined cities; and before he tried to sleep, the heir apparent finished the poems to his brother Cacama, who was far distant in the land of the Maya Kiche, and sent the messenger on his journey.

Prince Ixtlil was in a fury. During the upheaval he had assumed full control of his villa. He ordered Nopal and Tochtli to bar the entrances in case the flood water should reach the outer walls. The gates were further barricaded with free stone that had been brought at his request for a new terrace. The canal that ran partly beneath a wing of his palace was locked shut; and when his own villa was in readiness for the deluge, Ixtlil and a small band of youths climbed down from their walls and entered the city. The afternoon was spent in a multitude of adventures as the prince attempted to compel order. He hastened along the chief canals, futilely calling out to the nobles he recognized. No one would help him to close the floodgates; and after the water had risen too high to allow this to be accomplished, Ixtlil struggled alone with his handful of boy warriors to raise embankments across the avenues. One of his attendants had lost his footing beside a channelway, and had been swept from sight without appearing again in the surging water.

Ixtlil had limped back to his palace after the ordeal, his leg badly bruised. And in the evening, as he watched the barges cast away from the broken piers and float toward the lake, the prince vowed to take vengeance on the nobles he had recognized. Their cowardliness must be punished. As Temozin wrote his verses, Ixtlil compiled his list of the proscribed. Not content to wait, he summoned his band of followers and went out again into the city. Only one of the condemned could be found on the avenues. The prince himself had driven the barbed shaft through the cacique's chest, as Nopal and Tochtli murdered the noble's attendants.

On the following night two other nobles were accounted for, hunted down in the streets as they left the villas of their friends. On the third night another was slain on the quay below the terraces of the Imperial Palace. He had been bidding good night to a group of friends when Ixtlil descended on him from the stairway behind. In their surprise, the caciques fell to their knees before the prince. None arose. Those who had not immediately been impaled on javelins, or pierced by the first flight of arrows, were speedily dispatched with glass knives. Several in the group were experienced warriors; but a boy even in his twelfth year (and Nopal was already sixteen), if he were armed adequately, could easily effect a mature man's death. Nopal, momentarily engaged in a hand to hand battle with a powerful cacique, had managed to implant his knife.

This last foray against the offending nobles did not go unnoticed. Lord Itzco had been too concerned with re-establishing the general order to trouble himself over what he imagined were sporadic outrages. He expected rivals to take advantage of the confusion and pursue private vengeances. For blood to be shed on the very steps of the palace, however, was a violation that demanded his attention. When several more deaths were reported to him on the fourth morning, the Lord Marshal began to suspect an under-cover insurgence. He carefully noted the names and clique associations of the victims; but the result of his efforts indicated nothing. The murdered lords represented the major political factions.

Special precautions were taken. Lord Itzco, who had become the head of Nezahual's hitherto private agents, directed the secret corps to keep careful surveillance of the city after nightfall. He quickly reported to the Supreme Council that the dead nobles had belonged to various, unrelated parties; but the atmosphere of distrust that had entered into the sessions continued.

A day or so after Itzco had ordered his agents to police the city, the purpose of the murders was found out. Prince Ixtlil ventured from his palace on this particular evening to find the Baron Pallin, chief of the Arrow Warriors—an order highly respected in Tezcuco. The unsuspecting noble was overlong at his meal; and Ixtlil, waiting with Nopal and five other youths in the park across from Pallin's villa, impatiently fitted his javelin on the throwing stick. He did not notice the two nondescript tribesmen who had wandered out of a nearby alleyway.

The men paused beside the entrance to the knight's house, hidden from the street by the out-curving balustrades of the stairs. They had had no particular purpose in choosing this vantage to watch the street. Pallin was respected by the populace and honored by his brother warriors . . . nor was he sufficiently wealthy to encourage anyone to despoil his person. He had a pension from his knighthood, a small revenue from his clan holdings, an estate or so of his own in the mountains north of the valley. Though he held political power, he never wielded it; and he lived on such an unpretentious scale that his liegemen benefited more from his protection than he from their services.

Pallin himself had no premonition of what awaited him outside. His wife, however, kept insisting that he wait a little longer before he went to join his friends. "Another cup of pulque . . . ?" she questioned, holding out the decanter.

"My dear wife," Pallin answered, "I will stagger in the street. Very well, just a half cup." As he watched her pour, the cacique smiled thoughtfully to himself. He was very well aware that his wife was frightened by something, but he waited for her to confess. She, on her part, was ashamed to admit her sense of danger. Pallin, in order to prove that her fears were groundless, would all the more insist on going out; so his wife, instead of forewarning him. concentrated on filling his goblet—hoping he would grow sleepy on the effects, and decide to retire early.

The celebrated warrior was in his early forties, over six feet tall, and quite heavily built. His features were distinguished, if not exceptionally well-formed, his belly more than ample for his height. After his wife had filled his cup to the brim, he rose beside his chair and scowled at the ceiling. "I might not play patolli this evening after all."

"Oh?" Cuitzin replied offhandedly. "Very well, we can spend the evening together on the roof and watch the fireflies."

"We could . . . but then again, unless I really had a good reason for disappointing them, it would be unfair to Catzin and the rest." He looked down at his wife, caught her eye, then stared at the ceiling again. Every week he went on this particular evening to the merchant-lord's villa.

"Pallin . . ." she asked, after a brief deliberation, "are you not my husband?"

"Yes," he assured her guardedly, contemplating the burnished, honey-orange plaster over his head.

"And have you not put aside all your courtesans and concubines for me, though I have borne you only daughters?"

"Five beautiful daughters, Cuitzin. Yes, I desire only you."

She decided to risk confiding in him: "Then, if you do love me, not only as your wife but as your companion, Pallin, listen to me and respect my feelings. I sense danger in the night for you . . ."

"A vision?" he chided her gently, walking to her chair and touching her shoulder.

Cuitzin stared up into his eyes intently: "No . . . not actually a vision, Pallin—no sign I might relate to you in warning. But I sense something sinister in the streets tonight, something violent, intent on murder."

"You have been listening to palace rumors. Why should anyone wish my death?" He strode to the doorway and called out to an attendant to bring his mantle.

174

"But Pallin . . ." his wife insisted anxiously, rising to go to him, "I feel as though someone were brushing against me, just beyond my sense of touch. I *know* someone is waiting for you in the dark. His eyes are watching the doorstep now—" She began to weep.

The cacique took her in his arms and rocked Cuitzin back and forth. His manner had changed, however. A quizzical expression had come into his eyes. Pallin accepted the basis of his wife's fear: someone was most likely waiting for him in the darkness outside his walls. As the slave entered with his mantle, he abruptly asked the man to bring his battle mace. "Summon five of my guard," he added, "and see that they're well armed." He raised Cuitzin's chin with his thick forefinger: "They can wait outside for me with my own weapons while I play patolli." Pallin laughed reassuringly. "I'll go forearmed to quiet you . . . but Catzin would be amused at our fears."

"Please don't go out," Cuitzin murmured, accepting his decision. Pallin kissed his wife tenderly, and playfully slapped her posterior. Cuitzin did not react with her customary, pretended annoyance. She watched him pass into the hallway skirting the patio, then sat at the low table—idly studying his empty goblet.

Before he crossed his threshold, Pallin hesitated. He thoughtfully examined his warriors, taking account of their lance blades. The cacique nodded to himself, and ordered the gate thrown open. He paused again on the platform above the stairway, peering intently into the street. Now he felt the warning; the fine hair along his massive arms bristled. His very curiosity now drew the Baron Pallin down onto the avenue.

Nothing happened, however. He passed into the merchant section, where Catzin's villa stood. The two agents, to avoid explaining their presence near his house, had withdrawn further into the shadows. They were about to leave their vantage when one of them caught the movement in the park opposite. The men tensed, and waited. After a moment, Ixtlil and his own warriors cautiously strolled out onto the avenue. The agents, not recognizing the prince, remained in the indent behind the stairs for a moment longer; then one quickly hurried toward the palace. The other followed at a safe distance behind Ixtlil.

The prince, with the natural insight of a hunter, knew his quarry anticipated him. Pallin could not possibly have known who his intended assassin was, nor could he have imagined Ixtlil's purpose. The cacique's manner on the stairway, at once indecisive and alert, put the young prince on guard. The night's mission would prove difficult. As Ixtlil skirted the intersections behind the chief knight, he turned over in his mind the possibilities of accomplishing Pallin's death. It would be a game. Pallin's very unsurety might offer an unexpected opportunity.

Nopal pressed closer to the prince and questioned in a low voice: "Excellency . . . this canal ahead. If we turn off, and hurry, we could reach the park outside Catzin's villa first."

Ixtlil shook his head. It was too obvious a place for an ambush. "He knows someone is after him," the prince answered, without further comment. He did not want to devise anything—just to follow the baron and wait. Pallin himself would indicate how he should be slain. The youths walked quickly with the careful unconsciousness of trained stalkers, their thin sandals glancing with an even balance of weight on the rough pavement without the slightest scuff. All seven were clothed in dark cotton tunics, and their bare skin was rubbed with charcoal. Even the *itztli* blades of their weapons were coated with dull paint. Ixtlil wore a thin obsidian crescent attached to the delicate septum of his nose. Another jewel, a labret in the shape of a striking serpent, hung from his compressed lower lip.

In the twilight, the boy prince's small, compactly muscular body seemed more in the proportion of a man's. His shoulders were broad, his chest deep; and below his narrow hips, the thighs curved out in sturdy strength. There was no awkward, hesitant approach of adolescence in him. The attendant youths about him, though taller and more physically mature, were ungainly and vulnerable in comparison. There was the careless impatience of awakening, male brutality in their attitudes as they hurried along the avenue.

Ixtlil, his body bent a little forward, his head slightly down, projected the deliberate purposefulness of the hunter. He was at one with the darkness, the sound of the wind, the odors of humus, stagnant water, and flowers. Once he raised his hand in warning to his followers: calmly, without personal alarm. A few moments later Nopal and the others heard the approaching footsteps, and agitatedly waited until a group of merchants passed. Ixtlil felt no quarrel in himself with the uncertainties. For him, there was no pleasure in the inflicting of pain—no fear of his own defeat.

After the merchants disappeared behind them, the prince coldly watched Pallin and his warriors cross the small fountain square at the north of the avenue. The baron paused near the center; and Ixtlil knew that he had considered the danger of entering the overgrown park that lay between the fountain and Catzin's villa. Without satisfaction, Ixtlil saw the warriors turn aside and cut back on a diagonal to the northwest corner. As Pallin followed the narrow street skirting the dark gardens, his young assassin nodded to Nopal and the others to continue behind him.

A minute or so afterwards, another figure paused near the end of the same building. He quickly ascertained the direction Ixtlil had taken, then sped back the way he had come. It would take Pallin at least ten minutes to reach his destination. The way he had chosen was backed by a high wall on one side and a deep canal on the other. No one would attack him until he reached the edge of the Square of the Lions beyond.

Pallin also realized the uncovered position he would find himself in on entering the plaza. There was a steep stairway that led down from the square. Only one man at a time could make the descent; and an archer or javelin thrower situated below could pick off his warriors one by one. Pallin, not actually sure of his danger, was nevertheless enjoying the excitement. His attendants were able veterans. As he passed along the canal, the cacique deliberated on his approach to Catzin's home. If enemies were indeed bent on destroying him this evening, they would have chosen the park as the logical point of assault. Seeing that Pallin had chosen another route, they would now be hurrying to reach the square before him through the gardens. Very well, he would backtrack along the canal and take the path through the park after all.

The order was given and Pallin began to retrace his steps. He had satisfied the necessity of protecting himself; and the baron was now wondering how he should explain his tardiness to Catzin. A sudden encounter that would have startled both parties was avoided by Ixtlil's own foresight. The prince, not expecting the baron to change his direction, had been wary of trailing him along a path that offered no cover in case of surprise. He had followed Pallin on the opposite side of the canal. On catching the sounds of the baron's return, he had restrained his attendants and waited.

Ixtlil glanced at his lieutenant Nopal in blank surprise when he realized that the warriors passing several yards away from them were Pallin's. Quickly evaluating the situation, the prince paused long enough for his quarry to pass beyond close earshot, then began running at an even pace toward the opposite end of the canal. He crossed the bridge, and reached the stairway Pallin had feared to descend, before Pallin had entered the farther edge of the gardens. Ixtlil led his warriors down into the square and along the row of buildings toward Catzin's residence. Without hesitation he continued up a low flight of the terraced stairway, turned left on the first tier, and took a path that led up behind the villa. He would wait for Pallin near the rear entrance.

A moment after Prince Ixtlil disappeared in the heavy grove above the embankment, a group of perhaps twenty warriors filed from a side street into the square near Catzin's villa. Their cacique, one of the Lord Marshal's, issued a brief command; and the guard silently took up posts about the surrounding buildings.

12

WITHIN five minutes the onslaught began. Pallin, on nearing the rear gates of his friend's estate, hurried ahead of his warriors. He was still acutely aware of possibilities, however; and even before the faint rustle in the underbrush beyond him could have reached his ears, the baron seemingly lurched from the path—with the deft co-ordination of a warrior, flung out his battle mace for leverage and in a continuous sweep threw the weapon into the overgrown shrubbery. The weight of the glass-piked club pivoted him away as a scream glanced in sharp echoes through the garden. A javelin shaft whirred viciously past him, imbedding itself in a branch near his surprised attendants.

Before Ixtlil could fit another javelin to his throwing stick, Nopal had leapt into the clearing and hurled himself on the cacique. His knife sliced into Pallin's left shoulder and wedged in the bone under the hardened muscles. The powerful knight, still recovering from his initial lunge, carried the youth backwards with him. In another moment he had let go of his mace and crushed Nopal against his belly. The young lord collapsed as Pallin released him.

Without hesitation, Pallin ripped the knife from his own shoulder; and armed again, turned savagely toward the trees. In the moment of the first encounter neither group had moved forward. As Pallin rushed into the underbrush, his own warriors cried out their war call and attacked behind him with lowered blades. Ixtlil threw out his hands in a silent command for his band to scatter, and fell to his knee. Pallin fell against the branch beside him; and the prince, unable to cast his javelin, drove it forward with a tight grip. Lord Pallin would have mortally impaled himself had he not instinctively broken the light shaft the instant it had pierced his side.

Ixtlil, unarmed, rose defiantly to meet his victim, then quickly leapt aside as the knife curved out toward his belly. The prince lost his balance on an outcropping of stone and sprawled in a slight hollow under the brush. Tochtli, like a deer hysterical with fright, lunged at Pallin, flailing at the older warrior with his hatchet. Pallin seized the fifteen-year-old boy by the arm and sent him into the bushes after his prince.

The skirmish had lasted only a few minutes before the palace warriors had found their way up from the square. Not knowing the assailants from the assailed, they immediately seized everyone that remained on his feet. A moment afterwards, Lord Catzin and his attendants emerged, fully weaponed, from the nearby villa. Ixtlil, who had been hidden, was at the point of releasing his javelin into Pallin's unprotected back when one of the agents unknowingly blocked him. Catzin immediately demanded that his friend be released; and the situation was at least partly explained. The captured youths sullenly refused to speak—and were on the point of being dragged off to the palace when Ixtlil stepped into the clearing.

Pallin himself was the first to recognize his would-be assassin. No one knelt, however, as he called out the prince's name. Ixtlil stared at him in contempt. Catzin came forward: "What is the meaning of this outrage?"

The prince pursed his lips and said nothing.

The merchant-lord studied him for a moment, then turned to Pallin as though dismissing the boy. "Come with me, my friend. The attendants will look after your warriors." His gaze fell to the streams of blood that flowed easily over the other's tunic. Catzin, as he took the wounded cacique by the arm, called out to someone behind him: "Send for the physician Quantzin. Tell him to come immediately." He turned to the agent obviously in charge; but the man, who had been standing a little to one side of Ixtlil, was gone. The palace cacique stepped forward and knelt in respect to the old merchant.

Catzin spoke tersely. "I suggest that you accompany Prince Ixtlil to his own palace. Place him under guard, and immediately inform Lord Itzco of the situation. I myself will take responsibility for Prince Ixtlil's arrest." With this, he gave his attention to Pallin—who, outside of his bloody condition, seemed none the worse for wear—and the warriors parted as the two men walked toward the villa.

"Send for my wife," Pallin requested as they neared the gate. "She knew . . ."

By the morning session of the Supreme Council, Lord Itzco was still undecided. Prince Quauhpo, chief of the electors, refused to commit himself. The Lord Executioner, now the brutally efficient Zalmec, surprised his companions by demanding the death penalty for his ward. One of Ixtlil's companions had confessed his part in the four previous murders, though Zalmec kept this intelligence to himself. The fourth elector insisted that the affair should be turned over to Nezahual. The outcome of the previous night was unknown to the general body; and it was with outraged surprise that the assembled nobles heard of the attack on Lord Pallin.

The chancellor evasively related the incident. No one had been slain. Pallin himself was not in a critical condition. Nopal's cousin, who was commandant of the palace, was startled to hear that the youth had suffered a dislocated back—and immediately sent a messenger to Nezahual's rural estate. Fortunately Prince Tochtli, the grandson of the king of Tlacopan, had not been injured badly.

A quiet, decisively superior voice interrupted him from the end of the dais: "My Lord Chancellor, is it really so important—that the King of Tlacopan might be offended? The nobles of Tezcuco have suffered a disgrace. Are their titles and their persons so mean that an unruly prince should ridicule their authorities and viciously attack them in their very city?" Zalmec had risen. He hesitated, staring out into the hall.

The chancellor, his wandering mind suddenly focused by the other's presuming to judge a prince of the royal family, pounded the dais with his staff. "Lord Zalmec, my nephew's son is not to be passed judgment on by such as you." The unusual anger in the old prince's voice startled even the impassive Itzco. The chancellor paused, and rose falteringly to his own feet to confront the executioner: "In Ixtlil's infancy he punished a slave girl for misconduct. Not knowing his reasons, our lords directly condemned him. It was you, taking the liberty to answer one of the fourteen great barons himself, that asked us to wait in our judgment. Now . . ." he caught himself on the arm of his wicker throne, and an attendant steadied him, "now, Zalmec—without understanding Prince Ixtlil's motives—you are the first to demand his death." The anger went out of his voice, and the Lord Chancellor allowed himself to fall onto his raised stool.

Zalmec timed his hesitation, then addressed the hall: "In the last days, since the lake upheaval, four high nobles have been slain in the streets—together with their friends and their attendants, murdered. The effects of these brutalities have been felt in this very chamber. At the time when we must work in unity and confidence, our nobles have been set against each other in fear. Prince Ixtlil has been cursed by the gods. He is an alien, malignant spirit in our city. He has come to disrupt us, to turn noble against noble, to destroy the rule of the Nahua." Zalmec did not directly state that Lord Pallin would have been Ixtlil's fifth victim. He waited for someone to contest him.

"In the beginning, at the hour of his birth, the priests revealed this to the people. His early sacrifice was demanded, to deliver us from what should be the inevitable consequence—disaster. The great Nezahual*pilli* has asked us, his electors and spokesmen in the capital of Acolhuacan, to rule in his esteemed name. We are the protectors of that rule. To send for Lord Nezahual's judgment is to betray his confidence. How shall a father condemn his son? Let us be equal to the trust our Sovereign Lord has placed in his ministers."

Lord Zalmec paused, taking the measure of his audience. The nobles had submitted to him. "Princes must not be punished as common offenders," he admonished them, as though they had called out for Ixtlil's death. "No . . . for their disgrace is shared by the people. Rather, let us condemn him to strangulation by the garrote, consign his body to a pyre of cedar wood . . ."

There was one in the hall, however, who had not been intimidated. Itzco rose in turn to his feet: "You are no magistrate, Zalmec. You misjudge your rôle." The marshal strode to the edge of the dais. "The Prince Quauhpo, our Lord Chancellor, has stated his indecision. Moreover, further session is invalid without my presence." He stepped down into the hall. Near the portal he turned back to the nobles and clan speakers. "We will convene again in the second hour of afternoon."

"I should not violate the seclusion of the Lord Nezahual," Zalmec called after him, temporarily defeated.

"The Prince Ixtlil must speak in his own behalf," Itzco replied, passing into the court.

But Ixtlil refused to comment on his actions. As he mounted the dais again in the afternoon, the Lord Marshal was resigned to accept the council's verdict. As the session was opened, however, the Lord of Chiconauhtla breathlessly entered the tribunal. He crossed to the dais, genuflected quickly; and receiving the chancellor's permission, strode to the platform. He conferred with the electors, then turned to the waiting nobles: "I have just returned from Prince Ixtlil's palace. My youngest son, Lord Nopal, was painfully injured last night. It is still doubtful whether he shall walk again. My son has given me the reasons for the prince's seeming outrage. The deaths of the four nobles, which have alarmed us, were brought about to a man by Lord Ixtlil. We should not be angered, my peers—but *ashamed!*"

The speakers, who had begun to murmur loudly at this last admission, grew quiet. "Ashamed," the cacique of the elite guard repeated, lowering his eyes. He was not only defending Ixtlil's actions, but the life of his only son. "Would you know the reason Nezahual's son holds our dignity in such contempt? Why a child has taken it upon himself to punish us?" The cacique then told them of Ixtlil's desire to protect his father's city during the cataclysm. He related how the prince had frantically searched through Tezcuco for someone to help him, and had himself attempted to close the chief canals and build waterbrakes.

". . . And none of the nobles whom he recognized as his father's protectors would listen to his calls. The greatest among us were paralyzed with cowardice. Do you understand a child's fury when his elders betray their ranks?" The baron told his listeners how Ixtlil had compiled a list of cowards, that the child prince had then set out himself to avenge his father's disgrace. The list was read before the assembly; and those who heard their names, instead of becoming enraged, withdrew from the hall in their shame. The others watched them go, conscious of their own inaction in the face of disaster. They remembered their impotence.

"Condemn the Prince Ixtlil and his brave young companions if you will," the Baron of Chiconauhtla concluded, hiding his fear in rhetoric. "But, to honor the great lord whom you have betrayed, allow me to carry this report to Nezahual*pilli*—that he should know the cause of his prince's anger. Surely Ixtlil had no right to slay the unfortunate nobles. No one would have condemned *them* for their outrage against our rule. Who among our judges would have courage, when we are all proven cowards?"

With this, the baron knelt to the electors, to the assemblage, and left the hall. As he passed through the doorway, Lord Tizoc rose unsteadily to his feet. The great plumes of his headdress did not hide the thick bandages. His further attempt to indict Ixtlil was brief; for the high priest knew that the lords could not now be persuaded. The Baron of Aticpac, who remembered his earlier fear of Ixtlil, was more vehement; but his harangue accomplished nothing. Catzin, who had not been present in the morning, said little when he was called upon to speak. The Lord Executioner was no longer concerned with the laws of Tezcuco, but with his personal safety.

An oppressive stupor of accepted guilt lay over the nobles. When Itzco at last rose and put an end to the afternoon's session, the speakers left the tribunal with averted eyes. On reaching the courtyard, they hurried to quit the palace. No verdict had been reached; it was tacitly agreed that the matter should be forgotten. Itzco went to Ixtlil's palace in the early evening and released the guard himself. The prince, when it was explained to him that the nobles throughout the valley had acted in much the same manner, granted the impracticality of putting them all to death.

Itzco was amazed to hear in turn that Baron Pallin, on being told the reason why the boy sought to kill him, had visited Ixtlil to ask either forgiveness or immediate assassination. The marshal, not given to speculation, was incapable of understanding the knight's behavior. The four murdered nobles had become martyrs, had symbolically received the punishment due their kind. It was a purge of the general conscience . . . and now best forgotten. Pallin's humility had preserved him, however.

Before he left the prince's residence, Itzco received Ixtlil's promise not to continue the punishments. The list, if not the memory of it in the minds of the council, was destroyed. In parting, the marshal reminded the royal child that there were many powerful lords at court who had preferred his death. In warning, certainly not to indicate an object for Ixtlil's future wrath, he mentioned his uncle Tizoc. The prince didn't appear antagonized. "Baron Aticpac—who you know, Excellency, is among the really formidable lords at court—has waited since your fourth year to indict you. And the Baron of Acolman, also. Montezuma the lord would see you sacrificed, for the priests have proscribed *you*."

The eleven-year-old boy stared past the marshal, his attention wandering out into the court beyond the apartment. He half-lay against the pillows on his throne, one knee drawn up and clasped in his arms. Ixtlil was clothed in a short, white tunic embroidered with turquoise and silver jaguars, and a linked necklace fell over his chest. Attendants had just set the torches in their sconces, though it was still light outside. The prince seemed merely a thoughtful, shy child not yet of the world. Without glancing at the commander, Ixtlil asked in a low voice: "Why do the priests and nobles want my death, Itzco?"

He seemed so unaware of the havoc he had caused. The marshal studied him for a moment, wondering how he should answer the prince. That the child was a death-dealer was apparent: like a young jaguar or a fledgling eagle, Ixtlil seemed committed to violence. Why should he question himself with the fears of others? He only acted according to the dictates of his nature. Itzco gazed down at the prince, his arms akimbo and his small head tilted ferretwise. "The people are afraid of you, Lord Ixtlil. At your birth there were forewarnings that you should lead the enemies of Anahuac. Are you actually a betrayer, Lord Ixtlil?"

The prince looked up into his face, his boyish, curved lips impassively cruel. His already deep-set eyes glistened coldly in the torchlight.

A shiver of mistrust ran through Itzco, though he knew that he himself was safe from the boy's vengeance. He suddenly regretted having mentioned his uncle, though the high priest was invulnerable. And Ixtlil, his own thoughts turning to Tizoc, asked in an off-hand tone: "Will the Lord Tizoc go to my father?"

"Nezahual*pilli* receives no one. Your father would not ask your death." After all—the cacique considered his apprehension and answered himself—Tizoc's hatred of Ixtlil was no secret in Tezcuco.

"Nor would you, Itzco." It was a statement, not an oblique threat. The marshal, his own nature inclined to vindictiveness and calloused blood-letting, understood the sympathy between them. Itzco's conscience was Nezahual's will; Ixtlil's, the uncoded rule by which a civilization knows its transgressions against itself. The young doomster could never be brought to account by his people.

"But Tizoc, Aticpac, and Acolman have all spoken against me." The prince turned on his throne and glanced toward another boy, who sat on a pillow behind him. Tochtli nodded his head. "And what were these nobles doing when the city was falling?" Ixtlil asked the minor prince.

Itzco knelt and rose quickly: "I must return to the palace."

"My teacher Zalmec . . . has he come?"

"He came with me, Excellency. Good night, my lord."

"Good night, Itzco."

The marshal left the apartment and crossed the central court. He was joined at the gate by several caciques; and together with his warriors, Itzco returned to the Imperial Palace. He sensed that the retributions were not over. He gave no thought to the outcome of the Lord Executioner's defection from the prince. The Lord Marshal felt an obligation to Tizoc, however—and on entering the palace, immediately dispatched a messenger to the high priest.

As the courier sped through the city toward the temple of the War God, Ixtlil approached the chambers of the unforewarned. Zalmec anticipated him, however; but though he knew that he should gather his belongings and flee, the elector found himself unable to move quickly. He took overlong in examining his chests before allowing the attendants to carry them away. He was frightened, and exasperated with himself for such unnecessary scrupulousness. "Wait, wait," he would call, unfastening a lid. Zalmec knew that nothing was mislaid but he carefully pulled back the coverings and reached to check the bracelets and finger rings. He turned to another box, hardly rising—and another.

Then the executioner straightened, aware that Ixtlil had come. There was no sound. The attendants had not looked up from their tasks. Zalmec turned slowly toward the doorway at the far end. The prince stood several paces into the room. It was dark beyond the immediate area of the torches; but the man could see the small group of boys behind his assassin. There was no exchange of words. Several of the young warriors strode across the long apartment and closed the doorways. The attendants stopped their packing and stood quietly waiting; the desperateness of Zalmec's situation had not been explained to them.

Ixtlil deliberately approached his teacher, dismissing the slaves with a casual gesture. The doorways were opened for them, then closed again. They confronted each other silently: the cruel but logical arbiter of the known rule, the equally relentless, subrational equalizer of a collective conscience. Ixtlil was the requiter of ancient evils, a crime's restatement after long durance. If, indeed, the factor of disruption—of violence and eventual collapse—has entered a civilization even before its fulfillment in a golden age, then the child prince now signaled the latter days. Atavistic, and yet a harbinger: Ixtlil presented a terrifying accent on the present tense. He somehow broke the continuum, the imperceptible flow of the past into future time. And as a long-building wave, seemingly a far distance from the shore, unexpectedly strikes an impediment—and mounts into a crest, rushes with a wild acceleration to an apex and collapses in an inward curve that carries its force of ten thousand miles into a tightening spiral toward logarithmic nothingness—so Tezcuco felt the forward energy that is itself the essence of a state stemmed on the sudden, destructive appearance of a prince not destined by birth even to be known.

It was inevitable that Zalmec should betray his ward. The established rule is threatened by an untoward reminder of its primitive ethos. There was a profound spiritual bond between teacher and unregenerate student. Even now, as they faced each other over Zalmec's opened boxes (their contents strewn in a disarray of woven plumage, jeweled miters, gold and amber gorgets of authority), Ixtlil had no need to tell the offending noble that death was approaching.

Zalmec suddenly looked very old. The fanatic energy that had given his face an expression of vitality was gone. The deep, vertical wrinkles that drew down the corners of his mouth were lax, the staring eyes no longer penetrant with vague accusations. His color was ashen; and as the Lord Executioner absently drew his mantle about his neck and fingered the slack folds of skin before letting his hand fall, he bowed his head in acceptance of death. Then, abruptly frightened, as though begging a moment longer, he raised his head again and gazed sternly into the prince's eyes. Ixtlil had not moved. The boy returned the stare. Zalmec's momentary vigor flooded away from him before he could call out. But it was past the time of explanations.

The prince slowly fitted an arrow to his bow string. Zalmec caught the movement, and involuntarily winced. Through bleared eyes he watched the cord tighten and curve the bow into itself. The shaft was leveled, the long, glass barb aimed. The stricken man murmured something in an inaudible voice, the sudden release of the bow interrupting him. With the slightest impact, the arrow pierced into Zalmec's chest just below his throat. He clutched at the protruding stele and fell solemnly to his knees. For a moment he played with the tufts of feathers. He coughed slightly, and his thin nostrils brimmed with a froth of blood. Without opening his eyes, Zalmec collapsed slowly to the floor.

Ixtlil watched for a moment longer, his child's face expressionless. Without any attitude of satisfaction, he turned and strode as deliberately as he had entered toward the doorway. The young warriors left their stations in the room and followed him out. In the courtyard beyond, Lord Tochtli had gathered some twenty adolescent nobles. Several of the warriors that had accompanied Ixtlil in the just-completed assassination joined their companions outside.

Tochtli and two other youths stood a little apart from the others. They had waited in a tense quiet; and at the appearance of the three accomplices, the grandson of the Tlacopanec king nudged one of his lieutenants and indicated with a nod what he wanted. The other quickly left the group and approached the new arrivals. He conferred with them briefly, then returned to Tochtli. The Prince Ixtlil had gone to his chambers to put on his fighting gear. He would join his warriors shortly.

And in the temple of the War God, Tizoc was informed that a messenger from the palace had arrived. "What insignia does he bear?" the high priest questioned offhandedly, looking up from his accounts.

"The Order of the Eagle, Eminence. He is sent by your nephew, the Lord Itzco."

Tizoc seemed mildly curious. He glanced up at his chief vicar, whom he had apparently been reprimanding, then smiled humorlessly at Cihua, his prefect, as he rose. "Bring the messenger to me," he ordered, adjusting his long robes and ignoring protocol. The man was brought immediately into the private apartment of the high priest himself.

The courier knelt, and Tizoc impatiently gestured for him to rise. "What do you have to tell me?" he asked.

"Lord Itzco fears for your personal safety, Eminence. Prince Ixtlil knows of your speech against him in the Supreme Council this afternoon."

"All Tezcuco has known for eleven years now that I would have the prince dead," the high priest answered quarrelsomely. "What does Itzco intend that I should do?"

"The Lord Marshal is convinced that Prince Ixtlil will make an attempt on your life—"

"So!" Tizoc exclaimed in a tone at once amused and scornful. "What does my nephew propose? Shall I take myself to the top of my pyramid, and wait for a child's wrath to spend itself on someone else?"

"Prince Ixtlil promised to desist from his previous course of executions, Your Eminence. Lord Itzco has a premonition that he will now avenge himself on those who spoke against him in the session."

"Who else is endangered? Zalmec? He should be done away with. The temporal laws are not *soul*-binding—not inflexible, as though they were absolute canons of behavior. . . . Really, Zalmec is a vicious influence in the city. He undermines the rule by enforcing it so rigidly. And Baron Aticpac: is he to be assassinated also? And the Lord of Acolman? I am more sympathetic in their behalf."

"All of these men are in danger, Eminence," the messenger replied.

"But they haven't the protection of an entire knighthood, have

189

they?" the high priest asked sarcastically. "Will Prince Ixtlil attack me here, in the midst of my warriors? How do you imagine he will scale my walls?" Tizoc turned away and walked to his dais. He mounted the steps and paused on the platform. "Return to Lord Itzco. Tell him I am moved by his concern." He sat down as the messenger knelt; and after he had departed, Tizoc glanced at the two dignitaries. It was nonsense to fear Ixtlil's attacking him here. He discarded the possibility.

"Cihua," the high priest called out, "send for a decanter of chocolate. Are the vestments prepared for the ceremonies tomorrow morning?"

"Yes, Eminence," the prefect answered, crossing the apartment to the corridor. He returned shortly and approached the dais, his mind also on the important rites to be conducted in the morning. The scarification of children figured as a celebration of the first magnitude in the priests' calendar.

"Very well," Tizoc said in a weary voice. He had been retiring early since his accident. "We shall have our chocolate before I dismiss you." They waited silently for the attendant to come; and after the under-priest had entered and gone, Tizoc commented in a thoughtful voice: "If I should die unexpectedly, it is my will that you, Cihua, become high priest in my stead."

"I, Your Eminence?" the prefect questioned in surprise. He glanced at the chief vicar, who was in line of succession. The other priest lowered his eyes in embarrassment. Cihua quickly recovered: "I am not equal to the task, Eminence . . . and besides, we shall both die as old men."

"Be that as it may," Tizoc answered with decision, "you shall succeed me . . ." He had finished his drink, and rose to dismiss his attendants.

The high priest slept intermittently through the night; and arose, still weary, to begin the morning sacrifice. Immediately afterwards the rites of scarification would commence. As he descended the pyramid after the blood offering, Tizoc was interrupted in his thoughts by a commotion in the compound below him. He recognized the messenger who had come to him the night before, and anticipated the further news. Both the lords of Aticpac and Acolman had been slain. The death of Zalmec had been discovered; and the Prince Ixtlil was nowhere to be found. He had deserted his palace, along with his attendant nobles.

Tizoc had no immediate reaction; but after the rites were finally completed in the forenoon, he summoned Cihua and the cacique of his guard to him. "I have decided to take a journey," the high priest informed them.

"It is easier to guard you here in the temple confine, Eminence," the chief answered, imagining the cause of his master's decision.

"I am not concerned with my well-being," Tizoc stated. "The chief ceremonies of the month are finished. I delegate my powers to you, Cihua, in my absence. Not only will you celebrate the morning sacrifices, but the affairs of the priesthood will rest in your hands."

"Where are you going, Eminence?" the prefect asked in a low voice, turning his head away.

"To visit my uncle in Coatlinchan. I am not afraid of the Prince Ixtlil . . . but I think it best that no one know of my decision. Tell even my priests that I am ill and confined to my apartments. I shall leave my personal attendants here; and they are to take food to my chambers, and behave as though I were still with them." Tizoc turned to the cacique of the temple guard: "I shall leave the second hour after nightfall. No more than ten warriors and my litter bearers are to accompany me. You will take your orders from the Lord Cihua. Now leave me. . . ."

After the priest and warrior had gone, the High Priest of Huitzilopochtli summoned a scribe and dictated a short note to his nephew Itzco. The paper was folded and sealed, and the scribe himself sent to deliver it. The marshal, as he left the tribunal for his midday meal, was met by the black-robed priest on the stairway. He read the brief explanation of Tizoc's intended journey, and quickly gave a verbal message to be returned to him. As an afterthought, however, he asked the scribe to accompany him to his apartments overlooking the inner court. He took something from a jewel coffer, wrote several rows of ideas in the picture script of the three cities, and wrapped his present to Tizoc in the paper.

The scribe knelt, and knowing the message, hurriedly left the apartment. He crossed through the two courtyards and passed into the great plaza outside, quickly losing himself in the crowd of bartering merchants. At the edge of the fountain square in the merchants' section, he was spoken to by a young noble, who demanded that the scribe accompany him to his villa nearby. The scribe refused; but the lord insisted, saying that his father had been suddenly stricken and had called for a priest. The scribe would have immediately brushed past him and continued along the avenue, but a caravan had just crossed the intersection and he was forced to wait, ignoring as best he could the insistence of the noble.

Several of the youth's companions joined him; and loudly calling out their complaint to passersby, they began forcing him into the square.

In exasperation, the scribe explained his refusal to accompany them. He bore an important message to the great Lord Tizoc. The nobles ignored his words; and roughly seizing the scribe by the arms, all but carried him into the park behind. "We caught him!" one of them called out, and the scribe's indignation gave way to fear.

In the temple a short distance away, Tizoc fretted at his priest's delay. Enough time had elapsed for the man to have returned and left again on another errand. It would take all the remaining time until sunset to reach the fortress of Coatlinchan; and the high priest wanted to forewarn the old baron of his coming. That he might be endangering his uncle's life also occurred to him. Whether he would or no, Tizoc decided angrily, the scribe should be sent alone to the frontier city along a dark highway in advance.

When the hour of his own departure neared, however, and the messenger had not yet returned, it was apparent that something drastic had befallen the young priest. Not even Cihua had been told of Tizoc's note to Itzco. The high priest was amused that the bravery of his decision would go unnoticed. Ixtlil undoubtedly knew of his plans to quit the capital. Nor did Tizoc ask the cacique of his guard for more warriors; but calmly bid Cihua farewell, and closed the curtains of his litter as the side gate was opened. The brief exchange of voices outside on the avenue nevertheless caused the prelate to all but leap from his cushions.

Before the litter bearers came to a stop, Tizoc had seized his ceremonial staff and thrown the curtains apart. He would have leapt to the pavement had not a cacique beside him touched his arm in reassurance. At least fifty warriors had been sent at Itzco's insistence to accompany the high priest on his journey. The streets leading to the city gate were already under the surveillance of the marshal's agents, though Tizoc knew nothing of this. Once he called out to ask why such an unusual route was taken to the walls; and the cacique who had assumed charge of the company gave him an evasive answer.

It was apparent that Tizoc's messenger had been intercepted on his return to the temple. Outside of Itzco's offer of protection, what else had the marshal's reply contained? Tizoc wondered if he would ever know. As he rode through the night, he idly questioned his own perversity. When a man knew someone was hunting him, why should he leave the security of his own walls and chance the unsurety of a dark highway? Then again—the night could be an advantage to both hunter and hunted, Tizoc thought to himself.

To pass the time, he considered the impulse that had caused him to leave his temple. The moment Itzco's warning was brought to him he had felt restricted—had chafed, not against the actual threat that hung over him, but against the oppressive need of protecting himself. After all, he was a high priest, a spokesman of his god, and under the jurisdiction of Hummingbird Wizard alone. How could a mere disordered prince challenge him? Let Ixtlil descend with his brutal companions and see how a high priest might defend himself.

And even more when he realized that his messenger had been intercepted, and his plans revealed to the outrageous child, Tizoc knew he must go out from the physical invulnerability of his temple and encounter the enemy. He understood the baleful genius that directed the prince. With the same anxiety, the need of participating in violence as an instrument of his god's that had compelled him to join in the lake cataclysm, the high priest willfully abandoned himself to the dark highways.

Tizoc was infuriated by his nephew's meddlesomeness. Not even Ixtlil would have the temerity to attack such an escort. The high priest imagined that the prince was nearby in the darkness, watching his intended victim pass from the dense groves that lined the highway. Actually, Ixtlil had already reached Coatlinchan, and waited in the ravines above the city. He was less impatient than Tizoc. It was one thing to slay a mere arbiter of the rule, an executioner who had usurped the authority of rightful judges—and Tizoc was indeed the spokesman of a god, a priest who offered nourishment to the sun with his hands. He must be brought to account with more ceremony.

The journey to Coatlinchan was accomplished without incident. Tizoc arrived in his uncle's palace during the hour after midnight. On the following day Itzco's warriors returned to the capital, though the commander made it quite clear to the old baron before his departure that the city would be held responsible if any harm should befall the high priest.

The baron, more out of affection than fear of Itzco's displeasure, practically imprisoned Tizoc in Coatlinchan. And when the prelate ventured out into the countryside, a host of warriors accompanied him. Tizoc found it impossible to meditate beside the great, unfinished statue of the goddess of waters—which lay in a ravine a half hour's walk from the city—and begged his uncle to be allowed to visit his private shrine by himself. How could he commune with the ancient forces that ruled over the valley, when fifty warriors watched his every gesture? It was proper to mount his pyramid with measured, self-conscious steps—but in his private worship, the slightest posturing would only cheat himself.

The baron was obdurate. Tizoc could not go alone to the ravine, and that was that. "But I know the groves better than the avenues of Tezcuco," the high priest complained. "I wandered about these slopes in my youth. Every stand of cypress is familiar to me, every brake of fir trees."

"You were brought into the world here; I have no intention of allowing death to strike you in Coatlinchan. If you want to die violently, then return to Tezcuco." The old man spoke gruffly—but, after a pause, said in a gentler voice: "I want you to have my city as your own, Tizoc. I have no sons; and you among my relatives please me. Come here when you are also weary of honors, and find a quiet death among these slopes."

The pleading of the old man quieted the high priest for another day or so. And it comforted him to be spoken to as though he had not quite reached his majority. After all, Tizoc had passed his fifty-fifth birthday five months ago. For years now everyone had addressed him as though he were a universal father, a symbol of paternal wisdom and severity. At times he felt a great need to be chastised himself.

Early on the third day after the baron's refusal to allow him his liberty, Tizoc arose early from his couch and listened intently. He could hear the quiet breathing, the muffled coughs of his attendants asleep in the adjoining room. The prelate waited for another moment, then stealthily crossed to the small antechamber at the opposite end. He robed himself in full ceremonial vestment and paused before a mirror of glazed obsidian to study himself. In the half-light, Tizoc appeared as though he were a very young man again.

Despite his restlessness of the night before, his expression was one of complete repose. The tenseness was gone, the sharp elongation of his features softened. He fastened a gold crescent on his narrow septum. Heavy jade pendants hung from his long, stretched lobes; and a labret of clear amber glistened under his dark lip. Tizoc closed his heavy lids, his hand instinctively reaching for the jeweled gorget on his chest. Then he objectively appreciated himself once again—not closely, but for the indistinct impression of gold and vermilion, the intricate brocades of metal, feathers, and jewels. Beneath the sweeping, stone-encrusted plumes of his high miter, the high priest's thin, boyish face seemed ethereally sensitive, remote in the planes of deep shadow and half-light, almost wantonly mystical.

Then Tizoc turned quietly, and was gone. Almost at the echo of his footsteps the palace awakened. The slaves stirred, and arose to the day's chores without quite loosening their dreams. The attendants outside the high priest's apartment clothed themselves, murmured instructions to those passing in the corridors. Tizoc's personal attendant entered to awaken his master, and returned to his companions in dismay. The lord had doubtless been unable to sleep, and had wandered out on the terraces. Slaves were sent to discover his whereabouts, for the city priests would arrive shortly. It was only proper that the great prelate, chief of Hummingbird Wizard's cult in Acolhuacan, should honor the city by officiating at the morning sacrifice (though the common citizens were not informed of his august presence).

But Tizoc was nowhere to be found. The guards had not seen him pass the gates. Perhaps the high priest had gone of his own accord to the pyramid in the center of Coatlinchan; and the priests and the nobles hastened to the temple. But the Lord Tizoc was not there either; there was nothing to be done but celebrate the first sacrifice without him.

As the fluttering heart was lifted up in oblation atop the pyramid, the blood of flowers welcoming the day, the errant high priest paused on a slope high above the river. As the sun appeared, a chill of ecstasy rose from inside him. He raised his empty hands, offering himself to the god of heaven. A flood of tears brimmed his eyes. How beautiful the world was! The end of spring, the fifth month nearly past . . . the wakeful night finished; and the sun, orange-vermilion in a wan sky, struck a cosmic moment that held entire the day to come.

The coldness that swept up through Tizoc's heart was the shadow of the burning sun disk, hastening out of the dark entrails to follow the bright god at a closer pace. For several minutes the high priest stood without moving on the narrow outcrop of stone. His senses were painfully acute; the fretfulness of the night had worn his nerves to a painful sensibility. The apprehensions he was prey to, the fears of visceral disorder that accompanied his sleepless nights, surged out of him with the chill.

Tizoc had heard the dread call of the cuckoo on awakening, the four insistent notes that warned the listener of calamity. Or had he, actually? Perhaps he wandered in the fitful dreams that often fall upon one in the last hour before dawn, had dreamed he walked again in some garden of his childhood. He had left the rock ledge and lost himself in a copse of cedar. Everything about him was extraordinarily familiar—with a strange immediacy of childhood memories, as though not reawakened in the least, but happening again. The bank a pace beyond him, newly fractured with the weight of the night's rainfall, and the stone catching the light in a thousand crystal fragments: this very moment he had certainly experienced before.

The ominous, clear cry of the cuckoo rose from the brush above him; but Tizoc listened in delight, expecting the precise instant of its call. The high priest paused now, undecided, at the edge of the obstructing slide. The odor of wet earth was sweeter than the scent of the wild honeysuckle that trellised itself on the slopes. The woodbine tentatively awoke to the first warmth, and impatient kneading of early bees. Tizoc was lulled for a moment by the hum of insects, the sharp, trilling runs of bird calls. Then the delay suddenly oppressed him, and he carelessly strode over fresh earth that caught at his feathered sandals. A little farther, now, and he would turn down into the ravine.

It seemed to Tizoc that some incident of his childhood awaited him near the Water Goddess, who lay embedded (through centuries of dim emergence) in her matrix of stone . . . some incident that he must at last recover, a boyhood quest he had long forgotten and that held the final secret of fulfillment. A great, painful urgency to change, to arise out of himself with a deep breath and soar in a rebirth of spirit, possessed the scarlet-robed prelate. He quickened his step. The narrow cleft of a dry creek bed cut down from the path; and Tizoc, with the carelessness of an earlier year, chanced the steep descent—unaware that sharp branches tore at his jeweled mantle, and the plumes of his miter caught on thorns. He fell once, striking his thin knee on a ledge, but seemed not to feel the pain.

At last the high priest reached the bottom of the slope, and turned onto a long-disused trail without consciously remembering. He forced aside the underbrush with his plumed staff. The air was filled with the dry fragrance of sage, the humid, rich fetidness of leaf mold. The sudden conviction fastened on him that he wanted never to return to the outward pomp of worshiping the gods. Throughout his life Tizoc's mind had turned in his distress to this ravine. And in this season especially, he dreamed of his childhood. In the ninth year of the last cycle, in his own ninth year (for he had been born on the first day of the second week after the fire kindling), some strange, portentous awakening had occurred here. The ninth year of the past cycle: a year date that haunted him; and when he was writing his temple pronouncements, the high priest had often written it without awareness of error.

In an impatient sprint, holding up the skirts of his robe, Tizoc broke through the green, still-flexible brushwood. He hesitated at the edge of the clearing, his heavy-lidded eyes focused in awe on the goddess. The high priest adjusted his vestments and approached her, crossing his arms over his chest. A direct ray of sunlight pierced through the branches, glazing over the pitted, massive contours of the stone. Silhouettes of leaves moved back and forth over the worn engravings; and deep, changing shadows merged into the dark formlessness of unworked rock.

Tizoc halted a few paces away, agitated by a sudden inability to direct himself. He seemed on the verge of completing something. He stared intently at the goddess, drawing a deep, restricted breath. His whole consciousness was engrossed in his effort. A wild vertigo seized him, but still he refused to release his breath. He had no thought, just an indeterminate, passionate yearning. As he watched, the atmosphere about the stone became coagulated; part of the idol that had been broken away became material before his eyes. The goddess was returning his stare from her great, oval sockets.

Then Tizoc knew what he had come for. With the deliberateness of one directed in a trance, the high priest strode to the idol. He knelt beside it and quickly swept away the leaves from a hollow carved under the stone. The forest debris of almost half a century obstructed him, and his fingernails broke against the packed earth. A short distance away, an eleven-year-old boy stood quietly watching. At last Tizoc murmured an exclamation. For a moment he rested his head against the stone, his shoulders limp, then wrenched himself away from the idol. In his fist Tizoc held a small war ax fastened to a haft of ironwood. The high priest, as though with the practice of a warrior, reassured himself of the balance, executing a swift cut and turn through the air—the razor edge immediately poised for another slash. The ceremonial staff lay discarded below the goddess.

At this moment Tizoc saw his assassin. Ixtlil, himself appareled in brilliant plumage and jewels that glistened scarlet and orange in the sun, advanced. In his right hand the prince held a thin-bladed, copper hatchet surmounted by feathers. They slowly encircled each other, as though engaged in a pantomime of battle. Tizoc quickly straightened his body and leapt to the side, recovering with an exact balance. Ixtlil moved farther to the left, flinging out his hatchet for a curve that should bury the blade in the high priest's kidney. Tizoc pivoted toward him, raising his own weapon over his left shoulder; but the prince, knowing that the other's weight was greater than his—that the impact of the priest's haft would knock the hatchet from his grasp—sprang backward to the left. Tizoc anticipated the prince's intention of another thrust into his side, and whirled after him with a heavy slash of his ax.

Ixtlil had not struck out, however; and taking advantage of the high priest's instant of off-balance, stepped in for the attack. His hatchet barely missed the other's throat. The projecting end of the shaft, however, struck Tizoc just above the clavicle. The prince leapt back, poised to counter the high priest's expected lunge. Tizoc lay stretched on the earth, carried down by the weight and movement of his own body. He was quite dead. Ixtlil had accidentally struck the most vulnerable of nerves. The high priest had died of an instantaneous cardiac arrest.

Ixtlil contemplated his fallen enemy. Lord Tochtli and two other youths, who had watched the combat from the edge of the clearing, approached the prince and knelt before him. Ixtlil withdrew a small, folded paper from his tunic. He unwrapped the packet, and for a moment studied the carved stone in his hand. It was a piece of black lapis, as thin as his boy's fingers and shaped in the form of an ax blade. The lower crescent edge was filed to a razor sharpness; and the narrow, upper stem was fastened to a chain of native-silver wire. The jewel had an odd design. Ixtlil thoughtfully rubbed his thumb along the sharp edge. He was too inexperienced to know that it was a warrior's amulet retrieved from the burial caves in the valley of ruined pyramids.

The prince examined the ancient jewel a moment longer, then cast it on Tizoc's stiffening body and walked away. One late spring afternoon many years before, the boy Tizoc had knelt in this little ravine. It was here that he reached his decision to become a priest, and buried the obsidian war ax his father had given him under the idol as an offering, not only of his heritage of an only son but of his manhood. The high priest, though it was allowed him, had never taken a wife. And his father, angered and bereft of an heir, gave the amulet (which had passed from generation to generation of warriors, from eldest son to eldest son) to the two-year-old Itzco, the son of Tizoc's sister. By some premonition, Itzco had sent the symbolic jewel to his uncle. It had been at last returned, by Tizoc's assassin.

13

NEZAHUAL, scowling in exasperation, turned abruptly to face his son: "What do you mean, Ixtlil—this wanton butchery . . . why did you murder Tizoc? I know there is no sign of violence on his body; but you did slay him, didn't you?"

"Yes," the boy answered, returning his father's stare without insolence.

"And your teacher, Zalmec, and the lords of Aticpac and of Acolman. Are you bent on utterly disrupting my city? You have slain one of the fourteen great barons, a pillar of my throne."

Ixtlil assumed his father wasn't nearly so angry as he pretended. "I garroted the two barons because they came to you with lies."

"No one could accept the truth in you, anyway," Nezahual stated in momentary bitterness, and rose from his chair. He immediately repented, knowing his son's destiny. The prince could not in fairness to him be held responsible. The ruler strode to the doorway past his son, then paused beside Ixtlil: "Must you be so brutal?" His voice was less harsh. He searched the boy's face for some indication of remorse. "Ixtlil . . ."

"Yes, Father?"

"Answer me. Must you carry out your vengeances so brutally? Why did you have to drag the two lords into the square and strangle them yourself? The people are horrified."

"If they suffered death, it was no more than what they intended for me," the prince answered, lowering his eyes. "I have done no more."

Nezahual took his son's shoulder: "The day is not too distant, Ixtlil, when all the cities of Anahuac will call out your name in despair. Your violence is premature. Allow me these last years of my reign, a peaceful life in my gardens. I want to hear no further cries of anguish in the city." He raised Ixtlil's chin with his forefinger. "I will endure your disregard of the rule no longer. Your next offense, Ixtlil, is to be punished by death. I have sought to avoid interfering with your bitter destiny. Don't press my patience. I have already committed another that I loved to the executioner. Zalmec is replaced. After the rule is forgotten, Ixtlil, the executioner persists."

With this, the Lord Nezahual dismissed his son. He stood quietly by the throne for a time, listening to the echoing footsteps in the long corridor beyond the door. His solitude was rarely disturbed. After a time he absently crossed the apartment and paused outside an anteroom. *Yes,* he murmured to himself, thinking of the dead Tizoc. The high priest had unwittingly managed his own death: had actually possessed the foresight to take his own leave of the valley. No one in the three cities, not even Montezuma himself, could have dispossessed him.

Nezahual rehearsed the brief scene in the palace throne-room eleven years before—when Tizoc had come in the third hour of morning, the falcon's hour, to demand the death of the newborn. In the very beginning the high priest had foreseen the consequences of Ixtlil's birth, if not his own death at the prince's hands. Eleven years, and Tizoc was at last, now, given his answer. As he paused outside the anteroom, the ex-Emperor recalled the fastidiously clad prelate's standing arrogantly in the dark throne-room of Tezcuco. With his miter of sweeping plumes, his mantle of cardinal plumage, Tizoc was akin to the long-crested birds that fluttered down the walls devouring jeweled insects.

In his memory Nezahual heard again the measured, slow knells that had announced to the city his empress's death. "Tecui," he said aloud to himself—calmly now, without the bitter ridicule of his own despair. He had resented Tizoc's perpetual interference; and yet, as he reconsidered the dead prelate, Nezahual realized that there had always been a peculiar intimacy in their relationship. When Tizoc was but a mere priest, he had played a deciding if indirect role in the young Emperor's life. *A peculiar sympathy . . .* Nezahual was genuinely saddened by the high priest's death.

As he pulled back the heavy curtain that closed the doorway, the ruler answered his sense of bereavement. He smiled to himself as he thought again of the physician's cruel denouncement. Quantzin had utterly humiliated Tizoc by exposing the prelate's weakness. The high priest then had not possessed the foresight to withdraw before the onslaught. Tizoc had died before the final, complete humiliation that should debase the greatest chiefs of men and spokesmen of the gods.

Tizoc's was a timely death, well-proposed and urbanely carried out. He had received the death stroke in full ceremonial dress, in the scene of his childhood at his own request. Nor would the Empress Tecui have to see the degradation of the people she had helped to rule. In her death she had lain on cedar and rosewood; and her ashes were strewn with copal. But Maxtla. . . . Nezahual winced at the thought of the youth who had companioned his early rule, and had been termed *boy consort* by the jealous courtiers.

"Maxtla," the forty-six-year-old sovereign murmured, involuntarily shaking his head, for the name brought an echo of pain. The noble's life, as Nezahual's own youth, had met a shameful end. The ruler stepped deliberately into the small treasure room and carelessly surveyed the coffers of jewels and brocaded plumage. Five shields plated with gold and plumed with scarlet feathers lay against the wall. Nearby, the wrappings still half torn away, were several bolts of cotton—yellowed now, though once embroidered white on white with jaguars and herons. In other boxes were bolts of cloth woven with hummingbird down and overlaid with serpents and birds. They were intended for young concubines now quiet matrons long unthought of. The war of the northern invaders, and Maxtla, had come before Nezahual could turn to them. And between the two, that strange siege of madness—or "spirit weariness," as Quantzin called it.

In the days that just preceded his affliction, the young king had desperately sought for the identity of himself. "I am a great sovereign, the son of Coyotl," he had told his physician sadly, in vain reassurance of himself. "The tribes that dwell in the farthest mountains speak of Nezahual the Lord." But in his acts, he could no longer perceive what he had become. He had known himself in boyhood, known his dreams and the warmth of the summer sun on his naked skin. But in his ascendancy he became no more than a hunter-king—possessed of terraces and palaces, certainly, but nameless in succession, a leader of wanderers continuing the dream of forgotten chiefs.

In the early years of his rule, Nezahual gazed into mirrors and saw but the reflection of an anonymous prince. "But where is Nezahual?" he asked. "I yearn for myself, Quantzin. . . ." The physician could not answer him. He told the Prince of Tloque Nahuaque, the cause of causes, the Unknown God to whom but flowers and incense might be sacrificed. Tloque was the god of Nezahual's father, the one god, whom no one but a very few in the valley heeded. His high priest should know the secret of the Emperor's ill.

And the boy ruler would have sent for Coatl the high priest; but Quantzin answered that the prelate could not come, and repeated Coatl's prophesy. "After the god revealed himself in a vision, then you should seek his temple." The vision never came. Princess Papan had seen the angel Tloque on the Plain of Death, had noted his full, sweeping wings that shone with resplendent plumage—but Nezahual hadn't. On state occasions he summoned Coatl to officiate as the favored prelate (much to Tizoc's discomfort); but the ruler never had gone himself to the temple, not even at the times of his most profound despair. Coatl had often come to the palace as a representative of the priesthoods, not as a minister of the spirit.

As Nezahual stood in his treasure room now, however, he seemed very much in possession of himself. He was a handsome man: strong-featured, sensitive. The casual, defiant affectations of his early manhood (when he often pretended a passive boy's inadequacy, to catch his listeners off guard) had gone; and the cruel banalities of self-ridicule, which characterized his middle thirties, no longer concerned him. His attitude was one of bemused speculation—touched at times by bitterness, perhaps, as when he answered Ixtlil that no one could accept the truth in him anyway; at others, by the weariness of recurrent melancholy. There was a faint fanning of white at his temples, which if anything accentuated the youthfulness of his skin. His features were perhaps a little sharper.

On the whole, his middle age found Nezahual calm and rather

difficult to provoke. Although he was much slenderer than in his prime, his health was excellent. Quantzin was rarely called to the palace of the Plumed Towers. The lord was never again beset by the fits of disordered wandering—when the corridors of the palace seemed endless, eternally changing. He spoke to his attendants civilly, if not often, and took an interest in the planting of flowers and trees. One would not at all have thought that Nezahual was on the verge of a momentous discovery in himself.

He stared down now at the mass of treasure, which he considered his private hoard despite the vast warehouses in the royal palace that were filled beyond accurate count with jewels and precious fabrics equally his own. The ruler's eye fell on a small tiara wrought with emeralds and violet, iridescent shell. He suddenly remembered its significance, and bent to take the little coffer of jewels beside it in his hands. Nezahual eagerly opened the box. Yes, they were still here: the pearl ear pendants. He picked them out and closed the coffer. The child's tiara and the earrings would perhaps delight the Princess Nicte. The ornaments once belonged to another courtesan, whom he had loved with the ardor of his first need. . . . Mecatl, who had taught the boy Emperor the meaning of his verging manhood, and whose death had caused him to reject the love of women for a time—though not his essential maleness.

Nezahual left the treasure room and crossed the private audience chamber to the doorway onto a court. "Comtzin," he called, and after a moment his favorite slave knelt beside him. The ruler, without any premeditation whatsoever, rested his hands on the man's shoulders: "Comtzin, I confer on you the barony of Acolman." On the eve of a battle many years before, Nezahual had promised himself to ennoble this son of a childhood companion.

Comtzin stared up at him in confusion. He knew the king was not indulging in his strange humor (Nezahual once had given him the fantastic title of Lord of the Three Reservoirs and Keeper of the Hummingbirds). For a moment the suddenly manumitted slave could think of no words. If anything, he was more appalled than delighted. "But . . . but, Excellency, I know nothing of governing. What should I do with a barony? For thirty-one years, since my birth—"

"You have attended me since your childhood, *Lord* Comtzin. You have been at my right hand during every crisis. Day by day through years, you watched me guide the decisions of my councilors. You know more of governing than my princes. I have carried you with me on long campaigns. You have listened to the great Ahuitzotl and myself planning battles in the Oaxaca raid. Now rise . . ."

Comtzin rose hesitantly to his feet, his eyes downcast. Nezahual, seeming to forget the tiara and earrings he held in his hands, studied the slim, dark-skinned young man. "We must find decent clothing for you, Comtzin. Your station is now equal to your name."

The man stammered something in confused gratitude. The ending of his name, *tzin,* signified a lord; and the other slaves had often mocked him. He followed the ruler into the corridor, frightened and elated. A baron . . . ! They turned into a room where Nezahual's own robes and mantles were kept, and the confused attendant could barely keep his attention on Nezahual's words. ". . . And your father, before he was sent as a tribute captive to my city, lived in a village high in the eastern mountains. His grandfather, the chief Huemac, once entertained me in my youth. Here . . ." the king interrupted himself to pull out a loincloth of white brocaded cotton fringed in gold . . . "take this." He searched for a moment, and found a sheer tunic. He handed the pieces of clothing to Comtzin as he came upon them, finally throwing a cape of delicate orange-and-white plumage about the young man's shoulders. As he gave Comtzin a headband, he ordered him to go to his rooms and properly apparel himself.

"Return to me as quickly as you can, Lord Comtzin. I want you to take these presents to the Princess Nicte. Then you are to present yourself to my son, Prince Temozin. I will give you documents. You will attend my heir apparent, and become his lord steward."

Comtzin, as though not quite awake, turned in the doorway: "Excellency . . ."

"Yes, my lord?"

"May I . . . may I take my mother Chimotl with me? She is an old woman, and of very little value."

Nezahual glanced at him in surprise, then laughed: "Certainly . . . though she is of great value, Comtzin. But you are quite wealthy now, my lord. You could afford to pay twice, and many times, her worth. And I also present you with that young woman I gave you on your twentieth birthday . . . and your two boys. I release your uncle to you, and his wife. You should consider buying a little villa near Lord Temozin's palace for them. Tomorrow I shall send your own steward to you. Now go along. The afternoon has begun, and I want Princess Nicte to have her presents by nightfall."

Once in the corridor, the new baron quickened his step in a sudden, ecstatic anxiety. His mother could explain what had happened to him. For the moment, his confidence, the actual insight into government he had learned from Nezahual, deserted him. He needed the old woman's reassurance. Chimotl, with a feminine facility, would experience no difficulty in becoming the head of an important household overnight.

Later in the afternoon, the Lord Comtzin was announced to Princess Nicte. She received him with some surprise, and immediately conducted him into the patio outside her private apartments. It was a sultry day; and Comtzin, though he felt rather awkward in his new capacity, was glad to rest himself awhile. The court was shaded by a giant pepper tree, much older than the villa itself— which had only been finished in the fourth month of the year preceding the lake upheaval.

"A baron . . ." Nicte murmured, hesitating at the gateway in the low wall. She glanced at him appreciatively, then turned to the girl who had come. "Some chocolate, and maize wafers—and a jar of xtabantún honey." The princess moved toward her guest. "Do you want a little mescal, Lord Comtzin?"

"Oh, no . . . no, Your Highness. Chocolate is enough." He had forgotten he was allowed to drink mescal whenever he chose.

Nicte returned to her wicker chair beside the fountain. With an absent, habitual gesture, she trailed her hand through the cool water, then drew designs with her wet forefinger on the smooth stone. "I'm supposed to go with the Princess Acatli to her palace in Mexicaltzinco," the royal concubine said in an offhand way, as though Comtzin were an intimate. "I really don't want to go— though I do suppose I should." She had come to know the baron quite well in the year she and Nezahual lived in the royal palace together and Comtzin was their personal attendant. But he had been but a mere slave then; and Nicte, though she was by nature thoughtful in her demands, hardly granted him identity.

Now that the young man was a noble, however, the princess immediately received him on familiar terms. All the observations she had unconsciously made of him during the second year past were immediately accredited, without the least reluctance. He had moved into perspective. Comtzin, with the intuitive perception of the mountain tribesmen—that strange combination of docility and fierce devotion, which also characterized his father—had passed a more serious judgment on the ministers and nobles of Nezahual's court than most of the barons realized. The ruler, casually questioning his slave after audiences, had often based his decisions on Comtzin's reaction.

Nicte, though she had unconsciously considered this before, now felt a complete confidence in him. She glanced at the exquisitely fashioned tiara on the ledge beside her, then picked up the pearl earrings and fastened them onto her lobes. The jewels were very old, and a creamy, golden glaze mottled them. Nezahual the Lord had thought of her, and these were his presents. Nicte was delighted: "Did our lord send these jewels for me to visit him in Tezcotzinco?"

Comtzin looked down at his hands. "No, Princess."

Nicte seemed a little disappointed, and quickly changed the subject: "Shall you remain in attendance on his Serene Excellency?"

"No," the young man answered again. "I am to become Lord Steward in the palace of Prince Temozin."

"The heir apparent . . ." Nicte nodded her head, and rose as the slave entered with the chocolate. She indicated where the girl should place the heavy tray of lacquered wood, and commented: "I have never seen Nezahual's son. He is at least eleven by now—" The princess turned to the baron, her head tilted quizzically.

"Lord Temozin was eleven in the third month, your Highness." Nicte poured the thick chocolate into wide-brimmed cups, and the two sat quietly eating the sweet confection with shallow spoons. At last the time came when Comtzin had to go. He took his leave of the beautiful concubine of the Lord Nezahual. Nicte saw him to the gate of her villa, then returned to her apartment. She sat alone for a while in the little patio outside, content in her secluded life. The princess was twenty-six now—though little different from the young girl of fifteen who had danced before the court on the afternoon of Ixtlil's naming ceremony.

In the usual sense, Acatli never seemed to age either; but the courtesan of the golden age did change. Her life progressed from early youth to full maturity, through the middle years toward a quiet retirement. The effect of her amazing beauty was the constant, not the loveliness itself. Acatli's features had the refinement of a carefully wrought mask: time could not easily ravage the cold symmetry of cartilage and bone. But mere symmetry is not a woman's beauty; and gradual though it was, time altered the courtesan's appearance. Acatli knew the necessary illusions men require, the artifices that coax the male's sympathy (when cold loveliness itself, a subtle threat, could cause aversion) and give familiarity to his need.

Through bereavements, the courtesan herself changed in the depth and warmth of her understanding—learned even more how to evoke correspondences. This was the effect of beauty. Acatli was still desired when other women of her age had passed into the category of the benign, communal mother. On her rare appearances at court, even the adolescent nobles were restless as she passed—self-conscious, awkward in their eagerness to have her merely speak to them and dispel their sense of impotence before the courtesan of emperors.

Nicte, as though completely remote from the experiences that add emotional dimension—and, perhaps, erase a little of the freshness from the cheek—seemed not very different for the eleven years that had passed since Ixtlil's birth. Even then, though she was certainly a young girl, no one thought of her as such. As the princess sat beneath the pepper tree, idly throwing berries into the fountain, raising her eyes quickly to watch the flight of an oriole or a thrush over the court, she appeared absolutely childlike, awakening but not yet aware. Like Ixtlil, she was outside the usual maturing process. Experience could not break the continuum; and one year perfectly anticipated the next—strengthening the initial pattern, without changing it in the least. In both of them, what had seemed prodigious in childhood merely became more effectively expressed in later years, with no further vision or direction.

And Nicte was beautiful, if one did not approach her. Her dark eyes were large, and strangely unfocused, under heavy lashes. Her lips, full and slightly pursed, were sensual in an expression of child-hood remoteness—as though no one had used them for his pleas-ure, had taught her the sensations of love. After a time she rose, as it was growing dark; and in a moment of caprice, danced about the fountain: utterly complete in herself, voluptuously enjoying the movement of her body. With her peculiar innocence, Nicte swept her arms above her through the air, and felt the slight fric-tion of the fabric over her full, conical breasts. "Tomorrow," she said to herself, "I must go away with Princess Acatli."

And slightly after midday, in the seventh hour—the hour of the butterfly—Princess Acatli took leave of her villa in Tezcuco for what was intended to be a stay of several months in her palace near the great dike. Baron Catzin accompanied the courtesan and Nicte, though he would return a day or so later to superintend the beginning stages of reconstruction. Acatli could never have brought herself to alter the stairways and terraces, however the memories might occasionally oppress her; but the lake disturbance had demolished the reminders of a past the princess would as soon forget.

Acatli embarked on her journey of thirty-odd miles over the lake in a mood of quiet exultation. Nicte, still reluctant but passive to the will of the celebrated courtesan, soon found herself in high spirits; and by nightfall when they arrived at Mexicaltzinco, every-one was in such a festive humor that a feast which lasted until sun-rise of the following day immediately began. The Lord of Cul-huacan and his sons joined in the celebration and promptly invited all the chieftains of the surrounding villages. A caravan that was approaching the great causeway had paused on the outskirts of the city; and Catzin, who recognized the name of its leader, himself went out to fetch the merchant and his companions.

Nicte, despite her exhaustion, agreed to dance for Acatli and the Lord of Culhuacan—and later admitted to the older princess that at one point she became utterly possessed, which was quite unusual. For at least an hour she had performed without being conscious of either the music or her body. Throughout the following week, however, Nicte was all too aware that she had overexerted herself; and like an ailing forest creature, kept sullenly to her own apartments. The beginning of Acatli's visit set the pace of the entire stay. For three months, one feast only anticipated an even more sumptuous one on the night following.

Nobles came from Tenochtitlan, drawn by rumors if not actual invitations, to pay homage to Acatli of Tulán. Even Montezuma and his brother Cuitlahuac, on a pretext of visiting the Hill of the Star, arranged to spend five days of feasting in the princess's villa. An envoy of the independent king of Michoacan, a ruler who held most of the western coast beyond the plateau in subjugation, was received by the Aztec emperor during an evening's carousal. The Lord of Tlacopan, the least of the three kings of Anahuac, became so attentive to Acatli that a social disaster was barely averted. Catzin, his warnings growing less and less veiled on the tenth day of the king's stay, informed Tochtli's venerable grandfather that a man too old to play in the ritual ball game should be content to watch from the edge of the court.

The lord, turning to the group of young courtiers who had observed his displays of ardor throughout the last days, remarked: "Yes . . . yes, and perhaps an old lion, who fears as much for himself as he does for the loss of his mate, prefers to quarrel with another old lion—while a younger one frisks with the lioness." One of the listening nobles, who had taken an innocent walk with Acatli earlier in the evening, smiled self-consciously and lowered his eyes.

Catzin muttered something to himself, unconsciously glancing about him. Restrained by his sense of the ludicrous, however, he held his tongue.

The king laughed; and the princess, who had just returned to her admirers, nodded to him with a smile. "What amuses you, Your Excellency?" she asked. Acatli seemed even more beautiful than usual this evening. She was robed in a cotton batik of pale sepia and white stitched with gold herons, and over her forehead, a lacework of gold set with pastel jewels, rose a tiara in the form of two quetzal birds—the fragile sweep of their plumes lying against her temples.

Catzin forgot his annoyance at her approach, his eyes catching the graceful movement of her hands as Acatli spoke. The full, soft firmness of her arms revealed the beauty of the courtesan's body: the rounded, ample contours that yielded to the touch, and yet were gently taut, resistant. The pale color of her jewels subtly accented the mauves and cool ochres of Acatli's skin. It wasn't that his beloved seemed so very young for her years, the baron thought to himself as he watched her smile calmly at the Lord of Tlacopan. No . . . she possessed the beauty and completeness that should belong to every woman throughout her life: a beauty that sustained itself on quiet eagerness, the need to share in a man's quest of her.

As Acatli asked the Lord of Tlacopan the reason for his laughter she tilted her head, her gaze passing in quick appreciation over the group of nobles. The king, answering her slight bow, said: "What amuses me, Your Highness? The effort two old men will spend, and not even convince each other, to reassure a beautiful woman of their flagging interest."

"Your Excellency . . . !" the courtesan exclaimed, feigning dismay. "A man is only *old* when he feels no further need of vigor."

"Perhaps . . ." the king answered, flattered by her words. His manner was momentarily introspective. Perhaps the illusion of a need was more compelling after the actual yearning, and the means, had passed. Man's disposition was so perverse. . . .

"And then again," Catzin retorted in a mildly acid voice, restraining his fury, "a man who was even in his youth faint-hearted should be pleased with age. It offers him some excuse for weakness."

"Weakness!" exclaimed the ruler, forgetting his previous attitude and equally belligerent. He flicked his hand in the merchant's face. "I am still chosen to accompany the Emperor in battle—"

"So was the feeble Lord of Coatlinchan required to attend Nezahual*pilli* . . . to show our king's disdain for his enemies."

"Feeble!" With this, the Tlacopanec's hand fell swiftly to his side and grasped the ceremonial knife hanging at his waist. Catzin, himself unarmed, clenched his fist. The younger men were appalled by the undisguised rivalry. The seventy-year-old lords were both remarkably active and quite capable of carrying out a challenge; and each was powerful enough that no one dared to interfere—but Acatli. The princess, though she was frightened, calmly stepped between the two nobles. She raised her hands to their arms, and stretched back her head as though completely delighted: "Ah, my lords—only the gallants who remember the age of the great 'Coyotl know how to please a woman's vanity. Would you quarrel over me?" She glanced at them in turn, her eyes serene and yet melancholy in understanding. The tension passed. The king and the merchant-baron turned at the same moment, avoiding each other's gaze in embarrassment; and the three of them crossed the hall together, each with the courtesan's hand on his arm.

The younger nobles watched them pass onto the terraces, quiet in their awe and envious of Catzin and the king. And so the three months passed. The musicians in Acatli's villa played only the music of another era; dancers performed in an outmoded style; an archaic elegance of manner was unconsciously adopted in Mexicaltzinco. Acatli frequently recited the poetry she had written in her early years; and Catzin often thought of a comment that had been made of the courtesan in the beginning of Nezahual's reign. Undoubtedly the ancient empresses of Cholula were as she: never aging, just becoming tired and eventually deciding to die.

The reconstruction of Acatli's villa in Tezcuco was completed; but as the day drew near for her return, the princess avoided mentioning her plans. And then one evening Acatli casually told her guests that she would leave Mexicaltzinco on the following day. She would not return to Tezcuco immediately, however, but spend a few weeks alone in her small palace of 'Telco on the lake above Tlacopan. This had little significance to most of her visitors, who were not aware that the ancestral home of Acatli's family had been vacant for over twenty years.

Later in the evening Catzin remarked on this; and the princess explained that she had kept a wing of the palace in repair.

"But the gardens must be in ruin," the merchant remonstrated.

"A ruined garden is often more beautiful in the fall than an ordered one," she answered. On the following day she was gone, unattended except by several favorite slaves. She departed in the early hours by boat, and only Catzin was at the wharf to see her off. "When shall we be together again?" he asked her quietly.

"Soon . . . soon, my gentle lover," Acatli replied. "And we shall walk along the new terraces, give our own meanings to unfamiliar pavilions."

But fall passed into winter. Acatli did not return. It was said afterwards that in the space of a few months she became faltering. Her mind wandered from the present, and she often called her attendants by strange names. One afternoon in the month Fall of the Waters, she was stricken by a fatal agony. Something wrenched within her, constricted for a moment of internal violence. Attendants discovered her unconscious on a stairway below the palace, and brought the princess into her apartments. When Acatli recovered, she was too weak even to support herself against the pillows. Her breathing was difficult, and she asked an attendant to hold her. For several hours the courtesan of the golden age awaited death.

Perhaps she complained a little, fretting at the ache inside her—attempting to share the pain, and comforting herself with shallow tears of lassitude more than of anguish. Then she was still, the ordeal of breathing over. Her eyes closed with the briefest flutter, and her lips parted with a gentle sigh, softly rasping as though a rod had been lightly drawn over notched deer-bone. Acatli, Princess of Tulán, the Baroness of Coatepec and beloved of conquerors, was dead.

And on the following day, when news of her passing reached the three courts, there were many lords who burst into fits of weeping—and fiercely disconsolate, fled from the capitals to remote villas above the valley. Nezahual himself, already retired from the immediacies of loss, trembled before the messenger as his eyes brimmed with tears. He had no reply, but turned and strode quickly away. Nor could he eat for that day, nor for the two succeeding, without bitterly weeping as he sat down at his table. How unreasonable, this despair for Acatli! But no one, regardless of his cynicism and anticipation of grief, can really prepare himself for an intimate's death. Deep affection lies below the intellect, in the region shared by one's memories of childhood. And the hurt of loss, as though it were a visceral wound, overwhelms the frail disciplines of intellect—sweeps up from the recesses, bitter and cold, to catch in the throat and flow acridly from the eyes. How childlike, vulnerable and passive the loser is!

The year of the lake cataclysm passed: through the season of serenity, the month of resuscitation (with the bird sacrifices at Cuauhtitlan), the five unlucky days of the *memontemi*. Another year began; and in the third month, when Nezahual's boy princes celebrated their twelfth birthday, the people journeyed from cities throughout Anahuac to the shrine of Coatlicue at the northern junction of the causeway. In her aspect of the Mother Goddess, *Tonantzin*, Coatlicue was worshiped every year by a pilgrimage to her temple at Tepeyac.

On the eve of her feast day, the Lord Cuauhtemoc returned from his raid into the lands of the Maya Kiche. Prince Cacama, in his eighteenth year, immediately crossed the lake and presented himself to his father. His companions, Tepech and Macuil, accompanied him. The three youths had already distinguished themselves in battle, and from the bands about their foreheads hung the two tassels of a cacique. Nezahual, with an unusual display of enthusiasm, entertained his eldest prince for five days before he dismissed him. In the fifth month, during the god-impersonation ceremonies of Smoking Mirror, the Baron Catzin died of some seemingly inconsequential ailment; and his family of merchant-lords fell into complete obscurity.

Within the same month, Baron Pallin—whom Ixtlil had attempted to assassinate, and then forgave—was sent as an envoy to the court of the Mexican kings. The baron's wife, a niece of Princess Papan's, managed to gain Montezuma's permission to visit the secluded vicereine of Tlaltelolco. The old princess seemed quite contented in her confinement; and in her letter to Nezahual, the baron's wife mentioned that Papan*tzin* was eagerly awaiting the strangers who should come to devastate the land. Apparently Acatli's demise had not surprised the Aztec princess, who knew the night before the courtesan's attack of her approaching death.

During the little feast of princes, a tower on the chief Aztec pyramid burst into flames; and for nine days the stone itself burned—guttering like wax down the stairways. Nothing would extinguish the weird fire. The stench of hot blood filled the city. Then the omen passed: and the matter, at least ostensibly, was forgotten. The princes seemed to have become inured to the threats—or utterly confused by the contradictory explanations.

In the twelfth month (of the harvest, and the return of the gods to the valley), an incident occurred in Tezcuco that rather surprised the court. The Lord of Chiconauhtla, who was cacique of Nezahual's private guard, dispossessed his only son. Nopal would not recover from the injury he had received during Prince Ixtlil's attack on the chief of the Arrow Warriors. The seventeen-year-old youth would remain an invalid throughout his life, confined to a chair or a litter. A city as important as Chiconauhtla could not be governed by a cripple. His father relinquished title; and in Nopal's stead the young Lord Tepech was established as lord of the warden city. Tepech's twin brother, Macuil, received Nezahual's confirmation as Baron of Tepechpan. At twenty-four, the sons of a dead marshal were suddenly removed from the household of Prince Cacama and given two of the highest titles in Acolhuacan. Together with the new Baron of Acolman, the recently manumitted Comtzin, they ruled the northern provinces of the kingdom. Nezahual had previously ceded the fortress cities of Zumpango and Citlaltepec to their father; and the young lords ruled the end of the northernmost lake jointly.

14

THE SECOND YEAR after the lake disturbance was duly recorded in the codices of the priests. Nobles died, or came of age and contracted marriages. The old chancellor finally offered himself for sacrifice, during the Feast of the Mountains in the thirteenth month; the acceptance of death was apparently contagious. Pallin was recalled from Mexico and made chief of the electors. The physician Quantzin, whose youngest son was found one morning in the street outside his father's villa (obviously murdered) was stricken with apoplexy. Despite his advanced age, Quantzin lingered some four months and died during the seed time of the next year. Yet another peculiar phenomenon appeared in the second festival of the almanac, on the day of the chief physician's death. A comet arced over the valley at noon, ". . . and the air was filled with a terrible whirring noise." A fourteen-year-old boy had been standing on the roof terrace behind his apartments when it happened.

The whole sky was suddenly in flame. I became so frightened that I crouched on my hands and knees. The sound was deafening, like a thousand bull-roarers thrashing around me. The stone under me shook with the piercing wind screams.

Then it was quiet—and completely dark, as though the sun had fallen. I stared out over the city, and my eyes were blind. Inside, with an internal vision, I could still see the great ball of fire, with its tail streaking out behind.

Lord Temozin thoughtfully bit the end of his writing brush— then laid it down and stood up. He walked to the wide, low doorway. It was the day after the comet that the young prince felt calm enough to describe the incident in his journal. Everything that happened since his seventh year had found expression in the careful little pictures he drew.

An odd pastime for a boy, this absorption in a chronicle. It seemed as though experience were really outside of him, until the events and his reactions to them could be written down. He stood in his doorway for a while, his hand outstretched to catch the tactile warmth of the sun. *Macuilhuextlil, tlilzocotli coetpantlitlan* . . . "Five dark willows, dark fruit-lancets along the wall of serpents . . . *xochitepanyolanti—*" The idea-terms, as so many fragments, fitted themselves together into complex words.

Temozin turned back into the room and quickly strode to his writing bench, murmuring the one word that meant *under the walls of the flower garden. "Cotlitecoetpanyo macuilhuextlilantimanco . . ."* he wrote, rearranging his key references to *cotli,* or fruit, and *panyo* and *huex,* which were "wall" and "willow." And so the heir apparent contrived the poem that had occurred to him a moment before, as he stood gazing at the willow seedlings against the wall across the court. It was difficult to transcribe the complicated ideas into pictures. Sometimes one merely drew a willow with five dots in black paint; the reader could easily arrive at the word and pronounce it to himself. Often, however, the young poet had to pause—and using a method of rebus writing, think of a group of objects he could portray whose names in the spoken language were similar to the sounds of the word he wanted.

Simple actions were conveyed by formal signs. Footprints indicated travel or movement; a shield and a club were for war; a bundled corpse represented death. With these elements, Prince Temozin gave his own reality to the happenings of his life. Before he was finished with his morning's poem on his willow trees, Lord Comtzin appeared in the doorway leading into the court. "Excellency," he called softly. There was no answer. *"Excellency . . ."*

Temozin started from his writing and glanced up.

"Your dinner is prepared."

"Is it midday already, Comtzin? I'll be there shortly. Let the meal begin without me."

The steward waited, deliberately folding his arms.

"Very well." The prince rose. He stood for a moment, lost in some last reflection. Then he bent down, drew something hurriedly, and left the bench. Before leaving the apartment, Temozin washed his hands and face, adjusted the white, knee-length tunic, and slipped a thin diadem of gold onto his forehead. "There are no visitors . . . ?" he questioned, as though it were a comment.

"No, Excellency."

The prince followed his chief steward across the patio, up a flight of stairs, along a veranda, and down a long stairway into the central court. The attendant nobles knelt as he entered the hall. An hour later Temozin retraced his steps up the stairway and along the length of the veranda. He hesitated a moment before descending into his private quarter of the palace, however, and stood gazing down over the serpent wall. "Summer will come too early this year," he thought, noticing how the fruit trees were already putting out tentative, pale wisps of blossom. The spring should stay long in the earth to collect its vigor. "Harvest will come prematurely, and the fruit of late summer will be dry and tasteless."

It would soon be the ninth year of his residence in the little palace Nezahual had built for him. *"Chiucnauhxihuitl,"* he repeated several times aloud. "Nine years . . ." He was given to murmuring words to himself, merely to hear their sound.

Temozin was a handsome youth—perhaps more delicate than sturdy, though he had the strength of awakening in him. His manner was both shy and determined. In the last months a restlessness had increasingly disturbed him: a yearning for something he could not quite comprehend. He would start from his sleep at night and leave his couch to walk through the dark court outside. It was like a fever, this need to discover the meaning of something that had happened inside him. Though he tried to ignore it, Temozin had become decidedly ill at ease with himself. Why Nezahual did not anticipate his son's ripening, and send a concubine to assuage the prince's fitfulness according to the custom, was open to conjecture. It was common knowledge that this protected a youth from promiscuity and kept his heart susceptible for the love that would come in manhood.

As he stared down at the fruit grove—idly indicating to himself which trees were medlar, which were guava, and plum, and capolin —the prince felt the early warmth of the sun against his throat.

There was an uncomfortable, straining excitement in his blood, like the early vigor stirring in the trees below him. No . . . no, he didn't want to stay here. Some other boys undoubtedly were playing ball, but he didn't care to join them. He raised his eyes, and his gaze passed over the outer walls. The royal palace, tier on tier, terrace on terrace, lay a short distance away. He could see the crowd of merchants and barons in the great square; and suddenly Temozin made up his mind. He would go out and wander about the city. But first he must discard his crown . . . and call Cozca, his personal slave. No one must know he intended to go out into the streets, or Lord Comtzin would insist on sending a detachment of warriors with him.

The prince quickly descended the short stairway, and went immediately into his apartment. He removed his diadem; and while he was searching for a mantle that did not bear the royal crest, Cozca presented himself. "We are going out into the city," Temozin informed him.

The slave was surprised. "I was just speaking with the Lord Steward—" he said.

"I don't want Comtzin to know. What can you do, surrounded by a hundred warriors? The wind's a little chilly, despite the sun. Go get your mantle, Cozca."

The other youth hesitated, unsure whether he should protest, then hurried away. He was eager to leave the palace also. And a quarter-hour later, the two walked quickly through the fruit grove, cautiously opened the small gate at the farther end, and passed into a side street. Within a few minutes they were mingling with the citizens along the main thoroughfare. No one recognized the prince; and Temozin, as though he were a mere noble's son, was free to wander where he chose. Once he and Cozca were forced into a doorway as a caravan neared. Behind the merchant and his guard came the apprentices and slaves, their heads bowed against the press of their tumplines.

The crowd closed as the caravan passed. Someone roughly grasped Temozin by the arm. "Where is the villa of Lord Cuitla?"

The prince glanced at the men standing beside him. They were short and burly; and by their robes, Temozin knew the nobles were from Cholula, a city in another valley south of the lakes.

"Cuitla . . ." he repeated, shaking his head. Temozin turned to Cozca, who had gone pale with rage. The prince silenced the slave with a frown. After the men, shrugging in disgust at the youths' ignorance, let them go, Temozin stated simply: "They don't know who I am. It's no affront, Cozca."

A little beyond them were several black-robed priests, who were irritably forcing their way along the avenue. Behind them, in a wicker cage borne on a litter, was a captive intended for some ritual. No one paid them any heed. Suddenly, a strident blast of a conch trumpet warned of the approach of some great personage.

> . . . and a moment later [Temozin recounted in his journal that evening], at least five hundred warriors entered the square. In their midst, borne on a jeweled palanquin, was my brother Cacama. Everyone about me fell to his knees as the prince passed . . . and I knelt also, because I wanted to pay homage to him. *Omacoc ihuelitiliztli:* He has come into his powerfulness. Cacama*pilli,* whom my father has just made governor of Tezcuco.
>
> He was robed in the imperial tilmatli of our house; and the canopy above him was woven of the same quetzal plumage embroidered with gold and seed pearls. His crown was a helmet of plumes and jewels. Over his chest hung the jade crescent of his office. And after he had passed, and his retinue of chiefs after him, the square seemed dark and commonplace. The citizens crowded together again; couriers sped on their errands. The priests, with their shredded ears and hair matted with blood (from the penances they inflict on themselves, Cozca tells me), again tried to hurry faster than it was possible through the congestion. Outside of occasional clan leaders, who peered in idle curiosity from the terraces above the avenue, everyone seemed intent on carrying out his own particular function in the city—knowing only his allotted part and nothing else.
>
> The canals that sided the avenue were filled with barges, bringing in the produce of the fields, the tributes of my father's cities. There is a clustering, droning quality about the streets that I have never understood before: an insectlike intensity of purpose. No one but the priests actually hurries—or turns aside.

There is a terrifying, almost inhuman vitality. Beyond the thoroughfares the streets become no more than narrow paths that run along canals. The houses are built terrace on terrace next to each other. The waterways are spanned by innumerable bridges from tier to tier.

I have known only the palaces, with their quiet courts and spacious fruit groves . . . the temples set back on vast plazas. What a strange, complex intimacy the citizens live in!—when one's roof is another's courtyard, and one has to journey through a labyrinth of dark stairways, corridors, narrow courts, along the summits of walls, in order to reach home. At least, with all their bondage, my father's people are never lonely. To-morrow I plan to go into the city again. Cozca told Lord Comtzin that I spent the afternoon in the fruit grove.

As an afterthought the prince drew a sprawling palace, its outer apartments merged in the honeycomb of tenements.

She is more beautiful than any woman I have ever seen [Temozin's entry of the following night began]. Cozca and I found ourselves in the square where we saw Cacama yesterday. It is near a park, outside the merchants' section. A fountain is on the northern edge; and on the west lies a pyramid to the goddess Tlazol. We were standing near the gate of the compound when she entered. It was in the seventh hour, the hour of the Flower Prince.

Oh, how can I describe her? She is a longing inside me. A strange burning flutters on my lips, like a night moth. A part of me has become alien and new—and she is its meaning now. Perhaps I understand a little, though not what my change will yet do to me. Because I have seen her, my loneliness can no longer be quieted. And yet, how should I spend this anguish within me? It is a solitary thing, grown somehow from my unawakened season.

Her skin is the most delicate earth color—an umber, dusky and warm, diffused with gold. She was robed in white and pale orange; and her hair, long and as fine as the spun cotton of Cuetlaxtla, was caught at the back of her head by a jeweled comb. Oh, she is beautiful . . . she is beautiful. I can write no poem for her. When I first saw the woman with the jeweled comb in the gateway, my breath caught inside me. My heart turned cold, and was sick. There are no words for her, but the most ordinary and banal; yet a melody soars higher and higher within me—as though to fling the simple words in an ecstasy over the gardens: unashamed, because the heart is no contriver.

Oh, I am sick with my love of her. Surely, she is a princess who escaped her attendants to visit the goddess's shrine in quiet. Shall I ever hear her name? No . . . there is no reason to discover who she might be. Some other prince must have already possessed her and found his own meaning. Her secrets, which I shall never know, are familiar with sharing—perhaps familiar enough to be commonplace. But how? What does a man actually do with such a beautiful woman, without profaning his love? I surely have misunderstood. My reason is confused. A voice calls loud from my senses, suggesting satisfactions that appal me. Another, as though it were the spirit of my childhood, confirms a past innocence.

His hand had wavered; the brush executed several pictographs of vague insinuations, then became firm and controlled again.

Does she wait alone in her gardens at night, while her husband wanders the streets in search of a coarser excitement? [he continued, with an insight strange to an adolescent boy.] And should we know each other's name—? In a city names divide and bring together, not as the heart would, but as function and expedience demand. *Temozin* is a prince, the heir apparent to the throne of Nezahual the lord. He is not merely a young man. Princes have no right to search for beloveds. I shall wrap my love in careful shrouds. My longings, like golden chrysalids—which might have risen for fulfillment, one by one— are caught in silken tombs. This fluttering inside my lips will still.

I shall forget. But for tonight, I am sick with love of a princess who is all unknown. And she is beautiful . . . beautiful. Tomorrow I will write a few verses of a woman who has umber skin. Her loveliness shall then remind me of a thousand images;

my love of her will doubtless have become a mirror that reflects
and yet is nothing in itself. . . .

Though Temozin's first taste of love was bitter to him, he went
out of his palace on the next day. He and Cozca waited near the
gate of Tlazol's temple. But the woman of the jeweled comb did
not return. Nor did she come on the day following, nor for the rest
of the month—though the prince and his attendant waited at the
seventh hour for the princess.

One afternoon in the beginning of the third month, shortly after
Temozin celebrated his fifteenth birthday, the extraordinarily beautiful woman appeared again on the avenue below the goddess's
pyramid. As before, she was alone. It was Cozca that saw her first.
He touched his prince's arm; and Temozin, as though he had forgotten the purpose of their vigil, glanced at his companion with an
expression of rather distant curiosity. Cozca turned his head away
and stared intently at the approaching woman. The prince followed the slave's gaze, and began to tremble. His face blanched;
and Temozin, ashamed of his excitement, bowed his head and
closed his eyes.

After the woman had passed into the temple compound, he
placed his hand on Cozca's shoulder. "Let us return to my palace."

The other youth, surprised at Temozin's reaction, gave no immediate reply. Then he shook his head, suddenly determined. It was
not defiance; Cozca felt a deeper obligation.

"I want to go now," the prince repeated, without moving away,
however.

"We must wait," Cozca answered. "Excellency, we have watched
several weeks for her return."

"Then what should we do, Cozca? She will not speak to us."

The slave thought for a moment. "I will follow her, and discover
where she lives. At least you should know that, Excellency. She
may not return to the temple for another month . . . or she may
leave the valley," he stared into the prince's eyes, "and never come
back."

So the two waited outside the temple. In his journal that night,
Temozin wrote how Cozca had further insisted on the prince's giving him a note. By coincidence, a public scribe was passing in the

street. The prince offered a ring—of greater value than he knew—to the surprised man, and quickly chose a brush. The slave had followed the unknown lady into the walled garden behind the fountain; and when she paused outside the gate of a villa at the farther edge of the park, Cozca had approached her. The beautiful woman was not startled by him in the least. She had glanced at the note, then reread it with greater care. "Tell your master that I will answer him tomorrow," she promised. "Wait for me outside the temple . . ." the princess added, "with the condition that your lord himself does not speak to me."

Temozin, after he had related this, commented on the fear he had suddenly felt.

. . . a sudden intuition, as though something within me warned of disaster. An anxiety swept through me, even as I trembled in my happiness of seeing her again. Did I perceive my death in her? No: love and death are strangely intermingled. One emerges for fulfillment, only for the ultimate release.

And yet—as I think of her, there is this added fascination now. I seem compelled by my very apprehension to disprove my fear.

Princess of the Jeweled Comb [Temozin's first note began], why are you here in the city of the Alcolhua? There was a garden once, in a far place, and very long ago. Someone has built a pavilion for you in a land where no road goes. Why have you come?

The hand that was holding the note let it fall. "Why *have* I come?" Nicte questioned herself aloud. Was it really strange that someone should ask her this? It was nearing the hour when she often went to the villa of the late Catzin, yet Nicte delayed writing her answer. The princess had never considered her reasons for visiting the baron's family. She found an occasional comfort in one particular court, where it was said a previous empress of Nezahual spent her childhood. The Lady Tecui had once lived in Catzin's villa—before she left for her own city on the eastern coast, and returned to the valley to give Nezahual his heir.

Nicte creased the paper and laid it on the low wall. Wondering what answer she wanted to give, she idly dipped her fingers in the pool and then experimentally drew her thoughts on the stone. The princess had always felt in exile, though she had never known any land but Nezahual's. Nicte, even in her childhood, constructed an imaginary city of her own; and through the years, invested it with dreams she had come to believe—and no little reality. For there once was a city in the distant south. Ziyan Caan, the ancient rulers had named their capital on Lake Bacalar. Her father used to tell the princess of the cities their ancestors founded in the jungles. Before Mani, and Uxmal, and Chichen, the great Tutul Xius built the palaces and slender pyramids of Ziyan Caan.

Nicte drew a little pavilion in the primitive style of the Itzaes. She described the fruit groves beside the lake . . . and the warrior kings in their antique garb, as though she remembered them with the careless exactness of experience. "Yes," the princess answered both Temozin and herself, copying the little pictures she had drawn on the stone in neat squares across a sheet of maguey paper, "I am from a land where no road goes." As she was finishing, a slight wind blew through the court. Temozin's note glided into the pool. The blue and red inks quickly rose in thin trails of diffusing color. Nicte scarcely took notice.

Unfortunately, many notes followed in the succeeding months of the year that were not effaced in the shallow water below her fountain. Temozin expressed many sentiments that were easily misunderstood when the time of reckoning came. The destruction of their letters to each other should not have been left to an occasional accident. Nicte shared her yearnings for a bygone age with her unknown prince; and Temozin, as though he had completely given himself to her fantasies, added incidents of his own. Innocently captivated, using an unconscious pretense to assuage his longing, the prince described the love Nicte had aroused in him. Neither had the slightest conception of who the other actually was. It would have been, if not immediately ruinous, at least an obstruction to their dream. And Cozca, completely unaware of what he was committing, hastened back and forth between his lord and the princess. Throughout their correspondence Temozin never returned to the temple gate.

In one letter, written in the fifth month, the prince—as though he were recalling an actual episode—related their meeting on a stairway.

. . . and the steps were so steep, so overgrown with juniper and cypress, that we could hardly make our way down the terraces. The worn stone was like glass under the fallen leaves. You held my arm, for fear of the sudden disaster that might overtake us. Terrace by terrace we descended, through the ruined garden where no one ever goes now. Somewhere below us was the lake; but the stairway was broken before it reached the water.

There was conviction here, an earnestness in the only possible identity he could have assumed.

We took a side path through the trees. We hadn't forgotten. And we came at last to the pavilion, and rested on the bench outside. The lake was far below us, glittering in a thousand lights. Oh, that we might have stayed there always, sitting with our arms protecting one another! Our breath quiet, sustaining our excitement, we were at last complete.

You have belonged to no other prince. We have shared our meaning together; and the one who waits for you in the world outside our garden on Lake Bacalar—he will never understand this ultimate familiarity of spirit.

Temozin, with a facility yet of his childhood, a desperation that sought for the meaning of his new needs, abandoned himself to their fantasy. His journal was put aside.

And Nicte, imagining the brutal prince they had somehow agreed on (and certainly not referring, any more than Temozin, to Nezahual himself), answered that no one would ever know their secret of the dark terraces. It seemed that both were sharing in some past existence which had actually occurred. Her own letters were concerned very little with her new companion. She accepted his additions to her private world, but mainly wrote of her reveries. In Nicte's letters, Temozin accompanied the princess of the Tutul Xius in the palaces of the lost Ziyan Caan—but merely as a shadow, an adjunct. In an odd way, she gained through her private concept of Temozin the completion Acatli had found within herself.

One morning in the fourteenth month, in the season of the quail, Cozca returned to his lord in a peculiar agitation. No one had been at the temple gate to meet him. The slave waited until the ninth hour, and then left his place near the gateway. As he passed along the avenue, Cozca told the prince, he had the sensation that someone was following him. He paused several times in doorways, turned into side streets and waited behind buildings after he had crossed canals. No one had appeared; and yet, up to the very moment he entered the palace, Cozca knew someone was watching him.

But the actual disruption had occurred five days previous to Cozca's last errand for Temozin. The last four days had been spent in general penance. Even the old people, who were licensed because of their service to the clans, abstained from liquor. Husbands could not approach their wives; the strange correspondence of the heir apparent and Princess Nicte (which was certainly outside the conventional time and place) had also ceased.

On the day before the penance, Nicte's slave duly appeared in the gateway to the temple. She had given the princess's message to Cozca without a word, then turned and disappeared in the crowded avenue—with, perhaps, the most casual backward glance. The girl might have very well realized the seriousness of Nicte's and Temozin's offence. She doubtless knew that her mistress was a royal concubine and forbidden by strictly enforced laws to associate, except under formal circumstances, with anyone outside Nezahual's harem.

Nicte herself had been given unusual leeway, to be sure. She was not restricted to the palace of the king. Nezahual had given her a private residence suitable for the Lady Ilan herself, though the queen was confined to the women's quarters in the palace. Nicte was free to travel wherever she chose: to her new estates of Mexicaltzinco and Coatepec, or to the villas of Nezahual's barons. It was understood that she must be accompanied by her attendants. As the particular favorite of the Tezcucan lord, she had been granted up to this time an amazing immunity—and in her own mind, the princess transgressed against no one. The letters she exchanged with the heir apparent were outside the pale of actual commitment. After all, she had not troubled herself to discover Temozin's identity in the world of Tezcuco.

Cozca had observed to his master that the slave girl always behaved as though she were frightened. She refused to answer even his impersonal greetings, undoubtedly for fear that he should become friendly with her. Even in their brief moment of contact, when she either gave or received a letter, the girl would furtively scan the passersby in the avenue. Once, out of mere curiosity, Cozca had hidden himself in a recess of the wall beyond the gate. He often arrived early, as he had no particular reason to fear someone might take note of his repeated visits to the pyramid.

The girl had approached the meeting place so cautiously that Cozca was surprised to see her suddenly pass inside the gate. He waited for a few moments, watching her agitation—and then, ashamed of his carelessness, left his niche. Before Cozca could reach the gateway, the girl had hurried out into the street. He ran after her; and as the youth caught her arm, Nicte's slave moaned sharply in utter despair. In her fright she did not immediately recognize him. Cozca, startled himself by her reaction, pressed Temozin's letter into the other slave's hand and quickly lost himself in the crowd.

On this afternoon preceding the four days of penance, however, Cozca was in the mood for another experiment. Temozin was unconcerned; but the girl's attitude seemed increasingly ominous to the prince's attendant. Cozca was determined to find out the actual identity of their princess of the jeweled comb. Perhaps he would not have attempted to follow her on that particular afternoon. It was the sudden, backward glance (as though she had intercepted his thought) that convinced him.

Cozca waited for a moment, then took advantage of a group of passing merchants to enter the avenue after her. She had almost immediately passed from sight; but the young man, anticipating her direction, quickly forced his way to the center of the plaza. Then, instead of turning toward the fountain, he acted on impulse and crossed the avenue—though the memory of Nicte's earlier return through the park behind him should have caused the youth to search for the girl in that direction. The avenue bordered the south of the square; and along its farther side, separating the glazed pavement from the warehouses, ran a narrow canal spanned by portable wicker bridges. From the center of the thoroughfare a broader channel cut off toward the south, eventually connecting through a series of canals with the lake.

With an odd certainty, Cozca knew the girl intended to leave the main avenue by the western path along the channel. Just as he reached the edge of the narrow canal siding the square, the bridges swung up one after the other down the length of the waterway. Cozca immediately turned to the right, discarding his caution; for the passing barge would allow him to cross on the west of the channel first. In his anxiety, the youth ran onto the bridge before it was firmly in place; and forgetting that he was now directly behind the escaping girl, did not slow his pace once he had gained the other side.

In his haste, Cozca jostled the merchants and slaves clustered in little groups outside the warehouses. He passed open courts and alleyways without glancing into them, and at last—nearly out of breath—turned the corner of a building onto a by-street. About twenty yards away from him, a steep stairway led to a higher level. The girl was nearing the top. Cozca, suddenly aware that she might glance down into the street and see him, stepped back. There was an immediate howl of rage, and several merchants seized the careless youth by his arms. He had inadvertently collided with one of the slaves unloading a nearby barge; and the heavy coffer the man was carrying fell to the pavement. The air was filled with the dark aroma of chocolate.

It was a serious loss. One of the merchants called out in a strident voice for someone to summon an official. Cozca struggled desperately to escape, crying out that he would return before nightfall with the payment. The merchants, too intent on holding him, would not listen. "My master is the Lord Temozin!" the angry youth insisted, turning and twisting in their arms. Suddenly he struck one of the men in the belly with his elbow. The merchant, bending forward in pain, released the agile slave. Cozca's body was wet with the sweat of his exertion. The other merchant managed to hold him for another moment; then Cozca flung himself away and was gone.

The girl had since disappeared. She had turned at the first sound of disorder. Instantly recognizing Cozca, and surmising his reason for being in the street behind her, Nicte's attendant was seized by a momentary panic. Instead of fleeing while opportunity afforded it, however, she paused uncertainly. Her dismay abruptly changed to concern. A narrow, low gateway pierced the thin parpen wall beside the street; and the girl, without further hesitation, stepped into the courtyard beyond. An embankment planted with sapota trees rose to the level of the wall on her right. A graceful stairway faced with alabaster, translucent white against the dark retaining wall, connected the terrace with the court. Quickly surveying the garden, she crossed to the stairs and ascended. The edge of the terrace overlooked the street two levels below, and was hedged with woven cane and thick bougainvillea—enough of a screen to hide the girl as she watched Cozca's dilemma near the canal.

Cozca doubtless should have waited quietly with his captors until the official could be summoned. Once it was clear to everyone concerned that he was the favorite slave of the Lord Temozin, the merchants would have not been content to merely apologize, but would have given him some token of their esteem to carry to his prince. But the youth had been too intent on his chase; and now, as he broke away from the angry merchants and ran toward the stairway at the far end of the street, Cozca himself became the pursued.

He quickly outdistanced the apprentices who followed him; and the girl, losing sight of Cozca from her vantage, turned back toward the court. Her smile of satisfaction, however, was cut short. She herself had been too intent on Cozca. There was a small pavilion at the corner of the terrace, above the stairway joining the two streets outside. Several young men had been closely watching both the confusion near the canal, and her interest in it. As the slave girl turned from the hedge, her eyes suddenly met theirs. She gasped in terror, and for a second was unable to move. The youths merely looked at her, making no attempt to leave the pavilion.

Then the girl moved slightly toward the stairway. There was no gesture to stop her. She moved more deliberately, and suddenly ran forward. One of the older youths leapt from the open building and blocked the stairway. Nicte's slave fell dumbly to her knees before him. Her wide eyes, filling with tears, held the most pitiful expression. She opened and closed her small hands spasmodically.

"Bring her here, Tochtli," someone called out in the low, alto voice of an adolescent boy.

"Yes, Excellency," the youth in front of the stairway answered. He took the girl by the shoulder and raised her up. She followed him, without speaking, to the pavilion, her eyes lowered and her mind too stupefied with fright to grasp the significance of the title. There were not many in Tezcuco who might be called *Excellency*.

"What do you think of her, Nopal? Why do you suppose she was fleeing the young slave, then became so anxious for his escape from the merchants?" The question was put in the most offhand manner. There was a cold irony in the alto voice . . . as though the speaker were well aware of the girl's offense. She raised her eyes as the prince spoke, and immediately recognized the Lord Ixtlil from the descriptions she had heard of him. Only those of the ruler's immediate family might wear the mantel of quetzal plumage. The girl began to tremble violently. All the city knew of his cruel punishments—how, when he was only three years old, Ixtlil had murdered his nurse because she had allowed a man to possess her.

After the prince had spoken, the other noble leaned forward to examine their captive. He moved in an awkward way, and it was apparent that the nineteen-year-old Nopal was badly paralyzed. "She's rather pretty," he answered the prince. "By her clothing, it is obvious that her mistress is of high rank. Who is your mistress?" Nopal demanded, his tone becoming harsh.

"Princess Nicte," the girl answered, hardly knowing that she spoke.

"My father's favorite concubine," Ixtlil murmured to himself.

15

WHEN the prince left Nopal's villa several hours later, he had succeeded in discovering at least part of Nicte's indiscretion. He knew nothing of what her letters to the mysterious suitor contained; but the girl's sense of guilt assured him that the correspondence had not been innocent. He at first accused the slave of an immoral association with Cozca; and in her fear of Ixtlil's retribution—which might have been immediate —she could only confess her actual reasons for fleeing through the city with a boy in pursuit.

Ixtlil did extract enough to convince himself that his father had been betrayed. Nopal suggested that the prince leave the girl with him. She was young, and had a touch of beauty in her face. After all, the youthful noble was confined to his father's villa with nothing to do all day but watch the activity in the alleyways below. Ixtlil peremptorily refused.

In the eleventh hour, which was the hour of afternoon given to the Death God Mictlantecuhtli, the prince presented himself at the villa of Lady Nicte. Perhaps the princess thought that his arrival at the moment of her slave's return was a coincidence. Nicte was not particularly given to awe, whatever the situation; and she received Ixtlil immediately in her private court. She had been drowsing beneath the pepper tree, and did not stand when the prince unexpectedly entered. The royal concubine greeted him with court formality, however—addressing him by his various titles, as though to announce him to herself.

"My greetings to you, Lady Nicte," Ixtlil answered, staring coldly as he stressed her own titles. The prince laid particular emphasis on ". . . princess, and *consort of Nezahual*pilli."

Nicte returned his gaze with an equally detached curiosity. If anything, she was amused by his self-contained arrogance. She casually gestured for the prince to seat himself on the wicker bench beside her. Ixtlil ignored Nicte's offer. He stood a few paces away, his arms crossed, and continued watching her—his eyes slightly narrowed in accusation. His behavior produced no effect. The princess merely relaxed against her pillows and yawned. She noticed that the slave girl was still waiting near the gate.

"Do you want to take something, Excellency?" Nicte asked in a mildly solicitous voice. "Some chocolate, or guava jelly and wafers?" Her manner was a little condescending: after all, Ixtlil was half her age. Though he was a prince, he was not destined to rule; and in her own mind, Nicte was a princess of the Tutul Xius. Moreover, something had happened since her first exchange of letters with Temozin. Her vagaries were specific now, held to a definite sequence. A strangely convincing memory had been revived and elaborately—as though she had indeed lived in another time, had actually experienced the incidents her unknown suitor related in such detail. The references were to happenings too intimately familiar to be fantasy alone.

There was a peculiar confusion of personages and courts that sometimes accosted the princess. The youth before her decidedly did not belong to Ziyan Caan. This was Tezcuco, Nezahual's city— a separate existence; and each had its own reality. As Nicte glanced at Ixtlil, waiting for his answer, she was aware of a vague, floating sensation—of a suspension between two worlds. It was a diffused, pleasant confusion that allowed a certain willfulness. There was always an awareness of the other sphere, regardless of the one she might find herself involved in.

As Nicte watched her ominous visitor, waiting for him to give an answer one way or the other, she enjoyed an ability to dismiss him by merely changing her mental locale. It was much easier to erase an occurrence after something distasteful had happened, however . . . despite her dancer's faculty of creating whatever companions a situation demanded (and in the last months her alter-existence was one of recall, not caprice).

The princess was not disconcerted by Ixtlil's insolence. She waited another moment for him to speak, then called out to the girl: "Very well, Toçi—bring a little decanter of muscadine juice for me. Prince Ixtlil is obviously not thirsty." Nicte seemed completely unaware that the slave was frightened almost to insensibility. Nezahual's son could stand there as long as he chose. He certainly wasn't very talkative.

Ixtlil abruptly demanded: "Toçi, come here." He had not moved, and his eyes were still fastened on the princess.

Nicte was taken aback by his harshness; and the young attendant, hesitating a moment in the gateway, suddenly cried out in hopelessness. She darted across the court and threw herself at the princess's feet. Nicte was further surprised. She frowned in annoyance, and smoothed the nape of the girl's neck in automatic gentleness as she murmured something to comfort her.

"*I know* . . ." the prince stated with a terse insinuation, an odd cruelty edging his voice.

Nicte carefully released herself from the slave's arms and stood up. With her own detached arrogance she confronted the ill-mannered youth: "What do *you know*, Lord Ixtlil?"

"Your wantonness, Lady Nicte," he answered, his tone casual and sarcastic.

Nicte glanced down at Toçi, wondering what the girl could have done to anger a prince. It was inconceivable that he should have come to accuse a princess of some incontinence. "He must hold me responsible," Nicte thought, and touched the kneeling slave's cheek, resolved that no misfortune should befall her. "I punish my attendants in my own way, Lord Ixtlil. You forget yourself."

"It is you, Lady Nicte, that have forgotten. The girl is no concern of mine. *Your wantonness, Lady Nicte*," he repeated, "has brought me here. Your attendant has betrayed your confidence. I know of your letters."

Instead of reacting as Ixtlil had anticipated, the princess turned to the girl. "Toçi," she asked in quiet concern, "have you betrayed me in something?" Her manner was absolutely innocent. In Nicte's mind, her forbidden correspondence belonged to the other world —was certainly not in violation of Nezahual's trust. The slave moaned something between her sobs, and stared briefly at the princess; but it was Ixtlil who recognized the warning and confession of guilt in Toçi's eyes, not Nicte.

The prince was suddenly angered by what he thought was the concubine's deception. "Don't dissemble, Nicte*tzin*," he muttered, straightening out his arms and holding them stiffly at his sides. Ixtlil bent forward a little: "You are found out. For the last eleven months you have deceived my father, you have encouraged a traitor among my father's nobles. Your crime is punishable by death. Unless you immediately confess to me . . ." The prince raised his hand to the knife in his waistband.

Nicte was enraged by his threat. "You are a brutal child! I have heard rumors also, Ixtlil*pilli*. Nezahual's youngest prince is vicious and disordered. He is a slayer . . . like the jaguar, he kills beyond sanity or normal appetite. No one knows the cause of his vengeances. Nothing is sacred: neither great noble, nor venerable prelate. He despoils altars and thresholds." The princess had approached him, and stood but a pace away. Ixtlil hadn't moved; and his dark eyes were wide in amazement. Nicte paused, regained her composure, and stared at him coldly. Then, her voice inflected by mockery, she asked: "Have you come to frighten me with your madness? *My wantonness.* . . . Really, Ixtlil*pilli,* Ixtlil*xochitl*pilli, you are only a boy destined for nothing in his father's city. And yet you come, as though to challenge a daughter of great and ancient kings. Indeed, what is your line of princes, who were a century ago but petty, nomad chieftains?"

Nicte turned toward the fountain, then confronted him again: "You are still an evil child, Lord Ixtlil. What do you know of a woman's indiscretion, when you haven't the vaguest notion yet of your own function?" She studied him for a second with an attitude of exaggerated carefulness. The princess intuitively knew that he had not experienced a woman's love, despite the early maturity of his body. Though of small stature, the prince was physically already a man . . . but his potency was for death, not life.

"I have seen dogs together in my courtyard," Ixtlil replied, a sneer on his broad yet sensitively curved lips. Her observation had not intimidated him in the least. He casually raised his left hand to his hip. The prince gazed at Nicte speculatively, rubbing his right forefinger against the cleft in his chin.

Nicte laughed outright at his comment: "Do you imagine this is the extent of love? A youth in his sixteenth year, Lord Ixtlil, is supposedly prone to idealization. If this is the height of your romanticism . . ." The princess turned again to the fountain, and without facing her accuser, stated: "But I am tired now, Excellency. I will tell your father how you have honored his favorite with a visit. Good afternoon to you, Lord Ixtlil."

"The letters, Princess Nicte—" the prince demanded, his voice threatening again. The princess was silent. Ixtlil, remembering his last encounter with Nezahual, could not take retribution into his own hands unless he had actual proof. Nicte's ridicule had not touched him: his were not the normal vulnerabilities. He considered the situation a moment longer. "Lady Nicte, give me the letters from your admirer." Again there was no answer. "If you will give me proof of your suitor's guilt, I promise to give you my protection in return. No punishment shall befall you; for your 'innocence' would convince the judges—" *if not myself, he implied.* Unlike his previous vengeances, the one at hand would be carried out with partiality. It was inconsistent indeed that the princess should have been given an opportunity to escape her share in the consequences.

Ixtlil waited for a reply, but Nicte had removed herself to another world. "Very well," the prince concluded, turning to leave the court. "Nothing that happens in this city goes unnoticed. I will discover your lover, Lady Nicte. You both shall be strangled."

As Ixtlil passed through the gate, he felt a hand pull at his mantle. Toçi, aware that she had already given the prince enough information to expose the unknown poet, made a last bid for her mistress's safety. "Excellency . . ."

The prince, instantly knowing her proposal, smiled at her sardonically. "Could you find the letters?"

"Yes, Excellency—" The girl paused, and in her despair for Princess Nicte found the courage to barter. "And for the letters . . ."

Ixtlil anticipated her again: "For the letters, your Lady Nicte's life."

"I'll bring them to you."

"When? Within the hour?"

"Before you leave the palace. Wait just outside the entrance."

"Are they so near at hand?"

"Yes, Excellency," Toçi answered, and was gone.

Within a half hour, enough evidence of Temozin's guilt was in his brother's hands to convict him before the most lenient judges. The whimsical letters, which alone could have implicated the heir apparent, were carried to Ixtlil's villa; and five days later—after the general penance that commenced the season of the quail—someone other than Toçi waited near the gateway to Tlazol's temple. Whether Cozca had been as prudent as Nicte's slave or not, his sense of being followed ought to have had greater significance. Later in the afternoon, the name *Temozin* was affixed to the sheaf of correspondence. It was an inevitable moment.

Ixtlil wasted no time in indicting his brother. The lords Pallin and Itzco were immediately summoned. The chief electors were appalled by the evidence, which was seemingly conclusive, and begged leave to present it first to Nezahual himself. Ixtlil, however, insisted that the letters be shown to the Supreme Council. He had given *them* the proof of Temozin's guilt, not his father; and the treason could only be brought to the ruler's attention now through judicial channels. Pallin and Itzco, though the chief judges, must inform the other two electors of the crime. Then, as a body, the electors were obliged to indict the prince before the council of speakers.

Thus presented, the possibility of a crime's commission against the state established, a formal trial was unavoidable—even if the heir apparent's innocence were obvious. Then, as spokesman of the Supreme Council, Lord Pallin might ask the intervention of Nezahual. As the nobles returned to the royal palace, with nothing to do but make the offence public on the following day, Ixtlil dispatched an attendant to Temozin's villa. Tochtli was to inform the heir apparent of the situation before the council could place him under arrest. Ixtlil could not have expected Temozin to commit himself further in his anxiety. Perhaps it was to allow Nezahual's favorite among the princes ample time to destroy Nicte's letters—regardless of what the princess herself might have expressed.

In his journal of the evening, Temozin had expressed a peculiar prescience that troubled him.

> Again [he wrote], I feel as though some disaster were pending. My senses seem unnaturally acute. The slightest sound star-

tles me. What am I waiting for? I have an almost uncontrollable desire to flee my palace, to summon Cozca and lose myself in the darkness beyond the city. It is a terrible apprehension. Cozca himself seems frightened, though he pretends to be unconcerned. On one excuse after the other, he has remained near my apartment all evening.

Why should he have been followed this afternoon? Perhaps the Princess of the Jeweled Comb is curious of my identity in the city. Hasn't my meaning in our private world been valid enough? The time might now be near for us to know each other in Tezcuco . . . though I would as soon continue as we are. . . .

He referred to the sudden intuition, the anxiety that had swept through him on the day in the third month when their exchange of letters had begun.

I seem warned again of death. But even if death pursued me, where might I hide? I am perhaps more fascinated by the warning inside me, than frightened. Were I sure of disaster, I should be compelled to wait and adjudge it.

Temozin was interrupted by Tochtli's appearance. The next entry was the last in his journal. Throughout the subsequent trial he found no further need to give his own reality to the happenings of his brief life. A single row of careful little pictures expressed the situation that confronted him. There was no dismay, no fear, and no sorrow.

The Lord Tochtli, grandson of the king of Tlacopan, was just with me. Lady Nicte, my father's favorite concubine, is my Princess of the Jeweled Comb. My love of her is punishable by death. Nicte*tzin*'s letters must be destroyed. I have given Cozca his freedom, and a message to carry to Lord Tepech in Chiconauntla. He is gone.

Later that night Temozin was placed under house arrest by Itzco's warriors. The Lord Marshal had no alternative. And on the following day, the young prince's crime against his father was brought

238

to the attention of the Supreme Council. Cozca had been intercepted on his way to the fortress city; and both he and Toçi were
forced to stand witness against the heir apparent. Lady Nicte was
not summoned. Though the speakers themselves were biased in
favor of Temozin, they were keepers of the rule. After all, it was
certainly expected that Nezahual would set aside their verdict and
show his heir clemency. Such an action was within his right. Both
state and ruler would have behaved properly enough.

On the seventh day of the fourteenth month, a courier was sent
to the secluded palace of the Plumed Towers. It had not been until
late afternoon that the judges reached their verdict; and the messenger arrived in Tezcotzinco during the ruler's evening meal. He
was immediately presented to Nezahual, which was unusual, in
the chief hall.

The ruler sat with a small group of nobles. Nopal's father, the
cacique of the elite guard, was at his right hand. Macuil, son of
the great Lord Tepechpan, waited at his left. Comtzin and Cihua
the high priest sat a little beyond them. Several musicians stood
to the left of the throne, and a handful of slaves quietly refilled
goblets or attended to the torches. The courier's entrance seemed to
occasion no surprise. Nezahual gestured for the man to rise, without taking the cup from his lips.

The nobles stared at the ruler in anticipation, their attitudes
feverish and tense. Comtzin had come from Tezcuco in the morning; and the circumstances of the trial were known. The ex-slave
had succeeded in discovering the full implication of Temozin's letters—though the prince was too prompt in destroying the evidence
against Nicte, which might very well have revealed the peculiar
nature of his love, and his innocence. Several of the ministers, especially Pallin, were not without insight. At least the imaginary
aspects of their relationship could have been understood, in part,
and forgiven.

Macuil and Cihua, who detested Ixtlil, cautioned their lord to
distrust the proofs of the heir's treachery. The cacique of the
guard was in an anguish of remorse for the accidental part his son
had played. Nezahual had listened to them and said nothing.

And now, as the courier from the Supreme Council stood before him, the Lord of Tezcuco seemed appallingly disinterested. His gaze slowly passed from one of his nobles to another. "Speak," he commanded in a low voice.

"I come, Nezahual*pilli,* Lord of Acolhuacan, as a spokesman of the Supreme Council."

"What would my councilors ask of me?"

"The life of a traitor to yourself, Serene Excellency, and to the people of Tezcuco. The clans are of one voice; the chief councilors have judged."

"What has the unfortunate man committed against me, that he should die?"

"He has profaned your honor, Serene Excellency. He has violated one of the royal concubines, a consort of the august Nezahual the lord. The rule is broken, the gods offended."

"Is there proof enough of this to convince my council of speakers?"

"Proof enough, Serene Excellency. We have discovered the most explicit evidence. The guilt has been admitted."

"Which of my consorts is corrupted?" Nezahual asked, as though he knew nothing of the offense.

"The Princess Nicte. She appears to have been unaware of her lover's identity, but—"

"Who is my betrayer?" the lord interrupted, still studying his nobles and refusing to glance at the courier.

"Temozin, your son and heir, Serene Excellency."

Nezahual was silent for a moment, and then asked: "Does the council also demand Nictet*zin*'s death?"

"No. Though the princess allowed Temozin to write to her of his love, and probably to possess her in secrecy, it is proved that in the beginning of their correspondence she stipulated they should never meet. The responsibility is the prince's. Nictet*zin* provided the evidence of her lover's guilt; and by the law, she is exempt. Her punishment is not the concern of the judges."

Nezahual rose, raising his hand to the gold medallion that hung on his chest. He stared down at it, flicking the edge with his thumbnail. The man knelt below him. "If your lords offend you, Serene Excellency, rebuke them. Prince Temozin is very young. He is your heir, and beloved by the people." Macuil had risen from his pillow and knelt. His voice was sharp with earnestness.

The King ignored him. "Why, when the verdict has been justly reached, do you ask my leave? Do the ministers question their own judgment?"

The courier was startled by the question. "It . . . the crime, Serene Excellency . . ." He glanced at the surrounding nobles. Surely Nezahual realized that the final verdict in so serious an offense was often pronounced by the ruler himself. Temozin was second only to Nezahual in Acolhuacan. Though it was within the jurisdiction of the electors to punish the prince, the nobles expected the sovereign to veto their decision. Then the chancellor could suspend the sentence himself and merely reprimand Temozin before the people. Nezahual had certainly exonerated Ixtlil of more serious infractions against the rule.

"Why do you ask my leave?" Nezahual insisted. "Prince Temozin has defied our rule." He stared for the first time at the man.

"He has, Serene Excellency," the courier answered in an awed voice. Temozin had not even denied the intimacies described in the letters. He knew that Nicte would escape punishment and he would not relinquish the identity he had assumed in his love of her.

"You demand his death."

"Yes, Serene Excellency."

"By what means?"

"By the garrote, Serene Excellency," he said, falling to his knees again. The usual method in such cases was stoning, but this was a prince.

"Has the hour been set?"

"No . . . the electors beg you to pronounce judgment." The courier's words were scarcely audible.

"Then inform Lord Pallin that I shall come to Tezcuco on the ninth day of the month. I will convene my nobles in the Tribunal of the Gods in the ninth hour."

"In the hour of Feather Serpent, Serene Excellency? The hour of finality? Will you send the fairest of our princes into death?"

"That is the judgment of my councilors." Nezahual abruptly turned away and strode from the hall. The messenger, suddenly aware that the ruler had gone, rose to his feet. He paused for a moment, then hastened into the corridor also. Macuil seemed to contemplate following him, but the situation was hopeless. Slaying the courier would merely postpone Temozin's death if it accomplished that. The old cacique was stricken with remorse, and moaned over and over again that his son Nopal should have died.

On the afternoon of the ninth day, the chief barons of Acolhuacan were assembled in the Tribunal of the Gods. It was a dark, oppressive season. The first rain had fallen in a steady downpour since the early hours. Inside the hall, the restless nobles waited for their ruler to arrive. The tapestries of jewels and plumage rustled against the damp stone in the draft, glistening in erratic bursts of light from the torches. Along the walls stood the palace guard, the glass blades of their lances glancing streaks of fire.

The harsh moan of a conch trumpet announced the approach of Nezahual; and as the ruler entered through the serpent doorway his barons and priests knelt and touched their foreheads to the pavement. He was accompanied by only nine of the great lords. Five had already deserted him. The steward came forward to greet Nezahual as he neared the throne, offering his arm to the king of Tezcuco. The ruler's face was expressionless, almost stylized in its composure. He seemed anonymous—a representative of the nameless hunter-chieftains that had led their tribesmen from the northern wastes.

Nezahual deliberately ascended the dais. He was robed in the ceremonial vestments of his ancestors: the quetzal mantle and cotton sash embroidered with flowers. In his left hand was the thin, scepter arrow of gold tipped with obsidian; the coin of sovereignty hung over his chest, the token of the hours past counting that followers through generations had spent to erect the throne of the Acolhua. On his brow was the diadem of Tezcuco alone.

The forty-nine-year-old king seated himself on his throne, and waited. It was not long before another trumpet call was heard: a long, strident blast, an echo of the jaguar's voice in the mountains. Lord Pallin entered and advanced to the throne. He knelt; and at a gesture from Nezahual, the chancellor rose. He received permission to speak. Again the final verdict of the judges and the Supreme Council was given to the ruler.

Nezahual quietly left his dais and strode to the center of the hall. He halted before the pedestal. As he raised his hand, four warriors entered with Temozin. They approached the ruler and knelt. At a command from the steward, the guards withdrew—leaving the young prince alone before his father. For several moments they confronted each other. (How perfunctory it was, this final judgment on Tezcuco! . . . as though nothing more devolved from the sentence but the death of a youth.) Then Nezahual placed his hand on the polished skull of an ancient chief: "It is the verdict of the Supreme Council of the judges and lords of Tezcuco that Lord Temozin, prince and heir apparent to the throne of the Acolhua, shall pay the penalty of death for his transgressions against the people." He hesitated, and stared into his son's face. Temozin returned the gaze without flinching, his eyes clear and intense, then bowed his head in acceptance. It was done.

At the far end of the hall, set back and to the left of the main throne, were two chairs of state. Prince Cacama had half risen, his body thrust forward and his hands tightly gripping the wicker arm rests. Below the lord, their shoulders touching him, sat Macuil and Tepech. As he watched his condemned brother, Cacama shook his head in despair and murmured something over and over again to himself. Beside him, Prince Ixtlil sat quietly with his eyes closed—as though he were almost asleep.

"You shall be taken to the chief square before the royal palace on the morning of the eleventh day, of the month Quechollo. In respect to your birth, the executioner shall use the garrote—and your body be burnt on a pyre within the courtyard of the palace." Nezahual's voice was low, his words mechanically distinct. Once before the lord of Tezcuco had committed another that he loved to death by strangulation. Tizoc would have understood the moment.

With this, Nezahual removed his diadem and placed it on the skull. He raised his hands in oblation to his forefathers as the warriors led the doomed prince from the tribunal. Clothed in a white robe embroidered with leaves of pale-green plumage, Temozin (who had created the image of a goddess to attend him in his final

243

days, and spent the secret yearnings of his youth in fruit groves never to be sown) had now been consecrated by his father, not condemned. He was the part Nezahual offered of himself to his assassin.

—and your body be burnt on a pyre . . . my own flesh, the pain I have projected among men as a son! The conflict of Nezahual's dual nature was resolved.

And on the eleventh day of the Quail, Temozin, poet and prince, was put to death before the people of Tezcuco, sent by his father into a night of past seasons past memory. His transgressions were forgiven by the people, who paid homage through him to the martyr princes of an ancient time. As the thin cord cut into his throat, and the vertigo swept his life into darkness, the dying boy heard a familiar voice calling out to him. *Temozin, Temozin . . . I will follow after.*

To a land where no one goes . . . ?

The unquestioned heir to Acolhuacan was dead. Lord Cacama was tentatively proposed as Nezahual's successor. Temozin had died by the law of his people. His obsequies were for a prince; and all but Ixtlil and Nezahual wept at his passing. In the stillness as his body was consumed, the watchers heard a shrill, distant sigh of a whistle echo from the palace.

And there was no one left for Nezahual to love. Only the malignant expression of his nature remained at large in the city.

Nezahual returned for the last time to Tezcotzinco. He would never again leave his quiet gardens as the ruler of the Acolhua. Temozin's palace was walled up, that it should never be occupied by another. Princess Nicte passed into obscurity. The year of the first comet completed its cycle.

It was not until the following spring that Nezahual recalled several of his barons to him. Shortly after his son's death he had become very ill, and it was feared in the capital that the ruler might die. Nezahual was unattended except by a single slave. Only a few gardeners wandered about his estate; and no one else was allowed entrance to the palace of the plumed towers.

Then came the months of recovery: the long, slow walks

through the terraces. In the world outside, the affairs of men continued according to their use and wont. Prince Cacama had already established himself as a particularly successful governor of Tezcuco. He was stern when occasion demanded, yet lenient and generous to the citizens whenever the rule permitted. The lords Macuil and Tepech were his constant companions; and their eventual rise as war chiefs was anticipated by the other nobles. Cacama accepted the role of heir apparent without reluctance, determined to fulfill his obligations to Tezcuco. In a way, however, he could not consider himself his dead brother's, or Nezahual's, successor. Rather, Cacama held the memory, the explicit identity he had perceived within himself of Temozin as a guide.

The image of Temozin persisted; and in his private hours, Cacama still considered himself the spokesman of his brother. He would rule in the other's name. In another era, Cacama would have been the ideal chief of men. Unfortunately, this was a time for heroes, for the inspired soul that (god and demon both) is torn asunder yet contrives a balance of its opposite natures.

And Temozin, the gentle, lyrical intelligence, was dead.

Nezahual, hidden away in his seclusion, might effect a reconciliation of the energies within him that had brought about his downfall—but it would be a reconciliation of no practical value to his people. Ixtlil, the dire reminder of the established rule of a primitive ethos, the relentless equaler of a collective conscience, was manifest in the city.

In fact, Ixtlil had long ceased to regard Nezahual as his father. Nezahual might have stepped into the judgment hall from the jeweled and feathered tapestries, the foremost in time of the hunter kings, to pronounce judgment. Temozin was a martyr prince, again to be sacrificed. Even Cacama beside him was without individual, unique identity: merely an adversary, robed and crowned, continually projected from the past. To himself, Ixtlil had no personality. He encompassed ten thousand years' loneliness.

On the eleventh day of the Quail, Ixtlil watched the ritual murder from a balcony of his father's throne room. As the twirling rod gathered the cord about Temozin's throat, the dark prince felt a great, godlike buoyancy sweep through him.

16

BECAUSE of a trivial incident, an unnatural intuition, Ixtlil had come to watch his brother's body cast on a pyre. He at last realized his purpose in the city. It was not by the process of normal maturation, however. The earlier continuum of his life had anticipated and merely strengthened his awesome will to power. What had been prodigious viciousness finally reached a more effective level, without change. During the year of Nezahual's illness, the prince accompanied Itzco on a raid into the lands of Tlascala. The War of the Flowers proved to be especially successful; and Ixtlil returned a cacique, though he was only in his seventeenth year.

The chancellor and the marshal, acting against the advice of the other electors, then appointed him as the provisor-baron of the northern provinces—a formidable rank, which gave its bearer control of the tributes and levies of half Acolhuacan.

It was particularly odd that Ixtlil should be given the post, as Macuil and Tepech (whose hatred of Cacama's brother was well known) were the chief barons of the territory. They were also the immediate lieutenants of the new heir presumptive. Though he was seldom seen in the streets of Tezcuco, Ixtlil's presence was increasingly felt in the capital. He had begun to grow at a surprising rate since Temozin's death; and before his seventeenth year was out, the prince was among the tallest of the Tezcucan warriors.

None of this, however, reached the ears of Nezahual the lord. If he had been disinterested in the affairs of his kingdom before the execution of his chief heir, after his illness the ruler was completely detached from the world outside his palace walls. Indeed, Nezahual had completed the cycle, had returned to the palace of his childhood to become again but an emperor of terraces. He had relinquished his scepter, and his son. Only his right to these gardens was retained, to these empty halls. The gold amulet that hung over his breast, the sacred insignia the priests and nobles gave him as a mark of supremacy, had only this meaning now.

So Nezahual wandered through his terraces, paused by waterfalls that broke beside glistening pavilions, and slowly took his way again down seemingly endless flights of stairs. Over the gardens brooded a winged, stone lion from whose mouth peered the graven head of Nezahual's father. Once, a very long time before, the boy Emperor had gazed up the slope at the basalt figure, as another boy fastened the chain of the amulet about his throat. And several nights later—or had it been an eternity afterwards?—the lion with folded wings watched over the garden while Nezahual first tasted the love of a woman.

Most of the significant incidents of his life had occurred here. And as spring collected the warmth and the seed in its furrows, and the thick, amber blood of trees began to quicken, the lord pursued the meanings of himself in the recesses of Tezcotzinco. Beyond the terraces that descended the hill to the west stretched a forest of wilder seclusion. Without consciously remembering the slight, long-overgrown trails, Nezahual would turn from the stairways and lose himself in a luxuriance of fragrance and waxy color. Endlessly varied petals forever slipped on the winds; and only the murmur of leaves and hummingbirds' wings broke the silence.

Forgotten pavilions lay scattered over the slopes: the tombs of ancient courtesans. No one ventured into this desolation of forest after nightfall, in fear of the dread *ciuapipiltzin* who haunted ruined pleasure gardens. So much of himself had been betrayed in the little buildings! Nezahual felt no alarm of the baleful, golden-browed women, nor any fright whatsoever at the eerie lights that quivered occasionally in the darkness, when a feverishness led him out into the summer night. There was a sense of yearning spent, of ultimate release, in his aloneness.

A strange, pending excitement grew in him through the first year of his complete seclusion. Nezahual had the unusual capacity to turn sadness and despair to account. Within him was a private universe of reality, which gradually merged in the garden. Often he spent days without food, forbidding interruption and isolated on the cliff near the summit of his hill. He would fall into a deep sleep; and as though his spirit left his body, continue to wander through the outer terraces. At first, however, he had merely risen from his sleeping body. He would bend over himself, and carefully examine his features in an attempt to identify and give meaning to them.

Where was that part of him which was unique, the essential Nezahual apart from his role as hunter-king? It was time to cast off the magical prestige that had shrouded him since his birth—that had given him a tribal meaning, marked off and segregated from his people and from himself. It was too late to return to the community of men. So Nezahual stared down at himself, attempting to discern what he actually was; and discovering little, wandered spirit-wise into the gardens. In this state, his inner world became increasingly dominant. He would come upon those he had loved, who had waited sometimes a quarter century or more for his return.

And Nezahual, no longer a man in his fifty-first year, nor yet actually younger but somehow twenty and fifty at once, pursued the meaning of relationships he had not previously understood. One evening in the fall of the year after Temozin's death, the ruler was sitting quietly on the throne he had had carved in the cliff. A servant had just left him; and Nezahual, half rising to summon him back, almost called out the name *Comtzin*. At that moment, he caught a movement on the rim of the pool below him. He was not in the least startled, though someone would have had to pass beside him in order to reach the basin.

Instead, he rose from his stone seat and stepped down the stairway. The youth waited for him to reach the pool, then knelt. For the first time in many years, Nezahual felt a slight twinge of exhilaration in another's obeisance. An eager shyness swept through him, like a chill wind blowing up from his entrails. The moment of confused recognition passed. "Where have you been, Comtzin?" he asked, gesturing for the sixteen-year-old youth to rise. His eyes fell to the thin reed flute in the slave's hands. With a pained awareness, Nezahual realized that he could see the outline of the wall through Comtzin's body, and the quiet glimmer of the pool. The worlds had begun to merge, but only through him. The stone and the water belied the vision's reality.

"In the gardens, Serene Excellency," the boy answered, stammering a little in embarrassment and lowering his eyes as he rose.

"It has been a long time. Did it hurt, Comtzin?"

They both glanced down at the boy's thigh. The two small wounds, side by side, marked his skin where the snake had hung for an instant many years before. Nezahual suddenly caught a strangely familiar fragrance, a scent that belonged to a moment of flowering in some forgotten season. A sharp pain fluttered through his heart as he was confronted by the dead slave's innocence.

"Yes . . . for a moment, Lord of the Three Cities," Comtzin said, self-consciously fingering his flute. He stared briefly at Nezahual, his gaze full of devotion and understanding now . . . as though he had grasped the significance of Nezahual's boyhood pranks.

And Nezahual suddenly understood himself. There was a fleeting memory of an afternoon in late summer, of warmth, the fragrance of flowers, and the changeable moods of a flute. He recalled the moment when he had let his bright medallion slip into the reservoir—then called to Comtzin, and told him the talisman was lost in the water. He felt again the cool, wet fingers fastening the chain about his throat, and the warmth of the slave's nearness at his side.

Then a deep, hidden distress was resolved inside him. The desperate hurt of his childhood fell away. He understood his own innocence, his early dreams of rescuing an endangered flute from a horde of savages on the lower plains—and of holding someone in his arms as he wept. The later dream of a reed flute wailing one last sharp note as it lay broken on the earth, its melodies like streams of blood trickling from the finger holes, had no meaning now. He was no longer committed to the inevitability of loss, to the dire anticipations that had given a constant reality to despair throughout his life. For surely he had created his own ruin within himself.

Nezahual, not knowing what else to say, smiled sadly at his childhood companion: "I have commanded the squadrons of the empire, Comtzin. I have entered battle with the green panache of quetzal plumes falling from my warrior's helmet. All Anahuac has feared my anger, but . . . but I am no longer an emperor, no longer Lord of the Three Cities. Only Tezcuco listens to my voice; and another sits on the triple throne of my fathers."

Comtzin murmured something in sympathy, without comprehending Nezahual's loss. In the time of their actual boyhood, he had comforted the prince with the willingness if not the capacity to share in the other's hurt. It was enough.

"Play for me again," the ruler asked; and the slave boy, who had known his own meaning to Nezahual in terms of his flute, raised the primitive instrument to his lips. In its melody was the fragrance of rosin, the perfume of flowers as the wind changed. Nezahual was the flute's meaning: it sang for Nezahual, not for him. And as he played, Comtzin remembered his love of the slave girl Chimotl, and how he had lain with her the night before his death.

After a time Comtzin departed, and Nezahual found his way back to the palace in the darkness. Through the remaining months of the year the two encountered each other frequently on the terraces. Nezahual would hear the silent call of the flute. Once, on a morning in winter, the ruler had come to a little pavilion a quarter-league from the lake. Comtzin was waiting for him with another: the Prince Axaya, who had died a long time ago in his twenty-first year, before his marriage to a maiden of his father's court. The Aztec prince was clothed in a sheer cotton robe woven with rosettes of gold and plumage. His sleeves were brocaded with pearl, and a short mantel of blue cotinga feathers half covered his shoulders. The cape was drawn back, and strangely tied with folds of another plumage. Axaya was a bridegroom.

A long time ago, it had been said of Axaya that he held within himself the reflection of his yearning. As the slave Comtzin found identity in his serving maid—lying contentedly down to die—so Axaya discovered himself in his season. He was a hybrid flower, without pistil or stamen duplicated in the garden. He could only last for a brief time on earth, to depart without casting or receiving seed. Until midday he and Nezahual spoke together. The Aztec prince told his earlier companion that he now dwelt in a narrow valley high on the side of a great mountain. There was a community of youths and maidens here; and on the surrounding hillsides were built their houses and terraces. The buildings were of alabaster, jade, and yellow chalcedony. Each youth had his com-

panion, who had been joined to him spiritually first and then later
became bound to him in a season of ardor. They were as one, and
their exchange was of a greater delight than could be conceived of
in the physical world.

Even in his childhood Axaya had been betrothed to a maiden in
this community of spirits. He anticipated completeness—participated in his future fulfillment, beyond the division of sex. Nezahual, happy for his friend yet sad for his own isolation, inquired
about the two princesses that had shared his youth and early rule.
Princess Mecatl, he was told, had at last found the contentment
that was denied her in Nezahual's valley. Neither she, nor the
Princess Tecui, awaited him. Both had discovered other purposes,
and their needs had been conjoined in the offices of other bride-
grooms. Tecui herself dwelt in the same valley as Axaya. He described their present state in detail; and Nezahual, hearing of the
princesses, could not protest their contentment without him.

"Does no one that I have loved await me?" the ruler asked.

"One, Nezahual . . . one awaits you in a far place, in a desolate
fastness."

"But how?" Nezahual's eyes filled with tears of shame. He
glanced at Comtzin, who had been listening at the edge of the pavilion. The slave boy himself had not understood the conversation.
As he looked at Comtzin, however, Nezahual grasped the significance and spiritual consequence of his only actual love. The cause,
the misunderstanding of an early hurt, was unimportant now. The
balance was effected beyond nature. He knew his own innocence,
the meaning of the flute song that had accompanied his childhood
—a meaning apart from Comtzin's purpose to Chimotl, and the
outcome of their son. There was a love that carried two lovers
above the common, impersonal function of continuing mankind's
pain into the future . . . drawing them into a realm where they
approached the one god and were united in their needs, no longer
caught in the incongruities of body and spirit.

"But how . . . how could I find the way?" Nezahual asked,
turning to the spirit of Axaya. There was an intense silence; and
suddenly the air was filled with a low, all-encompassing whirr—as
though a thousand bull-roarers swept about him. Nezahual fell to
his knees in despair, crying out for Axaya to save him. Then there

was quiet again. Standing before the ruler was a youth in a long robe. His mantle was fastened with a jewel that glistened as brightly as the sun. His wings swept out about him, and the plumage shone in a myriad colors. His eyes were the translucent green of jade, their glance both shy and commanding. On his forehead was the sign of the four winds.

It was the vision Nezahual had long been promised. An instant later he was alone in the deserted pavilion. Neither Comtzin nor Axaya would accompany him again.

On the following day Nezahual secretly left his palace of the Plumed Towers. He entered his capital without being noticed, as though he had come in the darkness; and entered the temple precincts of the god Tloque. The High Priest Coatl received him, and conducted the lord into the deepest cellar under the pyramid. And later, when Nezahual stood on the high tower of his palace watching the valley that had once been his, change in the dusk, he understood his quest. He knew how he might find the way to the one that awaited him in a far place, in a desolate fastness.

Outwardly, Nezahual's behavior did not change during the year of the third comet. When he was with the few nobles he allowed to attend him, his manner was quiet and responsive. He spent a good part of his time tending the trees and flowers on his terraces, and supervised the repair of the aqueduct that carried water three leagues from the neighboring mountains. An embankment two hundred feet high connected the hill of Tezcotzinco with another hill to the east; an unexpected deluge had weakened the construction in the late spring.

Nezahual wandered less and less about the lower terraces in his physical state. He would seclude himself in his niche near the summit of the cliff. It had become an ordinary experience for him to rise from his sleeping body, a separate consciousness. Then he would betake himself down the long stairways and into the wild ravines beyond. A region he had never known before lay in the expanse of forest. And yet, this region had always been at the verge of the familiar—a common terrain that each individual spirit must charter (without laying claim) to discover itself.

During the late summer Nezahual came upon a small valley

high among the slopes of the surrounding mountains. There was a ruined village on the border of a lake; and the ruler knew he had found the first sign of his quest. The air was sharp and cool, for it blew between ice-sheathed peaks, catching, in passing, the pungent fragrance of pine forests. Through the remaining months of the year he searched through the gullies and foothills. And one day in the succeeding spring he followed a river bank far beyond the deserted village. He had paused opposite a little island midway in the torrent. Suddenly a voice called out to him: a sad, yet exultant voice. *Nezahual* . . .

"Maxtla!" he answered, and without hesitation threw himself into the icy current. Through the succeeding summer, a season that seemed to be without ending, the two companions rediscovered the meaning they had held for each other. The guilts and betrayals were forgotten; and a guest in a long robe, with wings that glistened in a thousand hues, came to anoint them.

But long before the angel of the Close Vicinity arrived on the island, midway in the torrent, several attendants had come upon the supposedly sleeping Nezahual in Tezcotzinco. Days had passed since he had isolated himself on the throne carved in the hillside; and the nobles feared that their ruler might have overspent himself in the long fast. Nezahual, lord of Tezcuco, was dead.

Once, recovering from a strange malady of the spirit in his early manhood, Nezahual remarked that he had sensed an immortality in madness, "a sort of entrée to death. I don't recall exactly what I used to think during those twilight months," he told his physician, "but I am sure it was beautiful . . . and if I had died, I should have continued to exist in that very personal world, unaffected by no longer having a body."

17

Nezahual is dead! The king is dead, and who shall succeed him?

Prince Cacama was passing along the chief avenue in the capital. His jeweled palanquin was preceded by the heralds, announcing the presence of the Lord Governor of Tezcuco on conch trumpets. Five hundred warriors attended him; and as the retinue passed, the citizens knelt on the pavement, touching the ground and then raising their hands to their foreheads.

Cacama was robed in the quetzal plumage of his house. His crown was a helmet of plumes and jewels, for the eldest son had come into his powerfulness. At his side were Macuil and Tepech, their glances threatening and austere. The procession was within a quarter-league of the royal palace when an excited courier intercepted the heir presumptive and his nobles. He had come from Tezcotzinco.

"Am I the first to know?" Cacama demanded, dazed by his father's unexpected death yet mechanically aware of his own position.

"Yes . . . yes, Excellency," the slave answered, catching his breath.

The prince turned to his lieutenants in apprehension; and Macuil stated his fears: "We must hurry to the palace and inform the electors ourselves."

"Yes," Tepech echoed. "Post a guard about the palace. The electors must proclaim you the successor this very afternoon."

There had already been rumors in the capital of Ixtlil's pretensions. An order was given; and the warriors broke into striding run, bearing forward the heavy palanquin with its canopy of woven plumage and gold.

By evening, Cacama was proclaimed Lord of Tezcuco. Ixtlil was not in the capital; but on the following day, a delegation of nobles presented themselves before the Supreme Council. Ixtlil was in revolt, and had gathered fifty thousand warriors under his ensign. The chieftains of the northern provinces, abandoning their loyalty to Tepech and Macuil, supported him. Acolhuacan was menaced with the disasters of a civil war. Cacama immediately turned to Montezuma, and the Aztec squadrons were sent to his aid. It was then that Nezahual's eldest son compromised his kingdom. He ceded half of his provinces, those that lay beyond the mountain range dividing Acolhuacan, to Ixtlil. The power of Tezcuco was at last broken.

Three years later, it was Cacama—a mere spokesman of Montezuma—who left the valley of the lakes on an unfortunate errand to the east. The terrible strangers had come, clothed in a bright metal harder than rock. They rode on unnatural beasts, and killed with fire those that defied them. In his hand Cacama carried three pearls of perfect color and unusual size. Shortly after this, the last legitimate ruler of Tezcuco was slain. Ixtlil, raised up by the vicious Spaniards, was created king of a ruined capital. The palaces and libraries had already been destroyed by the Indian allies of the conquerors, the Tlascalans, who had suffered in the continual Wars of the Flowers Montezuma had carried out against them.

Ixtlil commanded his own warriors against the last Aztec monarch, the brave Cuauhtemoc. To Ixtlil, more than to any other chieftain of Anahuac, must be given the title Destroyer of his People. Princess Papan, who managed to escape the violent death that accompanied the destruction of Anahuac, was baptized in the faith of the One God . . . and the story of her journey into the valley of the dead recorded in the journals of the new priests. Among the few of Montezuma's children to survive was the youth Cahua, who had sat with Nezahual and Papan on the night before the ritual ball game (on which the Tezcucan lord wagered his kingdom against three turkey cocks). Another of the royal children to outlive the conquest was the child Tecui, who had discovered Papan*zin* by the pool on the morning after her burial. From Cahua and Tecui descend the Counts of Montezuma and of Tula. One of the former, Don Joseph Sarmiento Valladares, ruled as viceroy over the lands that once were Anahuac.

So the history of the three cities ends. At the moment of Neza-hual*pilli*'s death, high on the side of his hill, the era was closed. To relate the circumstances of the conquest itself would be meaning-less. It has another, utterly disparate context.

Epilogue

AND NOW, these centuries later, when the pyramids are all leveled, the palaces destroyed and no vestige left of other thrones, this one persists: cut in a cliff near the summit of Tezcotzinco. To the south, in a deep ravine, lies a massive, unfinished statue of Chalchivitlicue, the Goddess of Waters whom the inhabitants considered their mother. Forever to be bound to its matrix of living rock, as though the stone itself had once tried to take her form, the goddess still strives as it were through the centuries to emerge.

The land is desolate now, a wasteland of parched gullies. But once there were terraces, and groves of cypress and fruit trees be-side the lake. Here a careless emperor had wandered, and listened to his young companion's flute. The earth was sweeter than the subtlest flower.

And yet, despite the aridness, the internal, visceral silence of a people now four centuries oppressed, the Valley of Mexico retains its calm, impersonal loveliness. Forests, birds—these are of merely fragile beauty. The latest architects now strive to build, not cause-ways and fortresses alone, but terraces and villas in the barren, jagged lava field just south of the present capital. The sharp crev-ices are filled with water for bathing pools. The walls conform and project; thin-rooted seedlings attempt to balance their stalks and brilliant blossoms.

A disconnection yet remains.

Teoloyucan ×

fortress city

Lake Zumpango

Lake Xaltocan

Cuauhtitlan ×

Swampland

canal

× Chiconauhtla

Tepechpa

47 miles

dredge marsh

Ecatepac

Lake Tezcuco

50 miles

Chi

Atic

ACATLAPAN

Tepeyac ×

CAUSEWAY

Tenayuca ×

Tlaltelolco ×

Azcapotzalco (slave market)

Telco ×

× Mexico or Tenochtitlan

Kingdom of Tlacopan

Tlacopan

Chapultepec —summer palace

× fortress

Mexicalt-zinco ↓

× Iztapalapan

Culhuacan ×

raised

me

Coyoacan ×

Great Dyke

waste land of lava fields

Cuicuilco ×

Swampland

Lake Xochicalco

MEXICO

volcano range

× Kingdom of

× volcano Xitli

19° 15'

19° 30'

Tepechpa